Just Got Real

JANE FALLON

MICHAEL JOSEPH

MICHAEL JOSEPH

UK | USA | Canada | Ireland | Australia
India | New Zealand | South Africa

Michael Joseph is part of the Penguin Random House group of companies
whose addresses can be found at global.penguinrandomhouse.com.

Penguin
Random House
UK

First published 2022
001

Copyright © Jane Fallon, 2022

The moral right of the author has been asserted

Set in 13.5/16pt Garamond MT Std
Typeset by Jouve (UK), Milton Keynes
Printed and bound in Great Britain by Clays Ltd, Elcograf S.p.A.

The authorized representative in the EEA is Penguin Random House Ireland,
Morrison Chambers, 32 Nassau Street, Dublin D02 YH68

A CIP catalogue record for this book is available from the British Library

HARDBACK ISBN: 978–0–241–54115–9
OM PAPERBACK ISBN: 978–0–241–54116–6

www.greenpenguin.co.uk

Dedicated to the wonderful people at Feline Friends
London who rescued my beautiful Pickle
www.felinefriendslondon.uk

I

She has no idea what she's doing here. Why she had thought this might be a good idea. She'd lain awake half of last night, wondering whether or not she could go through with it, kicking the covers aside because she had broken out in an uncomfortable sticky sweat, and then shivering as the cool air hit her damp skin. Restless. Anxious. No, scrub that. Absofuckinglutely terrified.

It's only a date. What's the worst that could happen? Actually, Joni doesn't want to answer that. She can think of plenty of examples: making a list of them wouldn't help. He has let her dictate all the terms: daytime, outside, a busy location, a café of her choice. She got there early, scouting out the seating arrangements, choosing an outdoor table up against the window where she could have a view of the whole terrace and be seen by the staff inside at the same time. She doesn't want to be taken by surprise when he arrives. If he arrives.

She takes out her phone and looks through her photos. As if his face isn't imprinted on her brain already. 'Always add at least ten pounds and ten years,' Imo had said when she'd persuaded her to sign up to the dating app in the first place. It had been a condition of her daughter's agreeing to leave home. 'Then subtract hair.

And maybe teeth. No one looks like their pictures, that's a given. Just don't be naive.'

'I don't know why you're so keen on me doing it if everyone on there's a liar,' Joni had said. It was the weekend before Imogen moved away to start a new life in Manchester, and she was clearly feeling guilty. Joni, if she were being honest, was feeling devastated, but she hoped she'd protected Imo from that knowledge. She wanted her to be able to throw herself into her training at a TV production company without worrying about whether her mother was lonely or not. She is, by the way. Heartachingly. Painfully. But that's another story.

A waiter is hovering, so she orders a coffee, cursing herself for choosing such an up-itself venue when he points to a list of about thirty versions of the same hot drink and asks her what kind. She'd wanted to impress Ant. To have him think she was the kind of woman who was at home in the smugster cafés of Kensington, when actually she'd just picked it because it was easy to get to from both her home in north London and his in Notting Hill, and it had tables outside.

'Just a latte,' she says, closing the menu and trying to ignore the waiter's dismissive expression. She feels as if she's let him down.

'Milk?' he says.

'Yes please.' She realizes her mistake immediately. Feels her face colour. Why is she so nervous?

The waiter puffs out his cheeks as if he's trying to suppress a sigh. 'I mean, what kind? Cow's, goat's, soy, almond, oat, pea, cashew, hemp or coconut?'

'Oh. Um . . . actually oat sounds nice.' She tries a smile on him. Hates herself for resorting to her harmless middle-aged-lady default position. Look, I'm old enough to be your mum, the smile says. Indulge a silly old woman. It doesn't work. Either he hates his mother, or he thinks oat is a terrible choice. The missionary position of the plant-milk world. When did coffee become such a thing? Didn't everyone already have enough decisions to make in life without adding caffeinated beverages into the mix?

'Chia, matcha or turmeric powder?' She looks at him, wonders for a second if he's taking the piss but his expression is deadly serious. She thinks about saying 'Chocolate sprinkles' just to get a reaction, but she fears he might throw her out in disgust. 'Just an oat latte,' she says. 'Oat milk, coffee and water. Nothing else.'

He finally leaves, oozing disappointment, and she checks the time. Five minutes to go.

If he turns up.

She has been talking to Ant for nearly two months. At first via the app, then text and finally on the phone. The first time it had shocked her how perfectly his voice had matched his face. She'd wondered if he felt the same. That sudden rush of relief. She knew she had a nice voice. Her ex-husband Ian had always told her she sounded as if she was purring when she spoke. Smooth. Soft. Obviously, that was before he decided he preferred the noises Holly made. Loud, confident, strident noises as if she was so secure of her place in the world that she didn't care who heard her. The Screecher, Meg had christened her. 'Imagine what she sounds like when they have sex,' she'd said. This, to be honest, had been the last thing Joni had wanted to imagine but she'd smiled anyway. 'It must be like shagging a goose.' Meg had always been able to make Joni laugh. But then Meg wasn't here any more.

She scours the other tables just to make sure she hasn't missed Ant. There's only one man sitting on his own. God, she hopes that slightly seedy-looking bloke with a greasy mullet isn't the person she had phone sex with last night. She feels a wave of both arousal and embarrassment. She doesn't know how they ended up there on their third phone call, how discussing the arrangements for meeting for the first time segued into uncensored lust, but it was both shocking and thrilling. What had she been thinking? She's a forty-nine-year-old divorcee who hasn't had actual sex for over four years, let alone simulated it over the phone. Ever. Certainly not with a virtual stranger. Except that was the thing about Ant. He didn't feel like a stranger. Not at all.

She watches as Mullet Man is greeted by a smiling woman. 'There's someone for everyone,' Imo had said to her as part of her online-dating sales pitch. 'That one perfect person.' Imo had always been a romantic despite also being wise beyond her years. And maybe it was true, although it seemed a bit random. What if you never came across that someone? And, even if you did, how would you ever know that in a world of seven billion people the bloke you said hello to every week in your local Tesco was the One? It made no sense. Joni had

4

always been much more pragmatic. There were probably thousands of people around the globe you could comfortably match with – tens of thousands even – it was just a question of settling for one who was reasonably local. And nice. She knows that 'nice' is a damning word. Too vanilla. Too beige. But, the truth is, it's what she wants. She's done with arseholes.

The waiter delivers her coffee in a bowl. Joni wants to ask him if they have any mugs she could decant it into but she's too intimidated, so now she'll have to wait until it's cold before she can drink it. She's furious with herself for letting it go. Is she getting old? Is that why everything suddenly seems so overwhelming? She feels her forehead. Is it the menopause? She's heard of women being consumed by rage as they sweat from places they didn't even know had sweat glands. Or is it just that serving boiling-hot coffee in a handleless vessel is a stupid fucking idea in the first place?

She checks the time again. Still a couple of minutes to go. A movement at the edge of the terrace gets her attention. A man. She feels her pulse quicken. It's unmistakably him. Ant. He's here. And not only that but he looks exactly like his pictures. No extra poundage, no surplus years. He scours the terrace; she assumes trying to spot her. She catches his eye.

She can see him scrutinizing her. She's the only single woman there after all. She almost smiles. Almost raises a hand to wave.

But she doesn't.

She looks away.

2

Joni buries her face in her phone, trying to catch her breath. Ant has decided she's not who he was looking for and settled at a table at the front of the terrace. She watches as he greets the waiter with a smile. She can't hear exactly what he's saying but she can tell it's friendly, polite. The imperious server even cracks a smile himself. You can tell a lot about someone's character from the way they treat waiters or shop assistants or bus drivers when they think no one is watching. It's so strange to see Ant animated. A mythical figure brought to life. He had suggested, on the second phone call, that they use FaceTime, but she had resisted. She didn't want the first time they saw each other to be made even more awkward by bad angles and unnatural lighting, she told him. She should have known for certain then that he was genuine.

'You can't be sure, though,' Imo had said when she'd filled her in. 'You could make all the arrangements and then on the day he'd claim he didn't have a strong enough signal and you'd have to settle for a voice call instead. But he'd know you now trusted him just because he'd suggested it in the first place.'

'When did it all get to be so complicated?' Joni had said. The last person she had dated had been Imo's dad, and they had been married for nearly twenty years.

They'd met in a pub through mutual friends. There simply hadn't been any possibility that either of them wasn't who they said they were. Unfortunately.

Ant looks up and down the street. Joni studies his profile. The straight nose, chin covered by neat stubble. His dark hair is cropped close, possibly to hide the fact that it's thinning, but it suits him. He's tanned – it's been a hit-and-miss summer so far, but he looks as if he has the kind of skin that tans easily. She can see the smile lines around his eyes that attracted her to his photos in the first place. Shit. Why does he have to be so perfect? So . . . him? She thinks about going over anyway. Introducing herself. Trying to explain. But what would be the point? They've talked endlessly about how much they value honesty, how there's no way you can build a relationship on deception. She should have come clean then.

She sips her now cool coffee. She can tell Ant is getting anxious. He looks at his phone. She reaches for her own and turns off the sound just in case. He makes a call, and she glances down and sees his name light up her screen. Looks on as he leaves a message. She can hear concern in his voice.

She can't watch any more. It's too painful imagining how it might have been. How she could have sat in the empty chair next to him and picked up where they last left off. (Well, maybe not with the orgasms. That might be a little inappropriate.) There's no point in her staying. She'll just have to learn from her mistake. Move on. She's thankful at least that she hadn't told Imo she and

Ant were planning to meet today. She couldn't face the inquisition.

She leaves a ten-pound note on the table, wishing she had the guts to wait and ask for change because there's no way the snotty waiter deserves the tip. She's always been an over-tipper. As if asking for her own money back might be seen as an affront. He picks it up and looks dismissively from the bill to the note and back. She ignores him. Ant is calling again. She hears him leave another message as she gets up, sounding slightly more irritated this time.

'I don't know how long to wait . . .' he's saying as she moves closer, towards the little gate out on to the street. 'Because it's already been nearly twenty minutes . . . did I get the day wrong?' She's just coming up beside him as he ends the call.

'You been stood up too?' It's out of her mouth before she can stop herself. She doesn't know what makes her say it, she just feels as if she wants to make a connection with him. He glances up at her. She holds her breath, waiting to see if he recognizes anything familiar in her. It's not out of the question. But his expression is blank.

'Looks like it. Date?' It takes her a second to realize he's asking about her.

She smiles ruefully. 'Friend. You?'

He sighs. 'Date.'

'Well, I hope they turn up . . .' she says. She wonders for a second if he might recognize her voice; she's made no attempt to disguise it, she realizes with a nervous jolt. But he just gives her a faint smile.

'I don't think so now.'

If this were a film now would be the moment where he would suddenly notice her, be struck by a lightning bolt of lust and ask her to join him. They'd bemoan their situation, but then find they had lots in common. Pass a long morning laughing and chatting and it would roll into lunch and then maybe a walk in the park. An arrangement to meet again. But this is real life, so Ant just turns back to his phone and Joni walks away with a cursory 'Bye, then.' He doesn't even watch her go.

She hadn't joined Keepers to deceive. Far from it. Well, only in so much as everyone else apparently did. Her conversations with Imo had left her feeling a little insecure. If everyone was presenting a carefully curated version of themselves using old pictures and editing out their flaws, wouldn't she be at a disadvantage if she didn't do the same? Wouldn't every other forty-nine-year-old woman on there look younger and firmer than she did? So she had trawled through old photos trying to find ones where she looked like the self she remembered in her head before life caught up with her. It was odd how few there were to choose from. Even with everyone maniacally snapping images of everything these days, from their breakfast to their bedtime-scrubbed faces, she had almost none. She had never been one for selfies and Ian had long since lost any interest in capturing her face on film. Meg would have had a selection, of course. They had often snapped each other on a night out, after a few drinks. But who knew where those were now? She should ask Meg's mum if she still had Meg's phone. They could go through the photos together, have a cup of tea and reminisce about all the fun times before Meg got into the car that would claim her life. She knew she should make more of an effort to keep in touch with her friend's mother but it was too painful, too raw. She pushed away the realization that she hadn't contacted her in months. Hadn't answered her messages.

She'd scrolled back and back, getting more and more frustrated. Surely there must be one decent snap of her somewhere in the world. She flicked past her sister, Lucy, laughing at a barbecue. Flicked back. She and Lucy weren't unalike – both with heart-shaped faces, deep brown eyes, a bottom lip much fuller than the top – but Lucy was the Hollywood version of Joni's B-movie looks. She was five years younger, with their mother's aquiline nose, abundant auburn hair and thick brows. Joni had their dad's neat snub, over-plucked brows that would never grow back, and her dark brown hair was barely shoulder length. If you put them side by side you would know, but apart – well, you probably wouldn't make the connection. Their smiles were the same. Wide. Straight white teeth. As deceptions went it wouldn't be the worst. She could probably convince most people that in five years Lucy had morphed into Joni with some hair dye and maybe a bit of rhinoplasty. It wasn't the same as finding a total stranger's image on Facebook and claiming to be them. Thankful that she had told Imo she couldn't create a profile with her breathing over her shoulder, she'd added the picture. Pressed save before she could talk herself out of it.

She'd known, deep down, that it would backfire, of course. Maybe subconsciously it had been self-sabotage. She could say she'd tried but online dating wasn't for her. But how was she to know that the first man she gelled with would turn out to be so real? So strikingly, handsomely, honestly real? She had assumed that he would have presented an unrealistic picture of himself too. A throwback to when he was in his prime. She wouldn't have agreed to meet him otherwise. They would have laughed when they realized.

She's an idiot, she knows that now. She's blown it with Ant. She walks home through Hyde Park, stopping at a bench to send him a message.

I'm so sorry, it says. *I wanted to come. I got cold feet. I hope you'll forgive me.*

A couple of long minutes later she gets a reply. *These things happen. It's been nice getting to know you. Good luck in the future.*

Maybe I could explain more on the phone, she writes. She waits for the 'delivered' notification to tell her her message has been received. It never comes. She checks on the dating app. He's already blocked her there too.

3

There's not even anyone she can share her story with. Imo is the only person who knows she's been online dating and she would disapprove wholeheartedly of Joni using Lucy's pictures. Meg would have found it hilarious. Teased her mercilessly. God, she misses her. That uncomplicated ease they had. None of the passive-aggressive resentments that lurk in families or the jealousy and point-scoring of relationships – in her experience at least. They had been friends since the first few weeks of secondary school, been through boyfriends and hangovers, recreational drugs, childbirth and divorce (hers). Death (Meg's). People talk about their fear of losing a partner but rarely a best friend. But they're a precious commodity. Irreplaceable. She has friends, of course she does – former colleagues, other mums from when Imo was little, one from uni – but mostly these days they're a duty. A once-a-year obligatory catch-up that both of them probably secretly hope the other cancels, where they talk about the facts, not the feelings. They could probably cover the exact same ground by sending out one of those awful Christmas-card letters, but for some reason they persist in meeting face to face. They're a box to tick, nothing more.

She lets herself into her flat, narrowly avoiding her

upstairs neighbour Flick. She freezes like a statue behind her closed front door when she hears Flick's heavy footsteps come to a stop in the hall. There's a knock, a shout of her name. It's not unknown for Flick to poke open the letterbox and peer through, but Joni can't move in case she makes a noise, so she presses back against the wall and hopes for the best. She loves her spacious, airy flat, but she sometimes thinks she lives like she's under siege avoiding her neighbour's well-meaning advances. That's the problem with living in converted houses instead of large blocks. There's some kind of tacit agreement that all the residents involve themselves in each other's lives. Gregarious – for that read nosy – Flick lurks on the first floor like a trap-door spider, sandwiched between Joni and the young couple on the top floor (she forgets their names. Jordan and Jaden or Megan and Morgan, something like that), waiting to pounce at the slightest sign of life. And Flick loves to talk. It doesn't seem to matter to who or about what, words just pour out of her mouth like an overflowing bath. There's never a beginning or an end to what she has to say. It's all middle. All the continuation of one big flow of consciousness. It's exhausting. Joni knows that if she opened the door now Flick would launch in with some non sequitur like 'He really shouldn't do that' or 'It turned out to be tomorrow after all' and expect Joni to somehow hop on board for the ride.

Eventually Flick gives up and retreats. Joni tiptoes into the living room, still wary of making a noise. She feels a rush of guilt, as she always does. Flick is harmless. She lives alone and she craves company. She has a son who she only sees when he wants money and a daughter she never seems to see at all. Really, they should bond, two single women living alone, but Joni would have to be hung from a bridge by her toes over a river full of hungry crocodiles to acknowledge she's part of the lonely-middle-aged-ladies pity club just yet.

She flops down on the sofa, fighting off the advances of Jasper, her ancient, scrawny black cat. Another tick in the cliché box. Kill me now, she thinks. I'm past all hope. She might as well give up, buy a kaftan and some over-sized artisanal jewellery and start easing into old age, sitting upstairs with Flick comparing ailments over a cup of herbal tea or ten. She curses herself for fucking it up so spectacularly with Ant. What are the chances she'll meet another genuine bloke she's actually attracted to and who likes her back (well, her personality anyway, and surely that's half the battle?).

The rest of the weekend looms ahead. She has a list of things she needs to do. Chores. But she finds she can't be bothered to move. What's the point of hoovering if no one except her is ever going to notice? If a crumb falls on a carpet and no one is around to see it, does it make a mess? She shuffles along the sofa to find the spot where the sun hits as it streams through the front bay window. Jasper follows. When did her life become this small? Work, chores, workout. And repeat. All that changes are the clothes she wears, according to the seasons. And even then not much, if she's being honest.

She looks round at her flat, her haven. The living

room flows into a kitchen that stretches across the back of the house. She has both the ground and the lower-ground floors. Three bedrooms, two and a half baths, a study. It's not what most people think of when they hear the word 'flat'. Someone once said to her that if a home looked too perfect it meant the person living there either had a full-time cleaner or no life. Joni only has a cleaner for three hours every Friday morning. When Imo was home it was different, of course. There was mess and noise and colour. She thinks about phoning her but then she remembers she's working. She's a runner on a new Saturday-morning live show for kids. Training on the job as part of a scheme to nurture new talent. She's earning next to nothing, living in an overcrowded house with five others from the same initiative, having the time of her life. Joni smiles. At least something's going right.

She allows herself to think about Ant again. Plays through the whole scenario in her mind. The thing is that she wouldn't have cared if his pictures had been old or filtered to within an inch of their lives. She'd actively hoped for it. Counted on it. They could have bonded over their well-intentioned deceptions. Except that her photos hadn't just been out of date and digitally enhanced. Her photos hadn't even been of her.

She's getting up to put the kettle on, her weekend ruined, when it hits her. What's to stop her bumping into Ant in real life? Her, Joni, with Joni's actual face and body? Striking up a proper conversation with him this time. He didn't exactly notice her when she spoke to him outside the café but then he was preoccupied. She knows so much about him from their two months of exchanges that she must be able to contrive a way.

She grabs a pen from the jar on the kitchen table and the notebook where she makes her to-do lists (tomorrow: 'Dry cleaning in, post Mum's card, buy tomatoes'. Another scintillating day on the horizon. She's not sure she can take the excitement) and makes a note of everything she knows about him: Anthony Simons, fifty-two, two children, divorced, owner of his own small chain of wellness centres – ultra-posh spas really – much beloved by West London's wealthy inhabitants who think nothing of paying four hundred pounds a pop to have a caviar facial, lives in Notting Hill near his ex-wife who is still in the palatial family home. She decides to go back to the beginning, trawling first through their exchanges on the app and then their texts in search of clues. She feels better when she sees the trail of breadcrumbs they have left for each other along the way. Ant, like her, loves the gym.

Where do you go? she'd asked. *I'm a Power Fit woman myself.*

Me too! was the reply. *Well, not the woman bit.*

Which one? was her next question, and he'd told her Notting Hill. She notes it down. There's a selfie of him with part of a street sign visible but she can only make out the word 'Avenue'. She tries not to look at the photos of Lucy she sent when he suggested they swap more snaps. He had added a picture of him with his dog Vinnie, a huge brown and white scruffy thing with a face like a snooty colonel. He likes Wagamama and *Line of Duty* and making bread. He has two brothers and his mum lives in Brighton. She's not sure any of this is helping much.

In their messages he mentions going to the cinema, the pub with his friend Pete and playing five-a-side football with one of his brothers. She likes that he's so down to earth, despite his successes. He talks about finding the perfect house when his divorce comes through. She has never even asked him what his company is called. God, she's been on her own so long she's clearly forgotten the art of polite conversation.

She remembers his Facebook profile – she has looked him up before, obviously. She's seen *Catfish*. She knows you don't let yourself get caught out panting into someone's ear on the phone if you haven't first checked they are who they say they are. There's precious little to see though. Just his cover photo – him, shirtless on a beach somewhere. They have no mutual friends. She has never sent him a friend request, obviously. Even if she was who she was supposed to be (she is in all ways other than looks, she reminds herself. Their conversations have always been completely honest. He knows the real her – so long as he keeps his eyes shut) she didn't really see the point. She's never on there herself; she'd stopped seeing the allure early on of everyone you ever knew and their fifth cousin being able to find you so you can exchange a few painfully awkward words. (*Hi! Remember me? We were at primary school together! I was Janine Mason then. What are you up to?*) Joni would rack her brain and come up with a vague recollection of a ruddy-faced girl with stringy blonde hair or a lanky redhead with glasses. At first, she'd replied

17

enthusiastically, despite not recalling ever having been friends with the person in the first place. *Yes! I remember you! How are you?* And then she'd be stuck in a seemingly interminable exchange of information about children and jobs and husbands and divorces that felt like homework every time she logged on.) She'd long since stopped checking her page. Left it to die a slow death. Imo had told her that Facebook was only for boomers anyway, which sounded like an insult. Instagram was the place to be. So, she had a page there too, with the same photo of Jasper as the header and her privacy settings turned up to the max so that she only had to interact with people she truly wanted to hear from. If Ant had ever checked on her in either place there would have been nothing that would have given her away.

This is hopeless.

She googles him. Again, she's done this before, just so she could tell Imo she had. Not that she'd found anything interesting. But she hadn't really tried. There was an actor with the same name in an American network show about lawyers and he took up the first six pages on his own. She'd given up in the end. She'd only been idly browsing anyway. Now she tries to be more forensic, searching for combinations of Anthony Simons, wellness and Notting Hill, but it turns out the actor had one line in the Richard Curtis classic and has also been on a voyage of self-discovery that involved several gurus and a variety of wacky-sounding holistic treatments. She changes tack and looks for spas in the general area but it's overwhelming. All she manages to glean is that the people of West London love to be pampered. With the more random ingredients the better.

Before she realizes it, she's gone down a wormhole of high-end treatments on offer at exclusive beauty salons, each one more outrageous than the last: exfoliation with diamond dust, vampire facials (where they take some of your own blood and inject it into your own face. The ultimate in recycling. Also, she figures, cheap. No outgoings), bee venom face masks; she even finds a guano treatment (for which read bird poop) to prevent ageing. It seems the more painful or disgusting the experience, the more expensive. Jasper paws at her arm in search of comfort or, more likely, lunch. She bats him away, moves her search to images. Again, the actor dominates the results, so she quickly scrolls through page after page, barely looking, to get to the less popular results. Why has she never asked Ant what his company is called? She keeps her finger on the down button as faces and film posters fly by in a blur. She goes past the photo without even noticing it, but something in her subconscious must take in more than she realizes. She stops. Scrolls back.

There's a picture of about fifteen coolly dressed, beautiful people smiling at the camera, a fairly even mix of men and women. Second from the right is a man who looks exactly like Ant. She clicks on the image and then through to the website it's from. Evoke Wellness. The caption reads *The whole team. Left to right* . . . and the fourteenth name on the list is Anthony Simons.

Bingo.

Now she just has to get her courage up.

4

It takes three attempts to set the alarm. Probably because Ant is fuming about the state of the place. The idea that the higher the prices they charged the worse the destruction left behind never ceased to irritate him. The greater the privilege the bigger the mess. Evoke had started to offer private group bookings in the evenings at the Kensington Church Street branch, in order to try and recoup some of the money lost from the months they were forced to close during the pandemic. You could charge a fortune for exclusive access to the hot tubs, sauna and steam room, but all they were really doing was catering to wealthy hen parties, it seemed. Gangs of women who sneaked in bottles of Ruinart and Cristal (they had a strict no-alcohol policy; they couldn't risk a lawsuit following a drowning in the Jacuzzi. Fancy booze-free cocktails were offered instead) and insulted the staff. People so entitled they couldn't even be bothered to hide the evidence. To be fair, most of them were fine, but every now and then the cleaners would report varying levels of carnage. Tonight – the twenty-first-birthday early-evening pre-party for the daughter of a music-business mogul and eleven of her friends – was possibly the worst he'd seen. A broken seat in the steam room. A smashed mirror. The birthday girl had apparently been

put in an Uber in tears. One of the therapists had threatened to quit, claiming she'd been verbally assaulted. The
branch manager only worked Monday to Friday, and
the evenings and weekends were generally overseen by
the head therapist, who was herself in tears in the back
room, and seemingly incapable of making any decisions.
Ant had been on his way home from a gym session when
he'd got the call. Only a few minutes away, so it wasn't
really a big deal, but it was certainly a waste of time. And
he'd wasted enough time already today.

He wasn't angry that Joni hadn't shown up. He
understood the last-minute nerves. It was a big step
taking something into the real world. She was probably
hiding something, that was the problem. An imperfec-
tion. Something she thought he wouldn't find attractive
In Real Life. People never believed him when he said
looks weren't important, but he honestly believed that.
Well, up to a point anyway. They weren't the most important thing. Far from it. The person was what mattered.
The connection they could make. And he had definitely felt a connection with Joni. She had sworn blind
to him on the phone that she was genuine – as he had
to her. It was a big deal to him, knowing that any woman
he was talking to was who she said she was. He'd waited
for nearly thirty-five minutes in the end, just in case
Joni was stuck on a tube somewhere with no reception,
but then he'd got her message and realized she wasn't
going to show at all. He'd been disappointed – he
wasn't going to lie. He'd thought they had something.
When he'd got her text he'd thought about trying to set

up another date, telling her that he understood, but he'd made a rule for himself when he signed on to the dating site that he wouldn't allow himself to be messed around. It was too easy to be seduced by the idea of someone only to find you'd been played.

He wanders towards Notting Hill. The flagship branch of Evoke Wellness sits proudly among the brightly coloured terraced houses, between a small Italian deli selling fresh fat artichokes and mouthwatering olives at staggering prices and a home-furnishings store that often features in the pages of *House & Garden*. It's a beautiful area. Hemmed in on two sides by run-down estates that allow the rich home-owners to maintain they are both in touch with real life and compassionately inclusive, while at the same time to turn only east or south whenever they leave their front doors and minimize the risk of having to actually rub shoulders with the locals.

It's quiet on a Saturday. Still too early for night-time revellers. Many of the houses are empty, their residents having fled to Suffolk or the Cotswolds the evening before. And it's been a beautiful day, not yet that over-ripe part of summer when everything starts to get a bit oppressive and overblown. He pushes open the door into the air-conditioned coolness.

'You weren't exaggerating,' he says to Amir, the receptionist. Amir had called him with the bad news because he knew that Ant always liked to assess any damage himself as soon as possible. Kensington Church Street had to be up and running – and looking beautiful – by the time it was due to open again tomorrow morning. The cleaners would do a faultless job overnight as usual, but the bench needed repairing, the mirror replacing. You couldn't have workmen clomping about in there while it was open, gawking at the half-naked clientele, singing along to Absolute 80s on their ever-present radios, ruining people's vibe. Evoke was big on energies, ambience, an all-round, holistic experience.

'I think these private bookings are more trouble than they're worth,' Ant says, heading for the back.

'Animals,' Amir says, leaning back in his chair. 'Absolute fucking animals.'

Ant feels a chunk of broken glass crunch under his foot. He kicks it out of the way. He'll get back on to the Keepers app tomorrow, he decides. He isn't going to let one disappointment put him off.

5

She can't just walk into a branch of Evoke Wellness and demand to see Anthony Simons. It needs to look coincidental, otherwise he'll think she's some kind of weird stalker. Which – in this instance only – she actually is. Joni needs to contrive to bump into him, start up a conversation ('Oh, it's you! Been stood up lately?' Might as well see if he can take a joke. He's funny on the phone but then they've never been laughing about his own misfortune). The company's three London branches are within easy walking distance of each other. She always tries to double her steps on her days off anyway, to make up for the fact that when she's at work she sits at her desk all day in a variety of back-crunching positions, so strolling back and forth between upper-crust areas of west London is as good a way to pass a Monday as any. It's not exactly a plan but, let's face it, it's something to do. She only works three days a week, job-sharing with Lucas in the accounts department at the head office of a chain of department stores. As the person who does 60 per cent of the work, Joni likes to think she has the slight edge in superiority, but she knows that Lucas would disagree. Although since Lucas seems to disagree with pretty much everything she says, on principle, there's no surprise there. They communicate via an occasional series of passive-aggressive Post-it notes attached to piles of work they have failed to complete by the end of their day. Sometimes the same documents will be batted back and forth for more than a week before one of them gives in and finishes whatever the job is. Usually her.

Joni tries not to think what Imo would say if she knew her mother was pacing around London hoping to bump into a man she barely knows in order to secure a date with him. The logistics of it wouldn't even seem like the most ridiculous part, probably. She heads for the main branch first. She's dressed in what she hopes is a cute-looking but practical outfit of loose-fitting jeans, rolled up a couple of times at the ankle, with pale pink trainers and a soft red cap-sleeve T-shirt. She doesn't go to the gym four times a week not to show off her toned arms. Maybe he'll turn out to have a tricep fetish and that'll distract him from her eye bags.

She stops short in the street. She can't do this. She should just go back on the app, change her photos for the real thing and write Ant off as a learning experience. But she knows it's an itch she needs to scratch. A 'what if?' that needs to be answered.

She'll just pretend she's spending a beautiful summer's day pottering. No agenda. No big deal. One day out of her life.

She turns into the pretty street, almost immediately stumbles across the Evoke Wellness window. She walks past without even looking in but then makes herself turn back. She's allowed to browse the list of treatments, isn't she? Nothing suspicious about that. She pulls her sunglasses down and tilts her head as if she's looking at the display while actually peering over the top at the people inside. The interior is decorated in browns and golds against mostly white walls. There's a waterfall cascading behind a reception desk, running over glittering mosaic tiles in matching shades. A large fridge with neatly lined-up bottles of water. No Perrier or Evian here. The bottles are clear green glass. No logo. Bespoke, she assumes.

A man is sitting behind the rustic wooden desk formed, it looks like, from a piece of driftwood. It's not Ant. Well, she hardly expected him to be the first person she saw. Or to be working behind reception, let's face it. It suddenly strikes her that as the owner of the company he might not even come in every day. If at all. Although he's often mentioned having been at work so, hopefully, he's the kind of boss who believes you have to lead by example. She gets the impression he built the company from next to nothing through sheer hard work. That he's very hands on. Two women stand talking to one side, one showing the other something on her phone, pointing out a detail with a long perfectly manicured fingernail. Dressed in almost identical slouchy soft trousers and thong sandals. Slightly cropped tops that show off a sliver of perfectly toned, tanned stomachs. Warm blonde hair in carefully messy beach waves. She watches as another woman in a brown, fitted T-shirt with Evoke written in discreet italics across the chest, and wide yoga pants in the same shade, collects them both and takes them through to the back. She's tempted to stay and see if they emerge later looking years younger.

She flicks her gaze back down to the featured treatments in the window. Basically variations on facials and massages with complicated add-ons: hydralifting and microbiomes, ultherapy and lipolysis. None of it sounds very relaxing, although it claims to be. There are no prices attached. If you need to ask you can't afford to buy, she assumes.

Evoke, she knows, also do global business in eponymous products. Scrubs and body creams with unlikely-sounding ingredients like gold leaf, saffron and white truffles. There are bejewelled vibrators (what if one of those diamonds came off mid you-know-what? was Joni's first thought when she saw them on the website. How would you ever explain that in A and E?) and dodgy-looking vaginal eggs made from smoothed crystals. It's a menu to rival Goop and, she knows, a very lucrative one. The spas, Ant has told her, are really a loss leader to advertise the brand.

Evoke is fronted by model/actress Bliss, who is actually neither of those things to any great effect, but she is the daughter of a grizzled old rock star and his It girl ex-wife, and has therefore lived a life of getting herself in the papers and thinking she's too special to have a real job. She has now fashioned herself as a holistic guru and is happy to disclose anything from the frequency and intensity of her orgasms to the frequency and consistency of her bowel movements to garner attention. Nothing personal is off limits: the more intimate and the greater volume of bodily fluids involved the better. Ant has told Joni she's a nightmare: rude, entitled, lazy. But all she has to do is put her name to products and proce-dures, and for the right amount of cash she's more than happy to do that.

There's a tiny café opposite with two tables outside. She's tempted to take up residence, but she decides to do a loop first, just in case Ant is in one of the other branches, a sitting duck waiting to be spotted. She wan-ders down Kensington Church Street, distracted by the shops. Evoke Wellness is about a third of the way down, a much smaller but equally high-end-looking shopfront. This one in shades of green. She does her 'looking at the treatments, but not really' trick again. There is only one woman visible inside. No Ant. She checks the map on her phone and swings back in the direction of Holland Park Avenue, repeats the whole process and sees only two women. Notting Hill is the only one of the three with a conveniently placed lookout opposite and she assumes that Ant is most likely to work out of the main hub, so she wanders back in that direction. This is a stu-pid idea. Ridiculous. She actually laughs out loud. But she's gripped by how well they connected, their long conversations. The way he listened to her.

She's hungry anyway so the empty table outside the café seems like a good option. She chooses a chair look-ing across the quiet road and orders an acai bowl and some kind of kefir water, settles in like a spectator at a cricket match. It suddenly occurs to her that she could have saved herself a lot of time and effort. The Evoke Wellness phone number is etched on to their window. She dials it on her mobile, gazing casually in any direction other than the building opposite. She worries for a brief second that one of the two people deep in conversation at the next table might be connected to the company, but as they've been talking about stock prices for the last five minutes she thinks it's unlikely. Still, she keeps her voice low when her call is answered.

'Evoke Wellness,' a man says, and Joni has to stop herself looking up in case he catches her eye through the window.

'Oh, hello. I . . . um . . . could I just check that Anthony Simons works out of this branch?' Is that an OK question? Does she sound odd?

'He does,' the man says breezily. 'He's not here at the moment, though. Can I give him a message?'

'No!' Joni jumps in far too quickly. 'Do you know when he'll be back? I have something that he needs to sign.' She likes that detail. No receptionist in their right mind would dare to ask what.

'He usually pops in at lunchtime. One-ish. But I can't guarantee it . . .'

'That's perfect,' Joni says. 'Thank you.' She jabs the button to end the call but then keeps the phone to her ear for a moment as if she's still talking. Just in case. In case of what she's not quite sure but she does it anyway. Her phone says it's eleven fourteen. She can potter down to Kensington High Street, maybe sit in the park for a bit, return to the scene of the crime just before one, hang around till two fifteen max and then slope back home to rethink her whole life. It's a plan.

6

Of course both tables outside the café are taken when she returns at nearly ten past one. She was aiming for five to, but she underestimated how far she'd walked in the other direction. Now she's sweating, and pink with effort. For all she knows she's missed him and now he'll be holed up in an office at the back of the building till home time at six or even seven. Later, maybe. The spa is open till ten.

She paces up and down looking in random shop windows. She could never be a private detective, she thinks, hired to follow some poor woman's cheating husband. The boredom would engulf her. All those hours of waiting. Hoping against hope to witness something that would ruin someone's life. She would probably end up falling asleep and then having to make stuff up to keep the client happy. Patience has never been a virtue of hers. Maybe she should cut this tragic mission short and go home before her self-esteem plummets so low she'll never be able to lift it up again. She decides to do one more pass of the street and then give it up as a one-off, never to be spoken of again, out of character . . .

It's him.

Her heart quickens. Now what? She's a hundred metres away, but she's sure. He's walking away from her, about to turn the corner at the far end. Dressed in . . . is that gym gear? Yes, and he has a bag over his shoulder. He's going to the gym. She even knows which one. They've talked about this – he said he goes most days, but it hadn't occurred to her it might be at lunchtime. There's no point following him, she thinks thankfully, picturing her sunny living room, the sofa, Jasper on her lap. She always goes to the gym on her days off. She joined years ago, when she needed somewhere to go that was just hers. Somewhere to channel all her angst about Ian and what he was up to. And now it's as much a part of her life as her job. More, probably, because the job is just something to fill her days, to distract her from the fact that Meg is gone. But Mondays, Wednesdays, Saturdays and Sundays she has an appointment with herself at four o'clock. An hour and a half. She listens to a playlist she has made on Spotify. Works her way round the equipment in an anticlockwise circle. Focuses more on legs on Mondays and Saturdays and arms on Wednesdays and Sundays. Half an hour's cardio on the running machine. She walks there and back to warm her body both up and down. She nods hello to the other regulars but no more. It's a serious gym – the members come here to work out, not to flop about in a steam room for half the session and chat just to tick it off their to-do list. It has no frills and that's its charm. It's sweat and power and hard work. It's the anti-David Lloyd. And twice as expensive. It's her second home. If she was struck down with amnesia she thinks muscle memory would still lead her there bang on schedule every time.

Her membership gets her entry into the chain's four other branches. She'll start heading for the Notting Hill Branch rather than her own in Swiss Cottage. One of these days she's bound to bump into Ant and, apart from moving her session to lunchtimes and travelling an extra twenty minutes for her workout, she won't be going out of the way of her usual routine so much that she feels like a psycho.

She turns and walks towards the main road, already looking for a cab.

7

Two days later she arrives at the gym at a quarter to one, stashes her bag in a locker and takes up residence on a running machine overlooking the main door. She's made an extra effort. Usually she hits the gym in whatever vaguely clean sweats she can find and no make-up. Posing in Power Fit means flexing, stacking up the weights, cinching in a powerlifting belt, not wearing an eye-catching outfit. Today, though, she's in her black Bo+Tee ribbed leggings that she knows are super flattering, an Under Armour coral racer-back vest and her hair is freshly blow-dried. She looks around. The layout is actually comfortingly familiar. Cardio machines along one wall, serious stacks of weights along the opposite, and state-of-the-art machines filling the space between. She jogs at a stately pace to avoid getting out of breath and sweaty. Waits.

Last night she had called Imo, prepared to leave a message. Imo had answered after three rings, a question in her voice.

'It's Mum,' Joni had said. 'I've got a new number.'

'What? Why?'

'I treated myself to a new phone.'

Imo had sighed. 'Why didn't you keep the old number? You'll have to transfer all your contacts . . .'

'Oh, I didn't realize you could,' Joni said, remembering full well the conversation with the woman in the shop who'd told her her life would be much easier if she kept her details the same.

'They didn't tell you? You should complain.' Imo had inherited her father's bolshiness when it came to consumer rights, one of his better qualities.

'It's all done now. Never mind . . .' Joni had wanted to distance herself from the woman who had phone sex and then stood a man up. Just in case she managed to bump into Ant again and, miracle of miracles, impress him enough that he asked for her number, she needed to have one to give him that didn't already pop up on his phone. She'd been due an upgrade for months, she told herself. Years probably. And it wasn't as if there were many people she would need to give her new number to anyway.

To steer the conversation into safer waters Joni had asked her how things were going and Imo, freshly home from the studios, and buzzing with her new life, had filled her in. Joni had been itching to tell her what she was up to – as if she needed another person to confirm she was acting like a crazy person and it was all going to end in tears. She didn't, of course, and Imo being eighteen and in love with the new world she had found herself in didn't ask. Instead, Joni had regaled her with a story about her day at work. She'd had to phone Lucas because of a mix-up over a contract that seemed to have gone astray.

'He actually said the words "I'm on my day off. Can this wait until tomorrow?"'

'Oh my God!' Imo had squealed. 'What did you say?'

'I said, "But then I'll be on *my* day off." Honestly, he's unbearable. Should I complain about him? I should, shouldn't I?'

She'd heard Imo sigh. 'You have to be careful. You don't want him to turn it round and make it sound as if you're the one who's out of order.'

'He does nothing all day. Absolutely nothing.' Joni took a long sip of her wine. She was trying to only drink at the weekends, but it took all her willpower not to pour herself a glass when seven o'clock and the prospect of another long dull evening rolled around. Tonight she'd given in. 'I should hide a Ring camera in the office, see how he manages to pass eight hours without actually achieving anything.'

'That's not a bad idea,' Imo said. 'But probably illegal. Also imagine what you might see . . .'

'Eew.' Joni choked on her drink. 'I have to share a desk with him, remember.'

'Wipe the seat down with an antibac,' Imo had said, and Joni had laughed until she felt sick. God, she missed her daughter.

After five minutes of door-watching, she's bored. She throws herself into her workout, trying to act as if it's a normal Wednesday, concentrating on what she's doing. She knows everyone moans about exercise, but for her it's like therapy. Time to think about nothing but herself. She's aware that sounds self-involved, but it's true. Sometimes you just need to do something to quiet the noises in your head. Mindfulness. Imo (who is effortlessly lithe but, Joni is convinced, could turn out to be one of those skinny fat people who looks fit on the outside, but whose organs are slowly being strangled by lard and who keel over from a heart attack walking up a slight hill one day) is always telling her to try jigsaws or colouring books. 'Much less effort,' she would say whenever Joni complained about her aches and pains. 'Or just get lipo if you're worried about looking good.' She knew Imo was winding her up, but deep down she also fretted that her daughter was of a generation who thought everything could be fixed by needles and scalpels. Joni stayed awake some nights worrying that Imo might decide to get hyaluronic acid injected into her perfect lips and then somehow be stuck looking like a beached fish forever, or worse, suffer an allergic reaction and drop down dead on the spot. But then again, she had also come to recognize that she was basically a catastrophist. Being the parent of an only child could do that to you. Ian used to tell her to chill (number three on his list of annoying phrases after 'Sweet as' and 'End of'. Well, and 'I'm leaving you for Holly,' but he only said that the once and within an hour he was gone, holdall in hand). He loved to be the laid-back parent, the annoying yin to her practical, appropriately concerned yang. While she stayed up panicking if Imo was still not home ten minutes later than the time she had said she would be, Ian would regale her with hilarious stories about his own misspent youth and the hair-raisingly life-threatening scrapes he'd got into. Meanwhile Joni's finger hovered nervously over the nine key on her phone. Then Imo would saunter in, full of funny stories about her evening, and Ian would say something really annoying like 'Your mum thought you'd been abducted. Again! Hahaha.' And Joni would want to kill him. It was one of the things they always argued about. How it was easy to be the irresponsible parent, the best mate, the wingman, but that that – so Joni thought anyway – wasn't what parenting was about. It wasn't a popularity contest. But for Ian, everything in life was about taking the easy road. He had never really grown up.

At five past one Ant walks in.

Joni almost loses her footing on the running machine. He walks right past her and through to the changing rooms, although he's already in workout gear so presumably he's just going to stash his bag in one of the lockers. Her heart starts pounding. This is it. One go, and then give it up. If he doesn't bite, she'll move on. She can't quite believe he's here on her first attempt. She'd thought it might take days, weeks even. Give her time to psych herself up. She's not sure she's ready to make a move quite yet. She can't miss this opportunity though. What's the worst that can happen? She stops the machine and moves over to the free weights, leaving herself ready to improvise when she sees where he heads first. He emerges two minutes later, bagless, and looks round as a man the size of a rhino, sitting at the squat machine, calls out, 'Hey, Ant.' They do the half-ironic post-Covid elbow bump and Joni watches as they chat for a couple of minutes. Then he slaps the rhino on the shoulder and heads straight for the rack she's standing in front of. She can't quite believe her luck. Of all the bars in all the towns . . . OK, well, that would work if she hadn't basically followed him here even though she'd arrived first. But still, the fact that he has appeared right beside her in this vast gym . . . if she believed in signs this would definitely be one. She decides she needs to, just for this afternoon. He reaches across for the fifteen-kilo dumbbells. Joni catches his eye in the mirror. Overacts shock and surprise so badly that she almost backs out and runs away before she even says anything.

'Hi . . . um . . . I know you, don't I?'

He squints slightly. No recognition. Nothing. 'I don't think so . . .'

She manages a weak smile. 'We've met before, I'm sure of it. I have a great memory for faces . . .'

He shakes his head politely. 'I don't remember, sorry.'

She pauses for a moment as if she's trying to recall. 'I know! From that café in Kensington last weekend! Did your date ever turn up?'

There are a few more agonizing seconds where she thinks he might just walk off, ignoring the crazy lady, but the penny must finally drop because he smiles back at her. Friendly. Open. Even if not that interested. Joni's confident mask slips a little. 'Oh, right. Yes. You were waiting for your friend. And, no. She didn't.'

'Well, you can't win them all,' she says lightly. 'Was it something you said?'

Thankfully he laughs, showing slightly crooked but sparkling white teeth. Prominent canines. 'Probably.'

Joni does a few half-hearted curls. 'Maybe next time.'

'I don't think so,' Ant says, scratching at something on his tanned forearm. He's so familiar to her. It's bizarre that he doesn't feel the same. She has to stop herself saying 'I know you hate blueberries, and that you're allergic to shellfish, and you have a dog called Vinnie.'

'Not who she says she is, is my guess,' he adds, failing to disguise a slight note of bitterness that pierces her heart.

He turns away to head for one of the benches. She can't follow him, and no way can she strike up another random conversation later either. She reminds herself she has nothing to lose. 'Ah, online,' she says, raising her voice a little so he can still hear her. 'I've always been too scared. God knows who you could be talking to.'

He turns back. 'You'd be surprised,' he says. 'Most people seem to be pretty genuine.'

'Just not this one?'

'Or she just freaked out. It happens.'

'What, when she saw you?' Joni says. She holds her breath to see if he'll laugh. Almost faints with relief when he does.

'Ha! Possibly.'

'So, I should do it?' she says. 'Online?' She notices him check her out briefly. Nothing sleazy, but a tiny flick of the eyes. She knows what she's wearing is flattering. She raises the weights a little, flexing her arms to show them off as subtly as she can. Pulls it back a bit so she doesn't look quite so much like a carnival strongwoman.

'Are you looking?' he asks.

She places the weights she's holding back on the rack even though she hasn't even really used them yet. 'Yes and no. I mean, I'm single. Well, divorced. But . . . not actively looking really . . .'

She almost laughs. Definitely not standing in a gym that she doesn't even belong to, at a time when she knew he might be here. Definitely not lurking outside the changing rooms. Not actively looking at all.

'Well, you know . . .' She's lost him, she can tell. 'It works for some people,' he says. He turns back towards the bench.

'Do you work round here?' she says, desperate to keep the conversation going.

He nods. 'I do. You?'

'No. Um . . .' Why did she say that? What reason does she have for being in a gym miles away from where she both works and lives? 'I only work part-time actually. I had to come over here to see a friend, so I thought why not use my pass . . . you know you can do that? Go to other branches?' Shut up, Joni, a voice in her head says. But she's nervous. She's so out of practice at anything even remotely like this.

'Lucky you,' Ant says. 'Working part-time, I mean.'

'Oh. Yes. Well. My husband . . . ex-husband . . . had a really good job, you know, in the City, so I gave up work, but then my friend died . . . I just do it for something to do really . . .' She peters out as she realizes how dull that makes her sound. She doesn't need to work but she has so little else going on in her life that she does anyway.

Ant takes a step away. 'Nice talking to you. I should . . .

'She takes the hint. Of course he's not interested in someone whose best sales pitch is that she's boring. 'Yes, me too. I hope you find someone who at least turns up next time.'

He rewards her with a smile. 'That would be something.'

Her heart isn't really in it any more, but she forces herself to go through the motions. Might as well salvage something from the day. At least she tried. Now she can put him out of her mind – clearly without her sister's face she's of no interest to him, and that's absolutely his prerogative: it's OK not to fancy someone. She doesn't fancy 99 per cent of the population. Ninety-nine point nine, probably. She's always been fussy. And she's definitely learned her lesson. There is no point trying to con someone into liking you. It can never have a happy ending.

She plugs in her earbuds, turns up the music and focuses on what she's doing.

She's stretching on the mat an hour later, having just about got through her session without gawping at Ant too much, eyes closed, wondering what to do with the rest of the day, when she feels a tentative tap on her shoulder. She jumps. Yelps. Ant stands back, hands in the air in apology.

She pulls out her headphones. 'Sorry,' he's saying. 'I was talking but . . .' He indicates her ears. 'I didn't mean to . . .'

Joni bursts out laughing. Partly from shock. 'Did I scream?'

'You did,' he says with a relieved smile. 'Really loudly.
I think they've alerted security.'

'Well, that'll teach you to go around poking strange
women.'

'You might want to rephrase that,' he says, looking
around nervously, and then they both snigger like a pair
of schoolkids.

'Did you want something or was it just random
poking?'

'Oh,' he says, rubbing his hand over his cropped head.
His eyes, in the flesh, are even more startling. Icy blue
pools. 'I wondered, well . . . if you'd like to have a coffee
or a drink sometime. Seeing as we're both, you know . . .'

'Sad?' she offers up. Her heart is pounding.

'I was going to say "looking"', but sad probably covers it as well.'

Don't be too keen, the voice in her head whispers.
'Yes,' she says without listening to it. 'I would. Like
to . . .'

'I have to get back to work now, but shall we swap
numbers? Maybe this weekend?'

'Yes,' she jumps in again. 'To both. Numbers and the
weekend.' She really must stop babbling. She rattles off
her new mobile number and Ant dials it so he's the last
call on her list.

'I'll call you beforehand,' he says, putting his phone in
the waistband of his sweats. 'Or, I mean, you call me.
Either.'

'Lovely,' she says. She can't quite believe she's pulled it
off. That her ridiculous scheme has worked. She allows

herself to breathe calmly for the first time since she arrived.

He turns to leave, waving a low hand, then turns back. 'Oh, I'm Ant, by the way . . .'

Shit.

Fuck.

She rattles through every name she can think of in her head that isn't her own. Why hadn't she thought of this already? The combination of her voice and her real name would surely be too much. She can't risk it.

'Lucy,' she says. Her sister.

He bestows a beautiful smile on her.

'Nice to meet you, Lucy.'

He's gone before she can even compute what she's done.

8

She decides to leave it to fate. She won't call him, but if he gets in touch with her, she'll make a decision then. Meanwhile, she'll try to forget Ant even exists. That he now thinks she's called Lucy. She's somehow lurched from one huge deception to another. Maybe it would be better if he never phoned.

She arrives at the office soaking from a sudden downpour on the way from the tube, and trepidatious as she always is on a Thursday as to what messes she might find, what fires she might have to extinguish. Working the last two days of the week, as she does, she always feels she has to tidy up all the unfinished business that Lucas has left before the weekend. Otherwise it feels like going out and leaving the bed unmade. It worries away at the back of her brain. A job not done. Loose ends not tied.

Annoyingly, it also means Lucas reaps the benefits when he comes in on a Monday morning to find a clean slate. She had thought job-sharing would be the best of all worlds. A focus, a sense of purpose, but also enough free time to give Imo the attention she needed. She had started thinking about going back to work when Ian first left – two years ago now, she realizes – unpacking the wipes she had stuffed in her bag last minute and cleaning

44

down the desk. He had been generous, she had to give him that. Financially anyway, because money was the thing that cost him least. Imo was just heading into the sixth form and Joni, alone in her beautiful new flat most days, thinking about her soon-to-be ex and his new girl-friend way more than was healthy, had started to feel as if she were losing herself. She needed to find a way back on to the career ladder somehow, after all these years. She needed to find her passion, her 'thing'.

She remembered saying to Meg that she hated meet-ing new people, didn't know what to say when they asked, 'So, what do you do?' as they invariably did.

'Tell them you're a fabulous best friend,' Meg had said. 'That's a vocation, right?'

They were lying on the grass on Hampstead Heath after an invigorating swim in the pond. Meg swore the freezing water had rejuvenating properties and so they tried to meet there once a week, weather permitting. They weren't so hardy that they could face it in the depths of winter yet. 'One day,' she remembered Meg saying. 'We'll come up here in the snow.'

And Joni had snorted. 'You wear bed socks in August. As if you're going to swim when it's minus two.'

'Watch this space,' Meg had said, stretching out in the warm sun. 'I'm a new woman. At this rate I'm going to look thirty-five by the time I'm fifty.'

That had been the week before she rushed up the motorway to see her mother who had had a mini-stroke doing her weekly shop in Aldi. She never got there. She was never going to reach fifty. She would be forty-eight forever. The police had given them all the clichés: she wouldn't have known a thing about it; she wouldn't have felt any pain; the accident was 100 per cent not her fault – a tired lorry driver, distracted by a ringing mobile. None of it had helped. Joni wipes a tear from her cheek. Fuck. When is this going to stop being so painful?

A couple of months after Meg had died Imo had declared that she was going to apply for uni courses in London. Media studies maybe. Joni knew why she was doing it. She also knew that she had her heart set on the on-the-job training in Manchester that she'd heard about. 'Why waste three years talking about stuff when I could actually be getting my foot in the door?' Imo had said when she read about it. Ironically the company was called Foot in the Door Productions. 'And they pay you and put you up in a flat.'

'Don't you dare,' Joni had said. She knew she'd been relying on Imo for company far too much since Meg died. Not only that but she was stifling her daughter, her natural catastrophist tendencies thrown into hyperdrive. She wanted to know where Imo was going to be every minute of the day, terrified that someone could be so alive one second and then dead the next, and she knew that – for Imo's sake – that had to stop. If Imo left home Joni was pretty sure she wouldn't worry any less, but Imo wouldn't have to witness it. 'I love you for even considering it, but no.'

In the end Imo had conceded but only to the extent that she would apply for Manchester first but, if she failed to get a place, London unis would be next.

Thankfully that decision had never needed to be made – she had aced the Zoom interview and been offered a spot two days later.

Lucas has left her a note. On the rare occasions he has to phone her he always calls her Joan, leaving her to fume that he doesn't have either the grace or the capacity to remember her name is actually Joni. Christened after Joni Mitchell. It isn't a pet name for Joan or anything else for that matter. She suspects that he does it to wind her up. The note has no addressee, it's just a curt instruction: 'Services breakdown for North East Region. Needs to be checked by close of play tomorrow.' She tears it up and throws it in the bin.

Her phone rings just as she's getting ready to leave for home. She knows it's Ant even before he says the word 'Lucy?'

'Hi!' She pushes the door of the office shut. Not that she doesn't want anyone to hear but she wants to concentrate. 'How are you?' She tries to put a bit of a twist on her voice. Just a tiny hint of her mother's West Country vowels.

'Good, yeah. Is this odd, me calling you? I said I would . . .'

She likes that he's not totally sure of himself. Ian was all bravado. Not really even bravado, actually; more a profound belief in his own worth. His mother had brought him up to think he possessed an almost godlike importance. She knows it's a cliché for a woman to butt

47

heads with her mother-in-law but, honestly, Sian really did think the sun shone out of her son and that he was selling himself short by marrying Joni. She'd all but said so. 'You fell on your feet,' she'd said to Joni when they told her they were engaged, even though Joni was earning nearly twice as much as him at the time in a job she loved at a City broker's. Joni had found his cockiness attractive when she'd first met him. God knows why. He was all swagger and confidence. Secure in his place as the king of the world. So, it's refreshing that Ant, for all his success, has a layer of self-doubt that matches her own.

'No. Of course not . . .' All of a sudden she feels tongue-tied. She's so terrified by the idea of giving herself away that she can't think of anything to say. 'Sorry, I'm at work . . .' Shit, she shouldn't have said that. She hasn't thought through what it is that Lucy does for a living that's close enough to the truth that she knows what she's talking about, but removed enough from anything she, Joni, may have told him about herself. Luckily Ant takes her statement as meaning she's not really in a position to talk and so he doesn't ask. Not this time.

'Oh, well, I won't keep you. It's just that we said we might have a drink and I was wondering about tomorrow night. If you don't have anything else going on . . .'

She knows she should put him off. That this can only end in tears.

'I would love that,' she says.

'Great. Well . . . you choose where, I'm easy. Somewhere you feel comfortable . . .'

It's such an Ant thing to say, it has the effect of relaxing her immediately. She racks her brain. Suddenly can't think of anywhere. 'I . . . um . . . I've gone blank . . .'

He laughs. 'I really did catch you at a bad time. How about we agree to meet tomorrow night at, what? Seven? And then we text later when one of us has a good suggestion?'

'Yes,' she manages to say. 'Good idea. Tomorrow at seven. Somewhere.'

'Somewhere.' He chuckles. 'I'll see you there.'

9

She spends the evening making a list of every fact she
has ever told him about herself. Her surname. Her age.
The fact that she lives in north London with an eighteen-
year-old daughter called Imo who has just left home.
Her job in accounts. That she's divorced. That only her
mother is still alive. The name of her gym. That's pretty
much it, but it's still the resumé of the important, immov-
able facts of her life. She could change gyms but she's
stuck with everything else.

She creates a CV for Lucy that sticks as close to the
truth as she can, hoping that, if she and Ant get on and
see each other again, she can start to blur the edges
between her two personalities and, eventually, come
clean. There's no other option. So, Lucy has a job as a
data analyst at the same retail chain that Joni actually
works for. She doesn't really know what a data analyst
does – beyond the obvious – but it sounds as mind-
numbing as her own occupation overseeing payroll,
checking up on the rent and the rates and the water and
electric of all the stores, at the head office in Cavendish
Square. Each branch manages their own infrastructure
but she – and Lucas – oversee the whole company and
handle executive wages and expense accounts. Luckily,
she had always told Ant her job was so dull she didn't

want to talk about it, so she has never divulged her employer. She – Lucy – lives in Steeles Village, which is one of those areas of London that people have heard of but don't quite know where it is. It's in the same general area as Joni's actual home in Frognal, so she won't have to get a taxi in the wrong direction when she leaves for home, until Ant is out of sight and it's safe to turn round. She's also divorced and has one parent still living. These facts seem generic enough for a woman her age to render them harmless. She gives her a daughter named Danielle (a name she had considered when she'd hoped she and Ian might have a second child) who is twenty rather than eighteen but doing the training that Imo really is doing because she's never shared that detail with Ant. She weighs up the pros and cons of telling him she's forty-seven or fifty-one (if he asks) and settles on it being better if he thinks she's older but looks good for her age rather than the other alternative. Maybe it'll be a pleasant surprise when she shaves off two years later.

That'll do, she thinks, rereading the list. Everything else can be the truth.

In the end he texts suggesting the Celestial Sphere, the new bar teetering at the top of a fifteen-storey hotel near Oxford Circus, and somewhere she's been wanting to try but didn't like to suggest herself because the minimum spend required to secure a booking felt presumptuous. Not that she couldn't afford it – Ian's meteoric rise in the financial world had left them well off even with her giving up work to become a full-time mum – but because she wasn't supposed to know that Ant could too (there were so many things she knew about him that she had to remember to pretend not to. God, she was never going to pull this off). She doesn't want to come across as the kind of person who has expensive tastes and assumes everyone else can afford to cater to them. But that isn't to say she isn't thrilled when he suggests it.

Perfect! she texts back. *I've been dying to try it.*

And then she agonizes for half an hour about what to wear. In the end she decides to ask Imo. She doesn't have to explain the whole story, and she knows Imo will be working now anyway so won't have time to ask too many questions. She dashes off a quick text: *Going to the Celestial Sphere tonight! What should I wear?*

Her phone rings immediately. She should have known Imogen would want the details, work or no work. 'Who are you going with?' she says before her mother can even say hello.

'I do have some friends, you know,' Joni says, laughing. 'Anyway, aren't you meant to be at work?'

'I'm on a coffee run. I'm always on a coffee run,' Imo says without a trace of disappointment. Joni's eyes fill with tears as they always do when she hears how happy Imo is. 'Isn't that all parents ever want?' she'd said to Meg once. 'A happy child who still loves them?'

'OK, well, this is not a big deal so don't try and make it one . . .'

'What?' Imo shrieks. 'Who is it? Is it a date?'

'Not really. I mean, I'm meeting Ant—'

She doesn't manage to get the rest of the sentence

out before Imo interrupts. 'Ant from the dating site? Oh my God!'

'Calm down,' Joni says, smiling. 'It's just a quick drink.'

'At the Celestial Sphere, though. Whose idea was that?'

'His.' Joni shuffles some papers round on her desk in an effort to look busy if anyone walks past. Her office has a large glass window on to the corridor. At one end there's an open-plan space where the assistants and all those not deemed worthy of their own private space – or the need for privacy while they discuss thrilling and sensitive topics such as why the overheads for the Redhill branch are so out of line with those of Manchester and Nottingham – sit and, at the other, the tiny kitchen, so there's a constant flow of traffic. She shoves a Star Wars miniature of Jabba the Hut that Lucas has left on the desk into a drawer. Recently he's taken to covering the already too small desk with his ridiculous action figures. She'd thought they had an unspoken agreement to keep the desk tidy out of respect for the other, but apparently not, and now every Monday and Wednesday he unpacks all his knick-knacks – figurines of Yoda and Gollum, and Daenerys with her dragons, along with a host of others Joni doesn't recognize – and so every Tuesday and Thursday she puts them away again. She's not sure how she missed Jabba this morning.

'Well, that's a good start. Make sure you sit near other people. And don't let him go back with you. Not yet.'

'Imo!' Joni gasps. 'I've never even met him . . .'

'Exactly. And don't even let him see you home. You

don't want him knowing where you live until you're sure he's not a psycho.'

'I don't think he is, but no, I take your point. No hot sex on date one.'

'Eew, Mum.'

'You started it.'

'God, I wish I hadn't now. So, wear that cap-sleeve shirt that you have. Assuming that your arms haven't gone to mush because you've been pining for me since I left . . .'

Joni digs out another antibac wipe. Worries at a spot on the desk. 'Well, I have been pining for you obviously. But I've been doing extra weights to make myself feel better. What with, though? The Zara skirt?'

'Mmmm . . . the black palazzos, maybe.'

'Black palazzos. Right.'

'Listen, I have to go,' Imogen says. 'But text me when you get home, OK? And I want a full debrief tomorrow. Oh, and Mum . . . remember he won't look exactly like his photos. Think about how far removed you're pre-pared to accept. If he's unrecognizable then leave. Immediately.'

If only she knew, Joni thinks. 'Bit fat and bald good, totally different person bad. Got it.'

Imo laughs. 'Love you. Be careful!'

Joni ducks out of the office an hour early, having worked through her lunch hour to get everything done. She picks out one task she can leave for Lucas just for the hell of it. Scrawls a note – 'Sorry, didn't get round to

54

this!' – and leaves it for him to find on Monday. She's home in twenty-five minutes, showers, makes up her face, decides it's too much, washes it off and reapplies. She's still trying to decide which shoes to wear when her Uber arrives so she plumps for the wedges she's currently trying on and leaves.

Ant is already seated at a table by the window when she arrives, so she has to walk across the whole room in her heels with him watching. She's tempted to do a comedy fall just to see if he laughs but she's scared she might actually end up breaking something – her arm or a table – so she tries to act natural, which turns out to be surprisingly hard. He stands up and greets her. He's looking good in dark trousers and a grey polo shirt, pale against his tan.

'Am I late?' she says, flustered. She hates arriving anywhere second. She knows it's a thing she has, and she usually tries to curb it, to stop herself leaving the house half an hour early 'just to be on the safe side'. Tonight, though, she had been hoping for the psychological advantage of being the one who was settled and owning the space when the other arrived.

'No. Not at all. I was early. Bad habit.'

'Me too!' she says. 'I mean, not tonight, obviously, but usually.'

'Oh good, we'll never miss a train then,' he says as she sits down. She knows it was only a throwaway remark, but it gives her a little glow nonetheless. The use of the word 'we'. The idea that they might go on a journey together one day. The waiter appears and she orders a vodka and tonic. Ant is drinking red wine and she wonders if he hopes she'll join him in a bottle, but she and red wine don't mix. Not since her fortieth birthday party. Actually, come to think of it, that was the last birthday party she'd had. She remembers having a great time, dancing on a table at the bar overlooking the Thames, knocking back the sangria that had been provided to go with the beachy theme, being sick in the taxi home. The next year Ian had quietly suggested they go for a meal, just the three of them, and she'd meekly agreed. She'll have a party for her fiftieth, she decided. A big stonking over-the-top blow-out. She'll dance on a table till she falls off and there will be no one to make her feel bad about it. She isn't sure who there will be to invite but she can worry about that later.

'The view from up here is amazing,' she says. She'd nearly asked him how the world of wellness was, but then remembered she wasn't supposed to know what he did yet. She needs to get the basics out of him before she trips herself up.

He takes a sip of his wine. 'Do you work near here?'

She nods. 'I do. Just round the corner, actually. Cavendish Square.'

'Let me guess—' he starts to say and she interrupts.

'God, no. Because whatever you say will seem insulting unless it's brain surgeon or supermodel.'

He laughs, teeth white. 'Well, those were the only two options I was considering so . . .'

'I have the world's dullest job.' She smiles at the waiter as he puts her drink in front of her. 'I'm a data analyst for Gibsons. The stores.'

'I'd ask you questions but I don't even know what data analysts do,' he says. You and me both, she thinks.

'Pretty much what you'd imagine. Ask me anything about the sales of second-tier designer perfumes in the first quarter of 2020 as compared to 2019.'

'I can't,' he says, shaking his head. 'The excitement might kill me.'

She takes a drink. 'Poor. Lockdown looming, all of that. It's thrilling stuff, really. Ask me about seasonal adjustments in pyjamas versus nightdresses in ladies' wear. I dare you.'

He holds a hand up. 'Really. My heart can't take it.'

'It's a laugh a minute, I can tell you. How about you?'

Ant looks out of the window. The view really is incredible. She can see the Shard in the far distance. She wonders if he feels awkward, about to have to admit to his hugely successful career when she's just confessed to having a shitty job. 'I have a wellness company. Spa kind of thing.' He's playing it down but, of course, she knows how impressive this actually is.

'Oh. Wow. Where is it?'

'There are four branches actually. Three in West London and one in Manchester – well, Alderley Edge. And we're just about to open a new one in Primrose Hill.'

'Amazing. So did you . . . I mean, how do you know about that stuff . . .?'

Ant holds up his hands, smiles sheepishly. 'I don't. Or at least, I didn't. I just employ good people. I had the chance to acquire a place years ago and I could see how much money there was to be made in it . . .'

Joni knows all this of course, but it's easy enough to talk about it again. 'But now you're an expert on placenta facials? Do you try them out in your spare time?' She peers at him. 'You do have very good skin.'

'Placenta facials are so 2020,' he says, laughing. 'We try to stay ahead of the curve.'

'So, what's the latest? Tell me everything. I can try and make my own budget version of it at home.'

'You sound like my son.' He laughs again. 'He's always asking me if I could put some kind of treatment made out of grass, or worms, or dog shit on the menu. He's definitely got an eye for maximizing profit.'

'You have a son?' Joni says, wide eyed. 'How old?'

Ant smiles warmly. 'Ten. Jack. And a daughter Amelia who's almost eight.'

'Gorgeous ages,' she says. She tells him about Imo – Dani – and the training course she's recently started. Tries to keep to an edited version because the truth is she could talk about her all evening given the chance. She doesn't want to bore him to tears.

'So, you're divorced?' he says once she's exhausted the topic. She nods. 'You?'

'Getting there.' He waves at the waiter. 'Same again?' he says, and Joni nods. 'Actually,' he adds, 'do you fancy getting something to eat?'

'Definitely.' She almost faints with relief. He must like her. The real her. Almost. Apart from a few small details. 'I mean, yes. That would be lovely.'

*

She wakes up in the morning with a smile on her face. Jasper is prodding at her cheek, hungry for breakfast and company. Joni gets out of bed, goes to the kitchen and feeds him, then makes a coffee and gets back under the covers. She wants to relive the evening.

Better still, she wants to relive the moment when he asked if he could see her again.

She can't quite believe she's pulled it off – or that she actually likes Ant as much as she hoped she would. They chatted about anything and everything – apart from work: thankfully somewhere along the line they declared it a work-free evening so that had cut down the lies she'd had to tell. In fact, she doesn't even know what they did talk about, but they laughed a lot which must be a good sign. She knows she didn't say anything she shouldn't. Somehow the deception, the fact that she knows him so much better than he realizes, had broken down barriers. There had been no awkward silences. No sentences that started with 'Soooo . . .' the speaker struggling to work out how to continue. He'd felt it too, she knew it.

She had cut the evening short at about ten, claiming a busy morning and the need for a clear head. She'd been worried another drink might loosen her lips and make her forget which version of herself she was trying to be. And the date had been so perfect she didn't want to risk ruining everything. Ant had insisted on paying, which had made her feel a little uncomfortable, but she'd tried to accept with good grace and not protest too much. He had walked with her to find a taxi and she had just been wondering if she was brave enough to suggest another meeting when he'd said, 'Would you like to do this again?' so casually she almost thought she'd misheard him.

'I would. It's been fun,' she'd said when she'd regained her composure.

And just like that they were having dinner on Tuesday evening. The Ivy Café in Marylebone, her choice.

Joni leans back against the pillows. A wave of absolute sadness washes over her. Why did she have to complicate everything? Why couldn't she have been honest with Ant in the first place? Last night was fabulous but she knows it can't have a happy ending. If she's sensible she should cut and run before she gets too involved, before it gets too painful. But she's sick of being sensible. She's had twenty years of being sensible and where has it got her?

She'll just have to wait and see what happens. Pick the moment exactly halfway between too soon and too late to tell Ant the truth. Cross everything and hope for the best.

10

Four weeks later

It's official. She has a boyfriend. Or at least she thinks she does. They haven't put a label on it, as Imo might say, but they've seen each other two or three times a week since that first night. Slept together – slept together! – twice already, both times at hers because his is piled up with all the belongings he didn't want to risk getting damp in storage while he waits to find his new permanent home, and mountains of his kids' things so that they feel at ease when they visit. 'I don't want them to spend all weekend wishing they weren't there,' he'd said, sadly. 'Their lives have been disrupted enough.'

Thankfully she had decided against Steeles Village when the question of where she lived came up – it was too small, too specific, pinned her down to just a few streets if he ever investigated – and settled on 'near Swiss Cottage', which was technically true even though Frognal was a much more accurate and salubrious description. But he hadn't seemed to notice as the taxi flew up the Finchley Road and past the pub that looked like a cartoon alpine chalet dumped in the middle of an A road; they had been too wrapped up in each other both times to be looking at the street signs.

Joni had known that sex was on the cards last week.

The tension had been building between them, bubbling up like an unwatched pot and threatening to boil over, for a while. When they'd kissed for the first time – on Piccadilly while they waited for a taxi to take her home – she had felt a bolt of sheer lust almost knock her off her feet. She had wanted to invite him back then and there, and, to be honest, if she'd had her waxing appointment that day instead of the next she probably would have (she wasn't going to go the full hog wax-wise, she'd decided, it was too much. And if Ant wanted her to look like a prepubescent Barbie doll down there then she really had bigger problems to worry about). It would be the first time she'd slept with anyone apart from Ian for over twenty years and that had been sporadic to say the least, not to mention an endlessly repeating perform-ance, stuck on a loop of familiar moves and a hackneyed script. But she'd found she wasn't in the slightest bit ner-vous. She couldn't wait. Could. Not. Wait.

And it had lived up to – was living up to – the expect-ation. Of course, it helped that they had had sex before, on the phone, even if he didn't know it, she thought, and then decided that that was too weird to even think about. She feels as if she's waking up from a twenty-year-long sleep. As if her life went into cold storage and now it's thawing out and her with it, unfurling in the warmth of the sun.

They somehow just gel. It's impossible to put her fin-ger on why. They have the superficial things in common, obviously: their love of the gym, good food, the cinema, but it's much more than that. Ant is so easy to get along with. There are no sides, no no-go areas. She and Ian had had topics that were red flags right from the get-go: any criticism of his family however badly they behaved, his thinning hair, the fact that she had been to university and he hadn't. She had learned to tiptoe around the minefield, but in retrospect it had been exhausting. Ant is secure in himself. Confident. She had never realized before how attractive that could be.

She wishes she had someone to confide in. As if sharing the facts would make them real. Imo is out of the question, obviously. Tempting though it's been, Joni has always tried to avoid the desire to try and be her daughter's best friend. For Imogen's sake. Joni is the parent: that's her job. It's not always easy but that's the way it is. Her mum wouldn't be able to get past the concept that her forty-nine-year-old daughter was dating again, let alone with someone she'd met on the internet. Maura always talked about the internet as if the word was in capitals: THE INTERNET! To her it was a mystical place full of unknown evils. She'd never even written an email, so far as Joni knew. Their three-times-weekly phone calls usually tick the same boxes: Imo; Joni's sister, Lucy; Lucy's kids; the neighbours. Joni loves hearing her mum's stories – Maura moved into a bungalow near to Lucy and her family a few years ago and immersed herself fully in village life – but they never really talk about anything deeper. Joni knows she always puts on a bit of a happy front with Maura these days. She doesn't want to give her mum anything to worry about. It doesn't seem right. And Joni and Lucy have never really been close. That is, they get on fine but they're not in each other's lives on a daily basis. Lucy lives an off-grid-but-only-because-she's-wealthy-and-owns-her-house-outright-so-she-can-afford-it life in the Cotswolds, with her hedge-fund-man ager-turned-alpaca-farmer husband and their three impossibly beautiful children. They spend their days caring for the animals (or, Joni suspects, watching someone they've employed care for the animals. Lucy's nails in her Facebook posts are always pristine), tending their vegetable garden (ditto), and home-schooling their kids (and again). They only noticed the pandemic was happening because the dinner-party invites dried up and Waitrose online was occasionally all out of Moët. They preach sustainability and carbon neutrality but they each drive a 4x4 and they have a swimming pool in their garden that is heated to hot-bath temperature all year round just in case any of them fancy an impromptu dip. Joni loves her, but they have very little common ground. She can't imagine confiding anything in her, ever. Let alone that she's been impersonating her in various ways to lure strange men into her bed. She shivers at the thought.

So, she keeps her news to herself. Feels a sharp pain at the Meg-shaped hole in her life. Sometimes she wakes up in the night and can't believe that this is happening to her. Even if she has to scour her flat for anything with her name on it and lock it away before Ant comes round. Even if she still has to refer to her daughter as Dani rather than Imo. Even if she knows it's unsustainable as it is. It's worth it.

'God,' he'd said to her a couple of nights ago, her

head on his chest, his hand stroking her back. 'All those months of trying to hook up with people online. It feels like a different world. What was I thinking?'

She'd propped herself up on one elbow. She had lit a couple of candles in the bedroom and the light was flickering on the dark grey walls. Jasper was banished to the living room, letting out an occasional mournful yowl. 'Did you meet up with many of them in real life?'

He'd shrugged. 'A couple. It really wasn't for me. Too many variables. And all that time wasted chatting back and forth only to then know within seconds of meeting that it wasn't going to go anywhere. Both of us, I mean. It wasn't just me.'

'Pheromones,' she'd said. 'If you could find a way to include them in online profiles you'd be a billionaire right there.'

'I'll bear that in mind,' he'd said, laughing. 'For my next venture. Seriously, though. I've never been so happy to cancel a subscription.'

She'd stifled the tidal wave of panic that had threatened to engulf her. Focused on the joy.

Ant always has his kids at the weekend. Even though his relationship with his ex seems to be fractious to say the least – she is still apparently dithering about going through with the sale of their huge house, allowing them to buy two separate places – they at least agree on childcare. He collects the two of them after school on Fridays and drops them back home on Sunday nights. On Wednesdays he watches his daughter's soccer practice and then takes them to the Electric Diner for tea. Joni has always found men who clearly adore their kids almost irresistible. She remembers watching Ian holding Imogen when she was a baby, cradling her tiny head against his, and feeling a wave of love for him so absolute her knees had buckled. She loves the effort that Ant makes to ensure his two are happy, but she's secretly quite relieved that he hasn't suggested she join them yet. Other people's kids are always hard work and rarely adorable, and anyway, she's enjoying the freedom of their relationship at the moment, the hedonistic lack of responsibilities – hers or his. It means that their evenings together are limited, but that suits her. She doesn't want her life to blend into someone else's. She's got used to her own space in her two years of being single – and about four more before that, in reality. Emotionally even if not practically. Her marriage to Ian was dying in the water long before he dealt the final blow. It's why she can't hate him for Holly. She was devastated, heartbroken, wounded, but she couldn't hate him. Not even at the time.

Besides, she still has to come clean with Ant. She can't leave it any longer. Imo is already asking about meeting him, planning when she can fit in a quick visit down south, joking about weddings and a new stepdad. Joni knows she's putting it off, the moment when she might ruin everything. Meg would tell her to get it over with. That the longer she leaves it the more it will hurt if it all goes badly. And she'd be right. This week. She'll do it this week.

She stretches, savouring her lie-in. The three-day

weekend ahead of her. She can hear Flick pottering about upstairs, talking either to herself or her impressive collection of houseplants. Sia the swiss cheese, Margot the money plant. Joni can't remember the rest, but she spent an agonizing afternoon when she first moved in, being introduced. It's sad really. Flick is allergic to cats and dogs – something she likes to remind Joni of often. In fact, Joni is convinced that she stands in the shared hall pretending to look at her mail sometimes, just so that she can sneeze loudly and make her point. Still, at least Jasper's presence means that Joni never feels she has to invite Flick in.

She thinks about what she's going to do with her day. Chores obviously. She always makes an effort to get them out of the way before Monday in the same way she used to try to get any weekend homework done on a Saturday morning and not in a last-minute scramble on a Sunday night that left her feeling resentful and stressed, the benefits of two days off wiped out. It's the same list as always: washing, dry cleaning, clean the bathroom. She leans over and unplugs her phone. There's a text from Ant already this morning – he'll be up early with the kids – *Miss you. Chaos here! xx.* She remembers that it's his daughter's birthday. Eight, she thinks. His son is slightly older. Ten? They're having a party at his old home this afternoon, him and his ex-wife putting on a front. He was dreading it. But this morning will be all about the three of them: Ant, Amelia and Jack.

Hope she's having a lovely day xx, she sends back.

She flicks backwards and forwards on her phone,

checking in with Twitter and Instagram, and Dark Sky to see when the rain will end. Her eye lands on the dating app. She still has her profile. Is still paying £24.99 a month for premium membership. In all the excitement of meeting Ant she forgot. She needs to cancel her subscription. She logs in, looking for the settings page. Cringes when she sees Lucy's photos. She's about to delete the whole thing when she remembers her and Ant's messages. Those tentative back and forths before they took it offline. She wonders if they'll still be there now he's deleted his account. She should take screenshots, keep them for posterity. She can imagine the two of them poring over them in the future, laughing at how formal they were with each other in the beginning, telling friends the story of how Joni used Lucy's pictures and the roundabout way they finally met. The whole story becoming folklore, a funny anecdote to be dusted off and aired after a few drinks.

She clicks on messages, noticing that she has a few new likes, a couple of hopeful virtual gifts (a bunch of balloons, a teddy bear. God, what is she, nine?). Ant's communications are still there, and she settles back to read from the beginning.

Something's not right though. She can't place it at first, it's just a vague unease, an unfocused anxiety. She tries to concentrate on the messages, one hand stroking Jasper's ear, but she can't relax into it.

And then it hits her.

Ant's profile photo has changed. It's been updated.

She clicks on it.

His account opens up. She's momentarily hurt. He told her he had closed it down, hadn't he? Offered up the information; she hadn't even asked him. He just hasn't got round to it, she tells herself. After all, hers is still up and running. He wanted to say something nice to her, so he said the thing about cancelling his subscription because he was about to do it. Meaning to. Or maybe he has cancelled but the site has a glitch and the account is still showing as active.

But it's the photo. Something about the photo.

And then she realizes. The picture is from a couple of evenings ago. The last time they met up. He must have taken it while he was waiting for her. She can see the geraniums, the space-age outdoor heaters of the pub where they ate outside. He hadn't been there before, he'd told her. She can see the muddy green T-shirt and black jacket he was wearing. The stubble that's grown into a short beard in the weeks she's known him.

Why would you update your picture if you were off the market?

She looks to see if there are any clues that he's been talking to anyone else, but the app's privacy settings are rigorous. She stares at the photo. 'If something looks too good to be true then it probably is,' she's said to Imogen before, anxious that her daughter's optimistic naivety would get her in trouble.

She should have listened to herself.

11

She knows she's overreacting. He's only known her a few weeks, even though in her mind – in reality – it's months. She reminds herself that Ant isn't in anywhere near as deep as she is. He has no idea how well he actually knows her. Maybe he's put his account on hold but he's still hedging his bets in case things don't work out, having been burnt before. Or maybe you can't just leave, you have to give notice so he thought he might as well keep his details up to date. Something prosaic like that. She wishes she could ask him but, of course, she can't. To see his profile she would have to be registered on the site herself and – in so far as Ant knows – she, Lucy, has never entered the world of online dating.

But she can't help feeling like a fool. A stupid, lonely, old-enough-to-know-better fool. Too trusting. Too gullible. She should never have let her guard down. He must have updated his picture yesterday. Or on Thursday night as she slept beside him. Did something happen that evening which made him think he had to keep his options open? The pub they'd been to was down in Kew. They'd sat outside in the sweltering evening heat, fairy lights twinkling in the trees. It had seemed magical to her. She remembers taking the mickey out of some of the services his clinic offered. 'So, you just carry it around?' she'd said about the crystals cleansed with Palo Santo Holy Wood smoke that they sold for eye-watering amounts. She'd been on their website. Ant had smiled, indulgently. 'Is it like having a Tamagotchi?' she'd carried on. 'Do you have to try and keep them alive?' And he'd guffawed. She remembered it clearly, how gratified she'd felt that he found her gentle ribbing funny. He'd held his hands up. 'We just give West London what West London wants.' He had a manager in place in each of the spas who kept on top of the trends, he told her. He had a healthily cynical attitude to it all himself, she was pleased to discover. She wasn't sure she could date a man who wanted vaginas to be steam cleaned.

Had he actually taken offence beneath those smiles? Did he think she was accusing him of being a charlatan? She wasn't, not at all. She would love to spend a day being pampered there herself. Had considered booking it but then wondered if that was weird now, and if she should maybe wait until Ant suggested it. There were just a few items on the menu that seemed to her like unsubstantiated fads as, to be honest, there were in most of those places – and why wouldn't you offer those if people were willing enough and gullible enough to pay? Maybe his own cynicism was a defence mechanism though. Maybe he really was offended by the jokes she'd made?

But then she thinks about how the last few weeks have been. How attentive Ant is, how much they've laughed, the fact that they never run out of things to talk about. She's felt as if their connection has been growing stronger, not weaker. But it's the lie that gets her. Why bother bringing up Keepers at all if he was going to lie about cancelling his membership? If there's one thing she knows it's that she won't enter into another relationship with a liar. Ironic really, considering much of what she's telling Ant isn't true. But Ian's default setting was untruths. Even about the littlest things – whether he'd used the last of the milk or phoned and booked a restaurant. Lie first; think later. Things that didn't matter either way, she just needed to know the answer. It got so that she couldn't believe a word that came out of his mouth. Or wouldn't, just in case. Self-preservation. She hated the suspicious, cynical version of herself she'd become with him, always assuming the worst. She wouldn't go back to being that person again. Ever.

Her brain feels scrambled. She forces herself out of bed, wraps up against the rain and heads outside to try and walk it off.

Flick is dusting around the piles of junk mail when she gets back two and a half hours later, feeling clearer-headed. She'd gone to the gym early in the end to escape the weather. She hadn't had her membership card on her but luckily Samira was on reception and Joni had experienced that little thrill of being recognized as a regular, of being part of a tribe. Thankfully she'd thrown on her workout gear as she always did at the weekends if she wasn't going anywhere special. She lives her life in athleisure like half of the middle-aged women in London. But at least she does actually work out in hers.

All the flats chip in for a cleaner who whizzes round the

communal parts once a week. It only takes her an hour, but she does the house next door, so she just adds this on at the end of her morning. Any of the residents could do it easily but it saves arguments. Flick, though, is often to be found giving the hallway a once-over herself.

'Eleven pounds ninety-nine in the end,' Flick says, duster in hand. Joni racks her brain, comes up with nothing.

'I told them it was half that in Tesco, not that they cared.' She must pick up on Joni's blank expression because she adds, 'The potting compost. Remember I told you . . .'

Ah, yes. Flick is going to repot the geraniums that sit on the front step. Her geraniums, that she put there without consulting either Joni or the couple upstairs. Joni would be the first to admit they look cheerful, but she doesn't know how she's been roped into contributing to their upkeep.

'So that's basically four pounds each,' Flick says, looking at her expectantly.

'Oh. Well, I don't have any change right now. I'll put it through your door,' Joni says. She's aware she's leaving a puddle on the stone floor. The rain still hadn't let up, so she'd got as soaked on the walk home as she had on the way there.

'Those two upstairs will probably argue . . .' Flick lifts up a stack of letters and sprays Pledge underneath.

'I should . . .' Joni says, indicating her door. 'I need to dry off . . .'

'I can't carry it back from Tesco, that's the thing, so I'd

have to shell out for a cab and that would cost us all a lot more . . .' Flick is saying as Joni puts her key in the lock. She raises a hand in acknowledgement.

She's seeing Ant on Monday night. He's cooking her a risotto – his speciality, he says – and he's told her that he'll bring all the ingredients, she doesn't have to worry about anything except making sure there's wine in the fridge. She's going to give him the benefit of the doubt, she's decided, try to dig a little more maybe, just to put her mind at rest. Give him a chance to come clean. She won't be judgemental, won't make him feel bad. She'll just be relieved he's telling her the truth. At least, that's the plan.

He's right on time, ringing her doorbell at one minute to seven, smart work clothes on, a holdall in one hand and a carrier bag – which he offers her with a flourish – in the other. He's talking into his mobile and he throws her an apologetic smile. 'Yes, drop it round to Ossington Street,' he says. 'Camille's there now, I checked. You're a lifesaver. Thanks, mate.' He ends the call and grabs Joni up in a hug, kissing the top of her head. 'Life-or-death emergency,' he says. 'Amelia left her favourite toy dog at the spa when they stopped in to say hello on their way home from school. She can't sleep without it.'

'Oh no,' Joni says. 'But it's sorted?'

He nods. 'That was one of the therapists; he's going to stop by the house on his way home. I don't know if it's normal for an eight-year-old to still be inseparable from a cuddly toy but I think the divorce . . . you know . . .'

74

'I slept with my bear till I was about twelve and I didn't even have that excuse,' she says, wanting to make him feel better. She knows that guilt about how the breakdown of his marriage might be affecting his kids weighs him down sometimes. 'I've still got him somewhere.'

She knows already that Ant will have a quick shower, hang up his suit and change into soft baggy tracksuit bottoms. Because he's already told her he can stay the night – sometimes he gets a taxi home late if he has somewhere to be in the morning other than his Evoke office and, in fact, those nights are her favourite, lying awake into the small hours on her own, replaying the evening over and over again – she knows that in his bag he'll have a clean shirt, beautifully pressed for tomorrow. They have a routine. Already. She doesn't know if that thrills or terrifies her.

'Can I do anything?'

'Join me in the shower?' he says with a raise of his eyebrows. Joni blushes to her roots. She can't get used to being wanted like this. Can't get enough of it.

Half an hour later she's opening the wine while he chops onions and garlic. He slices with the precision of a surgeon. Slowly. Carefully.

'How's work?' she says, handing him a glass.

He nods. 'Good. We signed off on Primrose Hill today. Oh, but the big news is Camille has put finally put the house on the market . . .'

Ant's ex-wife is French. For some reason this makes Joni insecure. She imagines an impossibly chic woman, confident in her own gorgeousness, falling out of bed in

the mornings in a Chanel suit and a full face of impeccable make-up. A Gauloises cigarette that miraculously
doesn't make her breath smell rank hanging from her lip.
'That's great. What swung it?'

He shrugs. 'I think she just wanted to make me sweat.'
He pulls his phone out of his pocket and fiddles around
a bit. 'Here, look . . .' He hands it to her and she sees that
he's on the PrimeLocation app. The property is a white
stucco townhouse of majestic proportions. She tries not
to look at the price, but she can't help noticing there's
more than one comma in it and it starts with an eight.
She scrolls through the photos. She marvels at the proportions but, mostly, she's blown away by the décor. The
sheer opulence of it. But tasteful. This is a much-loved
sanctuary, not an interior designer's wet dream. 'It's
absolutely beautiful.'

'Obviously it's not usually that tidy,' he says, laughing,
taking the phone back. She wants to ask if she can look
again, if she can scrutinize the pictures with forensic
precision. She loves her own home but that's all it is, a
home. This place is like a monument to style. A temple
of success.

'Which one of you has the great taste?' she asks
although she's pretty sure he's going to say Camille.

'We did it together. That was one thing we did agree on.'

'I can see why she's reluctant to leave.'

'Well, yes,' he says, putting his mobile back in his
pocket. 'Me too.' She has never asked why his marriage
fell apart but, from the slight edge of bitterness that he
can't conceal whenever Camille is mentioned, she

assumes it wasn't entirely his decision. She thinks she knows him well enough now to pry. Just a little.

'Why did you split up? I mean, if that's not too intrusive a question . . .'

He shakes his head. 'Not at all. I think she felt she took second place to the business. Which, you know, if I'm being honest, she probably did for a while. Well, and to the kids too but no one minds that, do they?'

Joni smiles. 'Definitely not. Nothing more attractive in a man than that he's a good dad.'

'I had to work hard to build it up. And, let's be fair, she didn't exactly dislike the perks. But I get it. I probably neglected her a bit. I don't think we would have gone the distance anyway. Too different.'

'So, now you can start looking for a permanent place of your own?' She wipes down the counter where the wine bottle has left a damp ring. Ant grins at her.

'I can start looking. I mean . . . I should wait and see what interest there is. It could take a while to sell, I suppose.'

'I'm a very discerning property finder, just saying.' Joni tops up their glasses. 'If you want any help. What do the kids think?'

He sloshes oil into a pan. 'They're OK, I think. They accepted long ago that we're separated. All they care about now is staying close to their friends.' He reaches out an arm and pulls her in. 'I'm excited to make a new start.'

Joni feels a rush of excitement. Suppresses it. 'Are you going to stay in the same area?'

'That's the plan,' he says, taking a drink of his wine. 'It depends what's out there, I suppose. How's work? How's the lovely Lucas?'

It doesn't feel as if he's having doubts. If anything they're more at ease with each other than ever. She leans back against the counter, running a finger round the rim of her glass. She catches a whiff of something. She topped up her fake tan this morning and she's pretty sure she smells like Hobnobs. God, what if the water in the shower was coming off her brown, and he'd noticed? Maybe she should sneak off for another one before dinner. But she loves that he's asking her about her day – Ian never did. She would save up funny anecdotes and offer them up in the evening, but he would just grunt and carry on with whatever he was doing. Ant, though, laps up her stories. Loves the pass-agg relationship she and Lucas have. So she tells him about the new batch of figurines she found on her desk on Thursday morning.

'Maybe they're presents,' Ant says, laughing, when she describes the two warlocks and a witch. 'You know, like crows start to bring you little rocks and things if you feed them regularly.'

'You do know I've never met him. Let alone fed him.'

Ant stirs the rice, glugs in some stock. 'How is that even possible?'

She shrugs. 'Because the whole point is we work different days. I think it's him marking his territory. Like a cat.'

'Do you think he pees up the curtains too?'

Joni pulls a face. 'Thankfully there aren't any. But I think the toys are metaphorical peeing.'

'You need some of your own,' Ant says with a wicked smile. 'Something he'll hate.'

'That is genius!' Joni gasps. 'Something really cutesy.' She grabs her laptop and looks up 'cute figurines' on Amazon. She has a heart-stopping moment when she realizes it says 'Deliver to Joni' at the top of the page. She whips the computer around so he can't see the screen, praying he didn't notice, that he doesn't wonder why she's suddenly being so secretive. Thankfully he seems to be concentrating on the food, stirring the rice intently. She has to keep scrolling down before she shows anything to Ant but, before she knows it, she's ordered a glass rabbit holding a red heart, two ceramic squirrels wrapped in an embrace and a plastic baby elephant with huge cartoon eyes.

'I'll have to just get them out at night as I'm leaving,' Joni says, wiping away tears of laughter. 'I couldn't live with seeing them all day. Let alone what my colleagues would think.'

'Let the battle commence,' Ant says, tossing some grated Parmesan into the pan. 'This'll be five minutes.'

She suddenly feels as if she has to get out of there. 'I'm just nipping to the loo.'

She leans her forehead on the cool mirror in the bathroom. She has to tell him the truth. She can't take the pressure of the fear of being caught out. A tiny thing – an Amazon page with her name on it, Flick bumping into the two of them in the hall – could give her away at any moment. And she knows – she absolutely

knows – that there's a world of difference between confessing to something and being caught out. It's surely
not that big a deal? Part of her thinks he'll find it funny.
Be flattered, maybe. Still, she feels sick at the prospect.
By the time she's flushing the toilet for authenticity she's
made a bargain with herself: she'll bring up the dating
app and when he comes clean so will she. Surely he can't
be pissed off at her if he's having to admit to his own
white lies too?

Ant is spooning the risotto into two bowls as she
comes in. It smells incredible. Jasper sits at the kitchen
table patiently, as if he's waiting for his portion. Her little
man. Joni suddenly remembers Vinnie, Ant's dog. She
doesn't think he's ever mentioned him since they met up.
She assumes Camille must have him in the family home.
It was never in doubt that Jasper would move with her
wherever she ended up. Ian didn't even know what brand
of food he liked. The name of his vet. She can't imagine
having to give up a pet. She puts a sympathetic hand on
Ant's back as he serves. Divorce is a nightmare, even the
most civilized one.

'So, tell me your online dating horror stories,' she says
lightly after they've been eating in comfortable silence
for a minute or so. She doesn't want him to think she's
digging. She's opened the bifold doors on to her garden
and the smell of the late roses and the recently cut grass
is intoxicating. One of the things that attracted her to
the flat was the garden. It's unexpectedly long, a hidden
treasure. She has no clue what she's doing out there, but
she cuts the grass with an oversized mower that lives in

the tiny blue-and-red-painted shed at the end, and pulls up the odd invasive weed. Flick is always hinting that she could help out if Joni would give her a small patch of her own to grow herbs, but the only access to the outside is through Joni's flat and the idea of Flick knocking on her door every time she wanted to pick a handful of basil fills her with horror, so she just laughs off the suggestion as if Flick is making a joke and changes the subject. 'This is absolutely delicious, by the way,' she says, and it is. He's told her he cooks every night when he's home. No ready meals for him. 'I find it relaxing,' he'd said.

'Oh God, don't make me relive it. I've got PTSD.' He heaps more Parmesan on to his plate, twinkles at her with those pale eyes. 'Where should I start? Olivia who turned out to be married? Or Joni who stood me up altogether?'

Joni starts at the mention of her own name. Shit. This is her chance to say, 'That was me actually,' but there's an edge in his voice that stops her.

'How long were you on there for?' she manages to say.

Ant shrugs. 'Eight, nine, months? Not all the time . . . You know what? I thought it would be a way to get to know people without them prejudging me. You know, the business and all that . . .'

It makes sense to Joni. Ant is so successful that it must be hard sometimes to know if people are interested in the real person or the dollar signs. 'It's a minefield out there,' Joni says. She pours them both some more wine. 'There must have been some successes? I've known people who've found the love of their life that way.'

He scritches at his beard. 'There were. I think . . . it's just . . . the old-fashioned way is better for me, that's all.' He smiles at her. His warm, crinkly smile.

Here goes, she thinks. 'So, you can just cancel your subscription? They don't have you tied in for the rest of your life?'

'What, like one of those book clubs, do you remember them? You have to go on six dates a year for the next ten years?'

She laughs. 'My mum would never let me join one of them for exactly that reason! She thought I'd never be able to leave. Like a cult.'

'Anyway, thankfully not. I just cancelled the payment and that's it. Done.'

Joni swallows. Her pulse quickens. 'And they take it straight down? Your profile? I mean, you don't leave some devastated woman out there somewhere thinking you might be the one for her and wondering why you never respond?'

'I assume so,' he says, a slight frown appearing as if he's wondering why she's asking. Maybe she's pushing too hard? She's got her answer now anyway. 'I mean, I've got no way of checking because I don't have an account any more. It would hardly make sense for them to leave it up there, though.'

Joni pushes her plate away. She's lost her appetite.

12

Ant is a sound sleeper. He's barely said goodnight before his breathing slows. He likes to wrap his arms around her in a post-coital haze, but after their first night together when she'd lain awake till the early hours sweating profusely, her left arm going dead, not wanting to disturb him, she's started to edge out from his embrace as soon as it's clear he's unconscious. He barely flinches, rolling on to his side away from her. She's been awake for hours. Since their conversation over dinner she's been going through the motions, waiting for this time alone to process her thoughts. While he was brushing his teeth she logged into Keepers, just in case the only thing he was lying about was the timing, and there he was, still smiling in the pub garden. Blue eyes. Tanned skin. Waiting for her.

She just needs to manage her expectations, she tells herself now. Stop thinking that Ant might be the new love of her life and view him as a starter boyfriend. A practice run. Someone to sharpen her rusty skills on. But she likes him. *Really* likes him. She had never expected that to happen. Joining a dating app had been a diversion, a way to convince Imo her life was back on track. It was never meant to be serious. She hadn't wanted to actually start caring about someone. But they make each other laugh, all the important stuff. He makes an effort. Trails over to Frognal with his expensive deli bag full of arborio rice and aged Parmesan and porcini mushrooms. It's not as if he's phoning it in while he kills time waiting for a better option to come along.

She's going to drive herself mad. She needs to find out what's going on and if she can't ask him then there's only one way. She can see his account on her phone but only his public profile. There's no indication if he's talking to anyone new. She's never been a snooper. Not even when she suspected Ian was up to no good – maybe because by that point she had started to not care. Or because she 100 per cent knew what the answer would be, so she just waited for it to play itself out. It's the death of a relationship she thinks, sneaking around checking up on each other. And she's always imagined that once you started it would be impossible to stop. You'd scratch one itch and then another would begin to irritate you right away. Crack cocaine for the paranoid. But this is different, she decides. This is self-preservation. This is about making a choice – going in with her eyes open or walking away more or less unscathed. Or being proved wrong, of course, which is the outcome she's actually hoping for, even if it seems unlikely.

She slides out of bed. Ant's mobile is charging in a corner of the room. She feels sick at the prospect of him waking up and catching her, but she turns it on nonetheless. Holds it over his sleeping face to unlock it and then, finding the Keepers app, does the same again.

It works. She slips out of the room and locks herself in the bathroom. Here goes.

She goes straight to his history. Sees that he has sent likes to three women in the past week. A lump rises up in her throat. She feels sick. She moves to private messages. There's a conversation with a woman called Wanda from yesterday. Those tentative, early exchanges. *Where do you work? Do you have kids?* She looks at Wanda's profile. She's good-looking in a kind of showy way. Glossy hair (definitely not all her own); thick, microbladed eyebrows over long eyelash extensions. She has a heavy jaw, high cheekbones, a mahogany tan. Something about her caught Ant's eye in the past couple of days. He first sent her a 'smile' eight days ago. Eight days ago Joni and Ant had walked along the South Bank in the evening, after he dropped the kids back with Camille. They'd eaten pizza under gas heaters with the restaurant's red blankets over their thighs because the weather had turned. They'd held hands across the table.

Joni goes back to messages. Before Wanda there was a fairly short chat with a Milly. That petered out at the weekend after only a few exchanges. And before that . . . Joni's heart pounds as she reads the message. *Do you want to take this off app?* a woman called Saffy had said to him two weeks ago. *Definitely,* came the reply. And then Saffy had sent her number and that was that. The day after Joni and Ant sat up way too late drinking wine and just talking. They'd fallen into bed at about one o'clock and, despite the fact they both had work in the morning, they'd stayed awake for another hour at least. She reads back through Saffy's messages. Two weeks of back and forth. No mention of the fact that he was already seeing a woman called Lucy in real life and it was going – so she thought – amazingly well. Saffy is a divorcee, living in upmarket Highgate. She's forty-two and has an edgy short haircut with a floppy fringe and an undercut at the back, and silver rings snaking up one ear. She's head-turningly pretty in her photo, and in the two she sent Ant after they started talking. The word elfin comes to mind. Joni feels sick.

She clicks out of Ant and Saffy's chain of conversation and scrolls even further back. There she is: Joni. She keeps going, past a couple more non-starters. She lands on another series of chats that ends abruptly when they agree to take it offline a few weeks before he started talking to Joni. Mary. Mary is sixty-three. Widowed. She lives in St John's Wood in the house she shared with her husband who died suddenly of a heart attack two years ago. She has a nice face. Kind. Joni feels a pang of sadness for her loss. She has warm amber eyes and an icy blonde bob parted at the side. She looks natural, friendly, trusting.

Joni shifts from the side of the bath to the floor. The tiles are cold, but she welcomes the invigorating shock of it. She keeps her fingers moving on the phone screen to keep it awake. She needs to decide what to do next.

She knows she can't stay here too long. Ant never wakes in the night but there's a first time for everything. She goes back through time past woman after woman.

So, Ant is a Lothario. At least now she knows. He can't be trusted. She'll live. Put it down to experience. Turn it into a cautionary tale she can share with Imo. But there's something else. Something hovering at the outer edges of her brain.

She feels as if it's important to preserve the information she's found. Just so she can study it again when she has more time – and guaranteed privacy. She can't think rationally at 4 a.m. It's against the laws of the universe. And she doesn't want to wake up in the morning and wonder if she imagined the whole thing. Clutching Ant's phone in her hand she creeps to the kitchen to find her own, listening out for signs of life as she goes. Jasper appears from the shadows and rubs himself against her legs, purring loudly. She gives him a handful of kibble to buy his silence. She opens up the camera on her mobile and goes through Ant's account again, this time taking photos of as many pages as she can with a shaky hand.

She creeps back into the bedroom just as the first crack of light hits the sky. Plugs Ant's phone back into its charger, checking twice that she hasn't left the app open. Then she crawls back into bed and lies staring at the ceiling. It's over. She just has to tell him.

And then she realizes what it is that's making her uneasy.

All the women Ant is talking to are completely different. Her, Saffy, Mary. The others he's interacted with briefly along the way. She knows that 'types' are a construct. Fluid. No one rigidly dates only blondes or chartered surveyors. But there's usually a nod towards some common themes. She personally never finds herself attracted to pale-haired, pink-skinned men. It's not a deliberate decision. It just happens. Or doesn't happen, more like. Meg always refused to date anyone over six foot. When pressed she said she thought it might be because their gangly limbs reminded her of spiders. Everyone has their preferences. Except, apparently, Ant. There's a twenty-year-plus age span in just the women she's seen that he's struck up conversations with. They are tall, short, fat, thin, blonde, brunette, red-haired, black, Asian, Caucasian. There's no common thread that she can see. Maybe all he needs is a pulse and a vagina. Maybe he's that much of a sleaze. But she can't equate that with the Ant she knows. The man she's been sharing intimate conversations with for three months now.

Damn. She wishes she could have another trawl through his phone. She should have looked at his text messages. He's bound to have texted with Saffy before they moved on to phone calls – if they even have. That was the way it worked with her. App then text then phone. And then a request for FaceTime. Maybe he had a sudden change of heart and told Saffy about her before things went too far. She's assuming that Mary will have petered out a while ago. She just can't see how they're a match. She's eleven years older than him for a start, which shouldn't matter, but she can't help wondering what made Ant notice her in the first place. If they'd met in the real world and hit it off it could definitely have turned into something romantic. Mary is undeniably attractive. But would he look dispassionately at her details and enter into a flirtation with someone of over sixty? With nothing to go on except a photo and her stats?

By half past five she knows she's got no chance of going back to sleep. The alarm is set for a quarter to seven. Usually Ant leaves at about half past. He likes to get to his office by eight, put in the hours so he doesn't feel guilty about taking a long break to go to the gym or leaving early to collect his kids from school. Joni has always found it endearing that he worries about how hard-working he's being perceived to be even though he's the boss and he grew the company from a niche brand to a well-known name. So, she knows she has time. She unplugs Ant's phone again, uses his sideways sleeping face to turn it on. This time she takes her own with it into the bathroom and goes into text messages. She finds the number she recognizes as Saffy's. Labelled just SJ which she assumes are Saffy's initials. There are only a few texts. She doesn't even bother to read them, just photographs them with her own phone. Then does the same for Mary – MT. Mary and Ant have texted a lot. A. Lot. So, she scrolls as fast as she can, trying to catch them all. She finds a couple of other people whose names are only initials – an AW and an ON – and, realizing on a brief scan that they are also women he's met through the app, albeit a while ago, with no recent exchanges, she captures those messages too. She sees herself, JK, and her more recent self LM. Two of many. Neither of them anything special. She goes back to the home screen, turns off the phone, plugs it back in to the charger and goes to the kitchen to make a coffee. She has homework to do.

By the time she hears Ant stir she has written off AW and ON as non-starters – both conversations lost momentum early on, with AW making her excuses and moving on to find someone she had more spark with and ON – Olivia – owning up to having a husband – and gone through most of his exchanges with Saffy and Mary in chronological order from the first – so familiar – formal back and forths, to the easy chat of people who feel comfortable with each other. She has noticed, sitting in the warm living room as the sun creeps into the bay window turning the pale grey walls yellow, that Ant seems to mirror the tone of whoever he is speaking to. With Saffy he's playful and jokey – a bit like he is with her. But with Mary he's more respectful. Reserved. In both cases the meaningful chats last a week or so before Ant suggests they try a phone call. After that they're shorter, more prosaic: *Just getting on the tube. Call you in half an hour xx* from Saffy or *I might be seeing my son tonight so could we postpone till tomorrow?* from Mary after Ant has suggested FaceTiming that evening. About three weeks in Mary and Ant started to make arrangements to meet for the first time. She checked the date – eight weeks ago, while he and Joni were already talking on the phone. Doing God knows what. The meeting clearly went well because there have been many more. These days their texts are all about arrangements to see each other, or what they will do when they do. It's a relationship. It's real.

She reads through the last few days with Saffy. A clear reference to the phone sex they've had. She blushes. Feels sick. Stupid. That was three days ago. Friday. Did he shut himself away while his kids played in the other room or wait for them to go to bed? Or was he still in the office? As she wanders into the kitchen and flicks on the coffee machine she reads the last two texts. A suggestion of where to meet up from Ant. A date and time. A venue. An agreement from Saffy. It's this Saturday.

Ant calls out from the other room: 'You already up?' Joni clicks her phone off.

Saturday. They're meeting for the first time on Saturday.

13

Joni can't wait for him to go to work. She can barely look at him when he emerges from the bathroom dressed in his sharp suit and crisp white shirt open at the neck. Her mind is racing. She's been trying to think if Ant has been any different towards her since he made the arrangement to meet Saffy, and the answer is no. He's given nothing away, shown no doubts. Last night they made plans to see each other on Thursday. They never meet on the weekends because he has his kids. And yet he has a date in his diary for eleven on Saturday morning. Coffee with Saffy at Kenwood House. Maybe his children have play dates or Forest School or some other commitment that means he can drop them off for a few hours and sneak off and meet a potential new girlfriend? How convenient.

She's fuming. Filled with a rage born of feeling stupid. Played. Used. The twenty-odd years she spent with a man who routinely lied to her. The closed-down version of herself that she'd become, putting up with a bad marriage in the hope of making a good life for her daughter. She'd thought she was over it, but Ant has opened her up again emotionally and exposed all her well-hidden vulnerabilities. Well, never again. Now she knows, she won't stand for it.

She barely gets through the day at work. Makes

herself feel better by 'accidentally' throwing Obi-Wan Kenobi in the bin. Actually, she lobs Jabba in first, but then she feels sorry for him – his tubby, hopeful smile – so she fishes him out and chucks Obi-Wan in instead. Imo calls her at lunchtime while she strides round the Outer Circle of Regent's Park trying to get her steps up and burn off her negative energy and, for the first time in her life, she doesn't answer her daughter. Not even to say, 'I'm busy, I'll call you back,' as she often does, followed by a quick 'You OK?' Even apart from the fact that Imo would want to ask about how things were going with Ant – she's already completely invested in her mother's new relationship and loves to hear the details of their dates, the (until now) happiness apparently evident in Joni's voice whenever she talks about him – Joni would be unable to disguise her uneasiness whatever she changed the subject to. She'll finish with him on Thursday, she decides. They're meeting at the Alice House pub in West Hampstead for food and drink and then – as usual – back to hers. She wonders if the reason they never stay at his isn't because of the boxes and the kids' junk but because he's worried she'll bump into one of his other women. Because it's not just Saffy. He and Mary are still seeing each other – she assumes romantically – according to their sparse text exchanges: *5 mins late xx* and *I'm sitting at the back x* being the latest from, she noticed, last Wednesday evening. Daughter Amelia's soccer evening. None of it makes sense. There aren't enough hours in the week.

By the time she leaves for the day she's decided what

she's got to do. She feels a rush of adrenaline that carries her through the park and up Primrose Hill. She couldn't face being cooped up on the tube. Not in this heat. Not with the sweaty armpits and hot breath of the rush hour. Not when she feels this wired. She would end up getting into an argument. 'Middle-aged woman punches pungent man on Underground': she can see the headline in *Metro* now. She picks up a bottle of Pinot Grigio on Belsize Lane. She needs to arm herself.

By the time she gets home it's gone seven. She feeds Jasper, pours herself a large glass of the wine and slings a frozen macaroni cheese into the oven. This is not the evening to worry about her carb intake. She settles on the sofa and finds Saffy's number in amongst her photos. Here goes.

'Hello?' a woman's voice says after a couple of rings, in that suspicious tone reserved for an unrecognized number.

Joni manages to croak a hello back, clears her throat. 'Is . . . um . . . is that Saffy?'

'Who's calling?' the woman says.

'My name is Joni Kendall.' She listens for the line to go dead as Saffy assumes she's about to launch into a sales pitch. She needs to get to the point and fast. 'I'm . . . well . . . I suppose I'm the girlfriend of Ant Simons. We're seeing each other, anyway. We have been for just over four weeks.'

She hears an intake of breath. She's got Saffy's attention.

'Right . . .'

'He's . . . well, I understand you've been talking to him through Keepers. I'm not phoning to give you a hard time . . . I just thought you should know, that's all . . .'

She waits. Wonders if Saffy will just tell her to mind her own business or that she couldn't give a damn if she's treading on someone else's toes. Slam the phone down.

'That fucker!' Saffy says eventually. 'How did you find out?'

Joni breathes a sigh of relief. At least she doesn't have a fight on her hands. In fact, Saffy is remarkably quick to accept what she's being told. It's still early days for her, Joni supposes.

'Well, the short version is I looked at his phone . . .'

'Sod the short version,' Saffy says. 'I want the whole story.' Saffy has a cut-glass voice. The confidence of a life of money. Joni, who only came into it over halfway through her own, has always felt like an impostor. She pictures the Saffy she has seen in photos: the self-assured, almost confrontational gaze. The voice fits.

Joni hesitates, but then decides she has nothing to lose. She and Ant are done anyway. So what if he finds out that Lucy is Joni, the woman who stood him up? And, if she's being honest, it feels quite freeing to tell someone the absolute truth. She starts from the beginning. Saffy hoots with laughter when she progresses from Joni to Lucy.

'You don't seem too upset,' Joni says. 'I mean, that's good . . .'

'Sorry. It's much worse for you. I don't mean to

trivialize it. It's just that I was expecting there to be a catch. And, you know, selfishly, it's better for me that I find out now.'

'Well, good,' Joni says. She feels herself relax for the first time all day. 'I was worried . . . obviously—'

'Don't be,' Saffy interrupts. 'People like him shouldn't get away with it. Are you very upset?'

Joni carries her glass to the kitchen and tops up her wine. 'Honestly? Yes. And cross with myself for being so stupid . . .'

'Not your fault. Entirely his fault. Fucker.'

Despite everything, Joni laughs. 'Did he suggest the weekend? Doesn't he have the kids?'

She hears a crash upstairs as Flick slams the hoover round her living room. Jasper jumps off the sofa and goes to hide under the coffee table.

'He has them Sunday, Monday, Tuesday, doesn't he?' Saffy is saying. 'They do half the week each or something.'

'No. What? He's always told me he has them at the weekends and on Wednesday evenings.'

'Ha!' Saffy snorts. 'This gets better. So, hold on, he told you this before I was even on the scene?'

Joni sighs. 'Because of Mary, I suppose . . .'

'Oh my God!' Saffy squeals. 'Don't tell me there's another one . . . Wait, I have to get a drink for this. Honestly, to think I nearly didn't answer the phone because I thought you were a cold caller.' Joni hears a fizz as Saffy opens a bottle of something, the rattle of ice cubes. 'Right. So . . . Mary . . .'

96

Joni can't believe how much her mood has lifted in the time she's been speaking to this stranger. Something about the other woman's ability to see the whole thing as a bit of a joke rubs off on her. It's not as if Ant is the love of her life – either of their lives. So she can focus on being angry at him, not hurt for herself. It feels like a much healthier emotion. The saying 'Don't get mad, get even' pops into her head out of nowhere.

She tells Saffy everything she knows about Mary: the dry basic facts available to all on her profile. The tentative exchanges on the app. The texts. Her confusion that there's a more than twenty-year age gap between her and one of the other women he's taken things further with. 'She's a widow. I don't know . . . it makes me feel sad for her. Like she's gone through enough already and now this. Should I tell her too? I don't know if I can bring myself to break it to her.' She heads back to the kitchen and turns the oven off, opening the door to let the heat out. There's a slight whiff of burnt cheese. 'At least if we both back off she'll have him to herself, I suppose . . .'

'Till the next time,' Saffy says. 'Do you really think he's just going to stick with her? Give her a happy ending? I mean, he's still on there, isn't he? Still trawling.'

'Tell me what to do,' Joni says, picking up the wine bottle again and then thinking better of it. She needs to slow down.

Saffy sighs. 'I think you have to tell her. I am one hundred per cent grateful that you told me. You've saved me from potentially making an absolute tit of myself.'

'You're right. I know you're right. But I get the feeling she's going to be really hurt. Oh God.'

'Better coming from you now than from him six months down the line,' Saffy says. 'Do you really think he's planning on spending the rest of his life with her? No. He's just fucking about. This is probably all a big joke to him.'

'OK,' Joni says decisively. 'I'll call her. I might have to leave it till tomorrow though, in case he's with her now . . .'

'He has the kids . . . Oh wait, no, that's bullshit probably.'

'What are you going to do? Are you going to confront him or just not turn up on Saturday?' She feels a bit nervous about having to face Ant once Saffy has told him what she has discovered. She needs to get in first, tell him it's over.

'I think I'll stand him up. Build him up into a frenzy and then let him sit there like a saddo waiting for me. Actually, maybe don't tell Mary about me yet. I don't want to ruin the big moment.'

'Shall I hold off calling her till Sunday?' Joni says hopefully. She knows Saffy's right and she has to tell Mary but she's not exactly looking forward to it.

'No. God. Put her out of her misery about Ant. Just leave me out of it.'

Joni knows she should go and eat her congealing food. Let Saffy get on with her evening. Instead, she says, 'What do you think he's up to?'

She hears Saffy exhale. 'You know him much better than I do. He's just a sleaze, I guess . . .'

Something about that doesn't feel right to Joni. 'It doesn't make sense. He's a good-looking—'

Saffy interrupts. 'Ooh, does he look like his pictures?'

'He does,' Joni says. 'Do you, by the way?'

'Give or take a couple of years.'

'Well, I understand that it might be hard to meet someone in the real world who sees him just as him first and then all the money and success later, but if he's simply looking for hook-ups then I really don't think he'd have a problem.' She tips the rapidly cooling macaroni on to a plate. Prods it with a fork.

'It's a lot of effort just for a hook-up,' Saffy says. 'And wouldn't he be on one of those sites where that's what they specialize in? It's not as if there aren't any.'

'Like Tinder?'

'Way more upfront. On some of them you basically just make an appointment to shag. No questions asked.'

'Really? God.'

'Totally. There's an app for everything these days.'

'God, I feel so old,' Joni says, scraping the food into the bin. She's gone past the point of eating. She suddenly feels exhausted. Like she's taken a sleeping pill. Like she could go to bed and sleep for a week. 'Shall I let you know how it goes with Mary?'

'You'd better. You're doing the right thing, by the way.' Joni hears her pouring more liquid into a glass.

'I hope so,' Joni says. 'I hope I'm not about to ruin her life.'

14

She wakes feeling better than she has for a couple of days, her face plastered to the pillow. It's going to be another hot one. Saffy's reaction last night confirmed that she was right to call her. But then Saffy has never even met Ant yet. Mary's a different prospect altogether. Joni's mood crashes. If she's going to do this she needs to get it over with before the idea of it overwhelms her. Can she phone a total stranger at eight in the morning?

She's safe in knowing that Ant will already be at work even if he stayed over at Mary's, but what if Mary is a late sleeper? Can she really wake her up with this news? Equally, though, she wants to get her before she heads out for the day. She doesn't work as far as Joni knows – at least, she told Ant she didn't in their early communications – but she might have her days filled with engagements that mean she can't answer her phone. Joni decides to get up, have a shower and get dressed, then make a coffee and get it over with. She can't do it with sleep in her eyes and bed hair and three-day-old pyjamas on. She needs to be wearing a suit of armour if she's going to break this woman's heart.

She thinks about Mary starting the day in blissful ignorance. Maybe making plans to see Ant again. Marvelling at this new relationship that has blossomed on the heels of tragedy. Yesterday Joni sent Imo a message saying she would call her back today, thinking that she might be in a calmer mood, so she decides to do that now. Justifies it to herself that she'll catch her before she starts work and so not interrupt her day. Imo answers on the first ring.

'How's it going? I'm just walking to the bus . . .'

'I've got the ick,' Joni says. She's watched enough episodes of *Love Island* with Imo over the past few years to know that having the ick – that queasy feeling when you inexplicably stop fancying a romantic interest and are repulsed by them instead – is unchallengeable. It's also impossible to rationalize, but every teenage girl in the country accepts its existence unquestionably.

'Noooo! Mum!' Imo says. 'He was so perfect.'

'I can't help it. It's gone.'

She hears a siren rush past Imo's head. Can picture her in her combats and trainers, her long skinny limbs. She has her mother's colouring, her father's green eyes. 'Have you finished with him?'

'I'm going to. Tomorrow night. I should do it face to face, yes?'

'Yes! What else are you going to do? Send him a WhatsApp?'

'I thought a telegram. Or a carrier pigeon.'

'Do it in a public place, though. You haven't known him long. What if he's a psycho?'

Joni is always both gratified and horrified that her daughter has picked up her obsession with worst-case scenarios. It will keep her safe, but it might stifle her too.

She has always wished she, herself, could lighten up a bit. Take a few more risks. 'I don't think he is, but I will.'

'And then get straight back out there,' Imo says.

'Mmm . . .' Joni says, non-committal. She's pretty sure she's done with online dating.

She sits at the kitchen table and tries to compose herself. Reminds herself how grateful Saffy was. She just has to pick up the phone and dial. Say what she has to say before she bottles out. And then she can go out and enjoy her day off and forget all about Ant – until she meets him tomorrow night and tells him it's over, that is. When Meg had been alive they would plan things to do together while Imo was at school. Walks and visits to random areas of London one of them had never been to before. Meg had been a jewellery maker, fashioning beautiful one-off pieces in her spare room, earning next to no money but in love with what she did, and she always claimed she did her best work in the middle of the night, so her days were often free. One of them would pick up the phone in the morning and say 'Whet-stone' or 'Eastcote' and off they would go into the unknown. It had always felt like an adventure. They made a list of all the galleries and attractions they had never visited and tried to work their way through them. She had known that Meg was worried about her in the aftermath of Ian leaving. 'You should see this as a new beginning,' she'd said. 'Time to do what you really want to do for once.' But that was the exactly the problem. Joni had no idea what it was she wanted to do. So she'd allowed Meg to help her fill her days while she tried to remember who she was. What her passions were. But then three months after he walked out Meg had died.

They'd been planning to go on bigger trips once Imo left home. Researching all the cities in the world they had longed to visit but had never got around to. They were going to be 'Two spinster ladies who travel,' Meg had said, laughing. 'Like something out of an Agatha Christie.' Once Meg was gone Joni's days had seemed endless. Empty. She'd known she was leaning on Imo far too hard, that it wasn't fair to make her daughter feel as though she needed her to survive. She'd taken the first part-time job that would have her and her rusty skills so that Imo would think she was getting her life together and because, if she was being honest, she needed a reason to get out of the house, to get out of bed in the mornings. Except that then the pandemic had happened and she'd ended up spending the first year doing a job she didn't want to be doing but from her kitchen. The worst of both worlds.

Still, she wasn't going back to work to make friends. She didn't need any more people in her life to worry about. She did the job on autopilot while she waited for her devastated heart to heal.

She notes down Mary's number on a scrap of paper. Closes her eyes and wills herself to go through with it. She keys in the number, holds her breath and listens as the call goes straight to voicemail. She's obviously not going to leave a message. She tidies away the breakfast things, washes Jasper's bowl. She's procrastinating but she knows she should just get herself together and go out. She always does her big supermarket shop on a Wednesday too. She can try Mary later. It all feels like too much effort, though, and what's the point? She can't go through life just ticking off the days. She's only forty-nine but her life is a stagnant pool. Knowing her luck she's going to live till a hundred. She's only halfway through but she feels as if she's given up already. Her relationship with Ant was a ray of hope. A glimpse into a different future. 'Fuck,' she says loudly. She throws the tea towel she's holding across the room. Walks over and picks it up, embarrassed by her outburst. She'll try Mary one more time and then she'll force herself out of the door.

'Yes?'

She almost drops the phone, she's so shocked. She's decided she needs to play this slightly differently to the way she broke it to Saffy. Mary has been seeing Ant in real life for a couple of months. She predated Joni. If anyone deserves the honour of calling themselves his girlfriend, it's her.

'Is that Mary Theobald?'

'Yes. Who is this? I'm in a bit of a hurry.'

Oh God. This is not the kind of conversation you can have with someone who's in a rush. 'Oh. Um . . . maybe I should call you back later? Is there a good time?'

'What's this about?'

She can't. Not like this. 'My name is Joni. It's . . . um . . . it's a personal matter. I'll call you back later. Or you can call me, on this number. Assuming my number came up that is . . .'

She stops talking as Mary says, 'OK, thank you. Good-bye,' and the line goes dead. Now she doesn't know what to do. There's no way Mary will ring her back, she thinks. She wouldn't if she were in her position.

She's in the checkout queue at Waitrose an hour or so later when it rings. A mobile number that might quite possibly be the one she just rang Mary on. She jabs a finger at the green button to accept the call, heart pounding. Steps away from the queue and hovers by the chocolate aisle.

'Is this Joan?' a woman says once Joni has said hello.

'Joni,' Joni says on autopilot. She's relieved that Mary sounds friendlier. Less stressed.

'Joni, I apologize. Now, what can I do for you? I was on my way into a meeting with my bank manager earlier and you know you don't want to keep them waiting . . .'

Joni waits for a pause. She's completely forgotten her carefully rehearsed script. 'I don't quite know how to put this. I'm a friend of Ant Simons . . .'

Of course that's the wrong thing to say. Mary cuts her off. 'Has something happened to him?'

'No. God. No. Sorry . . . I thought I should tell you that I met Ant on a dating website. About three months ago. I didn't know he was already seeing you. I've been seeing him in person for a while. A month or so. Just over.'

'You . . .? I'm not sure I understand,' Mary says.

'I just thought you ought to know. That, you know, he was still on there after you got together. And that actually he still is.'

'You must have him mixed up with someone else . . .'

Joni ploughs on, uses the weapon she's meant to be holding back for later. 'It's not just me. There's another woman, Saffy, too. She didn't know about either of us.'

There's a silence. Joni waits. Mary needs time to digest what she's told her.

Eventually she coughs. Joni jumps. 'I think you must be mistaken. I'm sure you're doing ... whatever it is you're doing with the best of intentions, but I think you must have made a mistake.'

'I—' Joni starts to say, but Mary interrupts again.

'I have to go. I have another appointment. Goodbye.' And then the line goes dead.

Joni stares at her phone for a few seconds as if there might be some explanation other than that Mary has basically hung up on her. She shoves it in her pocket. Not my problem any more, she thinks. I've done my duty.

She manages to kill the rest of the morning doing house-work, putting the *Hamilton* soundtrack on Spotify and turning the volume on her headphones up to ear-splitting levels. Singing along at the top of her voice. Afterwards she forces herself out into the garden and starts ran-domly pulling up what she hopes are weeds. She knows that Mary is not her responsibility, but she can't quite put her out of her head. She sits on a shady bench and calls Saffy.

'There's nothing more you can do,' Saffy says when she tells her. 'You've done your bit. It's up to her.'

'It stinks though, doesn't it? That he's just going to keep on doing it. Whatever it is that he's doing.'

'It does. Are you still seeing him tomorrow?'

Joni waves away a wasp. 'Supposedly. I just wish I knew what he's actually up to. If it was sex wouldn't he be going after younger women? I mean, no disrespect to any of us, but, you know . . .'

'Maybe he has a wrinkle fetish.' Saffy laughs. 'Or a Botox fetish in my case.'

'You know what I mean.'

'You and I are divorced. Mary's widowed. Maybe that's it. He thinks we'll be desperate or grateful or something. That we'll be flattered.'

'God.' Joni moves off, heading in the direction of the house. 'In my case he was right. How sad is that? I guess pretty much every woman on that app over a certain age is either divorced or widowed. Maybe that's it. Easy pickings.'

'But he didn't meet you on the app, did he? Not as far as he knows.'

'No, but I probably had "tragic" written on my forehead. "Grateful for attention".'

'We should mess with his head,' Saffy says decisively. 'Maybe if it wasn't so easy for him to pull off he'd decide to dump Mary and start with a clean slate. That way we'd have saved her anyway. She'd get over him soon enough.'

'Catfish the catfish,' Joni says. 'Can you be bothered though? I mean, maybe we should both just finish with him and move on?'

'What else have you got to do?' Saffy says, laughing.

And that, Joni thinks, is a very good point.

15

She can think of things she'd rather be doing with her Saturday – poking hot needles into her eye, eating her own arm – but somehow here she is, waiting for Ant. She's intrigued to meet Saffy, though, to see if they can fathom out what common attribute caught Ant's eye, and to have some fun at his expense. She isn't sure how Saffy has talked her into this, but she has to admit the surge of adrenaline she's experiencing is a definite mood-booster. And there are worse places to spend the morning than the fragrant green environs of Kenwood House even if it is teeming with people and their dogs. She doesn't know why she doesn't come up here more often.

On Thursday she had texted Ant and claimed she had a stomach bug. She'd laid it on thick about how she thought she might have caught something that was going round the office and that she was sure she must be highly contagious, and thankfully he hadn't offered to come over and nurse her. She didn't have the strength, or the acting skills, to get through an evening pretending nothing had happened. They'd arranged a rain check for Monday. She has no intention of keeping that date.

She texts Saffy: *I'm here. Where are you?* It's still more than twenty minutes until Saffy is meant to be meeting up with Ant so she's confident she won't bump into him, but she keeps a lookout just in case, staying away from the outdoor café area and the busy path that looks over the gardens.

Round the front, Saffy texts. And then: *It seems like the back but it's the front. Where the drive leads out to the road.*

As Joni walks round the side of the beautiful Regency building another text arrives *Red baseball cap!* Clearly she's not the only one who's anxious. She spots a red hat right away but there's a long blonde ponytail sticking out from underneath it. She looks around.

'Joni?' The woman in the cap whips it off and the ponytail comes with it, revealing a dark crop underneath. The Keepers photo may not be bang up to date but Saffy is easily recognizable. She's smaller than Joni imagined – barely five foot – but the oval face and big brown eyes are in evidence. She's a stunner even in her oversize dungarees and trainers. Joni immediately feels inadequate.

'Saffy?'

Saffy squeaks a hello. 'Oh my God, is it you? You're gorgeous! Why did you use someone else's photo? God. He should be so lucky. Would he recognize me from my pictures, do you think? Did you? Sorry, I'm babbling. Nerves. Tell me to shut up.'

Joni's tempted. Instead, she puts her hand on Saffy's bare arm. 'Let's go and sit somewhere.'

She leads her to a shady bench behind a giant rhododendron. If Ant walks past them, they're in trouble, but it's unlikely.

'Are we really going to do this?' Saffy crams the cap back on, hiding her hair again.

'It was your idea,' Joni says lightly.

'I know. Yes. How long have we got?'

Joni checks her watch. Can't help noticing with a stab of satisfaction that her red movement ring is almost closed already thanks to her vigorous walk from home. 'Eighteen minutes. Did you say he's going to text you when he gets there?'

'Yes. Well, whichever one of us thinks they're there first. But it won't be me, obviously.'

'OK, so we just wait. You don't feel at all sad not getting to meet him?'

Saffy snorts. 'God, no. I had a lucky escape. How are you bearing up?'

'Better, I guess,' Joni says. 'Now I'm angry rather than upset and I think that's probably healthier. I just feel stupid.'

'Absolutely no need. We both got taken in. Have a big night out with the girls and move on.'

'Good idea,' Joni says although there are no girls. There never were. She has always been one of those people who is happier talking in depth with one person than bantering with five. Those big gangs of women have never appealed to her. The admin alone to keep up with them all equally makes the whole idea seem more like work than fun. And wouldn't there be factions? Breakaway groups? Rivalries? 'Actually, I don't really have girls.' She doesn't know why she confides this. 'Not, you know, like a big homogenous group of friends . . .'

'Everyone needs the girls. They're a vital commodity.'

Before Joni can say anything else Saffy jumps as her phone beeps. 'Shit. Is that him? Already?' She peers closely at the message and Joni wonders if she should be wearing glasses. *I'm here just in case you're early. I'm at a table just by the little shop.*

'I know where that is,' Joni says, standing up. She sits down again. 'Let's give it two minutes. Don't reply.'

'Of course not. Right, let me look at you . . .' Joni turns to face her. 'You look like a gorgeous strong woman in the middle of a walk on the heath. Perfect.'

'Are you going to wait here?' Joni asks. 'So I can find you later?'

'I suppose so. I wish I could be there – I feel as if I'm missing the punchline.'

'I'll commit every second to memory,' Joni says, standing again.

She spots Ant immediately. He's leaning with his elbows on the wooden table, sunglasses on, looking around. He's slightly hemmed into a corner by two other tables so casually sauntering by is not as straightforward as it could be. Joni's heart begins to pound. Why is she doing this? Just to give him a fright and make him feel what it might be like to get caught out? A prank, really. It suddenly all just feels a bit juvenile and pointless. But she can't back out now, not when Saffy is waiting in the flower beds for her to report back. She decides to make a beeline for the little brick house that contains the shop, selling fancy bits of gardening gear and expensive bottles of elderflower cordial and flavoured gins from independent distilleries. She just needs to look as if she knows where she's going in case he sees her before she's ready. She takes a breath and strides forward.

Three, two, one . . . 'Ant?' She says it a few steps too early so she's not sure if he hears, but then he looks up and the expression on his face makes it all worthwhile. Sheer panic.

He stands up. Fakes a smile. Even with his sunglasses on Joni can see that he's scanning the area, looking for Saffy.

'Hey. What on earth are you doing here?'

She allows herself to be hugged. 'Long walk. I often come up here on a nice day. Are you meeting someone?'

He ignores the question. 'Are you feeling better? You look great.'

'Oh. Yes. Much. Although today is the first day I've really been out. I might get a coffee. Do you want one?'

She can see him looking anxiously at his phone, which is face up on the table. Right on cue it beeps with a message. She knows it'll be Saffy texting to say she'll be there in a couple of minutes. He scoops it up and checks it. She sees him swallow.

'I'm going to have to go,' he says. 'The kids are at one of their friends' and Amelia's cut her finger. They think they need to take her for stitches.'

Joni wants to say 'What? They said that in that short message?' but instead she pulls a face of concern. 'Oh no. I'll walk with you. Where's your car?'

He waves a vague hand towards the car park. 'It's OK. I'll call you later. It's so lovely to see you. I've been worried about you.'

'I hope Amelia feels better,' she says as he gives her the quickest of hugs and, casting another quick glance around the café's clientele, rushes off, calling 'Monday night?' over his shoulder as he goes. It's all over in less than three minutes but Joni feels elated. A rush like she's never known before.

She finds Saffy pacing up and down between two trees.

'He ran away!' Joni says, grabbing on to her arm. 'He actually ran away.' She can feel a slight wave of hysteria come over her as she starts to laugh. She knows it's mostly nerves, relief, a dump of adrenaline but she's powerless to stop it.

'What, literally?' Saffy laughs.

'Pretty much. That has definitely ruined his weekend.'

'Good. Fucker. Oh, here he is . . .' She holds up her mobile as it rings. 'Shall I?'

Joni nods decisively. Saffy puts a finger to her lips. She plasters a smile on her face and answers the call. 'Hi! Where exactly are you? I can't see you . . . Oh . . .' She holds the phone away from her ear and rolls her eyes at Joni as he talks, spins a hand as if to say 'blah, blah, blah'. 'Oh no! Which hospital? Is it bad? Poor girl . . . how did it happen? No . . . No . . . Of course you do . . . Yes . . . Let me know, won't you? Bye.' She turns to Joni. 'He couldn't wait to get me off the phone. You've completely rattled him.'

'Mission accomplished,' Joni says. 'Maybe he'll think twice next time.'

'Oh, I don't think this'll change a thing except hopefully shave a few days off his life. What next? Shall we go and get a drink? The Spaniards is only up the road . . .'

It's a beautiful day. Joni can picture the crooked old pub and its pretty gardens with the little shady booths and mouth-watering lunches. She hasn't been there for years. Not since she and Ian . . . well, not since they still did things like go out for lunch together. Since meals were an occasion, not a chore. It would be fun to sit and offload about Ant with Saffy.

'I've got a lunch thing . . .' she says before she can stop herself. Her default mode these days is say no first and think later. It's easier that way. Far better than the other way round. Saffy doesn't seem to take offence.

'No prob. Which way are you walking?'

Joni waves a hand in the direction of the opposite side of the heath. She's suddenly desperate to be on her own, holed up in her flat with her cat and a good book.

'I'll walk with you,' Saffy says.

'Don't you live that way?' She flaps a hand towards Highgate.

'I need the exercise. I can get a cab back.'

Joni mentally plans the most direct route as they set off. The one that will take least time.

'Have you been to the spa?' Saffy is saying. Joni forces herself to slow down, walk at a sociable pace.

'No. I mean, I went and looked through the windows.'

'I have. I went to the main one. Notting Hill. God, it's fabulous . . .'

'Really? When?'

Saffy laughs. 'As soon as he told me what he did. I thought I should check it out. I figured if I bumped into him and he recognized me I'd just tell him that's what I was doing. That I booked in for a massage to see what all the fuss was about.'

'I wish I'd thought of that. I just lurked around outside like a stalker. How was it?'

'Unreal. I mean, absolute heaven. I didn't see him, obviously. Maybe we should both go. Together . . .'

Joni snorts. 'No! I just want to put him behind me . . .'

Saffy shrugs. 'OK. I think I might still meet up with him though.'

'Why?' Joni stops in her tracks and looks at her. Saffy continues on a few steps before she realizes she's walking alone. She turns back.

'I don't know. He's still getting away with it too easily, I think. Maybe I can make him fall in love with me and then break his heart.'

Joni raises a sceptical eyebrow. 'I don't think he's the falling-in-love kind. Don't waste your energy on him.'

'You're right. Plus that sounds like a bit too much effort.' Saffy sidesteps round a fallen tree branch. 'The story needs an ending though, don't you think? The bastard gets his comeuppance, that kind of thing.'

'Today was fun, but I think I just want to move on now. Forget he even exists.'

'Mmm . . .'

They walk on in silence for a few minutes, Joni leading them through the woods. The leaves have already started to fall, hastened by the heatwave, and they're brittle underfoot. She finds herself longing for the first cool breeze of autumn, a fresh start.

'They should have a ratings system on the website. One star means don't touch with a barge pole,' Saffy says eventually.

'Too open to abuse.'

'There must be something. It's just not right.'

'If we go up this way that takes us to Well Walk. Does that sound OK?' She feels as if she wants to change the subject. She's not sure Saffy's obsession with getting back at Ant is healthy. Not that she can't understand the impulse, she totally can, but what's the point?

'Sure,' Saffy says distractedly.

'The next one will be better,' Joni says after a while. 'There must be some good ones on there.' She's not sure she believes this. Or, at least, she does but she doesn't know how you weed them out from the chancers. It's just luck, she supposes, and she's never felt as if luck has been on her side. Not since she won first prize in the church raffle when she was nine – a bottle of wine that her parents immediately confiscated off her and gleefully drank that evening. Second prize had been a Cabbage Patch doll and that had been the one she really wanted. She'd tried suggesting her mum and dad put the wine away for when she was older and they'd laughed and said they'd buy her a bottle once she was eighteen to make up for it. I must remind Mum of that next time I speak to her, she thought fondly. With interest surely that would be a whole case by now.

'Was your marriage ever happy?' Saffy says out of nowhere as they emerge from the cool of the path on to the road.

'Yes,' Joni says without hesitation. 'I mean, I can't see what I ever saw in him now, but I did. See something in him. Was yours?'

'Blissful.'

That wasn't the answer she was expecting. 'Then, why . . .?'

A driver impatiently waves them across the street. Saffy glares at him. 'Why do they do that? Stop for you and then get angry that you don't cross fast enough?'

Joni doesn't answer. She feels as if there's something Saffy wants to tell her and she's intrigued to find out what.

Suddenly, Saffy sticks an arm out, narrowly missing Joni's face. 'There's a taxi.' She turns and hugs Joni as it pulls up. 'I'll ring you,' she says as she clambers in. 'We should have that drink.'

16

By the time she arrives home Joni is too knackered to do anything with the rest of her day beyond pull her lounger into a shady spot and doze in the garden until it's time to go to the gym. There's no way she would ever take to her bed in the afternoon unless she was ill, but somehow sleeping in the open air is permissible. Aspirational even. She wakes at about three o'clock to find Flick staring at her from the first-floor window and Jasper from the ground floor. Luckily she still has her large Jackie O sunglasses on so she doesn't have to acknowledge Flick's wave. She knows it would be followed by an opened window and an invitation up for a cup of tea. She screws her eyes half closed and waits for Flick to move away before she gets up and goes in to pacify her angry feline. It's not that he wants to come out and join her, it's that he doesn't want her to be out there at all. He wants her inside, catering to his every whim.

She checks her to-do list. Tries to find something on there that doesn't fill her heart with dread. Settles on putting on a load of washing and removing the chipped polish from her toenails. She finds herself thinking about phoning Saffy to try and recapture her euphoria from this morning, but the moment has gone. It all feels a little childish, looking back.

When she'd originally decided on her work days – Joni had been given first pick, having been hired before Lucas was brought in to fill in the gaps – she had thought the long weekends would be ideal, and while Imo had been at home they were. Who doesn't love the prospect of waking up on a Saturday and knowing they have three whole days to please themselves? Now, though, she sometimes found the prospect horrified her.

She reads the papers online, half-heartedly phones her mum and listens to a long story that involves an episode of *Countdown*, checks Imo's Instagram and Lucy's Facebook. She looks up Saffy on both and finds her on Insta. She suddenly remembers Ant's beautiful home and goes on to PrimeLocation for a snoop. She puts in Notting Hill and no maximum price and there – eventually when she's scrolled past mansions on sale for 30 then 20 then 10 million – it is. Four thousand five hundred square feet of perfection. She sees with a jolt of pleasure that there are twenty-five photos. She decides to make a coffee and indulge her curiosity.

She takes her laptop and drink back out into the garden, settling into the faux wicker armchair closest to the house, where she will be unseen by Flick unless her neighbour stands on a chair and cranes her neck at an almost impossible angle. It's not out of the question.

Joni knows that people – especially very wealthy people – often stage their houses for selling, dressing rooms that are usually filled with junk with hired-in beds and even artwork. Painting a perfect picture. But she can't imagine that if Camille was so reluctant to sell she would have gone to those lengths. And, besides, the woman she pictures in her head – largely formed from her own imagination and based on next to nothing – has impeccable taste and attention to detail without needing any outside help. She scrolls through the photos Ant showed her the other day. The stunning exterior, the light-filled living room with vast white sofas (brave with kids, she thinks), a huge stone fireplace, and oversize paintings on the walls. The state-of-the-art kitchen with floor-to-ceiling glass doors on to a perfectly swept patio complete with space-age-looking moulded furniture and flawlessly manicured architectural plants in large black containers. She looks round at her own garden: a riot of mismatching pots and bordering on out-of-control flower beds. She actually loves the anarchic nature of it, but there's something to be said for ordered perfection. She moves on to what she assumes is the principal bed-room. It's light, airy, quite feminine with pale grey and white bedding and white curtains at the windows. The bed has the obligatory mountain of throw pillows in shades of grey and silver. She assumes Camille must have some kind of housekeeper who picks them all up every morning and arranges them beautifully and then takes them off again and hides them away at night because, really, who can be bothered to do that? Joni had tried to replicate the look once at her and Ian's home, but all it resulted in was an obstacle course of cushions on the floor every day that neither of them could be bothered to pick up only to discard them all again at bedtime. She can't imagine Camille living with that kind of clutter.

She flicks through pictures of what looks like a guest suite (walls a pale ashy blue and a large abstract collage above the headboard) and then reaches the kids' rooms. Obviously there is none of the clutter that accompanies children wherever they go in these carefully staged photos, but she can see flashes of their personalities in the décor – a large heart-shaped mirror in what she assumes is Amelia's space, and fairy lights around the white metal bedframe, a dinosaur lamp and a state-of-the-art mini car racetrack that seems to go all round the perimeter of what she guesses is Jack's. She moves on; it feels a bit wrong to be snooping on the children's private spaces even if they have been photographed for exactly that purpose. She comes to another bedroom with a single bed draped in a rich red and gold cover, two guitars propped up on stands, a framed poster of Janis Joplin. It looks like the room of a hip twenty-year-old. Maybe Camille has an au pair or nanny to help out with the kids. Ant has never mentioned it. Or maybe the room has been styled that way to help prospective buyers to imagine how the space might be used. The décor seems an odd choice though. She moves on to the next photo. This one looks like a nursery. Pale yellow walls with a frieze of slightly drunk-looking cows, pigs and sheep. A white cot with a canopy up against one wall. Joni scrolls back again to the exterior, the main living rooms, confused. It's definitely the right house. She goes back to the nursery photo, keeps moving forward to the small but beautiful garden.

She goes onto Rightmove and types in Ossington

Street, hoping for a different selection of pictures. She finds the house immediately, added to the site on Monday, clicks on the link. The images are all exactly the same, but she scours them anyway. The room with the guitar, the nursery . . .

Before she knows what she's doing she's calling Saffy. 'How many kids did Ant tell you he's got?' she says as soon as she answers.

'I'm very well, thank you, how are you,' Saffy says, laughing. 'Two. Why are you asking?'

'Because there's something funny going on. Go on PrimeLocation.'

'Have you had a glass or two? What are you talking about?'

'No, but that's a good idea. I'm going to get one.' She heads for the kitchen and the chilled bottle of Sauvignon Blanc in the fridge. 'Are you on yet?'

'Getting there. Didn't we just see each other a couple of hours ago? Aren't you supposed to be at a lunch?'

'It got cancelled at the last minute. Right. Put in Notting Hill and go down till you get to one for eight million. Just over. Big white stucco thing.'

Saffy is silent while Joni assumes she looks. 'OK. Ossington Street?'

'That's it. Ant showed me it the other day. It's his and his ex-wife's house and he told me she'd finally agreed to sell.'

'Right. It's gorgeous.'

'It is. So . . . Jack and Amelia, right? Ten and eight.'

'Sounds about right.'

'Keep going through the photos until you get to the bedrooms.'

'Ooh, look at that gym,' Saffy says. 'That's much better than mine.'

Joni settles back outside, takes a sip of her wine. 'Don't get distracted. You need to get to about picture number eighteen.'

'OK. There's the main bedroom. Very nice. I'm not sure about that rug.'

'Keep going. Past the en suite.'

'I am. So, Amelia's room, I guess. Am I supposed to study the picture for clues?'

'No. Keep going.' Joni moves her chair into the shade slightly.

'Generic boy's room. Jack. Bit young for ten, but I assume they've styled it. OK, what's this?'

'Are you on the one with the guitars?'

'Mmm-hmm. I guess one of them plays. We once had a home stager turn one of our rooms into a dedicated art room when we were selling, because there was an old easel in there.'

She could be right, Joni knows, but she feels as though, if that were the case, they would have made a better job of it. 'Maybe. There's one more.'

'This is like Christmas. Except there's no chocolate when you open the next window. Is that a baby's room?'

'Bingo.'

She hears Saffy breathe out. 'That's weird. Again, staging maybe. If I'm being devil's advocate.'

'What do you think it means? That he has two more kids than he's letting on? Why?'

'Maybe Camille already had one when they met, and now she's had a baby with someone else since they split up?'

Joni thinks about it for a moment. 'He would have mentioned the older one. There's no way he'd have a stepchild and never ever mention them.'

'I agree, it's odd. There's only one thing for it . . .'

'Oh God,' Joni says. 'What?'

'We're going to go and see it. I'll ring the agent.'

'No. I mean . . .'

'There's no way Ant will be there. He doesn't live there any more and you said yourself that his relationship with Camille is tricky, so he's hardly going to be popping round for a cup of tea in the middle of the day when he's meant to be at work. Shall I see if I can get us in for Monday afternoon? Are you at work?'

'No, but . . .'

'Right. That's settled. It'll be fun, right?'

Joni wants to say no, what can this achieve? Why are they wasting their time? But part of her knows that the reason she phoned Saffy in the first place is because she wants answers. She wants to know who this man she's been sharing her bed with for weeks really is. She wants to know how duped she's been.

17

Somehow Saffy has convinced the obsequious estate agent that she is a genuine potential buyer for Ant's 8-million-plus-pound house. Maybe she does have the credentials, Joni thinks. She does, after all, live in Highgate. Maybe she's seriously wealthy. Property companies usually check these things before showing people a mega-million-pound home. She tries to remember what Saffy told Ant about her life in their exchanges on the app. Doesn't feel as if she can ask about the size of her bank balance without appearing nosy.

Thankfully it's another sweltering sunny day so Joni feels she can accessorize with a floppy straw hat and the enormous sunglasses that, she thinks, make her look like a fly. Just in case Ant decides to drop in and pick something up. Even though she knows how unlikely this is she wants to feel prepared. Buy herself time to hide in the bathroom before he gets a proper look at her.

Saffy is waiting on the steps when she gets there, in a short floral summer dress and thong sandals, a huge see-through Starbucks cup in hand. She produces another one from somewhere and hands it to Joni. 'Frappucino.'

'Fabulous.'

They both stand and look up at the house. 'Remember to ask questions,' Saffy says. 'I thought if we asked about schools in the area, that kind of thing, that'd get us into it.'

'I thought nurseries.' Joni flaps the brim of her hat to create a breeze.

'Nurseries! Yes! Oh, is this him?'

Joni turns and sees a young man in a smart suit, cut too tight on the legs, a snug waistcoat under the jacket despite the heat, approaching from the end of the road. His hair is slicked back in a thick, dark wave. She can hear the click of his shiny shoes. No socks. 'Money on it,' she says.

'Mrs Jacobson?' he says as he approaches, looking at a point somewhere in between the two of them so as not to offend.

'That's me.' Saffy sticks out a hand. 'And this is my good friend Joni Mountbatten.' Joni double-takes and then realizes that she has never told Saffy her surname. She shakes the estate agent's sweaty hand. He doesn't bother to fill her in on his own name. After all, she's not the buyer. She wants to take him aside and give him a pep talk: always include the friend. The friend is the one who will ultimately persuade the client one way or the other. If you piss her off, you're toast.

They follow him up the majestic white stone steps, Saffy chatting away about the weather and the lack of parking spaces. The agent – Lucian, she gathers his name is from the way Saffy keeps dropping it into her monologue – rings the bell and then waits approximately 0.01 seconds before putting the keys in the lock and opening the door.

'So, this is the entrance hall . . .' he says and Joni's heart sinks as she realizes he's going to describe everything they're looking at as if they were on the other end of a phone and not standing right next to him. 'Original stone floor—'

'Is there a chain?' Saffy interrupts.

He doesn't miss a beat. 'No. They're happy to wait to buy until they've sold this.'

'Really? Where will they live?' Joni almost laughs. All subtlety is out of the window, then. Lucian looks slightly thrown but recovers quickly. 'Um, well, they have a house in the country. I believe they're going to relocate there for a while.'

Saffy raises her eyebrows at Joni as if to say 'Did you know about that?' and Joni gives her a slight shake of the head.

'It's lovely,' Joni says, feeling they should give the agent something. They follow him through to a vast living room that's familiar from the listing.

'The property has been extensively renovated by the family . . .' Lucian battles on.

Joni feels as if she needs to do her bit. They're here on a mission. 'How are the schools?' Saffy gives her a thumbs up behind Lucian's back.

'Excellent, as you can imagine. There's—'

'How old are the sellers' children? Maybe I could ask them . . .'

Joni snorts and covers it with a cough. Saffy certainly doesn't believe in holding back.

'Oh. Um . . . well, they range from about sixteen

down to a baby . . . I'm not sure how old. But the parents around here are very discerning so there's no shortage of fantastic schools for all ages. You have children then, I presume?'

Saffy nods. 'Two.' Joni knows this isn't true. She remembers from Saffy's early exchanges with Ant on the app that she doesn't have kids. She's not sure whether from design or luck. 'How long have they lived here?'

They follow him through to the kitchen. Joni can see Lucian is desperate to point out the eight-burner stove and the Gaggenau coffee machine, his whole spiel thrown off by Saffy's questions. 'Are all the appliances staying?' she asks in an effort to show interest. Saffy glares at her.

'They are. Although I'm sure you'd want to put your own stamp on the space,' he says, smiling at Saffy and flashing suspiciously straight, gleaming teeth. Imo once expressed a desire to get veneers and Joni had gone into panicked overdrive, telling her she'd regret it later when the fashion moved on from obvious fakes to a more natural look, as it surely would one day. 'And by then your own teeth will be black and rotten – what's left of them anyway because they file them down . . .' She'd known she was protesting too much and that that would almost certainly produce the opposite to her desired effect, but she hadn't been able to stop herself. 'You'd have to pay for them yourself,' she'd said, somewhat desperately. 'I'm not being complicit in you mutilating yourself.'

'Oh, for God's sake, Mum,' Imo had said as she'd stomped out. 'Stop being so dramatic.'

Joni knew that her argument had no validity anyway. If Imo's heart was really set on it she would only have to ask Ian and he'd stump up the money. He never denied Imo anything, a fact that made Joni both irritated and worried for her daughter at the same time. 'How's she ever going to learn the value of money?' she'd said to him on the phone when he'd offered to pay for Imogen to go glamping for a month last summer instead of getting a holiday job. 'She needs to know she has to find a way to earn her living.'

'She doesn't though, does she?' Ian had said infuriatingly. 'I mean, eventually, when she finds her passion. But she doesn't need to work just for the sake of working. Not like we did.'

'She does if she's going to be a fully functioning adult,' Joni had said, furious. 'Or do you want her to turn into one of those kids who just piss about living on Daddy's money with no purpose in life?'

'I just want her to be happy,' he'd said sanctimoniously, and Joni had told him to fuck off and then put the phone down. Somehow Imo had come out of it unscathed. Her teeth remained intact. She was working hard for a pittance (although Joni was pretty sure Ian was subsidizing her, but she was prepared to let that one slide). God, she loved the strong, (mostly) independent woman Imo had become.

'Could we see upstairs?' Joni said now. The ground floor was giving precious little away; anything personal had clearly been put aside so as not to distract from the stunning architecture, and she wanted to move things along.

'Of course. There are six bedrooms, four en suite,' Lucian continues gamely.

'That's a lovely garden for a dog,' Joni says, looking out of the window on the way up the stairs. Saffy looks at her, bemused.

'Oh, you have a dog?' Lucian says to Saffy. 'What kind?'

'A . . . um . . . one of those doodles. Alsatian . . . doodle.' She shrugs at Joni behind Lucian's back.

'Really?' he says. Of course he's going to turn out to be the world's biggest dog expert. 'I don't think I've ever seen one of those. Is it big?'

'Huge,' Joni says. 'Do the owners have a dog?'

'What?' Saffy mouths at her.

'Er,' Lucian says. 'I don't believe so. I've never seen one. Right, this is the principal . . .' Joni doesn't listen. Her brain is racing, trying to process what is happening.

Saffy oohs and aahs over the bedroom suite that takes up the whole of the first floor. Frustratingly there is nothing personal here either, but Joni knows the real clues will be on the floors above. She looks at her watch as if to imply they're in a hurry. Luckily Lucian picks up on it and leads them back to the stairs. 'There are three bedrooms on the next floor . . .'

He stands in the doorway of the first one they come to and waves a hand. 'After you.' This is the room Joni assumed was Jack's but it's even more obvious in real life that it's young for a ten-year-old. There's a wicker chair that wasn't in the pictures piled with cuddly toys for a start. A Scooby Doo Playmobil set. She's looking around for anything that might have his name on when there's a burst of grime music, which appears to be the ringtone for Lucian's phone.

'Do you mind . . .?' he says, finger hovering over the green button.

'Not at all.' Saffy smiles. She watches until he leaves the room and then flings the wardrobe door open. 'Keep watch,' she hisses. Joni hovers near the door. She can hear Lucian one floor down talking about a 'sealed bid situation'. Saffy grabs a hanger from the rack and waves it at her. 'Nil desperandum, mate,' Lucian is saying. The hanger holds a tiny school uniform: deep blue jacket with a crest, white shirt, blue-and-yellow-striped tie. Saffy looks at the label. 'Age five to six.' She stares at Joni meaningfully, then crams the clothes back in the cupboard as they hear Lucian taking the stairs two at a time.

'Sorry about that,' he says as he appears in the doorway. 'Right. This is the guest suite . . .'

The last room on the first floor is the nursery. There are wicker baskets full of wooden toys. A push-along trolley full of blocks. Clearly this is not a newborn. Or a room that's been staged.

'Aah, they have a baby,' Joni says in her best cooing voice. 'How old?'

Lucian looks like a rabbit caught in the headlights. Apparently ageing babies is not his area of expertise. 'Not sure. He's crawling, I know that much. Gorgeous little chap.' Joni and Saffy exchange looks. Joni is dying

131

to get out of here, to go for a debrief, to work out what all this means. They need to see the rest though, get all the info they can.

'So, top floor is two en-suite bedrooms. Great for teenagers, or an au pair.'

They traipse up the narrower flight of stairs on to a landing with a door each side. On the left is the room that could be Amelia's. A little sophisticated for an eight-year-old, but who knew these days? Opposite is the one with the guitars. 'Nanny?' Joni says. It smells faintly of joss sticks.

'Teenage daughter,' Lucian says.

Joni nods. 'Great.'

They can't wait to ditch Lucian in the street. Saffy tells him she'll talk to her husband and see if she can persuade him to come for a viewing. 'He has his heart set on Richmond,' she says, and Lucian's face drops. A morning wasted. As if on autopilot they head for the nearest café without speaking, take a seat outside and order coffees from the young, punky-looking waitress.

Once they're alone Saffy exhales loudly. 'What the fuck?'

'I don't even know where to start. How long did Ant tell you it's been since he split up with Camille?'

'A year,' Saffy says without hesitation.

'Same here. So, if the baby's crawling it must be his. Unless she got pregnant by someone else and they split up when he found out. That was the catalyst.'

'You'd think he might have mentioned that though.'

Joni fiddles with a paper wrap of sugar. 'Maybe he thinks it's emasculating.'

'OK, even if I buy that, which I don't really, who's the teenager? And why is Jack five years younger than he's supposed to be?'

'Maybe he's just small.'

Saffy pulls a sceptical face. 'Right. Half-sized son, someone else's baby and a random adolescent . . . what if the baby is the teenager's? His eldest daughter got knocked up when she was fourteen and he's so ashamed he never talks about either of them. Camille stuffed a cushion up her jumper for nine months and they pretend it's hers . . .'

'He would have told us they have a baby at least, wouldn't he? If it was supposed to be theirs?'

'No, because then it would look as if they still had a fully functioning sex life . . .'

'Hardly, if the baby's nearly a year already – it would look like they had sex once in January last year.'

'Well, you come up with something better then,' Saffy snaps.

'OK, don't bite my head off,' Joni says. 'I'm just looking at all the possibilities. What if he thought having a teenager made him seem too old?'

'He's fifty-two, right?' The waitress arrives with the coffees and Saffy indicates two more, like a drunk in a bar who can't risk a gap between drinks. Joni feels too wired already, but she just lets it happen. She doesn't have to drink it.

'Right. So easily old enough to have a sixteen-year-old. I mean, he could have a thirty-year-old and you wouldn't question it. If he was going to lie about that wouldn't he lie about his age too? Make himself younger?'

'Maybe he's really seventy. He just uses a lot of Evoke stock. But if that was the case you'd show off about it, wouldn't you? Make yourself a walking advert for your brand.'

'So, it is his stepdaughter. Camille already had her when they met. And they don't get on. He's already decided he won't have a relationship with her after the divorce, but he thinks the women he meets would judge him for that, so he just keeps quiet about her.' She smiles at a toddler sitting at the next table. She had loved that age with Imo. She knows it was exhausting and frustrating at times, but now she only really remembers how easy it was to make her laugh.

'That's possible.' Saffy moves her empty cup ready for a new one. 'Weird, but possible . . . No. For some reason he's been lying to us about his kids.'

'Oh, and let's not forget the dog.'

Saffy looks at her. 'What was that all about? I thought you'd lost it for a minute there.'

'The dog. Vinnie . . .'

'What dog?'

'Ant's dog. I assumed he left him with Camille and the kids, but there was no sign of a dog living there.'

'He's never even mentioned a dog.'

'He hasn't to me since we met, either. But he did when we were online. He sent me a photo.' She picks up her phone and finds the picture, holds it up for Saffy to see.

'OK, he hasn't sent me that one. Maybe the dog died.

Or they gave it away. The kids are the bigger issue. I wish Mary would talk to us. She could probably clear this whole thing up.'

'Of course,' Joni says, with a sudden realization, 'there is another explanation.'

Saffy looks at her. Waits. 'What? Tell me!'

'That it's not his house at all.'

18

'That's it! It's not his fucking house,' Saffy shouts loudly and bangs her fist on the table. The toddler squeals and jumps up and down with delight at the noise. Joni smiles apologetically at his parents. 'Why, though?' Saffy adds, more quietly.

'The only thing I can think of is that he's still with Camille. That all the stuff about their divorce is bullshit.'

'How would that work? Doesn't he stay the night with you?'

Joni nods. 'Not every time, but he has done. And presumably with Mary too. Wait a minute . . .' she says as a memory suddenly pops into her head. 'I heard him on the phone to someone at work about dropping something off at the house. He said the name of the road – Ossington Street – as if they'd know exactly where he meant. How does that work?'

Saffy screws up her face. 'He really does live there, just not at the house he showed you?'

Joni shakes her head. 'Why, though? It seems a bit convenient, doesn't it?'

'Fake phone call? Did you hear it ring? Could you hear the person on the other end?'

'Shit.' Joni closes her eyes. Thinks. 'It was the day he

showed me the listing. He was already on the phone when I answered the door. Do you really think he staged the whole thing just so he could drop the name of the road he was going to pretend to live in into the conversation? That's almost genius.'

'It's fucked up is what it is.' Saffy waves a hand at the waitress again as she delivers their second cups. Joni holds a hand up. 'No, Saffy. No more coffee. I've got the jitters already.'

'Could we get some water, please? And one more Americano?' Saffy smiles at the waitress who smiles back.

'How can you drink so much coffee? I'd be a basket case.'

'It's my only vice.' She swats away a wasp. 'That and drinking and having sex with unsuitable men. Is he good in bed? Ant?'

Joni actually feels herself blush. 'I never know what that means as an objective question, but yes. He has skills. We have fun. God, what if he is still married, though? Poor Camille. Shit.'

Saffy puts a tanned, perfectly manicured hand on her arm. 'You didn't know.'

'It doesn't make it any better. Well, it does, but you know what I mean. I'm not that woman. I never have been. I know too much about what it's like being on the other side of it.'

'Oh, I have.' Saffy hands the waitress her empty cup as she puts down two glasses of water. 'Several times, actually. Not something I'm proud of. Listen, Camille's problem isn't with you or me. Or Mary. It's with him.'

Joni nods half-heartedly. 'So, he's not divorced. His house isn't on the market. He's just a cheating scumbag. That's what we think?'

'That about sums it up.'

'And, what? Camille is OK with him being out three or four nights a week? Staying away?'

'He'll have a story. They always have a story. I once dated a married guy who told his wife he was doing undercover work for the police that meant he had to be out all hours.'

'And she believed him?'

Saffy shrugs. 'People believe what they want to, I suppose.'

'Well, she must have been deluded then,' Joni scoffs. 'Sorry, that's a horrible thing to say. I didn't mean it like that . . .'

'What did Ian used to tell you?' Saffy says gently.

Joni toys with her water glass, running her thumb around the rim. 'Work. I don't think I ever really believed it though.'

'But you didn't ask?'

'No. I didn't ask.' She squeezes her eyes shut. 'We need to save Mary. Some good has to come out of this.'

'Mary doesn't want to be saved: you said that yourself.'

'Only because she doesn't know the whole truth.'

'And neither do we,' Saffy says. 'We just have suspicions.'

They sit in silence for a moment. Saffy stirs her coffee,

round and round. 'You have to keep seeing him,' she says eventually.

'You want me to keep sleeping with a married man, who's been lying to me for months, just so we can find out what he's up to?'

Saffy shrugs. 'Pretty much. You said the sex was good. A few more times won't hurt Camille any more than she'd be hurt already.'

'You do it. Have you heard from him since Saturday, by the way?'

'Grovelling message yesterday. He wants us to rearrange. Apparently he has the kids all week.' She does air quote marks round the words 'has the kids'. 'I haven't called him back yet.'

'You need to,' Joni says. 'If I'm doing this then so can you. We can compare stories. Trip him up.'

Saffy drains the last of her cup. Joni assumes she'll just order another, sit here all day on a caffeine drip. Instead, she waves at the waitress for the bill. Joni finds herself feeling strangely disappointed that the morning is over. 'We should go through all the other messages – see if we can find a pattern. Like why it fizzled out with the others but not with us.'

'Because they saw through his bullshit probably.'

'Maybe.' Joni reaches into her bag for her purse. 'I feel as if he was the one who lost interest though. I need to read them again.'

'Do you have them?' Saffy gets her own card out. Holds it ready for the waitress to reappear with the machine. 'I'll get this.'

Joni fights her default urge to protest. 'Thank you. No. I just concentrated on yours and Mary's because you were the ones taking it further. I'll need to go into his phone again. Is it worth it?'

'Definitely.'

'That's easy for you to say!' Joni laughs. 'What are your plans for this afternoon?'

Saffy raises her slim arms up in the air and stretches. 'I'm meeting a friend at Borough Market and then this evening I'm at the theatre. You?'

What is she doing? Drifting through the afternoon until it's time to go to the gym, then Ant tonight and work tomorrow. 'I think I'll go to a gallery,' she says. She won't, but she doesn't want to admit that she's just going to go and work out. She doesn't want to own up to being that uninteresting.

'Call me tomorrow. Tell me all about tonight,' Saffy says.

'There must be a better way to find out what he's playing at without me having to keep sleeping with him. I'm sure Miss Marple didn't have to keep putting it about to get answers.'

'You'd be surprised. Anyway, it won't be for long. Like you said, we just have to convince Mary.'

Joni sighs. 'OK. Just till we can get some proof . . .'

'Operation Save Mary,' Saffy says, giving her a quick hug. 'She'd better appreciate it.'

19

They're meeting at a restaurant, thankfully. Joni is grateful he's not coming round to hers. The distractions of other people take the focus off the two of them. She feels sick at the thought of having to sneak through his phone again tonight. What if he catches her? She barely knows this man – less and less, she realizes. Who knows what he's capable of? Before she left the house she made herself look at the two photos of Mary she'd copied the last time she went through his phone. There's a sadness to her, even in these pictures where she's smiling. A vulnerability. The lost look behind her eyes reminds Joni of the way her mother was after her father died – nearly twenty years ago now. Like a small child waiting to be told what to do. Someone who had no comprehension of how their life had turned out as it had or what to do now. Joni's mum had taken years to recover, whatever front she'd shown on the outside. Joni had been glad to see the back of Ian, but Mary had been robbed of a man she loved. She had told Ant early on in their exchanges that she almost couldn't go on. That it was only her children who tethered her to life. And now she was mixed up with this charlatan. This man who clearly didn't give a fuck.

He's already there when she arrives, deliberately late.

Anything to shave a few minutes off the evening. He gives her a big smile when he spots her, oblivious to what's been happening behind his back. Joni feels queasy. Weirdly guilty, as if she's the deceptive one. She has no appetite. None. But she's desperate for a large G and T. Huge.

'How's Amelia?' she says as he stands to greet her. He's sitting at the dark wood bar on a high stool. Every brand of alcohol that comes in a green bottle is lined up on the wall behind, a light on the shelf beneath them giving them an eerie glow.

'Fine. Better. Two stitches.'

She allows herself to be kissed on the cheek. 'Did you have to wait long at A & E?' She wants him to feel uncomfortable having to lie.

'Not too bad by the time I got there. More importantly, how are you?'

'Oh. Better. Fine.' She orders a drink and the waiter tells them that their table is ready. They follow him through into the other room, which is buzzing with diners. She's glad. The last thing she wants is to be in a quiet, intimate, romantic spot with Ant. Ever again.

'This is nice,' she says as she sits, trying to get the timing right with the waiter pushing in her chair. She'd much rather do it herself, but it feels rude to say so. He's probably on minimum wage, desperate to please for tips. Usually Ant pays for dinner when they go out. She has no idea how they fell into that old-fashioned cliché, she had tried to pay her way, but Ant always refused and it felt churlish not to accept. She always insists on paying the gratuity, though, adding way too much with all the self-conscious angst of the English middle classes. She's already decided that she'll give this boy extra.

Ant is talking to her about the Primrose Hill site. He's all hands when he speaks, expansive gestures that captivated her at first, making any story he was telling seem more dramatic, more entertaining. Now she just sees it as smoke and mirrors. A performance. She tunes out, tries to think about why she's here, what she wants to achieve. 'Intel,' Saffy had said. 'Get him to talk about his divorce, his house, his kids, whatever. The more facts you get out of him, the easier it'll be to prove he's a liar.'

'How's the house sale going?' she asks once he's finished what he's saying.

He fishes a green olive out of a bowl on the table and eats it whole. They need to order, she thinks. The sooner they eat the sooner they can leave and then she can claim the need for an early night. She picks up her menu while she waits for him to answer.

'Few viewings, I think. I don't think it's going to happen in a hurry. The top end of the market seems to move quite slowly.'

'And Camille doesn't want to stay there?'

Ant laughs. 'Well, yes, I'm sure she does. But we need to release the capital.'

'How long ago did you split up?' She can't believe she has never asked him this as Lucy. He told Joni it had been a year or so, and Saffy too apparently. She might as well see if he's consistent.

He shrugs. 'I want to say last August. Around then.' So he's telling them all the same thing.

'It's a big step, isn't it, with kids? Me and Ian probably hung on for years longer than we should have because of Dani.' She almost trips over the word Dani; it still sounds so alien in her mouth. But she's glad now that he doesn't know her daughter's real name. Or hers either, for that matter.

'It wasn't good for them. Hearing us arguing.'

'No,' she says. 'It's always the kids that suffer, isn't it? Ian and I never really argued. Neither of us cared enough. How long were you married for?'

'Twelve years,' he says, without missing a beat. 'Shall we order?'

'Yes. Just give me a sec.' She realizes there's no point interrogating him. He'll just get defensive. So she moves the conversation back on to safe ground, telling him how on Friday, before she'd left work, she'd unpacked her little figurines – the squirrels, the rabbit and the elephant; she couldn't work out which was the more cloyingly offensive – and arranged them on her desk for Lucas to find this morning. She has no idea how he'd reacted, of course, but she's pretty sure they won't still be there tomorrow. Ant laughs as she describes how she'd lined them up and then swept them into a drawer again when the department assistant, Shona, popped her head round the door to ask if she needed anything doing before she went home.

'I couldn't bear for her to think I put them there because I liked them,' she says. 'She'd have lost all respect for me.'

'So war is declared?' Ant tops up their wine glasses.

'Definitely,' she says, smiling at him and making eye contact. 'It's on.'

They get through the evening somehow, Ant not seeming to pick up on any awkwardness. It's just assumed he'll come home with her and she knows they're going to have sex because she wants Ant to think that everything is normal, but she actually hears herself – her forty-nine-year-old, mild-mannered accountant and mother-of-one self – say, 'It'll have to be a quickie. I've got an early start in the morning.'

'Ooh, I love a quickie,' Ant says, pulling her into him. 'Should we have a knee-trembler up against the wall?'

'God, no. My hips won't take it.'

'Spoilsport.'

He's asleep by the time his head hits the pillow. Joni makes sure she watches where he plugs his phone in, so she won't have to fumble about in the dark too much, but she still leaves the light on in the bathroom down the hall just in case. She waits, scared to fall asleep herself in case she doesn't wake up till morning. She might not have many more chances like this. After half an hour or so she's convinced he's dead to the world and, when he conveniently rolls over on his back, she decides now is the time. There's just enough light for the facial recognition to register. She retreats to the bathroom, via the kitchen where she grabs her own mobile, and locks herself in.

She goes into the Keepers app and then remembers

that she needs to scan his face for this too. Cursing, she tiptoes back along the hall. Jasper weaves himself around her legs, threatening to trip her up. He jumps up on the bed as she gets closer and stretches out along Ant's side. Ant trails a hand along his back, and Joni waits, breath held, but he's still sleeping. She holds the phone over his face – this is the bit for which she'd have no explanation if he woke up: she'd just have to claim plain old jealousy and insecurity – but the app doesn't open. She creeps over to the door and opens it a few centimetres more until the light hits his face, and then tries again. She's in. She practically runs back to the sanctuary of the bathroom.

She sits on the cool floor and tries to slow her breathing. She can't get caught now unless Ant gets up and decides he wants to use his mobile. He can wonder all he likes about why she's locked in the bathroom, but he won't have a clue what she's up to. There's nothing new from the last woman he messaged, Wanda. She goes right back through the months to the first conversations he had. Photographs every single exchange. There's no time to read them now, but she clicks on the page of each woman and takes a picture of that too. A couple of them are no longer registered. Hopefully they've found love, she thinks. Hopefully they didn't just give up because they got played. She has to stop herself from reading as she goes along. She needs to stay focused on the job.

Before she finishes she checks his texts for the most recent exchanges between him and Mary. Nothing revealing. They obviously do most of their talking on the phone these days. There are no texts to Camille, she notices. Not even a curt arrangement for collecting the kids. How had she not spotted that before? She flicks through his phone screens. There's a WhatsApp icon. He'd told her he didn't do WhatsApp when she'd asked. Barely seemed to know how it worked. She clicks on it but it's locked. There's no way she's going to risk trying to scan his face again. Third time unlucky. It's obviously where he keeps his family communications, though, tucked away from prying eyes. Useful to know.

She runs through her photos, making sure she's got everything she needs before she exits Ant's account. She's never going through this again; her heart won't take it. She had intended to go back to bed, to trawl through everything once he'd left for work in the morning, but she's too wired. She would never sleep now. She replaces his mobile and then goes to the kitchen with her own to make herself a tea.

She settles in an armchair in the living room, grabs a notebook and pen, wraps a throw around herself and tells herself to be methodical. Read every exchange, even the *How are you? Good, thanks, you?* ones. She's used to forensically studying dry facts at work, poring over pages of figures and dates. The first woman he made a connection with was called Sam. Joni looks at her profile page. There's not a lot of information. Forty-four. Divorced. Looking for a long-term commitment. She has wavy brown hair and an open, friendly smile. A small gap between her front teeth that gives her a vulnerable look. Joni notes down the details. There are only seven messages. Still she reads each one twice before she will allow herself to move on. There's no doubt the chemistry wasn't exactly fizzling between them, the conversation is purely information-based. Ant tells her he 'works in the wellness industry' as he did Joni when they first spoke. He doesn't mention that he owns the whole train set, wary of gold diggers. *What do you do?* (Sam works as a carer.) *Where do you live?* (Hackney.) *Any kids?* Sam asks. He doesn't reply. Two days later she sends him *You still there?* Nothing. He's ghosted her.

She moves on to the next. Vicki, thirty-six, also divorced. Short honey-blonde hair with a heavy fringe, grey-blue eyes that slightly droop at the sides, thin lips. She's not – if Joni's being uncharitable – someone whose looks would make her stand out from a crowd. She looks anxious in her photo. Unconfident. Joni's heart goes out to her. At least Vicki had the courage to use her own photo. Well, she assumes it's her own; she's not sure why you would pick this one if you had a choice. Their conversation lasts longer. Maybe twenty back and forths. Again, very factual. Vicky is also divorced, lives in Kingston. Joni can't help herself – she skips on to the end, telling herself she'll go back. The last three messages are all from Vicky: *Did you get my last message? Are you OK?* and *I'm guessing you've moved on, thanks for telling me.* Ant has ghosted her too. Joni looks at Vicki's final offering before the silence. Reads it twice. She moves on to the next woman, forgetting all about her resolution to be thorough. Scrolls through to the death throes. The woman, Parvati – delicately pretty, dark-haired mother of three –

reaching out to Ant after he has failed to respond to her. There's a pattern emerging. Joni's not sure quite what it is or why, but something is niggling at the edge of her brain. Something not right.

'Luce?'

She wakes up with a jolt and, for a moment, she doesn't know where she is. Her left arm is dead and her back feels as if it's been fused. Why is someone calling her sister's name? It all hits her at once. She's on the sofa, the notebook open beside her, her phone on the floor where it must have fallen out of her hand. She stuffs them under the throw just as Ant walks in wearing nothing but a towel.

'Are you OK? Were you there all night?"

'I couldn't sleep so I got up to read,' she says, realizing as she says it that there's no book anywhere in evidence. 'Well, that was the intention, but as soon as I sat down I must have dozed off. My back's killing me.'

'Come back in the bedroom and I'll give you a quick massage. I've picked up some skills in my time at Evoke.'

'You should have put that on your dating profile.' She stands up slowly, stretching her arms above her head. 'You'd have been fighting them off with a stick. Do you want a coffee?' she says, ignoring his offer.

'Please. I'm going to grab a quick shower.'

She waits for him to go and then shoves both the notebook and her phone in the drawer under the coffee table. She doesn't think Ant is the type to pry but then she would have said the same about herself a week ago.

She feels as if she only breathes out once he leaves about twenty minutes later. She makes another coffee and sets up camp in bed for an hour. She goes through every exchange, from start to finish, and then she calls Saffy.

'I just wondered if you were around tonight?' she says when the voicemail kicks in. 'I think we should meet up.'

20

She can't even appreciate the small victory that is her figurines shoved into the desk drawer while Jabba and
friends laud it over the desk. Now Lucas knows how
annoying it is, even if it doesn't seem to have made him
rethink his own behaviour. She hides his away too and
tries to concentrate on checking that the quarterly electri-
city payments have gone through for all the store's
different branches. She wishes, not for the first time, that
her desk was out in the general office with its distractions
and the chatter of people around her. Anything to take
her mind off things. As it is she doesn't have the kind of
relationship with her colleagues where they can sit and
gossip or pass the time sharing stories about nothing
much. She's one of Them by virtue of being behind a
glass door. She shuts the door now and dials Saffy's number. At least having her own private space means she can
skive off occasionally and make personal calls.

'I was just about to call you!' Saffy shouts as she
answers. 'Tell me everything.'

'I can't, I'm at work. And I need to show you stuff. See
if you see the same as me.'

'This is so fucking exciting. Oops, sorry . . .'

'Where are you?' Joni watches as Shona walks past her
window balancing a cafetière, a milk jug and four mugs.

She raises her eyes at Joni as if to say 'Do you want one?' and Joni nods, smiling.

'I'm at a kiddies' playground of all fucking things. And again! Shit, sorry.' She lowers her voice to a whisper. Joni can hear children playing in the background. 'There's a woman here with a stick up her arse giving me filthy looks. See, this is why I never had kids – how are you supposed to speak? My neighbour had an emergency and the nanny let her down . . .'

'Oh no,' Joni says, concerned. 'Nothing serious, I hope?'

'Hollywood wax. And she goes on holiday tomorrow. Anyway, so I have to entertain the twins for a couple of hours. Jesus, it's exhausting. I tried to persuade her to take them with her, but she thought they might be scarred for life. I'm counting down the minutes . . . but yes, tonight. Where do you want to meet? Or come over if you like?'

'Shall I? It might be easier than being somewhere noisy . . .'

'Absolutely. Come straight from work, if you want; we can order in from the sushi place. I'm a hopeless cook. I'll text you the address.'

The taxi weaves through the beautiful residential streets on the way to Highgate, with their immaculate front lawns and sports Bentleys on the driveways. It's less showy than the nearby private roads with their security manned wooden huts at the entrances, but the area still reeks of privilege.

Joni and Ian used to live in a house like these. More space than they could ever need. They had moved there when Imo was eight and Ian had suddenly started to make serious money. Away from the cosy but still roomy semi in Muswell Hill, away from Imo's friends and their parents, and the neighbours that Joni had formed easy acquaintances with over the years. Away from real life. She had tried to stay in touch with some of them, but her sudden new wealth made people feel uneasy. Invitations were suddenly prefaced by 'I know you probably won't want to . . .' or 'I know it's a bit downmarket, but . . .' and however much Joni tried to protest that she was still the same Joni, that she still enjoyed the same things, she knew her friends thought differently. Only Meg had remained unfazed, teasing her relentlessly about her new status. 'You should write to an agony aunt,' Ian had said facetiously when she'd confided that she was feeling like an outsider. '"Dear Coleen, my friends don't like me any more because I'm rich,"' he'd said in a whiny voice. 'Very relatable.'

'They're just jealous,' he'd added later with a certain relish. He'd loved the idea of being someone who stirred envy in others. But Joni knew that wasn't what it was. It was just awkwardness, an adjustment. And she should have worked harder to get past it.

That move had been the start of it all going wrong, she'd realized later. The beginning of Ian's dissatisfaction with what he already had. Ian and Holly still live in the house. Ian, Holly and the baby that's on the way. The second baby that Ian never wanted with her after Imo was born. Not that he didn't adore Imogen, he always had, but he'd been adamant that one child was enough. Now he was going to be a dad again at fifty, and Imo had told her proudly that he 'couldn't wait'.

Number 12 is a three-storey white-rendered brick and glass box with an intricate architectural pattern of box hedging in front. It's stunning, there's no doubt about it. Saffy opens the front door before Joni has a chance to ring the bell.

'Oh my God, I've been dying for you to get here. What have you found? Is he a serial killer?'

Joni raises an eyebrow. 'I didn't bring anything, sorry. I should have brought wine . . .'

'God, no. I have a cellarful. Come in.' Joni follows her through the spacious hall to the kitchen at the back of the house, her shoes clicking on the dark, almost black, wooden floor. The sun is streaming through a wall of glass but the aircon brings a delicious chill to the air.

'This is lovely,' she says, and it is. The cabinets are a sleek pale grey with gleaming black work surfaces. There's a huge table by the glass doors at the back.

'Red or white?' Saffy says, picking up a bottle from the counter and brandishing it. 'That's about as technical as I get. This one's a . . .' She peers at the label. '. . . Malbec. Or I have others.'

'Any old white's fine. Thanks.'

She watches as Saffy sloshes wine into two enormous glasses. Red in her own, a Pinot Gris that she grabs from the fridge in Joni's. Joni thinks about telling her to go easy, but the way she feels at the moment she could happily down the whole thing in one.

'Do you want to go out in the garden?' Saffy says as she hands her a glass. Joni's torn. The cool of the kitchen is such a relief, but the garden is lush and she can see a table with two chairs beside a water feature in the shade beckoning to her.

'Yes. Lovely.' She grabs her notebook and phone from her bag and follows Saffy through the bi-fold doors. She jumps as she almost treads on a tiny, growling, gum-baring chihuahua that's flat out on a cushion just inside the window.

'Don't worry about him,' Saffy says. 'He's harmless. Only because he's got no teeth left, to be fair.'

'What's his name?' Joni says, stepping round him cautiously.

'Tyson. Because he's furious.'

It takes her a moment to get it. She laughs. 'What about?'

'Everything. He's very old. He hates it.'

The garden isn't big but it's a haven. The grass has been replaced by flawless white stone tiles. Huge planters hold even huger plants. It feels almost tropical. She can hear the rhythmic tap of people playing tennis somewhere over the back. They settle at the table and Joni lays the notebook and phone side by side in front of her.

'Just tell me,' Saffy says. 'I'm fucking dying here.'

'I want to see if you see the same as me,' Joni says. She brings up photos on her phone, scrolls back. 'So, this is his very first exchange on the app. Sam. Read the whole thing – it goes across a couple of photos.' She hands Saffy her mobile and she scans it greedily.

'Not exactly scintillating, is it?'

Joni takes the phone back, lines up the next conversation, with Vicki. Saffy screws up her eyes as she reads. Hands the phone back to Joni, looking confused. 'So he has a low boredom threshold. I mean, it's a bit rude the way he just cuts them off, but haven't you ever done that?'

'No, actually. What's the common link? What does he ask them just before he disappears?'

Saffy grabs the phone back and looks again. 'OK.'

'So, go on to the next one. Parvati.' She watches as Saffy reads Ant and Parvati's nine snippets of conversation. When she gets to the end she looks up. 'Oh.'

'So, the short version is: they all follow pretty much the same pattern until he gets to Mary. Here . . .' She takes the mobile back and finds the pictures that show Mary and Ant's exchanges. 'Look. Here's just before he suggests taking it off app.'

'Oh,' Saffy says again. She downs a big gulp of wine.

'And then there are a few more mishits before he gets to me. Look . . . Julie . . . here's the last page . . .' She holds it up for Saffy to see. 'Cerys, ditto.' Again, she holds it up. Saffy pulls her hand closer, screws up her eyes. 'I've got all the details noted down in here,' Joni says, indicating the notebook. 'I'm not imagining it.'

'No,' Saffy says. 'I don't think you are. But . . . I don't get it . . .'

'Me neither.'

'He basically dumps all the ones who aren't rich? Is that what you're saying?'

'That's what it looks like, isn't it? As soon as they say that they have a low-paid job, or live in a poorer area, he's gone. And then Mary basically says her husband left her very well off and at least the house is all paid for and next thing you know he wants to take it further. I tell him Ian worked in the City and that I bought an – and I quote – *absolutely beautiful flat* outright when we separated.'

'Shit. What did I say?'

Joni picks up the notebook and flips over a few pages. '*At least he was loaded so the house is paid off. And, to be fair, he was incredibly generous.*'

Saffy opens her eyes wide. 'Fucking hell. Did I say that?'

Joni nods. 'And you'd just told him you lived in Highgate.'

'It makes no sense though.' There's a shout as one of the tennis players wins a point. 'He's stinking rich. Why does he care if we are?'

'Well . . .' Joni draws a circle with her finger on the table, leaving a faint mark. 'If we were being generous we could deduce that he's just trying to avoid gold diggers. I mean, he must know that me, you and Mary aren't after his money . . .'

'And if we're not being generous?'

Joni sighs. 'He's not who he says he is at all. He's the one who's a gold digger.'

21

Neither of them says anything for a while, as if it's all too much to take in.

'I'm getting the wine,' Saffy says, standing up. Joni waits for her to come back, listening to the wood pigeons and the back and forth of the ball. 'That was fucking in!' someone shouts.

'So . . .' Saffy says as soon as she exits the glass door with the two bottles and a cooler full of ice. 'You're saying he doesn't own Evoke? Or he does but it's secretly really unsuccessful?'

'I don't know. I mean, that second one seems unlikely, doesn't it?'

'You've been to his flat though, right?'

Joni shakes her head. 'Never. He told me it was a mess, remember. That he's storing all his stuff there while he waits for the house to sell so he can buy a new one.'

'The house he showed you that isn't his?'

'Shit,' Joni says, closing her eyes. 'Am I really that stupid?'

'You and me both,' Saffy says.

'So, who the fuck is he?'

'Your guess is as good as mine.' Joni rubs at her eyes with her hand. Remembers too late that she has mascara on. Looks for something to wipe her fingers on. Opts for her skirt, hoping it'll blend in with the flowery pattern.

'You've googled him, though?'

'Of course. I mean, not forensically . . . have you?'

'Same,' Saffy says, standing up again. 'I'm going to get my laptop.'

Joni can't believe how naïve she feels. She protested to Imo that she'd done her due diligence with Ant, but in reality what did she actually know about him beyond what he'd told her? That his social media profiles were all private and – he claimed – inactive. That his face was in a picture of the Evoke 'crew'. She saw just as much as she wanted to see and took the lack of any counter-evidence as proof that what he'd told her was true. She's suddenly flooded with relief that Saffy – and presumably Mary – have been as easily taken in. She doesn't think she could bear it if it was just her.

She edges her chair more into the shade. Closes her eyes.

'Right.' Saffy's voice makes her jump. 'Anthony Simons. I'll try different spellings.' She studies the screen for a while, clicking on to a new page every now and then. Joni has to resist the urge to take over. She's never been very good at delegating. She'd always rather do things herself. 'So . . .' Saffy says eventually. 'I'm guessing this is the picture you found? I managed to miss this when I looked.' She turns the computer round so Joni can see the screen.

'That's it. I thought that validated him. God, I'm such an idiot.'

'You're someone who thought they'd met someone nice and wanted to believe it. Same as me.'

'I just didn't question it because if you googled me you'd get the same results. Private social media, the odd mention of where I work, maybe. Nothing else.'

'I can't find anything much about Evoke,' Saffy says, tapping away on the keyboard. 'It's owned by a company but there's nothing really on who's behind it. I mean, I'm sure it's all on there somewhere but I'm fucked if I know . . . Let's have a look at Camille. Do you think she uses his surname?'

Joni shrugs. 'Do you think she even exists?'

Saffy looks up. 'Shit. I have no idea. It's not going to be her name, is it?'

'I doubt it.' Joni swills the last of the wine round in her glass. She knows it won't help but she feels like finishing the rest of the bottle and then opening another. 'This is a beautiful house,' she says, apropos of nothing. 'Where does your ex live?'

'He's working in LA. Couldn't have got much further away from me if he tried. Anyway, what are we going to do?' She clearly wants to change the subject, so Joni doesn't push it. When Ian first left she couldn't bear people asking her about it. Not because she was heartbroken, but because she felt humiliated. She didn't want to be seen as the poor abandoned wife traded in for a shinier model. She's not sure if it's the wine or the desire to show that she's not trying to pry, but she finds herself saying: 'You do know we have Mary's address.'

Saffy's head jerks up like a dog who's heard the treat tin. 'Do we?'

Joni nods. 'She texted it to him the first time he was going to go round there. '

'Fuck.' Saffy empties the rest of the wine into their two glasses.

'Where does she live?'

'St John's Wood.'

Saffy jumps up again. No wonder she's so skinny, Joni thinks. She never stays still for more than a second. 'Let's go,' she says, banging her glass down decisively. 'We can show all this to her.'

'What? No. We're half-pissed.'

'Exactly. Let's do it before we bottle out.'

'No way,' Joni says, staying doggedly seated. 'What if he's there?'

'Oh yes, I hadn't thought of that. OK, well, when then? Are you at work tomorrow?'

'No. You know, the weirdest thing is that he never expects me to pay for stuff. I mean, I've offered . . .'

Saffy sits back down. 'Oh. Well, that is odd.'

'He must be building up to something. Otherwise what's the point?'

'He's playing a long game,' Saffy says. 'He's lulling you into a false sense of security.'

'Do you think I should tell the police?' Joni says, hooking her hair behind her left ear. She suddenly feels a bit scared, as if she's flailing in deep water with nothing to grab on to.

'And say what? I'm going out with a man who I'm

worried might end up trying to sponge off me? My guess is he's not planning on anything illegal. He doesn't need to. He's got rich women falling for his shit left, right and centre. It's not his fault if they offer to help him out when he needs it. He's been seeing Mary longer than you, so he might have made a move on her already. For all we know she's about to pay for the two of them to go first class to the Bahamas.'

Joni puts her head in her hand. 'I don't know, Saffy . . .'

'We can't just leave him to fleece her. We can't, can we?'

'Shit. OK. We'll go and see her tomorrow. Show her all the evidence. You know she might just tell him, though?'

Saffy shrugs. 'Then at least we'll have tried.' Her phone beeps with a text. She grabs it up from the table. Shows Joni the screen. 'It's him. Nice timing. *Hi gorgeous.*' She raises an eyebrow at Joni as she reads. '*Are you around? Do you want to chat?* Phone sex,' she says. 'That's what he's after. I'll just ignore it. I can tell him I was out later.'

'Tomorrow, then,' Joni says. She really should make a move, but she's enjoying sitting out here in the cooling air.

'What time should we go round?' Saffy snaps a leaf off a plant in a pot next to her and rubs it between her fingers. Joni can smell the aroma of mint.

'I always go to the supermarket on Wednesday mornings. I could meet you there after. Half elevenish?'

'What are we going to do if she's not in?'

Joni thinks for a second. 'I have no idea.'

'We'll have lunch. Isn't there an Ivy in St John's Wood?'

There's something about Saffy's upbeat attitude that Joni envies. It would make life so much easier always to be able to see a positive outcome to any situation. It's raining? Let's go in that pub and have a drink! My date hasn't turned up? All the more wine for me! My leg has fallen off? I can use up all those single socks that I keep finding in the dryer! Joni doesn't so much see a glass as half empty, more as an indication that the bottle is probably finished, and the off licence is almost certainly closed already.

'I . . .' She stops as her own mobile dings with a message. 'I don't believe it,' she says laughing. '*Hi gorgeous. Are you around? Do you fancy a chat?* Ha!'

'Fucking tosser,' Saffy says. 'We should both say yes and see what he does.'

'He'll try Mary next. Hopefully she'll reply.'

'Do you think she'll listen this time? I'm getting more wine, by the way. You don't have to leave yet, do you?'

Joni loves her flat and her peaceful evenings watching TV or reading. Just her and Jasper, but she can't face it tonight, she realizes. Her own thoughts will be too much. 'Go on then,' she says, surprising herself. 'Your guess is as good as mine. She definitely wasn't having any of it when I phoned her, but it's hard to argue with the evidence.'

'Well, we'll know soon enough,' Saffy says, heading for the kitchen. 'One way or the other.'

22

Joni wakes in the morning with a pounding head and a feeling of anxiety that she can't quite put her finger on until the realization comes crashing in. She and Saffy are meeting at Mary's. It had somehow seemed a good idea when Saffy, with all her bravado, had been egging her on, but in the harsh light of day, and with her pores sweating white wine, Joni knows it's bound to be a massive mistake. She drags herself out of bed, ignoring Jasper's scratchy cries for breakfast, and unplugs her phone. She needs to call Saffy and abort the mission. She needs to drink a pint of water, go back to bed and sleep for three hours. She's not used to drinking a bottle and a half of wine and forgetting to eat – they had never got round to ordering out for sushi, or anything else for that matter. In so far as she can remember anyway, but there's a black hole where her – presumably Uber – journey home took place, so who knows? Saffy's number rings straight through to voicemail.

'Call me,' Joni says. 'It's Joni. I think this is a bad idea.'

Waitrose, she realizes, is out of the question, and she curses herself for messing up her carefully orchestrated routine. Maybe she'll feel up to it later in the day. Much, much later in the day. After her extra sleep and a huge fry-up. She checks the time. Realizes with a shock that it's already nearly ten. No wonder Jasper is shouting at her.

She feeds him, gagging at the pungent smell of fish in his food, and then stands under a warm shower trying to wake herself up. She tries Saffy again as soon as she's out but there's still no answer. Maybe she's overslept too, Joni thinks hopefully. Maybe she's forgotten all about the plan they made. She knows she can't take the risk, though. If she doesn't hear from Saffy she'll have to be there at half past eleven. She can't just stand her up. She can talk to her outside, persuade her they shouldn't go through with it.

She's out of the house by five to, in enough time to walk to Mary's and still be early. She can at least get her steps up so the day isn't a total washout. She's feeling a bit more human since her shower and a pair of paracetamol, but still a little fragile. The air will do her good.

She reaches Adelaide Road and turns into the neat streets of St John's Wood. She's early but when she gets to the turning into Queen's Grove she can see Saffy up ahead, sitting on a bench. She looks like a teenager from this distance: skinny tanned limbs in a cut-off romper suit and neon-pink trainers, hunched over her phone. Joni suddenly feels protective of her. Pushes the thought away. That's the last thing she needs.

'Fuck, Joni, I only just got your message,' Saffy says as she looks up. Joni laughs. If someone had told her to put a bet on the first word out of Saffy's mouth she would have just won a fortune. 'My stupid phone's been playing up. Are you OK? You look terrible.'

'Thanks. Aren't you hungover?' She flops down on to the bench.

'Not in the slightest. Did we drink a lot?'

Joni doesn't even want to think about it. Her mouth feels furry inside and even the thought of wine is making her gag. 'I would say so, yes.'

'Well, we can't bottle out now.'

Joni groans. 'Which one is her house?'

Saffy points to the opposite side of the road, a couple of houses along. A large red-brick detached with Virginia creeper threatening to engulf the whole thing. 'The one that looks like a bush with a door.'

'Have you seen anything?'

'No. But one of the upstairs windows is open. I guarantee you Mary would not go out and leave a window open.'

'Maybe she has a housekeeper.'

'Maybe she's at home,' Saffy says. 'We won't know until we ring the bell.'

'Can't we just think it through ... Where are you going?' Saffy is up on her feet and crossing the road towards the house she pointed out. 'Hold on. Wait!' Joni jumps up and follows her. 'We need to plan what we're going to say if she's there.'

Saffy stops and turns around. 'OK. Let's sit back down for five minutes but then we're going in. I think we just come straight out with it. What's the alternative? Pretend we're Jehovah's Witnesses and hope she invites us in for a cup of tea?'

'She might just slam the door in our faces.'

'She might.'

Joni sinks back down on to the bench as if that might delay the inevitable.

'Come on.' Saffy reaches out a hand to pull her up. 'Before I lose my nerve too.'

'Do you ever? Lose your nerve?'

'All the time. I just don't let on. Right, you ready?'

Joni nods. She isn't, but she doesn't think she ever will be so she might as well get it over with.

Mary's front garden is paved with swirls of cobbles and surrounded by neat flowering borders. A gleaming black 4x4 sits in the middle like a modernist sculpture. The creeper is trimmed neatly round the windows and the pillared front door. Joni hits the bell and she and Saffy both stand to attention like a pair of naughty schoolkids waiting to see the headmistress. Joni can feel her stomach flipping, whether from the alcohol she consumed last night or fear of what's to come she can't tell. She just knows that she wants to be at home, living her old uncomplicated pre-Ant life. There's a rattle inside and the door opens a couple of inches. A woman – unmistakably Mary with her pale blonde bob and flecked amber eyes – peers through the crack. She looks younger than she does in photos. Joni has been thinking of her as an older woman but sixty-three isn't the sixty-three it used to be. Sixty is the new forty, which makes fifty the new thirty and forty the new twenty, although that seems a little unlikely. Maybe they're like dog years. Not everyone is equal. Otherwise twenty-year-olds would still be in nappies.

'Can I help you?'

Here goes, Joni thinks. She opens her mouth to speak but Saffy gets there first.

'Are you Mary? I mean, I know you are, I recognize you from your photos. I'm Saffy and this is Joni. She called you. About Ant Simons. She called me too. We're both dating him. Well, I haven't actually met him yet, but I was supposed to last weekend only I stood him up . . .'

Joni can tell that Mary is about to shut the door. She puts a hand on Saffy's arm and Saffy stops talking as abruptly as she started, like the talking doll Joni had when she was little.

'Mary. Please hear us out for a second. I'm really sorry to just turn up on your doorstep with no warning but I didn't think you'd want to speak to me if I called again. We have something you really need to see. Five minutes and then you can tell us to go and we will.' She gives Mary her best pleading look. She looks at Saffy to see that she is doing the same. Eyes like saucers as if she's channelling the cat from *Shrek*.

'I've told you already,' Mary says, looking at Joni. 'I'm not interested in what you have to say.'

'It's not just that he's still using the app to pick up other women. He's a fraud, Mary. We have proof.'

Mary doesn't budge. 'I can't just let you in. How did you get my address anyway? You could be anyone.'

'That's true,' Joni says. 'And quite right, you shouldn't. How about if we go to a café round the corner? I promise that once we've shown you what we have to show you we'll leave if you want us to and we'll never ever contact you again.'

Mary sighs. 'I don't know. I'm waiting for a delivery.'

They all stand there for a second. Joni wills Saffy not to break the silence. Eventually Mary caves first. 'Look, go round the back to the garden and I'll meet you out there. But I haven't got long.'

A high gate leads to a narrow path along the side of the house with three steps down to the garden. Like many of the majestic homes round here it looks as if most of the land has been sold off at some point to squeeze in another ten-thousand-square-footer with almost no outside space behind. It's perfect, though. A tiny neat lawn is getting a drenching from a sprinkler. There's a flawlessly trimmed leylandii hedge just the right height to screen out the neighbours at the back and hydrangeas and something bright orange that Joni thinks are dahlias. Beside the back door are raised planters brimming over with aromatic herbs neatly laid out in rows. Saffy sneezes. 'This is why I don't have grass,' she says in a loud whisper just as the back door opens and Mary appears. Joni had thought she might be the kind to make even the most unwelcome of visitors feel at home by bringing a jug of water or home-made lemonade, but she's empty-handed.

'It's gorgeous out here,' she says but Mary ignores the compliment, indicating a table and four chairs under an oversized umbrella.

'Shall we sit?'

They do as they're told. Joni wonders how many times

Ant has sat in this garden. She racks her brain for how to start. Mary has been gracious enough to give them time but there's definitely a frosty air coming from her direction. And she obviously has no intention of being the first to speak. The silence feels heavy. Impenetrable.

'Well, you couldn't exactly say he has a type,' Saffy suddenly says out of nowhere. Joni almost laughs but she stops herself when she catches Mary's cool expression. She needs to take charge. Say what they came here to say.

'OK. We're really not here to upset you, Mary, but since I spoke to you on the phone we've found out more about what Ant's doing and we feel as if we have a duty to tell you. It's up to you whether you believe us or not, but at least we will have tried.'

'I'm listening,' Mary says. Joni looks back through the pictures on her phone to get to the beginning of the story. She has to make sure she does this right.

'So,' she says, taking a deep breath. 'It looks like Ant joined the app about nine months ago and started talking to you in about April – does that sound right . . .?'

Mary listens without saying anything but her expression gives her away. Joni talks her through it as gently as she can, ignoring Saffy's occasional muttered 'Fucker' and 'Absolute arsehole'. She starts by showing Mary how he continued to pursue other women even after he'd taken it offline with her. 'But that's nowhere near the worst bit . . .' she says. 'So, then . . .'

Mary stands up. 'I think I should make us some coffee.'

'Oh. Right. Thanks.' Joni watches as she walks abruptly off, then turns to Saffy. 'What do you think?'

Saffy swats away a fly. 'She's listening, I suppose.'

'What if she's phoning Ant right now?'

'What if she is? There's no way he could deny it if he was confronted by all three of us together.'

Joni leans her head back and closes her eyes. She just wants this to be over. To say what they need to say. She wants her conscience to be clear, to have done what she can to put things right.

'Oh, that's more like it.' She opens her eyes as Saffy speaks. Mary is carrying a tray with a bottle of what looks like whisky and four glasses, one filled with ice. Her stomach lurches.

'I thought maybe this was more appropriate. I can make coffee if you'd rather. I think I need a glass of this though.'

'If you twist my arm,' Saffy says, visibly perking up.

'I'm OK,' Joni says, holding up a hand. She would actually kill for a glass of water but it seems rude to ask. 'Can I carry on showing you what we found?'

'Yes, do. I just needed a moment.' Mary has a soft voice and Joni has to strain to hear above the low rumble of traffic. There's something fragile about her. Delicate. She can imagine men want to put their arms round her and protect her. Women too. She noticed that in her mum too, after her dad died. A sadness that has never really left. Mary pours a small measure of whisky in two of the glasses and hands one to Saffy, then offers her the ice. Saffy picks out one cube and plops it into her glass.

171

'Cheers,' she says and Mary gives her a small smile.

Joni steels herself. It's a bit like kicking Bambi after telling him his mother is dead. 'So, I'm going to go right back to the beginning. There's a pattern . . .'

Fifteen minutes later she's talked through the whole timeline. Mary has stayed quiet again, but Joni sees her swallow nervously when she points out what Mary revealed about herself in her and Ant's early conversations. She wonders how she'd feel if someone turned up at her house out of the blue and told her how they'd seen all her private communications with the person she was dating. Angry, probably. Embarrassed, certainly.

'So, you see, we're similar, us three. The three he's asked to meet. We're financially well off and we basically told him so.'

'But . . .' Mary says and then she stops. Saffy opens her mouth to speak and Joni gives her a small shake of her head. She wants to let it sink in. Mary is massaging the thumb of one hand with the other, pressing so hard she's leaving a red indentation on her pale porcelain skin.

'Are you OK?' Joni says after a moment.

Mary bites her lip. 'I just bought him a car,' she says in such a small voice Joni isn't sure she hears correctly.

23

The words hang out there. Even Saffy is stunned into silence. Mary has produced a tissue from somewhere and is tearing it into ever tinier shreds.

'Shit,' Joni says eventually. The understatement of the year.

'I'm actually going to kill him,' Saffy says.

'He's going to pay me back . . .'

'Of course he isn't. Did you get him to sign anything?'

'Saffy . . .' Joni says. She knows how much it must have taken for Mary to admit what she's just admitted. There's no point in making her feel stupid.

Mary clears her throat. 'No. No, I didn't. It didn't feel right . . .'

'That's what he was relying on.'

'It could have been any of us,' Joni says, hoping that Saffy doesn't contradict her. She has no way of knowing if she ever would have fallen for it herself. If things had gone differently and she hadn't realized Ant was a player – no, scrub that, not a player, a conman – so early on. She'd like to think she wouldn't have, but it's definitely possible.

'I don't understand why he would need to . . .' Mary still hasn't worked it out. That Ant isn't who he says is. That none of them actually knows the real him.

'Have you ever been to his flat, Mary?' Joni asks. She's pretty sure she knows what the answer will be.

'No. He always comes here. He's living in a temporary place . . .'

'While Camille sells the house. Yes.'

'He's trying to buy somewhere new, so all his cash is tied up until they sell the house, and then his car broke down . . .'

'And he couldn't just lease one like a normal human?' Saffy says. Joni scowls at her.

'He . . . I don't know.' Mary suddenly looks older, smaller, shrunken in on herself. 'Oh God, I hope my boys don't find out about this. They think I threw myself into the deep end too fast as it is.'

'There's no reason for them to know if you don't want them to,' Joni says sympathetically. She can't imagine having to explain to Imo that she'd spent thousands on a scam artist. The pity in her daughter's eyes would kill her.

'How much was it?' Saffy says. 'I mean, there's cars and cars.'

Mary looks at her hands, the table, anywhere other than at the two of them.

'Fifty thousand. Just over.'

Joni's mouth drops open and she can't seem to find a way to close it.

'You are kidding me,' Saffy is saying. 'Is it brand new?'

Mary closes her eyes. Gives a little nod.

Saffy grabs up her phone. 'Fuck this. I'm going to call Evoke and ask them what he does. I don't know why we didn't think of that before.'

'You don't think he owns the company?'

'We don't,' Joni says gently before Saffy can say any-thing. 'Not much he's told us seems to check out, to be honest.'

'More like nothing. Fuck all. OK, here goes.' She googles the number. They all wait in silence. A fat mag-pie lands on the bird bath and starts splashing around noisily.

'Hello? Oh, hi. I was just wondering, do you have an Ant Simons working for you? . . . You do?' She nods at Joni and Mary. 'No, no, that's OK. Could you just tell me what he does? . . . Oh. I see . . . Right . . . No, I'll call back another time. Thanks, bye.' She cuts the call off without waiting for a response and sits back, eyes wide. 'He's the fucking maintenance man.'

'Not really?' Joni frowns, confused. Mary just looks ashen-faced.

'Really.'

'We're all dating the maintenance man. Not that there's anything wrong with being the maintenance man except that he evidently thinks there is or he wouldn't have lied about it. Prick.'

'He's literally just after our money,' Joni says as it sinks in.

'Well, it seems he already has mine,' Mary says.

'This might sound like a stupid question, but can you afford to hand him fifty K?' Saffy pushes her sunglasses up on to her head. Rubs her eyes, which are starting to water.

'When I told him Andrew left me well provided for I

meant this place was paid for by his life insurance,' she says. 'I'm very comfortable, but it's not as if I'm rolling in money. He said he'd pay me back as soon as the house sale went through.'

'There is no house sale,' Saffy says bluntly. 'There's probably no house.' Joni shoots her a look.

'Listen, maybe we're wrong. Maybe he is selling his house, it's just not the one he showed me. And he does intend to pay you back. We don't know he won't. Yet. I mean, it does seem unlikely . . .'

'Ha!' Saffy scoffs. 'Just a bit.'

'Saffy . . .' Joni says.

'What? I'm not trying to make Mary feel worse. None of this is her fault. But let's not sugar-coat it. Unless he's secretly inherited something, or he's a bank robber, no way is a bloke who works as a maintenance man in a spa in a position to throw fifty grand cash at a new car . . .'

A bell rings loudly from inside. Saffy yelps.

'That must be my delivery,' Mary says, getting up. 'Excuse me.'

Joni waits until she disappears into the house. 'Don't be too hard on her.'

'I'm not,' Saffy says indignantly. 'I'm just angry at him.'

'Yeah. Well.'

They sit and wait for Mary to come back out, both staring out into the garden, not speaking.

'Did he insist on paying for everything at the beginning?' Joni says to her as she re-emerges.

'Everything,' Mary says, sitting down. 'Even though I kept offering.'

'Same here. I suppose he thinks what's the price of a few meals against an eventual fifty grand.'

'And then we started staying in more. Here. Because he loves to cook. I thought it was sweet. That it meant he was committed.' She stifles a sob. Joni goes to put a hand on her arm as Saffy does the same and they sit there, one on each side comforting this woman who was a stranger half an hour ago but with whom they apparently have so much in common.

'So did I,' Joni says. 'I actually liked that he wasn't being flash. That he wanted to spend evenings just with me. Playing house. God, I'm an idiot.'

'What do we do now?' Saffy says, quietly.

'I think Mary should tell him she suddenly needs the money back. Because if he gives it to her then we can forget all about him and move on.'

'He won't.' Saffy digs around in her bag for a tissue. Blows her nose.

'No, he won't. But I think we have to give him the chance.'

'He's only had the car a couple of weeks. I agreed he could pay me back when he sold the house. Won't it seem odd if I'm suddenly demanding repayment now?'

'You need to make up a crisis,' Saffy says. 'Tell him that he'll have to sell the car if necessary. See what he says.'

'All right,' Mary says, nodding. 'I'll try.'

'When are you seeing him again?' Joni asks. 'I'm not till tomorrow.'

'Tonight. He's not . . . You don't think he's dangerous, do you?'

'No,' Joni says, realizing as soon as she says it that she has no idea. 'Don't push it though, the money thing. Just let him know how much you need it and see what he says.'

'I could stay here if you want,' Saffy says. 'Just hole up in a spare room with a bottle of wine and come out if you need me.'

'Really?' Joni says. It's such a kind gesture. For all Saffy's bluntness she apparently has a kind heart. She couldn't imagine putting herself out like that for someone she's just met.

'It's fine,' Mary says. 'But thank you very much. I think . . . if you don't mind, I think I need some time on my own now.'

'Of course,' Joni says, jumping up. 'Let me give you my number. Will you call me tomorrow and tell us how it goes?'

'And mine,' Saffy adds. 'If you're worried about anything this evening text us and one of us'll come straight round.' She looks at Joni. 'Right?'

'Absolutely,' Joni says, although she can't really picture herself storming down here at three in the morning, PJs on. 'Are you going to be OK?'

'Of course. Thank you.'

They leave her there, sitting in the garden. 'That was so nice of you to offer to stay,' Joni says, once they're out of earshot. Saffy shrugs.

'I don't have to be anywhere. Are we going to go and have lunch?'

Joni feels exhausted, partly from the hangover but mostly from the hour or so they've spent with Mary. Emotionally drained. She's not sure she can face more conversation. She can feel her cool sheets. The delicious sleep. 'Do you mind if we don't? I'm absolutely knackered.'

'No prob,' Saffy says, without hesitation. 'Let's speak tomorrow, once Mary's called one of us.' She reaches over and gives Joni a hug. 'Feel better.'

Joni's phone rings as she's walking up Finchley Road. Saffy headed off in the opposite direction, to pick up a few things on St John's Wood High Street. It's Ant. On FaceTime. She's been avoiding him for a couple of days, but she needs to keep up the pretence that everything is normal. She smooths down her hair, holds the phone up and answers.

'Hey.'

'Hi, gorgeous. Oh, where are you?'

'Getting my steps in. Are you at work?'

'Just on my way to a meeting at Ken Church Street.' She can only see his face, not what he's wearing. She thinks about all the times he's turned up at her place, suit on, clean shirt in his bag. She can't imagine he's changing washers and cleaning hair out of the traps under the showers in his Tom Ford. He must change before he leaves the spa and then again when he gets there in the morning. Do his colleagues see him arrive dressed for an office job? Did he learn to cook just so he could transition from expensive nights out to cheap nights in while looking like the perfect boyfriend? She knows from personal experience how tiring deception is – remembering she's Lucy, her daughter is Dani, that she works in data processing – but the idea of fighting that war on a triple front is mind-blowing.

'I hate that I'm not seeing you till tomorrow,' he says. 'It's just, having the kids . . .' He'd told her that Amelia and Jack are staying with him for a few days while Camille has to pop over to France to visit her mum. Joni had been relieved. The less time she had to spend with him the better until they work out what to do about Mary's money.

'Are you doing anything special?'

'I just want to enjoy staying in and hanging out with them,' he says. Father of the Year. Boyfriend of the Century. 'A bit of normal family life, you know. I miss having them live with me.'

It's so tempting to say 'I know you're seeing Mary,' but she manages to restrain herself. She has no idea at this point if Ant even has children. She doesn't care. Actually, that's not true. For their sake she hopes not. She doesn't want to imagine them as pawns in whatever game Ant is playing. Either way, he definitely doesn't have them staying with him tonight. She wonders whose photos he might have been showing her, the cute red-headed girl and the boisterous blond boy. A niece and nephew? Is there a website where you can buy candid snaps of strangers so you can pretend they're your family?

'Well, have fun,' she says, crossing at the lights. She doesn't say what she really wants to add, which is 'While you still can.'

Because she's pretty sure that, for Ant, the game's up.

24

She can hardly concentrate waiting for Mary to call. She has to add up a column of figures four times to reach the same total twice. Yesterday she'd ended up sleeping on the sofa all afternoon – to Jasper's delight. She'd only got up to eat – heating up frozen Itsu dumplings and ramen because she couldn't be bothered to prepare any-thing from scratch – and to have a bath and change into her pyjamas. She had missed her gym session and she was angry with herself about that. She'd let life get in the way. She'd spent a while noting down all the extra sets she needed to add in to her sessions on Saturday and Sunday to make up for the lost time.

When she had arrived at work this morning she'd found a circle of Viking warriors – Ragnar and Lagertha among them – on the desk, surrounding her embracing squirrels, swords raised, and she'd actually laughed out loud. She took a photo and sent it to Imo and then, in an effort to appear as if everything were normal, to Ant. Really it was a way of testing the waters while she waited for Mary. To see if he'd got wind of what she was up to. Thankfully Mary had never told him about her phone call. 'I think I was in denial,' she'd said when Joni had asked her. 'I was hoping it would all go away.' Ant had returned her text immediately with a laughing face and

Lucas 1 Lucy 0, so she was pretty confident Mary hadn't told him about her and Saffy's visit either.

In the end she gives in and plays Minesweeper on her computer to distract herself, angling the screen away from the glass wall. Anything to make the time pass. She's on her fourth game when it's interrupted by Imo's voice shouting 'Answer the phone, Mum!', the ringtone that Imo had recorded before she left home, and Joni has no idea how to change. Mary.

'Hi. Are you OK?' She closes the door. 'What happened?'

'I'm fine,' Mary says. It sounds as if she's in the garden again and Joni can picture her there among the flowers, the birds singing their hearts out to be heard over the distant traffic. 'Sorry I didn't try you earlier, I had to go—'

'Did you ask him for it back?' Joni interrupts and then feels rude. 'Sorry. Go on. What were you going to say?'

'Nothing. Yes. I told him one of my sons needed the money urgently. That something had happened – I was vague, but I made out it was basically a matter of life and death. I said I couldn't access any more cash because that's more or less what he said to me, so I thought two can play at that game . . .'

Joni paces. She always walks round her office when she's on the phone. It helps her think. 'And?'

'He said there was nothing he could do at the moment. That as soon as the house was sold he'd pay me back as promised. He kept apologizing and saying he couldn't believe he'd got me in this mess, but, of course, I didn't believe a word of it. I even asked if he had any shares he could cash in but he said his accounts are all frozen till the divorce is finalized. Could that be true?'

'Maybe. If they're locked into some kind of court battle. I don't know. It seems unlikely. Me and Ian just divided everything in two. And anyway, he told me his divorce has gone through. All they had left to do was sell the house and split the profits. But obviously we don't know if that's true either.'

Mary sighs. 'Well, it doesn't look as if he's intending to repay me any time soon. I feel like such a fool.'

'We'll think of something. Are you sure you don't want to tell the police? I mean, I know he'd just say it was a present, but it might make him think . . .'

'No. I couldn't cope if it got out. I can't believe I've been this stupid, but if my family knew . . . well, I just couldn't . . .'

'I understand,' Joni says, imagining herself trying to explain something similar to Imo. She actually can't. It would be too humiliating. Even worse if she was nearly fifteen years older like Mary, and Ant's senior. She thinks about those stories you read in the paper where a seventy-year-old woman has married a twenty-five-year-old man she met on holiday and is protesting that she believes it's real love even when it's obvious to everyone reading – and presumably her own grown-up kids and even the grandchildren – that he's taking her for a ride. Not that it's inconceivable that Ant and Mary would make a believable couple. Not at all. But she knows how the world sees things. Mary would be perceived as the silly, gullible menopausal victim. The butt of jokes. Joni can see it would be unbearable. 'I'm going to fill Saffy in, are you OK with that?'

'Yes, do,' Mary says so quietly Joni almost doesn't hear.

'Don't beat yourself up.' She says goodbye and then carries on pacing round her office. She doesn't feel as if she can settle to anything. She's so preoccupied with Ant. She sits back at her desk, stands up again and dials Saffy's number.

'I'm in John Lewis,' Saffy says when she answers. 'Shall I come and meet you for lunch?'

Joni hesitates. She likes to eat lunch at her desk, her door shut, her chair facing the window overlooking the square. Her back a metaphorical 'Do not disturb' sign for anyone approaching her office. She brings it in with her – a carefully balanced meal of avocado and salad sandwich on seed-laden granary bread. A bag of protein crisps. A bottle of blended juice. It never varies much beyond the ingredients of the salad or the type of fruit and veg that make up the juice. She knows it's healthy, it's what her body needs, so who cares if it's not that exciting?

'I'm literally two minutes away from you. We could go to the Langham.'

Her lunchbox is waiting, stacked up in the fridge in the kitchen with the other four that are always there, the milk that's usually a day or so past its best, a couple of old yoghurts and half a bottle of wine that's been open since last Christmas.

'OK. But make it By Chloe. I only get an hour. I don't have time to faff around with posh service.' She doesn't know why she suggests it. It's the only place she can think of off the top of her head, but she hasn't set foot in there for months. Eighteen to be precise. More, actually. Meg, newly vegan, had been obsessed with it, trekking over at least once a week and salivating over the burgers and fries.

'And it's healthy!' she would exclaim, stuffing in mac and cheese with fake bacon.

'It's definitely not,' Joni remembers saying. 'The calories must be insane.' She wishes she'd kept quiet now. Just let Meg work it out for herself. Or not. Whatever made her happy.

'Fine. Ten minutes?' Joni looks at her watch. It's twenty to one. Usually she waits till one, but only because that's a rule she sets for herself – if she takes her break any earlier the afternoons feel interminably long – and they stand more chance of getting a table if they go earlier. 'See you there.'

As it happens the café is already heaving, so she waits for Saffy outside and then they order a takeaway – quinoa salad for Joni, pasta with avocado and pesto for Saffy – and walk up Portland Place trying to find a bench. Saffy, dressed in her combat trousers, her big purple trainers and a slightly cropped vest top, looks like an escapee from the Spice Girls, Joni thinks. Sweary Spice. In contrast she's in her safe work clothes – a pale pink Orla Kiely skirt patterned with daisies, and a fine knit off-white short-sleeve top. Flat sandals. Nice, but hardly a masterclass in self-expression. She has a variation of the same for all seasons. A-line skirts, fitted tops, sensible but attractive footwear. Thick tights in winter. Thin cardigans in spring and autumn. A uniform.

Saffy has talked nineteen to the dozen since she spotted Joni waiting for her outside the café. Joni's not quite sure what about – what she's been looking for in John Lewis, she thinks. It's like an assault. After a quiet morning processing figures in her office it's too much all at once and it takes her a few minutes to adjust, tune in, pick the words out of the noise. She lets it wash over her like a foreign language, the odd phrase standing out here and there – 'four-seater' and 'modular' – which leads her to believe Saffy might have been shopping for a sofa. She spots a bench on a quiet side street and points to it.

'Right,' Saffy says when they get there, as if adhering to some tacit agreement that business talk wouldn't begin until they sat down. 'What did she say? I've been on edge all morning.'

Joni hears a growl coming from Saffy's bag. 'Is Tyson in there?'

Saffy fishes him out. Places him on her lap. 'The cleaner was off sick this morning and I didn't want to leave him on his own.'

'What were you going to do if there'd been a table free?'

'Oh, he'd have been quiet. He's a good boy, aren't you? No one would even have known.' Tyson looks up at her, his tongue lolling from his mouth. She plants a kiss on his head and he rumbles with another growl. 'So, tell me.'

Joni fills her in as succinctly as she can, trying to fend off interruptions.

'So, he has no fucking intention of ever paying her back, let's face it.' Saffy shoves a plastic forkful of pasta into her mouth and then picks up a few pieces in her fingers and offers them to Tyson, who snaps them from her like the world's smallest toothless crocodile. 'Good boy.'

'No, I don't think so. I mean, you'd offer to sell it straightaway if you didn't have the money, wouldn't you?'

'If you were an even vaguely decent human being, then yes. How did she sound?'

'Sad. Resigned.'

'Not angry?'

Joni thinks for a second. 'No. Not yet.'

'She should be. I'd be fucking fuming.'

'You and me both.' Joni has been trying all morning to imagine what she would have done. In her head she can see herself shouting at Ant, telling him she knows what he's doing, that he needs to get the money back to her or else. In reality she wonders if that's really how she would react. It's easy to be brave in your own imagination. Saffy, she's pretty sure, would have marched him to the bank right then and there whether it was open or not, dragged the manager out of bed if she had to. 'I wonder when he'll try and cash in with me. I imagine that's the point.'

'I would think so. I can't wait to hear what it is he needs next. A yacht? A plane?' Saffy puts the last remains of her lunch on her lap and Tyson dives in face first. 'We can't let Mary let him off just because she feels embarrassed or she doesn't want her kids to find out. He can't just walk away with fifty grand.'

'I know.'

'He knows she lost her husband, for God's sake. I mean, how low can you stoop?'

Joni turns to look at her. 'You're a big softy under there somewhere, aren't you?'

'No,' Saffy says, stuffing her now empty carton into the paper carrier bag along with her cutlery. 'I just don't like people taking advantage, that's all.'

'Even if we could get him to sign the car over to her that'd be something,' Joni says, still working on her salad. Tyson eyes it greedily. Joni gives him a stare that she hopes says 'Don't even think about it.'

'We need to find out more about him,' Saffy says. 'The truth about who he really is. He must have an Achilles heel.'

Joni nods. 'Everyone has something. We just have to find out what it is.'

25

Joni feels as if she's back where she started, hanging around outside Evoke in Notting Hill, only this time with Saffy in tow. The only things they know for certain about Ant are his name, his gym and where he works. They need to start somewhere. They're sitting inside the café across the road, watching from the window in the hope of seeing him leave for the day. Joni is pretty sure that he finishes at around six because it seems to be no problem for him to get to hers before seven, but they still got here at ten to five, just in case. Hopefully today he'll be prompt, because the waitress has already warned them she's shutting up shop any moment, and Joni doesn't want to risk him spotting her out on the street. She claimed an emergency dentist's appointment at four forty-five and left work at a quarter past four, something she has never done before. Not even for a genuine reason. She always arranges anything extra-curricular for her days off. And then she'd felt she had to act the part, so she put on a sad face and winced as she told Shona where she was going. 'Oh God, poor you,' Shona had said with genuine sympathy that made Joni's guilt even worse. 'You do look as if your face is a bit swollen.'

This morning the collectibles were back. This time the elephant was being held hostage by Jabba, Jar Jar and

Baby Yoda. Some kind of uniformed space warrior held his plastic gun to its head. Joni put them all away and then went on to Amazon and ordered a pink and white unicorn and a kitten with a ball of wool. Two could play at that game. She looked around for a note detailing whatever Lucas didn't get round to yesterday and found nothing.

She and Saffy have tried looking Ant up on 192, the electoral roll site, but Anthony Simons, London, throws up hundreds of searches including countless A. Simons who could just as well be Angela as Anthony. They need to narrow down the area he lives in if nothing else. They have to assume that everything he's told them about himself, beyond those three facts, is a lie.

Saffy grabs her arm, points with the other hand. There he is in his gym gear, striding down the street. 'Go on,' Joni says. They'd weighed up following him, but it seemed too fraught with pitfalls unless he simply strolled round the corner to his home. What if he got into a car or taxi? Or wasn't going home at all? They know he's not heading to Mary's – he's told her the story about having the kids staying for a week, but with completely different days that stretch across the weekend – but that doesn't mean he's not on his way somewhere else.

'He must need a night off though,' Saffy had argued. 'I mean, you'd be knackered, wouldn't you? Juggling two women and with another waiting in the wings. All that shagging. Do him and Mary shag, do you think?' Her own rescheduled first meeting with him has yet to be confirmed, but they've speculated as to whether he'll start to back away from Mary, now she's had the temerity to ask for her money back, and invest more energy into seeing what he can get from Joni and subsequently, presumably, Saffy herself. 'A fucking broken nose,' all five foot not much of Saffy had said. 'A knee in the balls.' Joni didn't doubt it for a second.

Now Saffy crams her ponytail-attached baseball cap on to her head and strolls across to the entrance to Evoke while Joni pays for their drinks. Joni watches as she pushes the door open and goes in. She's not entirely sure about leaving the task to Saffy, who she can imagine veering wildly off script, but they couldn't risk Ant doubling back and finding her, Joni aka Lucy, there checking up on him. She paces as she waits, watching the corner just in case.

After a couple of minutes the door opens and Saffy stomps out clutching a handful of sample-size bottles of something or other. 'Here,' she says, thrusting three of them at Joni.

'Did they give you those?' Joni asks, wondering if Saffy even managed to ask what she was supposed to.

'It said help yourself. They probably didn't mean to six but . . .'

Joni stuffs the samples into her bag. 'So . . .?'

'Oh. Yes. So I said exactly what we planned. I asked for him and when they told me he'd left I said I was his cousin and I was visiting London and I'd just dropped in on the off-chance. I'm pretty sure it was the same boy on reception as when I went for my treatment, but he didn't show any sign of recognizing me. Anyway, so then I said, "Oh, no worries, I'll try him at home, hopefully he's still at the same address . . ."'

'And?'

'He didn't bite. Just looked at me. I guess they have a policy about not giving out any personal information. So I said, "I don't really know London, what's the best way to get there from here by tube?"'

Joni wants to say 'Just cut to the chase' but she's knows Saffy's enjoying her moment, so she waits.

'And he was a bit more helpful once he realized I wasn't trying to extract anything from him that I shouldn't and he looked at a tube map on his phone and said, "Go round on the Circle Line to Victoria and change."' She looks at Joni proudly. *Haven't I done well?*

'To where?'

'Oh. Yes. He said, "You'd probably be best off getting out at Vauxhall. But it's a bit of a walk, I imagine. You might be better getting the bus." Anyway, to cut a long story short I got it out of him that it was Battersea. Where Ant lives. Because he said something about how it'll be much easier when they open the new station.'

'Excellent,' Joni says, and she means it. 'Well done.'

'So, back on 192?'

'Exactly. This must narrow it down. If he's listed at all we'll find him.'

'Shall we see if they've got a table at Ottolenghi? I'm starving. Being a detective takes it out of you.'

'I can't. I'm going out later.' It's a lie, of course. Her default response to any unexpected invitation these days.

'That's OK,' Saffy says, pulling her phone out of her

bag. 'One of my besties lives round here, I'll see if she's free.'

'I'll let you know what I find,' Joni says. 'It might be the morning.' She's going to have to keep up the pretence now that she was out and not trawling through electoral records all evening. 'Do you want me to wait and see if she's up for it? If not we can share a cab back. I have to go home and change.'

'No, it's OK,' Saffy says, grabbing her in a hug. Joni tries to relax into it, but she's never been a hugger. Certainly not with anyone outside her immediate family. Or Meg, of course. Meg had always been a cuddler. Joni pats Saffy's back as though she's patting a horse. 'If she's not I might see who else is about. Someone's bound to be at a loose end.'

'Have fun,' Joni says. 'I'll call Mary on the way home and update her.' She watches Saffy walk off in the direction of the main road and wonders what it must be like to have a slew of friends to call on. The girls. The gang. Exhausting, probably.

She spots a taxi with its light on. Flags it down. Pictures herself having a cool shower, enjoying a glass of wine in her PJs. Pleasing herself. The thought doesn't feel as comforting as it usually does.

26

Once she's showered, changed and Jasper has been fed, she opens the cold wine and pours herself a glass. Digs out a frozen thin-crust margherita from the freezer and turns the oven on. She tries not to eat pizza too often, but she's starving and exhausted and she wants comfort food. She sets a timer on her watch once she slides the pizza in and heads down the steps to the back garden and her favourite spot in the shade of an apple tree. Flick's windows are wide open and she can hear the strains of Bob Dylan competing with Adele from the floor above. It's not exactly peaceful. She's thought about moving before. Not because she doesn't love her flat – she does – but because her neighbours drive her to distraction. But then she could go through all the hassle of finding a new place, trying to sell this one – one of the five most stressful life events she thinks she read somewhere, but then so is divorce and she survived that one more or less injury free – and be in exactly in the same situation somewhere else. So, she just lives in hope that either Flick or the couple above her will decide to relocate one day. She reminds herself that she chose her home not just for the space, but for the garden. She'd never find somewhere like this anywhere else.

She fires up her laptop and logs into 192. Buys more

credit. She has to google the postcode for Battersea and then she searches Anthony Simons again. Bingo. This time there are only three. Two Anthonys and an A. She notes down the addresses and then all the other occupants of each property – none of them seem to live alone, but who knows who these other people might be. Out of interest she looks up her own address and finds herself listed as living with a Barbara Willis who, she knows, is the woman she bought the flat from two years ago, but who has obviously not kept her electoral details up to date. In fact, Joni's pretty sure she moved to Australia to be near her grandchildren. No ages are listed for any of the A. Simonses. Nothing to narrow them down further. She googles a map and locates the three addresses. Sends the whole lot to the printer.

Just to be sure she goes back to the main search and swaps the word Battersea and its postcode for Vauxhall, SW8. There's another A. Simons to add to the list. No sex, no age, no other details beyond the address, which is located in the opposite direction to Battersea from Vauxhall tube and so unlikely according to the details Saffy was given, but she writes the address down anyway.

Four possibles. How hard can it be to narrow them down? She's about to send Saffy a quick text update but then she remembers she's supposed to be out for dinner, so she forces herself to think about something else. She needs to try and relax.

She phones Imo expecting her to be out and about, ignoring her phone, but she answers immediately. Joni stands up and wanders down the garden as she talks. She's made the mistake of sitting below Flick's window and chatting before, only to hear most of the conversation regurgitated back to her a couple of days later. 'Oh, I heard about your mum's operation. How is she? And poor Jasper had to have a tooth out . . .'

'Hi!' Imo says, a smile in her voice. Joni immediately knows she's happy. Feels a weight she didn't know she was carrying lift off her shoulders.

'How's it going? How's work?'

'Fab.' Imo tells her a story about something that happened the day before involving them having to close down a cul-de-sac to film a segment for her project and an old man who kept popping his head out of his front door in the background – as well as working on the live show at the weekends, all the trainees are teamed up with a skeleton crew of technical students one day a week, and tasked with making their own show in the genre of their choice. Imo has chosen factual, the field into which she wants to progress once she graduates – 'He was so sweet,' she says. 'He just couldn't grasp what was going on. Are you down the garden? I can hear birds.'

'Hiding from Flick,' Joni says. 'She's got her windows open.'

'Did you ditch Ant yet?' Imo always does this, jumps from subject to subject with no segue. Joni used to love listening in to her conversations with her friends, her boundless enthusiasm to know anything and everything that was going on in their lives.

'No. Long story. I'm building up to it.'

'Poor Ant,' Imo says, not knowing how wrong she is. 'Just put him out of his misery.'

'I will.' Joni paces between two trees. She makes the mistake of looking up at the house and Flick waves. Joni raises a hand in response and turns away. 'Damn. Flick's spotted me. I'm toast.'

Imo laughs. 'No, you're not. Just stay on the phone while you walk back into the house. She can't talk to you then.'

'OK. Hold on.' She heads towards the back door, raising her voice as she goes. 'The thing is, Mum, you need to get tested. STDs can be serious . . .' She hears Imo laughing down the line.

'No! Poor Granny!'

'That'll give her something to think about,' Joni says as she shuts the back door, having snatched up her laptop and wine glass on the way. The kitchen smells faintly of burning. She checks her watch and realizes that she hadn't set her timer after all, just the stopwatch, which is now telling her her pizza has been in the oven for thirty -five minutes instead of the requisite sixteen. 'Shit, I've burnt my dinner.' She opens the oven door and wafts the smoke with a tea towel. The alarm starts to beep. 'Oh God, sorry, Imo, I'd better go. I'm around Sunday if you want a chat. Love you.'

'Love you too,' Imo says, still laughing. 'Don't burn the place down.'

She gets home from the gym at half past six on Saturday, as usual, and runs around the flat hiding any mail that has arrived since Ant was last here in a locked drawer. She just has time to shower before he arrives, bringing with him fresh ravioli and pecorino cheese. She sticks a bottle of Sauvignon Blanc in the freezer. She's dreading the evening. This cuckoo in her nest. This man she doesn't know at all. She texts Saffy: *I feel weirdly nervous.*

Saffy answers immediately. *Of course you do. The man's a fucking psycho. It's like* The Talented Mr Ripley. *Remember, he won't kill you though because he hasn't got anything out of you yet. That was a joke by the way. Text me later and let me know you're OK. Xx.*

Yeah, that's made me feel so much better, thanks, Joni responds although, in truth, Saffy's message had actually made her laugh.

He arrives at five to seven, carrier bag in hand, suit on. She can't imagine how she ever found him attractive. He's still good-looking, obviously, but everything about him repels her. She has to stop herself from flinching when he kisses her. She feels as if she wants to suggest they go out into the garden to give her a sense of space between them, but she's worried Flick might start calling her from the window, giving away her real name and her own deception. She pours them both a glass of wine and watches while he unpacks his wares.

'Join me in the shower?' he says. She wonders if he actually finds her attractive or if it's all part of the act.

'Just had one. Can I do anything?'

'Absolutely not. I'll be five minutes.' He leans down and ruffles Jasper's head on his way out of the kitchen.

The cat flips on his back and offers up his belly. He trusts him, Joni thinks sadly. He thinks he's a nice bloke.

She watches while he cooks, now in sweatpants and a fitted T-shirt. Bare feet. He smells of her mango shower gel. She racks her brain for things to talk about. Anodyne things that won't lead her into trouble. Tells him about Lucas and the figurines and he laughs. 'At least you know he has a sense of humour now.'

He suggests they eat outside and she tells him she's going to move the table down the far end where they won't hear the neighbours' TVs (and too far away for even Flick to think it was appropriate to shout). She insists she can manage on her own, grateful for the few minutes she can spend alone. She grabs the small café table that's folded by the back door and hotfoots it down to the end of the lawn where there's a secluded place between three trees with fairy lights strung between them. They're solar powered, set not to light up till dark, but they will be beautiful later on. There's a faint sweet aroma from the honeysuckle growing up the fence along one side that will only get stronger as the night goes on. It's idyllic. It's all wasted on Ant. He doesn't deserve it.

She goes back for two chairs and then wipes everything down with a damp paper towel, grabs a Kilner jar and fills it with a few flowers and covers the table with a sunshine-yellow cloth. She finishes just as Ant appears with two plates filled with delicious-looking pasta in a buttery sauce with shaved cheese on top.

'That looks amazing,' she says as she passes him on the way in to fetch their drinks.

'There's a salad too,' he calls after her, so she collects that as well. Ripe juicy tomatoes and thin slices of onion, a drizzle of olive oil and balsamic. Tiny micro herbs on the top. She has to give it to him: he's fantastic in the kitchen. Maybe she should just employ him as a chef. He'd get money; she'd get good food. It was win-win.

Ant stands up when she gets back to the table in a gesture that makes her cringe slightly. She's never been good with those gender-specific acts. Men opening doors and pulling out chairs. It doesn't feel like chivalry; it feels like something they've learned that women might fall for. A cynical means of point-scoring.

'Cheers,' he says, clinking his glass against hers. She can hear a wasp buzzing around although she can't see it. It's that time of year when eating outside can feel like being under siege. A good idea until you spend the whole meal flapping your arms like a drunk semaphorist. Or in Joni's case occasionally getting up and running away screaming.

She concentrates on the food. The ravioli parcels are soft and delicious, filled with ricotta and spinach. Ant is telling her a story about his kids. A couple of weeks ago she would have found it charming, this doting father. Now all she can think is, if these children actually exist, do they have any idea of the kind of man their father really is? She nods occasionally, no longer listening, the words washing over her.

'Luce?'

She realizes he's stopped talking and he's looking at her expectantly. 'Sorry. I was . . . What did you say?'

He gives her a smile showing his white teeth, the lines around his eyes crinkling. 'I was telling you about my car. How it broke down on the way to the model village at Beaconsfield. We ended up sitting on the M40 for two hours. It's on its last legs, I think.'

Joni jolts to attention. This must be what it feels like to go into fight-or-flight mode. For an animal who senses a danger they can't see. This is it. The moment she's been waiting for. 'Is it old?'

'Ancient. It's a classic seventies Jag. Like the one in *The Sweeney*. It looks gorgeous but it's totally impractical when I need to ferry Amelia and Jack around.'

'It's insured though, right?'

He drains the last of his wine. 'To an extent. But I need to pension it off, I think. Get one of those reliable tanks.'

'I'm surprised you don't have one already . . .'

He laughs a little self-deprecating laugh. 'I actually have three cars but they're all vintage. Beautiful and impractical. The thing is, it's not very safe driving the kids round in any of them. When they're working. Which, at the moment, none of them are. I need to get back on the road quick but in something grown-up and safe. I can't be running round like a boy racer any more. I'm a single dad.' He gives her a look – *aren't I charming?*

'So, what are you looking at?' She's itching to talk to Saffy. To somehow find a way for her to witness this conversation. Because she absolutely, 100 per cent, knows what's coming.

'Range Rover. But I've got a bit of a problem. All my cash is tied up while the divorce is going through . . .'

'Not all of it, surely?' She needs time to think, to decide how she's going to play this.

He rubs his hand over his eyes. 'Pretty much. Because Camille is contesting every penny. Her lawyers have frozen all our accounts.'

'That's awful,' she says, because it would be if it were true. 'I thought it was all sorted bar the house.'

'I didn't want you to think I was in the middle of some legal wrangle. I didn't . . . well, I didn't want it to look as if I was somehow trying to get out of paying her her due. I'm absolutely not. It's not as if I'm trying to hold anything back. She's welcome to half of everything. More, even. I don't care . . .'

Cry me a river, Joni thinks. Get the violins out. 'You can lease a car though, can't you?'

'I suppose so. I hate being tied in for years and told how many miles I can do, though.'

'Just in the short term, maybe. Until things are sorted out with Camille?' She's not going to make it easy for him. How would she have reacted if she didn't already know his form? she thinks. It still would have been too much, too soon, too big an ask. But, who knows? Maybe she would have fallen for it. She shudders.

'Maybe. I did have another idea, though . . .'

She waits. She's desperate for another glass of wine but she doesn't want to interrupt the moment. Let him ask. Let him prove once and for all that he's a user.

'. . . I wondered if you could lend me the money. Just in the short term . . .'

She can't stop herself from interrupting. It's so ridiculous. The logic is so skewed. 'Won't the bank do that?'

He holds his hands up. *You got me.* 'But then Camille would have to approve it and, you know, that would get complicated . . . I'd pay you back the minute everything was finalized with the divorce. With interest obviously.' Mary had poo-pooed the idea of interest, she'd told them, so heartily had she believed in Ant.

'Gosh,' Joni says. 'I don't know. I mean, how much are we talking?'

He grimaces. 'Fifty K. Fifty-two maybe.'

'Wow. Um. I need to think about it, is that OK? Check what I've got in the bank.'

'Of course! I wasn't expecting you to . . . It's obviously a big decision. But it wouldn't be for long. And you'd be earning me serious dad points.' He gives her what he obviously thinks is a winning smile. 'You're not upset with me asking, are you?'

'God, no. Not at all.'

'Good, because if you don't want to that's fine. Absolutely fine. I wouldn't want you to think I was putting pressure on you.'

'Not at all. Listen, if I can help out I will. I just need to check a few things . . .'

He leans across the table and kisses her. 'Thank you.'

'I'm just going to get the wine,' she says, standing up. 'Won't be a sec.'

Inside she shuts herself in the bathroom with her phone. Types a message to Saffy and Mary. *He's just asked* me to 'lend' him 50 grand! And guess what for?? TO BUY A CAR!!!!!!

Saffy responds immediately: *No fucking way!!! Call me later!!*

It'll have to be tomorrow, Joni types, running the water in the sink. She puts her phone on silent and hides it in the drawer in the coffee table with the mail as she walks back through to the garden.

27

He doesn't bring it up again all evening, probably because he's worried he's pushed too hard already. They sit outside finishing the wine as it grows dark and the fairy lights start to glow. Tiny bats fly above their heads. A skinny fox stops, startled to see them there, and then turns and runs into the undergrowth. Thankfully Ant is in a garrulous mood, so Joni doesn't have to think too hard to find things to talk about, she just lets him hold court and adds the occasional 'Mmm'. She leans her head back in her chair as if she's soaking up the warm evening, the food, the wine, and not simply avoiding conversation. Later she finds she enjoys the sex by divorcing the act from the man in her head. Focusing purely on the physical and not the emotional. As if they're friends with benefits, except that they're not even friends any more. Acquaintances with benefits. Two people who aren't who they say they are. With benefits.

She actually sleeps well, despite everything. Maybe her body understands she needs the night to be over as quickly as possible. She only stirs when Ant brings her a cup of tea and tells her he's leaving.

She drags herself upstairs and fishes her phone out of the coffee-table drawer. There's a message from Mary: *Unbelievable! What did you say?*

That I'd think about it, Joni replies now. *I need to string him along for a bit while we decide what to do.*

A few minutes later there's another, this time addressed to both her and Saffy: *Would you like to come over on Tuesday evening? I can cook us a meal and we can talk about what happens next?* Joni assumes that Saffy will have plans already. That her bulging social calendar will be filled this late in the day, so she's surprised when there's an immediate response: *I'm up for it.*

Me too, Joni finds herself writing before she can stop herself. *I can get there about 6.45. OK?*

She adds up figures, she checks payments, she signs off on payroll. She eats her lunch from the fridge sitting at her desk with a fan blowing gently in her direction. She passes the odd pleasantry with a colleague she bumps into in the kitchen as she makes herself a coffee or washes her hands at the sink in the toilets. *Do anything nice at the weekend? How's your mum? Hot today, isn't it?* The day drags on.

Just before she leaves she remembers the unopened Amazon package she stuffed in her bag as she left home this morning. She opens it and finds the kitten and the unicorn, both more hideous than she remembers. She unpacks every one of Lucas's figures from the drawer and places them in a line along the front of the desk. Finds one – Batman – who has movable joints and arranges him at the front of the queue in a prone position as if kneeling to a god. Head down, arms outstretched. Sits her unicorn at the front, the object of all the worship, a deity granting audiences. She smiles to herself, pleased with her work.

Saffy is already nursing a glass of wine in Mary's kitchen when she arrives. The inside of Mary's house is as beautiful as the outside. Lived in. A home. Dark wood and rich colours. A cluster of paintings on the wall. Candles dotted among silver-framed family photos. Joni can imagine holing up here on a rainy winter's day. Curled up on a chair with a book looking out over the garden. The bag at Saffy's feet sighs and moves.

'Tyson?' Joni says.

Saffy nods. 'He's asleep. Busy afternoon at the groomer's.'

'I can imagine.' Mary hands her a glass and proffers both red and white wine. She's looking better today. Less stressed. Joni indicates the white, holds out the glass while Mary pours. 'Is this where you brought up your family, Mary?'

'I've lived here for twenty-nine years. My youngest was born here.'

Mary, Joni knows from reading her early exchanges with Ant, has two sons: George, thirty-one, and Oliver, twenty-eight. 'What a lovely home.'

'Yes, I love it. It's too big for me really, now the boys are gone. Shall we sit in the garden again?' She moves towards the patio doors without waiting for an answer.

'If it's paid off, though, why not stay?' Joni asks, following her.

Mary grimaces as she puts her glass on the large faux-wicker table and moves a chair out of the direct line of the sun. 'Ant knows it is too. I imagine that was a big draw. Widow sitting on a goldmine.'

'Fucker,' Saffy barks, and Joni thinks how like Tyson she is. Tiny and furious. Although she does have teeth at least.

'I like the way you say it as it is.' Mary laughs. It's the first time Joni has seen her do so – there weren't many opportunities on the morning they broke the big news to her, let's face it. She has a huge mouth when she smiles. Half of her face is lips. A slash of red lipstick. It gives her a sensual, earthy look that's disarmingly attractive.

Saffy plonks her Tyson-filled bag in the shade. Joni makes a mental note to check that Saffy takes the bag with her when they leave.

'So, what am I going to say?' She looks between the two of them. 'I mean, no, obviously. Sorry, Mary . . . I didn't mean obviously . . .'

'It's fine.'

'Cars are clearly his thing,' Saffy says, drinking half of her glass of wine in one go. 'I assume – what? Did you just give him the money, Mary, or did you pay the car dealers?'

'I transferred the money to the dealership. He made a big deal about wanting me to know that it was all above board, that it really did cost what he said he needed. Why would he do that?'

'Because it makes it more convincing,' Joni said. 'I assume if he does the same with me he'll just sell it again immediately. He'd make a loss and it's a bit of a faff but he'd still end up with tens of thousands and, if I ever wanted to see the car for some reason, he could show me the one Mary bought . . .'

'Unless I wasn't the first and he has a garage full of them somewhere.'

Joni thinks for a second. 'No, I think you were. You were the first person he had success with on the app. I mean, who knows? Maybe he was on a different dating site before this. There were no signs on his phone though. I went right back through his texts.'

'It's hardly a way to cover your tracks though, is it?' Saffy is sitting, knees up, feet on the seat of the chair. She's in baggy soft trousers, a gold bracelet around her thin tanned ankle, silver polish on her toes. 'If anyone looked into it they could trace all the cars. It would be obvious straightaway.'

'And so, what? He hasn't done anything illegal. He asked someone to buy him a car and they did. Whether he asked more than one person and he sold some of the cars is neither here nor there. His story would be that the cars were gifts and he can do with them what he likes. Immoral maybe; illegal no.'

'And a lie, obviously,' Mary says. 'Given that the money was supposed to be a loan and not a present.'

'No proof though. Maybe I should ask him to sign an agreement? Tell him I'll lend him the money but my bank are insisting I get a written confirmation that it's just a temporary loan or something? See what he says.'

'He'd run a mile.' Saffy leans down into her bag, which

growls. She comes out with a pair of sunglasses. Puts them on.

'No, I think he'd guilt-trip you out of it. Make you feel you shouldn't have asked. Can I meet him?' Mary indicates the bag where Tyson is clearly now awake.

'I wouldn't . . .' Joni says as Saffy picks up the bag.

'He's a big softie really.' She reaches a hand in and the bag starts to rumble. Tyson comes out snapping like a Venus flytrap.

'Aww. Come here, sweetie,' Mary says, reaching out to take him as both Joni and Saffy shout, 'No!' Too late. She scoops him off Saffy's lap and places him on her own where he flops on to his back, belly in the air, and the growling stops as quickly as it began.

'Look! He loves you!' Saffy says.

'Lucky you,' Joni says. 'So, you're still up for checking out those addresses tomorrow?'

'Definitely.' Saffy drains her glass. 'Could I get us another, Mary?'

'Of course. Do you want me to . . .?'

Saffy jumps up. 'I'll do it. You look after Tyson. Joan?'

Joni opens her mouth to correct her, but then she realizes that Saffy hasn't got her name wrong, she's just abbreviating it. It gives her a tiny curl of pleasure deep in her gut. Meg used to call her Jojo. No one else ever did. 'Please.'

'Fill Mary in on the addresses.'

Joni does what she's told. Mary listens, stroking Tyson's head, fingers millimetres from being gummed to a pulp. 'Can I come?'

'Can you . . .?'

'Come. Tomorrow. It sounds like fun. I feel as if I have to do something proactive.'

'Yes. Of course. We just have to be a bit careful not to be seen . . .' She's not sure if it really makes sense for three of them to be trailing around looking conspicuous, but who is she to tell Mary she can't join in?

'Oh. Yes. Well, I don't have to if you think it might be iffy . . .'

'What might be iffy?' Saffy has returned with the wine bottle.

'Mary wants to come to check out those addresses with us. No. It'll be fine. Come . . .'

'I had an idea about that,' Saffy says, filling up the last glass, her own. 'Obviously I'm desperate to play detective again, but it is a bit risky when we have no idea whether he'll be there or not. But . . . we know exactly where he's going to be at eleven on Saturday. Meeting me for the first time.' She looks at Joni triumphantly. 'You could actually ring on the bells and see who's there. Talk to the neighbours. Whatever. Without worrying that Ant might spot you.'

Joni shoots a look at Mary. 'Are you up for that? Because I'm definitely not going on my own.'

Mary rewards her with another wide smile. 'I certainly am. Where are you meeting him, Saffy?'

'By the Serpentine. So he's going to have to leave home at ten thirty at the latest, I would say. I can keep him occupied until at least twelve. Half twelve by the time he gets back . . . You'd have two hours.'

'I'll drive us,' Mary says, more animated than Joni has ever seen her.

'Perfect. Now we just have to work out what we're going to say . . .'

It's pleasant sitting out there as the sun goes down, Joni thinks as she nibbles on an olive Mary has produced from somewhere. They have all drunk far too much, and now they're sharing stories of what led them to join Keepers in the first place. Mary's path is a classic tragic love story. She and Andrew had a happy marriage. One of those all-too-rare relationships of equals and best friends. Joni finds herself wiping away a tear when Mary tells them how she couldn't wake him one morning and discovered he had had a heart attack in his sleep. Sixty-one years old. For all the horror she must have gone through – the shaking him to try and wake him, the ambulance, the failed attempts at CPR and defibrillation – Mary smiles sadly and says that she's happy he went that way, knowing nothing about it. Hopefully dreaming about something lovely. Joni looks at Saffy, who is bawling like a teething toddler. She gulps loudly as she tries to get herself under control. Mary pats her on the arm. 'I'm all right now,' she says. 'Not over it. I don't think I ever will be. But I've moved on. I can look forwards. Finally. What about you, Joni?'

Joni's story feels so trivial in comparison. A cheating husband. A marriage on its last legs. No lasting scars. 'I'd like to have had what you had,' she says to Mary. 'I'd like to have experienced that.'

'Yes,' Mary says quietly. 'I wouldn't trade it.' Saffy sobs again.

'Saffy's story is pretty much the same as mine, I think, isn't it?' Joni decides to spare Saffy from having to speak. 'Except that she misses her husband more than I miss mine, clearly.' Saffy nods, still sniffling.

'There are good men out there,' Mary says. 'You just have to find them.' And for some reason this makes Saffy start sobbing all over again.

By the time Joni leaves, Saffy is unsteady on her feet. Joni had lost count of the number of times she topped up her glass after Joni and Mary moved on to mint tea. They had already decided to share an Uber, but Joni doesn't feel she can leave her to negotiate her way around her front door and burglar alarm. Nor does she want to go out of her way to drop her off in Highgate first. It would add half an hour to the journey. More maybe by the time she got Saffy inside. And she's feeling a little worse for wear herself. She just wants her bed.

'You can stay at mine,' she says reluctantly as she manoeuvres Saffy into the back of the sedan, having checked three times that she has Tyson in the bag. She can't even imagine what Jasper will make of him, but at least she knows he has no teeth to bite the cat with.

''K,' Saffy says, leaning back in the seat and falling asleep immediately. Luckily Saffy is so tiny that Joni doesn't need the driver's help – which he definitely isn't offering – to drag her out when they get there and manhandle her up the steps to the front door. Saffy perks up as the fresh air hits her and starts exclaiming loudly just as they enter the hall. 'Ooh, is this all yours? How lovely! Whose mail is this?' She picks up a pile from the table and flicks through it. 'Felicity Marmot, who the fuck is that? What sort of a surname is Marmot? Isn't that like a beaver? Felicity Beaver. Now that'd be a good name.' Joni gets her own door open and half pushes, half pulls her inside.

'This is nice. What a lovely room. Where's Tyson? I didn't leave him behind, did I?' She keeps up a running commentary all the way through to the kitchen. 'Shall we have another drink?'

'I'm going to make you a camomile tea,' Joni says, steering her towards a chair.

'Yuk.' She puts her bag on the floor and lays it on its side. Tyson staggers out and makes a beeline for what's left of Jasper's dinner. Joni shuts the kitchen door. Best her boy doesn't see this.

'She's lovely, isn't she? Mary.'

'She is,' Joni says, flicking on the kettle.

'It's so sad what happened to her. So, so sad.'

Joni exhales loudly. 'It makes you think our situation isn't too bad. We just got let down by a couple of faithless bastards.' She looks round as she hears Saffy let out another sob. 'Oh God, sorry, Saffy. I didn't mean to upset you again. You're far better off without him, you do know that, don't you? It might not feel like that now . . .'

'It wasn't him. It was me.'

Joni can hardly make out what she's saying through the wail. 'It . . .?'

'It was me. He didn't do anything wrong. I'm the faithless bastard. All Stefan ever was was lovely, and kind and devoted, and I fucked it all up. My life is ruined and it's all my fault.'

In the end Joni puts her to bed in the spare room, a huge glass of water on the cabinet beside her. There are already clean sheets on the bed. There are always clean sheets on the bed 'just in case' although Joni hasn't had anyone to stay in the room since she moved in two years ago. Just as there are on Imo's bed in the event she ever turns up unexpectedly. She plonks Tyson on the grass outside for a moment in case he needs the bathroom (he declines), and then drops him on the bed next to Saffy. She worries for a minute that if he tries to go anywhere the plummet from bed to floor could kill him but, when he snuggles contentedly into Saffy's arms, she decides it's so unlikely as to make it not worth worrying about. She turns on the light above the mirror in the en suite in the hope it will act as a beacon in the event of an emergency. She has no idea whether Saffy will remember where she is in the morning but, short of making a large poster saying 'This is Joni's house' and sticking it on the wall opposite the bed, she's not sure what she can do. She shuts the door behind her to maintain a barrier between cat and dog – Jasper is currently hiding from the big bad beast behind a chest of drawers in her room – and leaves them to it.

Most of what Saffy had been saying had been incomprehensible between the sobbing and the slurring, but

Joni had gathered that Saffy had had an affair – one that she now truly regretted, clearly. It had resulted in her marriage ending. That's as much as she knows. Her heart aches for Saffy. So much of her confidence, she can now see, is bravado.

Joni's bedroom is at the back of the flat. She loves this room with the little patio outside the glass doors, the steps up to the garden. The cool, quiet peace of it. She starts to worry about whether she should have turned Saffy on to her side. What if she's sick? She tiptoes back down the corridor, knocks tentatively. There's no answer so she goes in anyway. Saffy is flat out on her back so Joni risks the wrath of the dog to move her. Satisfied, she heads for bed. There's a weird warm feeling in her stomach. She thinks about what she might make Saffy for breakfast, what little parcel of products she can make up to present to her along with a fluffy towel for the shower, what clothes she might be able to lend her (she can't really think of anything, to be fair. Maybe one of her T-shirts as a dress?). Whatever the circumstances, it's actually nice to have someone here who needs her mothering skills, who needs to be looked after.

She wakes up with a faint feeling of needing water, the edges of a headache. Her first thought is Saffy. She can make them both a coffee. Maybe go back to bed for a bit: she's exhausted. Unused to drinking and late nights even if all they involved was sitting in someone else's garden. She pulls her hair back with one of Imo's scrunchies and potters up the stairs to the kitchen. Feeds Jasper. She knows that Saffy would rather have her drink black than share her oat milk. She checks the time – just after nine. She rarely sleeps this late, but it seems like a reasonable time to wake someone up. Downstairs she notices the door to the spare room is slightly open. She pushes it further and finds it empty. Pristine. The bed is made. The water glass washed. There's a note propped up on the pillow: 'Thank you so much. Slept like a baby! Call you later xxx'.

She feels a wash of disappointment. Checks herself. At least Saffy must be feeling OK.

28

Saffy is used to waking up with a hangover. It's become her default early-morning feeling ever since Stefan left. The nausea. The dry mouth. The free-floating anxiety. Rarely too bad, but there nonetheless. This morning's had been more severe than usual. She didn't usually have a blank where the evening had been, but after a certain point last night all she has are snapshots. Her crying. Joni reassuring. Fuckssake. She hates being caught letting her guard down like that.

She's in Joni's spare room, that much she knows. It's tempting to just stay here, allow herself to be looked after, but she can't face Joni's sympathy. She wants to put as much distance between herself and her confession as she possibly can. She makes the bed, washes her water glass, tears a sheet out of a notebook in her bag and writes a note. Then she scoops Tyson up and leaves. She can find a cab on the street.

Of course, this being north London she doesn't see one until she's practically reached Hampstead High Street, and then she almost loses it to a bloke in a suit who really has no idea of the extent to which he is dicing with death. 'I put my fucking hand out first,' she shouts so loudly she takes herself by surprise. She actually didn't, the man had clearly spotted the taxi before she did, but she needs a shower and her bed. Now. 'I've got an emergency. My dog is in here and he's sick.' She reaches in and shows him Tyson, who is perfectly content but, if she's being objective, always looks as if he's been the victim of a terrible accident.

'Oh Jesus,' the man says, turning away from the horror. 'Take the cab. Are you OK? Can I help?'

'No,' she says, trying to moderate her voice into something friendlier-sounding. 'I just need to get him to a vet. Thank you so much though.'

She almost cries when she shuts her front door behind her, she's so happy to be home. Her hangovers always come with an unhealthy dose of self-pity. No, make that self-loathing. She doesn't want anyone to see her like this. She knows that she'll spend the next few hours beating herself up about why she did what she did. Reliving the moments where she could have made a different choice, could have laughed in Rich's face and said of course she wasn't interested in him, and that she knew he wasn't really interested in her either – beyond his compulsion to try to seduce every female he met. She'll never understand why she didn't just throw him out. He had come round knowing that Stefan was working late, knowing that Stefan had been working late every night for weeks, sometimes till one or two in the morning, and that Saffy was feeling unappreciated, unnoticed. What a spoilt brat she'd been, loving the fruits of Stefan's hard work but resenting him doing that work in the first place. She'd known when she married him that she would only get a fraction of his time, and she'd accepted that. It had seemed worth it because the hours they did spend together were blissful: she'd been honest with Joni about that. Even though he was always tired and stressed he never failed to make an effort when he got some free time. He never came home from work angry or frustrated. He left it all at the door. That had been his promise: *I might not be home much, but when I am I'll be there 100 per cent.* And it had been true.

Rich had turned up one evening bearing a bottle of wine, feigned surprise that Stefan wasn't home but then suggested he and Saffy drink it anyway. He'd actually known she was home alone, he'd told her later as he kissed her up against the fridge and his hand slid between her legs. He'd always fancied her. It made him angry how Stefan never paid her enough attention, a stunning woman like her. She should have pushed him off then. Told him to leave. But she and Stefan had had a rare argument on the phone minutes before Rich had arrived, and she'd wanted to punish him. Rich's timing had been impeccable. Any other evening and she would have probably kneed him in the balls and told him to go fuck himself.

Sex has always been a shortcut for Saffy. A way to val- idate that she is attractive. Enough. She knows that now, but it took her most of her life to really understand it. A lot of introspection and being brutally honest with her- self. More to the point: listening to other people being brutally honest with her.

Of course, it all came down to daddy issues. She couldn't be anything other than a walking fucking cliché.

Not that her therapist had ever said so directly, nothing so crass, but Saffy had got there on her own. Her father – a distant, cold, disapproving workaholic – had left when Saffy was eleven and her brother, Ludo, ten. The man who had constantly criticized her mother for being frivolous and under-educated had exchanged her for a woman who could have won medals in vacuousness at the Personality Olympics. Saffy can remember being annoyed at her mother for being insufficiently alluring to win him back. She had shouted at her that she wasn't surprised her father had looked elsewhere when she made so little effort. Her poor mum. They were close now. Ludo's teenage descent into drug-dependent hell had united them in a common cause. Unfortunately he was still down there somewhere. Saffy had long since given up on him. Her mother never would. It broke Saffy's heart. He popped up every now and then when he needed something, money mostly. She kept telling their mum she should refuse him, that she was enabling his addiction, but seemingly she just couldn't bring herself to. Saffy's own reaction to her dad leaving had left fewer physical scars but probably just as many psychological ones, however many times she told herself she was having fun. Stefan had been the first decent man she had ever given the time of day. She couldn't believe it when he told her he loved her back. Couldn't believe she was worthy of it. Deep down, maybe she never had.

'You have zero self-respect,' her former best friend Bella had shouted at her when they were fifteen and Saffy had ended up in bed with Bella's boyfriend one afternoon after school. She'd once heard a gang of boys talking about her on the bus and one of them had referred to her as 'practice'. A way to improve their skills for when a girl they actually liked finally said yes. The words had stung so hard she'd almost burst into tears, but her stop was coming up and she refused to walk past them showing how much they'd hurt her. She'd held her head high and acted as if she hadn't even seen them as she made her way to the door. 'Oh fuck,' one of them said when he spotted her, and they all hooted with laughter, grabbing on to each other's arms. She could still hear them as the bus pulled away and she sat on the seat in the shelter and finally allowed herself to cry. She was the hot girl they all wanted to sleep with but none of them would ever even consider taking home to meet their mum. She didn't even want to meet their stupid mothers. Those women who had brought up boys to treat girls like commodities to be ranked on a scale of sinner to saint, shag to girlfriend. She just wanted to be accepted. Loved.

'You'll hate yourself in the end,' another former friend – Fran – had said once, when her fiancé had confessed to a 'horrible mistake' with Saffy on top of the coats at a party. 'That's what's really sad. You'll end up lonely and old and hating yourself as much as the rest of us hate you.'

It had taken fifteen years – ten of them the happiest she had ever been – but it had turned out Fran had been right.

She could almost forgive herself that one five-minute

wonder with Rich in the kitchen. Almost. It was what she did. What she had always done. But not the three afternoons in her and Stefan's bed that followed. She couldn't blame them on a moment of madness. They took planning and premeditation. They were a calculated deception, and she would never understand why she had done it. She'd come to her senses and stopped it before Stefan had found out. Had told herself she could live with the guilt even though it was eating her up. That she would never ruin Stefan's life by telling him even though it threatened to engulf her. The logic had been skewed, she knew that. He deserved to know who she apparently really was, this woman he adored and who, supposedly, adored him back. She didn't tell him because she knew he would never be able to get past it: it was as simple as that. If she had strayed with anyone else – literally anyone else in the world – there would have been a chance they could work through it eventually. But now the only course of action she had was silence.

And the only thing worse than her not telling him had been him finding out from Rich himself.

She feeds Tyson and gets into bed without even bothering with a shower. She pulls the dog up next to her and wraps her arms round him. He growls and wags his stumpy tail at the same time. He reminds her of herself: tiny, feisty, broken.

29

Mary is dressed like Secret Squirrel. That's the first thought Joni has when she opens the door to her on Saturday morning. Raincoat, cloche hat, sunglasses. Thankfully it is at least drizzling slightly.

'You wouldn't recognize me, right?' Mary says, raising the glasses.

'No, but I might be worried you were going to stick an umbrella tip in my leg and kill me. Maybe lose the coat.'

'It is a bit hot,' Mary says, peeling it off. 'I should keep the hat though, shouldn't I? Cover my hair.'

'Keep the hat,' Joni says. To be fair she, herself, is dressed in the most un-Joni-looking outfit she can find: shapeless jeans and an anonymous-looking black over-size T-shirt. Clothes she still has from before her workout obsession began, cut to disguise rather than flatter.

'I need to ask you about arms,' Mary says, following her inside.

Joni turns round, confused. 'Arms?'

'Your arms. I want them.'

Joni laughs. 'Go to the gym more. It's the only answer. Do you have a gym membership? Or one in your house?'

Mary looks at her as if she's just asked if she's ever won the Nobel prize. 'Well, no . . .'

'Join mine. I can show you what to do.' She says it

before she thinks. Does she really want Mary invading her space, her sanctuary?

'Oh yes, give me the details. You can knock me into shape. Gosh, this is nice . . .' She looks around at the large living room.

'Let me just show you the garden, then we should get going.' Joni leads Mary through to the back, unlocks the patio doors.

'This is incredible. Where does it end?'

'Two hundred feet away. It's why I chose this flat.'

Mary wanders off across the grass. 'This is magical. I'd live out here if this were mine. It's like being in the country.'

Joni smiles, enjoying seeing it through someone else's eyes. It reminds her of how special it is, how lucky she is. 'I should do more with it.'

'The semi-overgrown look is very in ever since No Mow May . . . you can tell people it's deliberate.'

'Why didn't I think of that? I'm doing it for the bees.'

'Exactly. Could I come back and have a proper explore one day? I mean, only . . . is that presumptuous?'

'No. Of course. Come round for a cup of tea,' Joni says, knowing she'll never get round to fixing a date. It's easy to look gregarious in the moment. But she's starting to feel close to both Mary and Saffy, she's come to real-ize. Could imagine them forming a true friendship outside of their connection with Ant. And that scares her. Sometimes life is easier if you keep people at a dis-tance. 'We should go.'

*

Joni barely recognizes Battersea from the last time she was here – visiting the rescue centre and picking out a nervous-looking black cat with big green eyes from a sea of other needy cats. Meg had told her that black cats were notoriously hard to rehome because people found it hard to get good photos of them to put on social media, which had made Joni determined that a black cat was exactly what she was going to get. Then the area around the animal home had been forgettable low-rise housing, the huge form of the power station dominant. Now even that iconic old building has been dwarfed by glass towers. It reminds her that Jasper is getting old.

They drive around in circles a bit, the satnav unaware of all the diversions and road closures the regeneration is causing. 'Look!' Joni squeaks excitedly at one point as they pass the glass swimming pool that connects two buildings high above their heads. A lone person is breast-stroking along, looking like an underwater shot from *Jaws*.

'Oh no,' Mary says, glancing up at it when they stop at temporary traffic lights. 'No, no, no.'

Joni smiles. 'I'd love to try it. I wonder if you're allowed or you have to live there.'

'No. I feel queasy just looking at it.'

The first address is a small terraced house south of all the new developments. A couple of streets further north and the owners would probably have made a small fortune selling to the developers, but this street looks sad. Run down. Forgotten. The houses look functional. No embellishments. No frills.

'Number seventeen,' Joni says, looking at her list. 'This one's definitely an Anthony.'

'It must be that one with the bins.' Mary parks up a few houses along. Number 17 has peeling paint on the windows and two overflowing wheelie bins on the concrete front garden.

'What time is it?' Joni says rhetorically as she looks at her Apple watch. 'Quarter to. Shall we leave it five just in case he's running really late?'

She texts Saffy to check Ant hasn't called to postpone or warn her he'll be late. *Nothing,* comes the reply. *Not since we confirmed last night xx.*

She had called Saffy on Wednesday afternoon to check if she was OK and Saffy had acted as if there had been nothing to talk about. She'd thanked Joni for her hospitality, said she had a bit of a sore head 'because we did chuck back a few', but had made no allusion to the crying mess she'd become, the sad admission about the end of her marriage. And Joni had thought she couldn't bring it up, although she had found herself thinking about it all day. Remembering how Saffy had once told her that her marriage had been blissful.

'OK. Shit,' she says to Mary now, pulling on a baseball cap and tucking her hair up into it. It says 'Justin' on the front, from when Imo had a Bieber phase at about thirteen, but it's the only one she could find so it'll have to do. 'Is this a really mad thing to do?'

'Totally. But what else have we got? Stick to what we planned.'

'What if he has a Ring camera and my face pops up

on his phone?' Joni says, panicking now. What was she thinking?

'You'll know before you get too close to it, so just abort. Are you sure you don't want me to go instead?'

Joni does. She wants it with every fibre of her being. But she can't do that to Mary. This was all her idea. Joni and Saffy had agreed between themselves that Joni should be the one to ring on the doorbells. Mary would be too easy to describe to Ant. Older, the amber eyes, the white-blonde hair.

'I'm fine. Here goes.' She gets out and walks unsteadily towards the house. They had toyed briefly with some kind of survey or official-sounding excuse, but on balance thought that that would make the occupants suspicious they were being cased by two very polite, middle-class burglars. Joni knew she would never fall for it herself so why would they? In the end they'd decided that they needed a more credible cover story. One that was unprovable in the moment. Joni was looking as unthreatening as possible. If a jealous partner came at her with a bread knife she was going to refer to Mary as her girlfriend and try to get out of it that way.

On closer inspection the house looks a bit more loved than from a distance. Yes, the outside is shabby but she can just about make out through the slatted wooden blinds at the front window that there's a cosy lounge with a small sofa and a brightly coloured fabric scarf of some sort hanging on the deep aubergine wall behind it. She wants to peer in and have a better look, but she's too scared of being caught. She looks back at Mary, who gives her a thumbs up. She checks the doorbell – there's no video attached of any kind, let alone a Ring, just a white buzzer on a small white plastic box. She takes a deep breath and presses it. It rasps like a rusty chainsaw.

She shifts from foot to foot while she waits.

And waits.

There's no one in. She feels brave enough to take a closer look through the front window, but there's nothing that she could obviously identify as Ant's. There's a low coffee table, dark wood, in front of the sofa. A big TV. Anonymous things that could belong to anyone. She looks over at Mary and shrugs. Makes her way back to the car.

'Let's try the next one. We can come back later if none of the others check out.'

They consult the list. The closest of the remaining three properties – as identified by Mary on the map she must have created last night – seems to be a flat. Home to one A. Simons. It's a five-minute drive, back towards the new development.

'I wonder how Saffy's getting on,' Joni says as they pass the same set of temporary traffic lights for the third time, seemingly trapped in a loop of diversions caused by the building work.

'He's going to love her. Oh look, here's the turning . . .' Mary swings the car round into a small side street, a cul-de-sac, with more of the same terraced houses on one side and a low-rise block of flats taking up most of the other. Nineteen seventies, Joni would guess. That era when they reclaimed bombsites left empty since World War Two with new housing, but with no regard to style or taste. Functional boxes. Places to exist in, not live.

'Maybe turn round before you park up so we can make a quick getaway,' Joni says. This street is making her nervous. It's unloved.

'Twelve to twenty-six,' Mary says, pointing. 'It must be in there. Flat fourteen. Do you want me to come with you? I could hide out of sight. Just in case.'

'No. Wait here with the engine running.' She knows she's overreacting, turning into her mum, who used to bristle with nervous tension when she passed a home-less person on the street, clutching her handbag close to her chest, despite happily boasting about her fundraising for a local shelter. She's judging a book by its cover.

Number 14 is on the first floor along an exterior walk-way. Joni picks her way through kids' bikes lying on their sides and drying washing. She knocks without hesitating, so keen is she to get away. She can hear noises inside, and the scrape of a chain being dragged into place. The door opens a couple of centimetres. If you were asked to draw a generic old lady this would be who you'd choose. Tiny, white-haired, kind-eyed, wearing a woolly cardigan even though it's in the high seventies today, wrinkled tights and fluffy pink slippers. She peers through the gap.

'Yes?'

'I'm so sorry to disturb you,' Joni says, feeling sud-denly ridiculous that she was expecting a Rottweiler and instead is faced with a miniature poodle. 'I'm looking for Anthony Simons.'

'I don't know who that is,' the woman says. She goes to shut the door.

'Um. It says an A. Simons lives here . . .' What says? Joni thinks. Luckily the other woman doesn't pick up on that.

'That's me. Amy. I don't know an Anthony, love.'

'OK. Thanks. Sorry . . .' Joni feels a wave of sadness. How awful to end up like this, afraid to open your door to strangers. She hopes this Amy has family or friends. People who check up on her regularly. Make sure she has milk and bread and pass the time of day with her now and again. She walks off quickly, keen to let Amy know that she's leaving and not about to try and force her way in to hunt for the family silver. She hears the door click behind her.

'Let's get out of here,' she says to Mary as she gets in the car.

'No good?'

'No good.' She tells Mary about Amy as they head for address number three.

'She probably has a couple of doting children and scores of grandchildren just up the road,' Mary says.

'Mmm. Or she doesn't see anyone from one week to the next and one day she'll be found dead on the floor when the postman smells something funny as he puts the letters through. Half-eaten by her cat.'

'You're a ray of sunshine this morning,' Mary says, but lightly, as if she's joking. 'Did you see if she even had a cat?'

'Sorry. It's just sad, isn't it? Ending up like that. Years

of being lonely.' She knows she's overreacting. Mary reaches out a hand and pats her knee.

'You have Imogen. I have my boys. We're lucky.'

Joni feels tears prick her eyes. What is wrong with her? But Mary considering herself lucky when she's lost the love of her life feels too much, too tragic. She wonders if she should tell Mary about Saffy's outburst, but it feels like a betrayal. She turns and gives her a smile. 'We are. Right . . . this one is the other definite Anthony . . .'

Number 3 on the list is another flat, also in a fairly modern purpose-built block, but this time with neat lawns out front, dotted with miniature acers. She approaches the entrance on the ground floor – a sign declares this as the door to flats 8 and 9 only. She can hear laughter coming from an open window, smell the unmistakable smell of a barbecue. She rings the bell and almost immediately a woman in her forties opens the door, still laughing. Joni can hear shrieking in the background. Raucous family life.

She goes through her script again: 'Hi, sorry to disturb you. I'm looking for Anthony Simons . . .'

'Oh,' the woman says. She has a smear of pink lipstick on her teeth. 'Tony!'

Joni jumps as she shouts. This wasn't what she expected. She's tempted to turn and run, but her rational self knows that this can't be her Anthony. Her Anthony – Mary's Anthony, Saffy's Anthony – is currently in Hyde Park about three miles away. She just needs to check this one off her list.

A lad in his twenties appears from nowhere. 'All right?'

'Are you Anthony?' Joni says, relieved.

The boy looks at her quizzically. 'Yeah.'

Her heart starts keeping normal time again. 'Sorry, the Anthony I'm looking for is in his fifties. He's not your dad, is he?'

'My dad's called Bob,' Anthony – Tony – says, still suspicious.

'OK. Thanks. I'll leave you to it. Sorry to bother you again.'

'I think it's that first one,' she says to Mary as she clicks in her seatbelt. 'Shall we go back?'

'What about number four?'

'It's out of the way, isn't it? Not really Battersea, strictly speaking. We can do it on the way home. There's something about that first one . . .'

'OK. What time is it?'

Joni checks her phone. 'Still only half eleven. Saffy's going to text me the second he leaves.' As if she's manifested it her phone beeps now. 'It's her.'

Having brunch in the Mandarin Oriental. Just ordered. I'll eat slowly. He's gone to the loo. He's fit, isn't he??? xxx.

Joni sends back a kiss in acknowledgement. She's nervous to actually write anything in case Saffy leaves her mobile on the table and Ant sees, even though they've all agreed to be extra cautious about that kind of thing. 'OK, we've got loads of time,' she says to Mary now as they pull away.

Back outside the Victorian terrace ten minutes later they park in the same spot. 'Something's different,' Mary says, peering at the house.

Joni looks, can't see anything. 'What?'

'The curtains upstairs are open a bit more open, look . . .'

'Who are you, Columbo?' Joni says incredulously. 'How did you notice that?'

'They are though, aren't they?'

'Maybe,' says Joni, who once didn't notice that Imo had dyed her hair red on a rainy afternoon when she was fifteen. It was only when Imo had pointed at her own head and said, 'See anything different?' in a slightly aggressive way that the penny had dropped.

'Someone's in. Or they have been.'

'Oh God. I need the loo now.'

'It's just nerves,' Mary says. 'Mind over matter.'

'Yeah, well, that's easy for you to say.'

Mary pats her on the arm. 'We'll find a café after. Or shall I go? I'll go . . .'

'No. I'm fine.' She remembers she brought a pair of glasses with plain frames that a twelve-year-old Imo once used for a school play. She was playing a doctor and her main character trait seemed to be 'wears glasses'. Otherwise she was just Imo saying the lines robotically. Joni has no idea why she still has them except that she hates to throw out anything that has a memory attached when it comes to her daughter. She puts them on.

She retraces her steps back to the front door, cap pulled down low. She can hear music coming from inside. Motown. The Four Tops singing 'Reach Out'. She takes in a slow breath through her nose and out through her mouth and rings the bell. Nothing happens. She rings again and the music stops abruptly. Joni suddenly understands what people mean when they say their heart is in their boots. Hers is somewhere around her knees and sinking fast. She feels light-headed.

The door opens. A woman with bobbed cherry-red hair, held back from her face with a red and white gingham scarf, looks at her. Joni would guess she's in her mid-forties, eyes set just a fraction too wide apart, straight nose, full lips. Striking rather than conventionally good-looking, but with a confidence that could convince you otherwise.

'Hi.' She smiles, showing an Invisalign aligner. 'Can I help you?'

Joni knows this is the right house. She can feel it. Behind the woman she can see a bike, an old sit-up-and-beg, as her dad used to call them, with a basket on the front. A vase of bright gerberas on a side table.

'I'm looking for someone called Anthony Simons. Is this the right address?'

A tiny frown flits across the woman's face. 'Um. He's not here at the moment . . . do I know you?'

'No. Are you his wife? I went to school with him in Bromley. Donkey's years ago obviously . . .' She sees the woman relax. She hopes she doesn't ask too many questions because beyond Ant having once mentioned the area where he went to school Joni is clueless.

'I am. I'm Deirdre.' Deirdre, not Camille. 'Do you want to come in?'

Joni would love to, to have a poke around, but she knows it would be a terrible idea. Apart from getting caught red-handed if Ant came home, she'd probably end up confessing everything she knows to this poor woman. Putting her out of the misery she doesn't know she's in.

'I'd better not. I have ten more addresses to check out this morning. I'm trying to organize a class reunion and you would not believe how hard it is to track some people down. At least I can cross Ant . . . Anthony – off my list.' Luckily Deirdre doesn't seem to notice her slip-up. Maybe people have been calling him Ant since he was at school but it's not worth taking the risk.

'That's a shame. He'll be back soon.'

'What does he do these days? I remember he was good at sport.'

Deirdre smiles at the image of her teenage husband. 'He works at a spa.' It's all the confirmation Joni needs. Belt and braces. 'Do you have kids? Sorry, that sounds nosy, but it's so interesting hearing what everyone has been up to.'

'No kids,' Deirdre says. 'From choice though, so . . .'

'OK, well, it's lovely to meet you. Maybe you'll come to the reunion? I'm going to send a letter round once I find everyone.' She notices for the first time that Deirdre has a wide paintbrush in her hand. A pale yellow colour at the tips. And that the retro boiler suit she's wearing that Joni thought was patterned is splattered with the same paint. 'It looks as though you're busy.'

Deirdre rolls her eyes around the hall. 'As you can see, it's in need of TLC. We've lived here for years but we've never really done anything to it. For some mad reason I decided now was the time.'

'Well, good luck. See you again, I hope.'

Deirdre smiles. 'Thanks for coming. What's your name, by the way?'

'Sharon,' Joni says. There must have been a Sharon in his year. 'Sharon Smith – well, I was then.'

Deirdre waves as Joni walks back to the car.

'That's him. And that's his wife. Deirdre.'

Mary raises an eyebrow.

'Exactly. She seems lovely.'

'Of course she does,' Mary says bitterly as they turn on to the main road. 'Of course he would have a lovely wife at home. Why screw over three women when you could screw over four?'

'And there are no children. No Amelia and Jack. God knows whose photos he's been showing us.'

'So now we know.'

Joni takes off the hat and glasses. Shakes out her hair with her fingers. Her mobile pings as they turn on to the Fulham Road. 'It's Saffy. He's just left.' She hits the number to phone her. Saffy answers immediately.

'I definitely would have if it wasn't for you-know-what . . .'

Joni laughs. 'You're incorrigible. Where are you? Shall we come and pick you up? We have news.' She looks at Mary for confirmation and Mary nods. 'OK. Wait there. We'll be about fifteen, twenty minutes, I think.'

'Albert Memorial,' she says to Mary once she's ended the call.

'So, what now?' Mary says.

'Now we know exactly what he has to lose . . .'

30

They find Saffy sitting on some steps opposite the Albert Hall, not looking out of place next to a gang of teenage skateboarders. She's dressed in a long, soft dusky orange skirt with sandals, a silver ankle bracelet with tiny bells on that tinkle when she moves, and a white vest top. Bracelets of beads snake up her skinny right arm. She looks like a child who's raided the dressing-up box and come as Stevie Nicks.

'So?' she says when Joni and Mary get close enough.

'Success. But you first. How did it go?' Joni sits down beside her and Mary the other side.

'The really shitty thing is that I liked him. I mean, not just fancied him, which I did, obviously, but I actually liked him. Absolutely no doubt in my mind that I would have been his next target. I mean, he comes across so genuine . . .'

'It's definitely his best skill,' Joni says. 'When are you seeing him again? I assume you are.'

'Wednesday. He has the kids on Mondays and Tuesdays in my world, remember . . .'

'Indeed. That's why I'm seeing him on Tuesday. Mary?'

'Not till Saturday. I got the "the children are staying the whole week with me" story again. I have a feeling I might get that more and more often now.'

'How do you think he squares all this with her?' Joni says, raking a hand through her hair. 'All the evenings out and nights away . . .'

Saffy does a double-take. 'With who?'

Joni raises an eyebrow. 'We found his wife. The real one.'

'Shit,' Saffy exhales. 'Stef used to work all hours. I hardly ever saw him. It never once crossed my mind that he was doing anything other than working. And he wasn't.'

Joni reaches over and squeezes her hand. 'There are no kids, by the way. We've had that confirmed.'

'*Quelle surprise.*'

Joni fills her in on Deirdre, with Mary interrupting every now and then. They're all a bit hyper, jabbering away like they're coming down from a high. It reminds Joni of being fourteen, euphoric with the excitement of nearly being caught shoplifting for the first time (to be fair, she only ever did it once. And then she'd felt guilty and reverse-shoplifted the Mac mascara right back into the shop the next day. That had actually been more nerve-racking than stealing it in the first place). The combination of fear and excitement making them hysterical.

'He's definitely not spending the money on the house,' Joni says. 'I mean, there's nothing wrong with it, I'm not saying that at all, but it didn't exactly look as if it was stuffed to the gills with high-end goods.'

'Because how would he explain them to Deirdre?' Saffy rubs a spot off one of her blue-painted toenails.

'He must have it stashed away somewhere. Maybe he's planning on dumping her when he's saved up enough.'

'Do you think she knows about the car?' Mary looks between the two of them.

'Maybe. If he tells her he's leased it,' Joni says. 'Or perhaps he's sold it already. That would be my guess.'

Saffy leans back on her elbows, face up to the sun. 'You should ask him to drive you somewhere, Mary. See what he does.'

'I don't think I'll be getting any more favours. Not now I've asked him for the money back. My guess is he'll start to back away gradually. Focus on Joni and then you.'

A pair of police officers on horses clop slowly by. Joni smiles as she remembers Imo following one such duo in St James's Park when she was little – she had a tendency to follow any animal she saw, arms outstretched as if to catch them – and an avuncular-looking policeman lifting her up to sit in front of him. She has a photo some-where, probably on an old phone or downloaded to a now defunct computer in the days before the cloud. Imo holding the reins as if she were the one in charge.

'I think I get the couple of weeks of dinners at res-taurants first, don't I? To soften me up for the kill. I'm looking forward to that bit. I'm going to order caviar – even though it's disgusting – just to see the look on his face. And white truffles on everything. See him trying to work out how much he'll have to fleece me for to make it worth his while.'

'Should we just tell her? Deirdre?' Mary says, a smile

on her face as one of the skateboarding kids successfully completes a flip.

'God, no,' Saffy says before Joni can answer. 'She's his wife. It's not like Joni telling one of us who'd only just met him. Or not even, in my case.'

Joni nods. 'I agree. We need proof. Actually, Mary, maybe you should send him a text about paying back the money. Get a reply in writing that at least acknowledges he owes it to you. That might help somewhere down the line.'

'Will do,' Mary says. 'Shall I do it now while we're all together? You can help me compose it.'

'Good idea. How about: *Give me my fucking money back, you absolute wanker?*'

'Nice,' Joni says. 'Maybe not so subtle.'

Mary snorts. She has a quiet laugh, nothing like Saffy's raucous cackle, but every now and then something catches her and she honks like a goose and then looks surprised that it's happened. Like a baby sneezing for the first time.

'Something like: *I wonder if you've had a chance to think about repaying me . . .*' Mary types obediently. 'Finesse it though. Make it sound like you.'

She and Saffy watch as Mary writes and rewrites several times. 'No rush,' Saffy says, raising her eyebrows at Joni, when Mary deletes the whole thing for the fourth time. 'It's not as if either me or Joni have a life to get back to any time soon.'

'Speak for yourself.'

'All right, how about this,' Mary says. '*How are you this*

morning? I was wondering if you'd had a moment to think about paying me back the money I lent you for the car . . . I thought I should be specific so that he can't argue later that I was talking about a fiver I lent him for a sandwich.'

'Good idea.' Joni shuffles along the step a bit to get out of the sun.

'*. . . I really do hate to ask you. I know I said there was no rush, but my circumstances have changed and it's become quite urgent. I hope you're having a lovely time with Amelia and Jack. Talk soon.*'

'Perfect,' Saffy says, 'although I think my version was more pithy.'

Mary's finger hovers over the send button. 'Shall I?'

Joni looks at Saffy just in case she has any more to say. She takes her silence as agreement. 'Do it.'

Mary stabs the key and they all stare at the phone for a moment, as if they think a reply might pop up immediately.

'Do you think he has two phones? I mean, he's not getting messages from us on a mobile Deirdre might see, is he? Jesus! Fuck!' Saffy leaps off the step and flaps her arms at a wasp. 'Bastard. What did I ever do to you?'

'Probably,' Joni notices Mary and Saffy both looking at her. 'What? No.'

'Just a quick look through his bag,' Saffy says. 'You said he sleeps like he's in a coma; he won't catch you. Who knows what else you might find out?'

'I'll try. Maybe.' She stretches. 'I'm going to have to go. I need to get to the gym.' She realizes she's reluctant to move. Tempted to skip her work out and stay here lolling about in the park. But she knows she'll be angry with herself later if she does.

'Those arms won't build themselves,' Saffy says. She turns to Mary. 'Do you want to have lunch? I mean, I know I've only just had brunch, but I didn't eat much.'

'That would be lovely,' Mary says with a smile. Joni feels a sudden unexpected pang, a wish that she could join them, spend the afternoon sharing stories and relaxing.

She gives them both a quick hug. 'Let me know as soon as he replies. Don't let Saffy talk you into telling him to fuck off. Not yet.' She watches as they walk off together, feeling a weird kind of pride, like she did when Imo made her first schoolfriend. Then she heads for the road to flag down a taxi.

Forty minutes later, as she's making a cup of fennel tea before she goes out again, Mary sends her a text. *He's replied!!! Now what? x.* There's a screengrab attached showing a message from Ant. Joni stares at the screen.

I need to talk to you, it says. *Can we meet this evening? It can't wait. X.*

31

Mary had thought that meeting in a restaurant instead of at her house would make the evening less intense – she had told Ant that her eldest son, George, and his wife were staying for a few days (Joni's suggestion. Saffy had gone with 'tell him you think he's being a cheapskate and you don't want his two-for-one-in-Asda tortellini') and that while she wanted them all to meet now was not the time because her daughter-in-law's father had just died and she was taking it very badly. It wasn't a lie that came easily out of her mouth – it was too close to home – but it felt like something he couldn't argue with. Now, though, she's wishing they were somewhere more private. She has no idea what to say.

She pushes the thought from her mind that George and Millie his wife have actually not been to stay since Andrew died. Except for the week of the funeral. They've been to London a handful of times, but Millie prefers to stay in a hotel. 'She doesn't want to be in the way,' George had said the first time and then, even though Mary didn't believe the excuse for a moment, it was just accepted that that was the way things were. She's seen them – they've met at restaurants or (once) for dinner at hers – but it's not the same. Millie is always friendly, but distant, staking her superior claim to George with a seemingly permanent hand resting on his arm.

Mary knows George loves her. He phones her all the time, at least twice a week. But he has his own life now. She'd always hoped that her sons would marry people she could dote on. New members of her ever-expanding family. But, so far, it hasn't worked out like that. She understands. Millie's parents live in Truro, not far from where they've settled. Girls need their mums more than boys.

She sees Oliver even less often, except on FaceTime. When his father had died he'd given up the sensible job he hated – 'We only get one chance, Mum,' he'd said – and gone travelling. When the pandemic hit he'd been in Australia and, rather than try to scramble his way back, he'd opted to ride it out there in a bubble of new friends he'd made. He's currently working his way round the country earning money by doing odd jobs for cash. He seems happy but Mary lives in fear that he might decide to settle down over there. Never come back.

Ant had insisted on champagne when they arrived and maybe Mary should have guessed then. Usually she ordered a Prosecco because, really, who could tell the difference? He was in an ebullient mood, telling her she looked beautiful, taking her coat and holding her hand. She had assumed he was buttering her up to tell her there was no way he could repay her the money he had borrowed. But this . . . This was much more alarming.

'Mary Elizabeth Theobald,' he says, looking into her eyes intently.

'Ant, stop . . .' she says quietly. Is he going to propose? Surely not. She tries to look away, but he pulls her hand towards him across the table.

'I've been thinking about it all day,' he says. He still hasn't mentioned her text reminding him she needed to be paid back. 'I want us to take the next step. Start setting up a life together. Move in together.' Not marriage, at least, she thinks. She wonders how she would have felt about his suggestion a few weeks ago, back when she genuinely thought their love was blossoming. Would she have seen it as the start of a new happy life? Quite probably. Would she have agreed just in case he never asked again or was offended by her refusal? Quite possibly. For a moment she's angry. Does he really think she's this stupid? Desperate? That she'll be so grateful she won't even question how he's reached this point so soon?

She thinks about Deirdre. Will he just walk out on her? On their life? And then she thinks: Why is he doing this? What's in it for him?

An image of Andrew pops into her head. Thirty-three years ago. Just the two of them, halfway up a mountain in the Scottish Highlands, the wind whipping their hair and turning their noses red. 'We should move in together,' he'd said. She'd looked at him and the way he was staring at her had made her heart flip. She hadn't even hesitated. 'We should. Would you like to?' 'Yes, please,' he'd said, taking her hand.

'I know it hasn't been long, but I love you,' Ant says now. A woman at the next table, who's been listening in, clutches her heart. 'It makes no sense that you're rattling around in that too-big house and I'm miserable in my rented flat. Let's set up home together.'

He sits back and looks at her. What is he expecting? she wonders Tears of gratitude? 'I don't know . . .'

'You can sell your house and we'll buy somewhere together. Fresh start. And you can use some of the money for your son. Maybe the bank would advance it to you if they knew you'd put your house on the market. You know I feel awful that I can't pay you back yet.'

Ah. We're getting to the heart of the matter, she thinks. 'I thought you had to wait to sort things out with Camille before you can buy anywhere,' she says, trying not to sound accusatory.

'This way we won't have to wait. We can buy somewhere with the proceeds from your place and then when my house sells I'll transfer my share of the money over to you. Or we just set up a joint account and pool everything in there.' She notices how he keeps saying 'we'. How she's missed that word. How she's longed to be part of an 'us' again. A team.

At what point would he ever even admit that he actually has nothing to add to their cosy nest egg? Maybe he'd hide it from her forever, carry on heading out every morning in a suit and claiming to have millions tied up in investment schemes. Pretending to be working evenings and weekends while actually spending the time with his wife in his own house. At least until he'd cleaned her bank accounts out completely, she assumes. Maybe sold the house they'd bought in joint names and taken his half. Of course, she realizes. That's the point. He has no intention of actually moving in with her; he just wants to persuade her into buying a home in both their names, effectively gifting him a few million. The really scary thing is that none of this would ever have occurred to her if it weren't for Joni and Saffy. She would have walked blindfolded – deliriously happy even – towards her own downfall.

She realizes that he's finished speaking. That he's waiting for a response. She would give anything to have either Joni or Saffy in her ear right now, telling her what she should do. Obviously buying a house for the two of them is not – will never be – an option, but how should she play it? She tries to think what they might say to her. Closes her eyes briefly, hoping it will look like she's overcome with emotion, picturing their faces.

And then she knows. There's only one thing she can do.

'Yes,' she says breathlessly, channelling all the acting skills she hopes she has buried in her somewhere, although the last role she ever played – Bottom in *A Midsummer Night's Dream*, as an eleven-year-old in her school production – is probably not helping much. 'I think that's a lovely idea. Let's do it.'

He leans forward and squeezes her fingers. 'It's the right decision,' he says. 'You've made me so happy.'

She can't wait to get out of there and phone the others.

32

Joni is out for an early-morning walk when Mary calls, halfway across Regent's Park at a pace that's only just short of running. She's grateful for the excuse to stop, to catch her breath.

'Are you up?' Mary says. 'Did I wake you? I tried you last night but you must have been in bed already.'

'I'm in the park. How was it?'

'You won't believe it. I can scarcely believe it myself.'

Joni walks to the nearest bench as Mary fills her in. 'I can't . . . I don't know where to start,' she says once she grasps what Mary is telling her. 'What about the kids? How's he going to explain away the fact that you can never meet them because they don't exist?'

'I know. I did the right thing though, didn't I? Accepting? I've been fretting about it all night.'

'Definitely. If he thinks he's getting somewhere he'll be on the back foot.'

'I'm actually shocked at just how naïve he thinks I am. No, not shocked. I'm angry. He thinks I'm so besotted that I won't even question the fact that his solution for him paying me back is for me to sell my own house.'

Joni's phone beeps. 'That's Saffy trying to ring me. Did you tell her yet?'

'Yes. I can't repeat anything she said. Answer her – I'll talk to you later.'

'OK. Take care.' She presses the green button to take Saffy's call and holds the phone away from her ear in anticipation.

'Absolute fucking fucker!' Saffy shouts, and Joni thinks she couldn't have put it better herself.

Flick taps on her door thirty seconds after she gets in. Joni is so distracted she opens it without thinking who it might be.

'How is she?' Flick has a look of concern on her face. For a moment Joni thinks she means Mary although her brain can't make the leap as to how she'd know what happened. Her confusion must show on her face because Flick follows up with: 'Your mum. Isn't she poorly?'

Joni almost laughs. Imagines calling Imo later and telling her. 'Oh. No. She's fine. What made you think that?'

'I just . . . I thought you said . . . Oh, well, that's good. Have you got time to come up for a cuppa?'

'I've just got in, Flick. I have loads to do, sorry. It'll have to be another time.'

Flick nods frantically. Her earrings jangle with the ferocity of wind chimes in a gale. 'Of course. Are you well? You look well.'

'I am . . . You?' Joni adds as an afterthought.

'Yes. Good. Well, apart from my knees, which are playing up something rotten—'

'Sorry to hear that,' Joni cuts her off. 'I should . . .' She points vaguely into the flat.

'Oh yes. I'll leave you to it . . .' Flick starts to back away. 'See you soon . . .'

'See you,' Joni says, shutting the door with a bigger bang than she intended.

On Monday she does all the chores she's somehow neglected all weekend. She strips the bed and irons sheets. Does two loads of washing. Cleans the bathroom and vacuums the living room. Irritation bristles off her that she's let things pile up, strayed from her schedule. Jasper spends most of the day hiding under the coffee table as if he can sense her mood. She gets to the gym late – at ten past four – and for some reason it's this that tips her over the edge. She bursts into tears in the basic changing room. No fancy products here, just a pile of towels and two hairdryers. White tiles on the floor and wooden slatted benches. Amenities for people who are so hardy they don't need cotton buds and body lotion. She has no idea why she's so angry except that it feels as if her life is slipping out of her control.

'Are you OK?' Joni looks up and a young woman is looking at her, concern etched on her face.

'Menopause,' she says, which, to be fair, is probably at least partially true. Things have been going a bit haywire lately. She's been trying to ignore it.

The young woman can't disguise the flicker of revulsion that crosses her face. Her inevitable future is standing in front of her and it's ugly. She backs away, muttering, 'So long as you're all right . . .' half under her breath. Joni gives her a weak smile. Flushes with embarrassment.

She didn't think she cared about being on her own. She had been glad to see the back of her marriage. But it still felt like failure. She hadn't realized she had put so much hope into her new relationship. That discovering Ant was deceiving her would hurt so much. It isn't just the shame at being taken in, however much she tries to make herself believe that it is. That is there, there's no doubt about it. But she had been starting to see a time when she might begin to fully open up again. To trust. It hurts like hell that that's gone. She thinks about his latest play, realizes with a jolt of surprise that she actually feels worse for Mary than herself. Ant is like a shark smelling blood, circling around, waiting to strike the fatal blow. He's a user, a fake, a merciless predator.

She wipes her eyes, takes a few deep breaths and heads out through the main gym to the little room at the side where the big bags hang. She pulls on a pair of gloves that are almost worn through with other people's sweat and pounding. They're gross but she doesn't care. She hurls herself at the bag and punches till it hurts her knuckles and she's struggling for breath. On her way home Saffy sends her a text. A photo of Tyson, tongue lolling out, the little tuft of hair on his head styled into a quiff: *He says hello!* Joni smiles for the first time all day.

On Tuesday she finds the ceramic kitten on top of what looks like a makeshift bonfire made of pencils and with orange paper flames dancing round it. Jar Jar and friends watch in awe. Joni has no patience for it. She sweeps the figures into the drawer and gets on with her work. She leaves them there when she goes home. She can't be bothered.

Ant is on a charm offensive when he turns up at seven. He's brought flowers. Brightly coloured gerberas just like the ones in his own hallway. Maybe they're the same ones, she thinks. He's saved himself £6.50. Of course, he's making an effort, he needs Joni to come through before – so he thinks – he half moves in with Mary and it all gets a bit more complicated for a while. She feigns delight. Overacts in an attempt to appear normal. She watches him prepare a curry from scratch as though she's got a front-row seat at a sell-out show. Fascinated. Captivated. Smitten. Inside she's a roiling mess of loathing. Fuck him. Fuck his cooking and his jokes and his compliments. Fuck his cruelty and his lack of a conscience.

They eat in the garden again. Joni made a list earlier of things they could talk about, so afraid was she that her real feelings would render her mute. So she regales him with anecdotes, mostly made up. She's the life and soul of the party. She can't wait for the evening to be over.

'I was thinking about the car,' she says when they sit down at the table. Ant has warmed a couple of delicious-looking naan breads and placed them next to a dish of raita.

He clears his throat slightly, trying, Joni thinks, to cover his eagerness to know her answer. 'Oh?'

"I want to help you. Of course I do. I just have to put the money on a month's notice with the bank because it's on a fixed savings thing . . .'

She sees him gulp.

'Is that going to be a problem?'

'No,' he says with indecent haste. He clearly can't believe his luck. 'Thank you, Lucy. That's incredible. I'll pay you back as soon as we sell the house. Sooner if I can, if Camille comes to her senses.'

As ever, she starts when he uses her sister's name. She'll never get used to it. It's a reminder that her relationship with Ant could never have really worked, even if he'd been genuine. It was always built on sand.

'That's OK. I'm just sorry I can't access it more quickly.'

He reaches over and takes her hand. 'You're incredible, do you know that?'

'I have my moments,' she says, glad she can let out a laugh that's been threatening to engulf her. She wishes she could have captured the moment on film to show the others. How happy he is that his plan has worked for a second time, a child opening his presents on Christmas morning. He just made fifty thousand pounds tax free. Well, maybe forty if he actually goes through with buying the car and then selling it off quickly. But either way it's a pretty good night's work.

Later she texts Saffy and Mary from the bathroom: *I wish you could have seen his face!*

Saffy answers first, before Joni has time to turn the phone off. Joni knows she's having a night out at the Ivy with her girlfriends. She can picture her there with Bec and Jude and Caro, sipping champagne and all talking at once. She imagines they're clones of Saffy. Twig-limbed, tanned and fabulous. *Just don't actually give it to him by mistake! Xx.*

Mary is hot on her heels: *Well done you. Xx.*

Once Ant is safely asleep – happily having passed out while she was still brushing her teeth thanks to the two more glasses than usual that he drank, presumably in celebration – she combs through his bag methodically, looking for hidden pockets concealing phone-shaped lumps. Nothing. If he has a second mobile then he doesn't have it with him tonight. Maybe all he does is tell Deirdre he's going to be out of contact, and she just accepts that. Otherwise wouldn't she be filling up his WhatsApp with messages he couldn't ignore, expecting him to call her back? Or, even worse, phoning him while he's in the middle of God knows what? Where does she even think he is three or four nights a week anyway? It's not as if he has a job that requires him to travel. Joni thinks about her when she's back in bed, lying beside his sleeping form. What's she doing now? Lying awake won-dering what her other half is up to? Or innocently dreaming, trusting his every word? She looks at him, lying on his back, snoring gently. Someone else's husband.

Somehow she has got herself roped into helping Saffy get ready for her date, even though she had tried to pro-test that she would be at the gym and therefore never make it in time.

'Go to the gym earlier,' Saffy had said when she called. Joni was emptying one of her kitchen cupboards in an effort to declutter. She was surrounded by a pile of detritus on the floor, seemingly unable to decide what

255

she should keep and what she should throw away. 'What else are you doing?'

'That's not the point. I go at four . . .'

'Why, though? It's not as if you have to book a slot.'

Joni huffs. 'I just do . . . Fine. I'll go at half three. I'll be sweaty. Just to warn you.'

'Eew. Don't you have a shower?'

She starts to shove the Tupperware back into the cabinet it came from, having lost the will to sort through it. 'No. I always wait till I get home. Their showers are grim.'

'OK, well, this is an emergency, I suppose . . .'

'I have to go, Imo's trying to get through. See you about half five.' Joni cuts the call short, not because Imo is calling – she's not – but because she wants some time to herself. She hates having her routine disrupted. It's what holds her together.

Her workout feels like a chore. She's still irritated that she had to come early. That she has somewhere to go afterwards. She can't lose herself in it as she usually does. But on her way up to Highgate she starts to look forward to seeing Saffy. To spending an hour talking nonsense and laughing. And without the usual Saffy-associated danger of most of a bottle of wine. She's meeting Ant at Scott's at quarter past seven. She's already researched the price of the most expensive items and, she told Joni, she plans to order them all. Beluga, Bannockburn steak, Dover sole, Dom Pérignon.

She answers the door with a towel wrapped round her

tiny frame and blobs of muddy brown contour cream all over her face.

'Have you been sunbathing?' Joni allows herself to be hugged.

'Thank God you're here. You have to help me decide what to wear. Come in. Have a glass of something. I'm on the Gavi . . .' Joni follows the babbling brook to the kitchen, relieved that she's not expected to add to the conversation. Saffy pours her a large glass. 'OK. Come upstairs. How are you? How was the gym? God, your figure is amazing. If I wear Lycra I look like a stick drawing. I've got no arse. Absolutely none. I don't know how I'm able to sit down for more than five minutes. Am I talking too much? I'm nervous. Fuck knows why.'

'Maybe remember to leave a pause for him to say something every now and then,' Joni says, laughing. 'Just stop every twentieth word or so.'

Saffy sucks in an exaggerated breath, blows it out slowly. 'I think I'm scared I'm going to say the wrong thing. Give us all away.'

'You won't. Don't drink too much.'

'You're right.' She puts her glass down on a small table on the landing and leaves it there. Joni does the same, feeling she should lead by example. She follows Saffy through into a huge, light bedroom with one dramatic deep pink wallpapered wall behind the bed. Tyson lounges on his back on the white duvet like a tiny Hugh Hefner. They walk through another door and into a wardrobe-lined dressing room, with a large banquette in the middle piled high with clothes. It looks like the world's poshest jumble sale.

'Shall I have a look through?' Joni asks, not quite sure where to start. 'You keep on doing your make-up.' Saffy sits in front of a lightbulb-surrounded mirror and scrabbles through an oversized silver make-up box, coming out with a small sponge and starting to blend the cream into her face furiously.

'How should I play it? I mean, usually I'd go into flirt overdrive but should I? I don't know.'

'Definitely,' Joni says, rummaging. 'That way he won't suspect anything. And drop hints about how much money you have. But subtly. How about this? This is gorgeous.' She holds up a silky halter neck dress with a swishy skirt in a black fabric with vibrant purple and blue exotic flowers. The whole thing is barely more than a metre of fabric and probably cost four figures.

'See, this is why I knew I needed you. I thought about this one but I talked myself out of it. Pick out something else and then I'll try them both on and you can choose.'

Joni carries on sorting through the pile. 'It should be a dress, I think.' She decides to push her luck. They're easy with one another now. She can't imagine Saffy getting offended by anything she says. 'You know when you stayed at mine the other day? Do you remember the conversation we had about your husband?'

'I don't want to talk about him,' Saffy says, shutting it down. 'Shall I put some music on?'

'Sure. I know. I just . . . if you ever do. You know.'

Saffy jabs at her phone and Chrissie Hynde starts singing 'Back on the Chain Gang'. 'Yep. Thanks. Did you find another dress?'

Joni knows when she's defeated. 'This one?' It's short and off-white with cap sleeves and a teardrop hole in the front. Simple. Beautiful.

'Oh yes, I love that one,' Saffy says with forced jollity. Joni feels bad that she's ruined her mood. 'Let me try them both on.' She drops her towel with no apparent self-consciousness and pulls the halter neck over her head. Joni doesn't know where to look.

They decide on the white in the end, even though Saffy has a panic that she looks as if she's expecting to play a set of tennis. She straps on a pair of Louboutin sandals.

'You look incredible,' Joni says. 'He should be so lucky.' She calls an Uber while Saffy finishes her make-up.

'I can drop you off,' Saffy says, spraying herself with Jo Malone Frangipani Flower perfume. 'We'll practically go past your door.'

On the way back through the bedroom she picks up Tyson and shoves him into her bag. Joni double-takes. 'You're not taking him? To Scott's?'

Saffy shrugs. 'He loves fish. No one will even know he's there.

Fat drops of rain hit the windscreen as they pull up outside Joni's house, and there's a deafening crack of thunder. She wants to say 'Call me when you're on your way home,' feeling suddenly protective, but she settles for 'Ring me tomorrow.'

33

Walk. Tube. Walk. Office. She puts her lunch in the fridge and makes herself a coffee. Plods along the corridor fighting off that sinking feeling that she has two days' work in a row. She really should resign. She doesn't know why she still does this. As ever, as soon as she thinks that, she feels guilty. Spoilt. Millions of people do jobs they don't enjoy and they don't have the luxury of doing them part-time. But the truth is she doesn't need the money. She took the job because she needed to have something in her diary, but now she's starting to feel as if she barely has a moment to herself.

She surprises herself by feeling a little pang of disappointment that there is no sign of any of the figurines. Not even Lucas's collection. He must have taken her lack of a response on Tuesday as a snub. There isn't even a token piece of unfinished work left for her to do. She sits at her desk, fires up her computer. Sighs.

Another day to get through.

She wonders what time Saffy will be up. Sends her a text that says *Call me as soon as you're awake!!*

Twenty minutes later, just as she's starting to worry, her phone rings.

'Jesus Christ, what a fucking night!'

'What?' Joni's heart stops. She stands up and shuts her door. 'Tell me.'

'I only left my bag in the sodding restaurant, didn't I . . .' She waits for the penny to drop. Joni gasps.

'Tyson?'

'Exactly. One of the waiters called me just as I was getting out of my Uber and said he'd found it and he'd put it in lost property so I could collect it today. Thank God he called then because I couldn't have got in the house without my keys. Anyway, so, I got straight back in the car and headed back down there. He said they were closing up but I told him he had to wait for me and then I asked him if he'd gone through my bag and he said yes, to see if he could find my name and number, which, luckily, was on my key ring because I'm always losing the bastard things, and I said, "Didn't you find a dog?" and, anyway, you can imagine . . . by the time I got there two of them were on their hands and knees trying to find him. I had to give them fifty quid each as a thank you.'

'And is he OK?'

'Best night ever. We found him under a table eating a fishcake. Luckily neither of them was the manager, and they thought the whole thing was hilarious, especially when I tipped them so well. And the Uber driver was well chuffed with how much he must have earned so it all turned out fine.'

By the time she finishes, Joni's stomach aches from laughing. 'And what about Ant?'

'You know what?' Saffy says, suddenly serious. 'If

things had been different then I probably would have ended up inviting him back. But . . . actually, all I could see when I looked at him was this big pile of bullshit. I laid it on thick though: you'd have been proud. He wanted to see me again on Saturday, which is . . .'

'. . . the night he's supposed to be seeing Mary . . .'

'Exactly. So Mary's a done deal as far as he's concerned, I think. He doesn't need to put the effort in any more. Not now she's said yes to buying a house.'

'So, are you? Seeing him on Saturday?'

'I didn't think I could pull it off again so quickly, so I claimed I had a friend staying. We've agreed next Wednesday for dinner. Thankfully not Scott's again. I don't think I can ever go back there.'

'I'll babysit Tyson,' Joni says and then regrets it immediately. 'Or maybe Mary can. He likes her.'

Imo is coming home for the weekend. That is, her slightly delayed weekend, which starts on a Saturday afternoon and ends on a Tuesday morning. 'I'll be knackered,' she says to Joni when she calls to tell her. 'I'm always knackered after the show on Saturday. So I might just sleep through the whole thing.'

'I don't care,' Joni says. 'I'll watch you sleep. It'll make me happy.'

'Weirdo,' Imo says lightly. 'I can't wait to see you.'

'Does Dad know?' Joni wants her daughter all to herself, but she knows she has to at least display a pretence of fairness.

'I won't have time to see him this visit. Next time.'

'There might be a baby next time.'

'I know. Weird, right?'

On Friday evening Joni rips the head off Jon Snow and attaches it to a piece of cotton she pulls from the hem of her top. She sellotapes it to the kitten's raised paw, puts the kitten on a little wooden box she has for paper clips, and raises the arms of all those others who have moving parts, standing them round the sacrifice in a semi-circle. She hopes she hasn't damaged Jon for life, but she decides it's worth the risk. She prints out a list of rates payments and sticks a Post-it to the paper. 'Couldn't be bothered to check these' she writes, hoping her boss doesn't stop by for an impromptu visit. She leaves in a buoyant mood, feeling better than she has in weeks.

On Saturday morning she scrubs the flat until it gleams. She scours the garden for flowers to put in a little glass vase in the kitchen, but everything is dying. Autumn is here. So she adds them to her massive shopping list and makes her way down to Waitrose. She finds herself picking out things Imo used to love when she was ten, or thirteen, or fifteen, but has probably never eaten since. Things she used to find at friends' houses and come home asking why they couldn't have them at home. Potato waffles and Mr Kipling cakes. Cheese strings and mini pizzas. Once her trolley is almost overflowing Joni makes herself go round and put half of it back. She'll stick to her list. She piles the shopping into a taxi and heads home.

Flick is coming down the front steps.

'I should have told them Saturday would be too busy,'

she says grumpily and Joni is in such a good mood that she gives her a big smile and says:

'How are you, Flick?'

'Oh. Not too bad, actually,' Flick says, and Joni feels bad that she seems surprised to be asked. 'And you?'

'Good. I'm good.' She doesn't want to say that Imogen is coming home, even though Flick is bound to spot her; it feels insensitive given that Flick barely has any contact with her own children. She doesn't want to rub it in. Flick picks up three bulging carrier bags in each hand and carries them up to the hallway.

'Thanks,' Joni says.

'I can't stay and chat,' Flick says as if Joni is the one who always tries to engage her in conversation and not the other way round. 'I'm late.' She waves goodbye as she stomps off down the street.

Imo's train is due in just after five and Joni finds herself watching the kitchen clock nervously just like she used to when she was a teenager and a date was coming to pick her up. Jumping every time she hears a noise. It was all she could do to stop herself going down to the station and waiting on the platform. When the key turns in the lock she's at the front door in milliseconds, swamping Imo in a hug.

'Jesus, Mum!' Imo dumps her bag on the floor and hugs her back.

'Indulge me. I'm a sad old woman with only a cat for company.' Imo rewards her with a laugh. 'Right. Tea, coffee or a glass of wine given it's nearly six?'

'Wine definitely. I had three coffees on the train.'

'I'm going to spoil you rotten, you know that? And you have to let me. It's the law.'

'Go for it,' Imo says, flopping on to a kitchen chair. 'You look well.'

'Do I?' Joni has already decided she's not going to tell Imo everything. It's too big a burden to place on her daughter and, if she's being honest with herself, she's looking forward to a couple of days not thinking about Ant. 'So do you.'

'I am. I'm loving it.'

Joni squeezes her hand. 'I'm so thrilled for you. When do you want to eat?'

'Now. I'm starving. Shall I help?'

'We just need to make a salad. Everything else is done. Tell me everything. Are you still getting on with your flatmates?' She knows the answer, she talks to Imo every couple of days after all, but she wants to hear it again, to pore over every detail. There's nothing better than knowing your child is happy. Hopefully it'll last forever but, just in case, she wants to savour every word.

Sunday is a perfect day. They sleep in late, having sat up till one in the morning chatting. Joni takes a cup of tea in to Imo at about a quarter to ten, and finds Jasper curled up in the crook of her knees like he used to every night before she left home. They walk down through Regent's Park to Marylebone High Street where they have brunch sitting outside Le Pain Quotidien, potter round the shops for a while – Joni insists on buying Imo a top she admires in Anthropologie – and end up at the Wallace Collection. Joni doesn't even fret that she's missing the gym two sessions in a row. With her daughter safe at home she feels relaxed, open to anything. For the first time in weeks she falls asleep as soon as her head hits the pillow.

'Did you know their house is up for sale?' Saffy is on the phone.

For a moment Joni doesn't know where she is and then she realizes that she's on the sofa, a knitted cushion pressed into the side of her face. Imo left after lunch and Joni, feeling as if all the lights had been turned out, must have sat down for a few minutes and drifted off. Last night they'd holed up with takeaway pizzas and *Rear Window*. It had been bliss.

'Who?' she says groggily.

'Ant and Deirdre. I was googling the address just to see if I could find out anything else and it came up. New listing. Did she mention anything about that?'

Joni sits up. Tries to clear her head. 'No. She just said the decorating was long overdue. How odd.'

'There are photos and everything. It's not as if it can have been a last-minute decision. When are you seeing him again?'

'Tuesday night,' Joni says, thinking about how much she's dreading it.

'OK. I'm going to make an appointment to go and see it. What do you think? Half six?'

'Oh God, really?' She tries to think of an objection,

but she actually can't. It's a good idea. 'I'm meeting him at Murano at seven, so even if for some reason he's not at work he would have to have left home by then.'

'He's buying dinner again? No home cooking?'

'He wants to keep me sweet till I give him the money, I assume. Bit more investment won't hurt. Wear the blonde wig, won't you? Just in case she describes you to him when he gets home.'

'God, can you imagine the state of their marriage if that's what passes for pillow talk?'

'Me and Ian got ours down to "Did you double lock the door? Yes. Night" by the end. It was pretty spectacular.'

There's a silence and Joni wonders if she's put her foot in it, reminding Saffy that her own marriage never stagnated, she had just detonated a bomb under it.

'Is he staying over? Can I talk to you once I've been? On Tuesday?' Saffy says after a moment.

'No. I told him Imo was staying a few more days. I couldn't face it.'

'Fab. Ring me when you're on your own.'

Joni phones as soon as she gets into a taxi. The evening had been weirdly OK, aided by fabulous food and the knowledge that they weren't going to have to spend any time alone together. Not caring about impressing him took the pressure off and it was actually easier to find things to talk about. Obviously, most of it was lies in one way or another but she didn't care so long as it passed the time. Her mind was really with Saffy, though.

She couldn't wait to get the meal over with and get out of there.

'Well?' she says now. 'How was it?'

'Oh my God,' Saffy says breathlessly. 'I mean, oh my fucking God. Are you on your way home? I'm coming over. I'm at Mary's. Actually, even better you come over here. Where are you now?'

'Still in Mayfair. Hold on, no. Tell me what happened.'

'You'll be passing here in fifteen minutes. Is that OK, Mary?' There's a pause. 'Mary says yes.'

'Fuckssake. It's half ten already.'

'Are you working tomorrow? No, you are not. What have you got to get up for?'

'The supermarket.'

'The Morrisons in Chalk Farm is open till ten at night. No excuses.'

'Oh God, Saffy, I'm knackered.'

'Come and have a drink. We can share an Uber home. It'll be fun.'

Joni sighs. She's too tired to argue. But Saffy's right. Will the world fall apart if she goes to Waitrose at midday rather than nine? Or at eight at night? Or to Morrisons instead? 'OK. Only because I'm dying to hear about tonight. It had better be good.'

She leans forward and tells the driver there's been a change of plan.

34

Saffy opens Mary's door as if she owns the place, big glass of deep red wine in hand.

Joni drops her bag in the hall. 'Have you been here all evening?'

'Since I left Battersea. We're in the living room.' Joni follows her through to a vast airy room painted pale sage green, with large glass doors on to the garden. Mary is sitting in a huge cream armchair looking slightly shinier-faced than Joni has ever seen her. Tyson is upside down on her lap, gazing at her adoringly. When she doesn't stand up Joni leans down and gives her a hug. 'Are you OK?'

'Never leave Saffy in charge of refilling the wine glasses,' she says, slurring slightly.

'Do you want me to make you a coffee?' Joni says, giving Saffy a look. Saffy shrugs.

'No,' Mary says. 'It's ages since I got properly drunk. I'm enjoying it. Just don't let me call Ant and tell him what I think of him.'

'Actually, give me your phone,' Joni says, hand out. Mary passes it over obediently.

'Here.' Saffy hands her a drink. 'Mary has heard it all already but she's up for hearing it again. So . . .'

Joni sits at one end of the pale sofa. Saffy settles, legs curled under her, at the other.

'. . . I met the agent outside at half six. It's a bit of a shithole, isn't it? I mean, not to be a snob, but . . . actually, fuck it, I am being a snob. That's one of my worst qualities. I take that back. It's a bit run-down. Anyway, I told her I was buying it for my son as an investment. The first thing I asked her was if she knew why they were moving, and guess what she said . . .'

'I can't. Tell me.'

'She said as far as she knows they're leaving London. That the husband has a new job down in the West Country and the wife is a hairdresser locally, but she can work anywhere.' She stares triumphantly at Joni as if to say 'Do you get it?'

'Do you think he's intending to just ghost us all?'

'That's exactly what I think. He's going to disappear off to God knows where and leave you fifty grand down each, and me too if he can pull it off, and Mary with half a house. Anyway, it gets better. So we went in and Deirdre was there. She was hanging out in the kitchen, trying to keep out of the way, but obviously I went straight in there and started chatting to her. She's nice, isn't she? Seems it, anyway.'

'She does,' Joni says, glad to get a word in. Mary takes another sip of her wine and balances her glass on the arm, putting the cream chair in mortal danger.

'She basically confirmed what the agent had just said, so I asked her if they'd found a new property yet and she said they were waiting until they'd sold this one and that they were going to rent for a little while down there while they decided exactly where they wanted to live . . .'

'Because he doesn't know how much money he'll have yet. That's what he's going to do, sell all the cars and put the money into the house.'

'Yep, that's what I think. It explains the cars, doesn't it?'

'I suppose so,' Joni says, working it out. 'The banks are hot on money laundering these days when you buy a house, but I guess if you sell something that was given to you then that looks legit. Won't Deirdre wonder how they can afford it though?'

Saffy shrugs. 'Maybe she lets him do all the finances. He'll just tell her the mortgage is bigger than it is. Or make up a story about an aunt dying and leaving thousands to him or something. And then he'll probably disappear out of our lives and keep Mary as a long-term project. Once she's bought a new house in both their names what does he care if he hardly ever sees her? In fact, it'd probably suit him better not to have to. He can tell Mary it's all over and they're going to have to sell the house again and, by the way, half the money they get is his, remember, because he's on the deeds. Why wait?'

Joni sighs. 'He's actually evil.'

'Deirdre said them not having anywhere to go wouldn't hold up the sale and they were actually keen to sell as quickly as possible.'

'So, he's given his notice in at Evoke, I assume. Oh, is Mary asleep?' Joni leans over and grabs the glass, putting it on the coffee table. 'He must have to give a month at least. And he's already got something else to go to.'

'By the sound of it.'

'We're never going to get her her money back, are we?'

Saffy looks at Mary's sleeping form. She gets up and eases her bejewelled sandals off her feet, plucks Tyson off her lap and drapes a throw over her. Puts him back. 'Should we try and put her to bed?'

'She's out cold. It's probably better to leave her there. I don't think she's used to drinking that much.'

'That's my fault. Shit. What's wrong with me?' Saffy plonks back down on the sofa. 'I wasn't always this much of a mess, you know.'

'You're not a mess. Well, a bit . . .' She looks to see if Saffy laughs and she's gratified to see a smile. 'You're just grieving, same as she is.'

'Not the same. Nothing like the same. Mary did nothing wrong. She doesn't deserve what happened to her. I do. That's the bit that's killing me.'

'You have so much going for you,' Joni says gently. 'You're drop dead gorgeous. You're funny. You're secure financially. You have loads of friends . . .'

'I don't have friends,' Saffy says so quietly Joni isn't sure if she's heard or not.

'The girls . . .'

Saffy snorts. 'Yeah, the girls. The girls all dropped me when they found out I cheated on Stefan. They were all married to his mates, you see. I don't know if they were disgusted with what I'd done or if they suddenly saw me as this loose cannon who might make a play for their husbands. Or they just wanted an easy life and not to have to worry about which one of us to invite to dinner parties any more. Either way, they all picked him. Even when he moved to the States, they didn't bother getting back in touch with me.'

'I'm sorry.'

'Don't be. I never liked them that much anyway. Actually, that's not true. Some of them could be a laugh but it's not as if we were bosom buddies. It didn't go deeper than mojitos at Harvey Nicks and who had the most expensive handbag. Or the best plastic surgeon. But I miss them, that's what's so stupid. The idea of them more than the actual people. The fact that they existed and I didn't have to think too hard. If I was bored I could call one of them up and go for lunch. God, I'm making myself sound shallow . . .'

'You must have other friends? From before?' She can't imagine garrulous Saffy not surrounded by other people. 'What about all those women you're always going off to have lunch with . . .'

Saffy shakes her head. 'Not really. I was so happy to throw myself into his life and I kind of lost touch with everyone. Not deliberately. And not because he wanted me to either. He wasn't like that. He would have been just as happy hanging out with my friends and their partners, but I just sort of let them slide. There are no lunches. I just . . . I didn't want you to think I was a saddo . . .'

'My best friend died. In a car crash . . .' Joni doesn't know why she says it. She never talks about Meg except to Imo. It's too raw, too painful. 'It was always just the two of us. We did everything together.'

'Fuck, Joni. I'm so sorry. Jesus.'

'It's OK.' It's not. It never will be. 'Who did you have an affair with?'

Mary stirs. Saffy reaches out and pulls the throw over her arm. 'It was barely even an affair. That's what's so fucking stupid. I mean, emotionally not at all. I think I was feeling invisible. Stef was working all the time – not that that's any excuse at all – and I was at home just filling my days with manicures and lunches and Pilates classes. I wanted attention, that's the bottom line. I'm not that perceptive, by the way. It took me a year of therapy to reach that conclusion. I needed to be reminded of my worth, something like that. Basically, I could have sat Stef down and told him I was feeling a bit lost and he would have listened. I know that. That's what's so stupid. But instead, I slept with the worst person I ever could have chosen . . .'

Joni waits. She doesn't want to break the moment.

'I slept with his brother, Rich. And not only that, his sleazy fucking creep of a brother who's always been jealous of him and who flirts with anything with a pulse. We used to joke about what idiots those women were to fall for his cringy chat-ups. It was always so obvious he was spinning them a line, just trying to get them into bed, and then I fell for it myself. I need another drink.'

'No, Saff. No more wine. I'll make us a tea.'

'Really? No. Coffee at least.'

'OK. Was it just one time? The brother?'

Saffy closes her eyes. Joni suddenly realizes how quiet it is outside. She looks at the clock on the mantelpiece.

It's gone midnight. 'A few. A couple of weeks. And then I came to my senses. You have to believe me: I didn't even fancy this bloke. He's like a bargain-basement Stefan. Not as good-looking, not as funny, not as smart. Not as kind.'

'And you told Stefan?'

'I didn't. The brother did. He couldn't wait.'

'Shit, Saffy.' She pats her on the arm as she gets up. Collects their wine glasses. Then she notices a tear roll down Saffy's cheek and she puts them down again and sits back next to her. Pulls her into a hug. 'It'll be OK.'

'It won't be though, will it?' Saffy says. 'It never will be.'

When Joni wakes up it's almost light. She shivers and pulls the cover back over her before realizing that it's a scratchy throw and she's still on Mary's sofa. Saffy is curled up at the other end, under a blanket like a baby bird in a nest. Mary is slumped in the chair. It all comes back to her: Saffy's revelation. Talking till two in the morning. Saffy falling asleep, cried out. It had seemed easier just to lie down where she was, and besides, she was nervous about leaving her two charges alone. Mary had drunk herself into a stupor and Saffy was an emotional wreck. It was like every teenage sleepover she'd ever attended. Only this time it was three middle-aged women who really should know better. She smiles to herself. She thinks about getting up. Pictures her soft, warm bed. But she can't be bothered to move. Not yet. She snuggles under the throw and goes back to sleep.

She stirs, she doesn't know how much later, to the

smell of coffee. Saffy's spot is empty. The detritus of glasses and bottles has been cleared away. One of the patio doors is open wide and the morning – is it still morning? – is sunny and cool. Mary sleeps on, Tyson on her lap. Mouth open. Her hair is sticking up at the back of her head, and she has mascara streaked down one cheek. Joni stands up, wraps the throw around her shoulders and follows her nose.

'God, you were both unconscious in there,' Saffy says when she sees her.

Joni gives her a hug. 'Are you OK?'

'Yes. And thank you. I don't want to talk about it.'

'I know. But if you ever do . . .'

Saffy gives a quick nod. 'I don't. Coffee?'

'Yes please.' She sits at the pale wood table.

'When did your friend die?'

Joni starts. 'Sorry?'

'You said you lost your friend . . . I'm not trying to be nosy . . .'

'Two years,' Joni says, quietly. 'Almost exactly.'

Saffy busies herself making the drinks. 'Do you think . . . I mean . . . Don't take this the wrong way: you know I've been therapied to within an inch of my life . . . Is that why you're a bit of a control freak? I really don't mean in a bad way . . .'

Joni gives her a weak smile. She doesn't want to talk about this. She can't. She's not ready to go there yet. 'Should we wake Mary, do you think?'

Saffy takes the hint. 'I don't know. She might need to sleep it off some more.'

276

'It probably wasn't a good idea for her to drink so much . . .' It comes out more accusatory than she means it to. Thankfully Saffy doesn't seem to take offence. She hands Joni a mug.

'You're a lovely person, Joni. Do you know that?'

Joni scrapes at a stain on the wood with her nail. 'You too.'

35

It's not that Joni had forgotten about the work party, it's more that she'd buried it in the back of her brain and built a wall around it. Head Office held one every year in the early autumn, before the holiday season began and everyone was too busy facilitating other people's Christmases to have time to celebrate their own. Last year, of course, the whole shebang got cancelled along with everything else, so this is Joni's first invitation. She's not sure why she's so adamant about not going. The people she works with – in so far as she knows them – are all pleasant enough. It's not a snub to them, it's more that she doesn't see why she should conform to the pressure to also see them outside of office hours. Life is, as they say, too short. She knows that better than anyone.

So, when she arrives at work and finds Captain Kirk on one side and Luke Skywalker on the other, holding up a note in their posable hands that reads 'Jone, please say you're coming to the awful party?' she laughs, but then throws it in the bin. A few minutes later she digs it out again. Jone, it says, not Joan. Short for Joni, not getting her name completely wrong. The same way Saffy does. Could that be it? She looks up and sees Caitlin from HR heading for the kitchen and picks up her dirty mug and follows. She's always got on with Caitlin – not that she's had much to do with her. But they've bonded a couple of times over their same-age kids when they've been waiting for the kettle to boil.

'How's things?' she says now.

'Manic,' Caitlin says, filling up the coffee machine with water. She has big pink hands that look as if she's been washing laundry all day in a bucket, not reading CVs and trying to mediate between Carly and Darren from Reception who are at war over who takes the most bathroom breaks and how long they last. 'You?'

They chat about Imo and Caitlin's son Sid – just started his first term at Durham and loving it - for a couple of minutes. When they've caught up, and the coffee has started to drip, Joni launches in. 'How old is Lucas?'

Caitlin frowns at her. 'Lucas Lucas? Your Lucas? My guess is as good as yours.'

'I don't have a guess seeing as I've never met him.'

'Haven't you?' She holds up the coffee jug as if to ask Joni if she wants one and Joni nods. 'Never?'

'We communicate through notes and the odd email or ten-second phone call. There's been no reason for us to ever meet.'

'Wow.' She hands Joni the mug and Joni roots in the fridge for the oat milk that she puts in there once a week. 'That's mad. I'm sure you were meant to do a get-to-know-you meeting when he first arrived. Haven't you even Zoomed?'

Joni shakes her head. 'The whole point of us is that we're an either/or. You never need both of us in the same meeting.'

'Well, he's about our age, I suppose. Maybe a bit younger. Mid-forties, I don't know. I must have known at some point because it was me who interviewed him. Why?'

'I'm just curious. I always thought of him a certain way and now I'm wondering if I got it wrong, that's all.'

'How did you think of him?'

'Geeky. Offhand. Bit lazy. Sorry, this is totally off the record, by the way. It's not me complaining about him. He's fine.'

'Duly noted,' Caitlin says in a slightly comedy voice. She has a tendency to slip into funny accents. It's the oral equivalent of acting out quotation marks around words. 'He is a bit of a geek, I'll give you that. But not so much that it takes over his whole personality. He can be pretty funny. I don't know about offhand. I'm pretending I didn't hear lazy.'

'See, I'm wondering if when I thought he was being offhand he was actually joking, and I didn't get it.'

Caitlin considers. 'He's quite dry. It's not always obvious.'

'I should make more of an effort. How's the Carly and Darren situation?' Caitlin completely lacks one of the essential qualities needed for a good HR manager: discretion. She's a terrible gossip and so half the company knows about Reception Wars. Although, to be fair, they're pretty apparent to anyone spending more than a couple of minutes in the airy glass-fronted entrance hall. The pair of them seethe and simmer and roll their eyes at each other like a couple of over-boiling kettles.

'Did I tell you they've started timing each other when they go on a break? And Carly's had a flare-up of her IBS so she can have some long visits, if you know what I mean. I shouldn't have told you that, obviously.'

'I shouldn't have told you that' is Caitlin's catchphrase, along with 'Don't tell anyone I told you.' Joni is fond of her but if she had a problem at work Caitlin is probably the last person she would trust with it.

Before Joni leaves for the day she thinks about how to answer Lucas's note. In the end she plumps for a cardboard speech bubble, precariously stuck to the squirrel's open mouth saying, 'I would rather eat my own eyeball.' She hopes it makes him laugh.

Saffy and Mary are sitting in her living room, drinking tea instead of wine because Saffy has declared her desire to turn over a new leaf, and Joni is trying to be supportive. She called them both from the office and invited them over. She'd suddenly felt the need to recreate some of the closeness, the camaraderie of the other night, and besides, time is running out. If Ant moves away, starts a new life, a new job, are they really going to scour the West Country looking for him, even if they could think of a way to try to force him to pay Mary back once they'd found him? Joni knows he'll keep in touch with her for as long as it takes for her to hand over her own enormous 'gift', and presumably he's hoping Saffy will come through a couple of weeks later (she's been laying it on thick about how wealthy she is, even, she told Joni and Mary proudly, telling him that she likes being generous with her ex-husband's money, it feels like a fuck you to him to give it to causes he wouldn't approve of), but then he'll be gone and the chance of justice will suddenly slip away. Mary's house is a longer-term project, but one that he can keep an eye on from a distance. He could go to ground for years. They need to up their efforts to find out everything they can about him while they still can. Just in case.

'Tell me what I would need to say again.' Joni has just told Mary what she thinks they should do next.

Joni jumps to her feet. 'OK. Let's think about this . . . anyone want more tea?'

Saffy pulls a face as if she's just been offered soapy water to drink. 'I think I'll pass.'

'Mary?'

Mary shakes her head silently. She's looking even paler than usual. Ashen.

'Just chat to her. See what you can find out. It has to be you; she's seen both of us before.'

'I'm not sure if I can.'

'Listen,' Joni says. 'If it all gets too much or you're worried you're giving yourself away. just change the subject. Talk about where you're going on holiday or *Strictly*. There's no way she'll think anything of it.'

Mary rubs at her wedding ring without even realizing she's doing it. Nods. 'OK. Let's get it over with.'

36

She needs to psych herself up. Psyching herself up is not something Mary is good at. She's passive by nature. A pleaser, a nurturer. When she and Andrew had their babies, her ambition was to be the calm, warm constant they could all rely on. A beacon in the dark. She had loved those years. While her friends had juggled madly feeling as if they could never give themselves fully to either work or home, constantly being pulled between the two, Mary had chosen motherhood. She had given up her job as a legal executive – all that training for nothing – two months before George was born, intending to go back one day, but it had never happened.

She knew how fortunate she'd been that she could make that choice. Andrew's family had money. Old money. She hadn't even known that for a long time after they'd met. Not until he first took her to his home to meet them, and she was faced with what, to all intents and purposes, looked like a stately home. It had been sold after they had died: neither he nor his two brothers had wanted to take it on with its constant upkeep and the absolute refusal of the local council to see beyond its Grade One listing and allow them to take proper, practical steps to ensure it didn't slowly crumble into a pile of very expensive rubble. Andrew had done very well from his share of the sale, but he'd still worked hard all his life. He hadn't wanted his whole existence to be a gift from his parents, he used to say. He'd wanted his children to look up to him as a man who had never rested on his comfortable, cushioned heritage. He had been desperate to have children, and so had she. And he had turned out to be a wonderful dad. There was something about a big man holding a tiny baby so gently. Something primal. God, he was a lovely man. She'd been lucky – they both had been, because he had always said he couldn't survive without her. It had just been too short. Decades too short.

Before he died Andrew had been talking about selling his share in the advertising company he had built up with one of his friends. Cashing in while he could still enjoy it. He'd been in the middle of a complicated deal when he went to sleep and didn't wake up. They had always been more than comfortably off, living in their beautiful house in St John's Wood, driving nice cars. But now Mary would happily hand it all over to anyone who could bring Andrew back. What was the point of it if he wasn't there to enjoy it?

It meant that when Ant had asked to borrow fifty thousand she hadn't really hesitated. Stupid, she realizes now. But she'd had no reason to doubt him. He was the first man she'd been interested in since Andrew – it had taken her two years to even look around and see who was out there. No one in her wide circle of acquaintances, it had turned out. She couldn't imagine getting romantic with anyone Andrew had known. It seemed like a betrayal. And then she'd seen an advert for Keepers. Smiling people walking hand in hand on beaches and clinking glasses in front of a real fire. It had looked safe, cosy almost. Comforting. Like a world she had lost.

Maybe if one of the boys had lived closer everything would have been different. But they had their own lives and she wouldn't want it any other way. George had offered to move back to London when his father had died. Or at least to the Home Counties. Somewhere closer than Cornwall. But Mary had told him in no uncertain terms that he shouldn't even think about it. She didn't want to become a burden. She knew that Millie would have vetoed it anyway. It was a sincere but baseless offer. And she wasn't even close to getting old yet; she was perfectly capable of forging a new life for herself. Except that she had spectacularly messed that up.

The idea that she doesn't miss the fifty thousand is ludicrous, but true. But that's not the point. The money was Andrew's. Mary always suspected that the stress of selling the company was what caused his heart to give out. It wouldn't matter if it was fifty pounds or fifty thousand. He didn't worry himself into an early grave so that she could hand his money over to a conman. She owes it to him to make sure Ant gets his comeuppance.

She had got home from Joni's at about half past ten and treated herself to a whisky before bed. It was sweet how Joni was trying to help Saffy cut down on her drinking, and she was happy to go along with it too when they were all together. Mary had never been a big drinker. She hated to feel out of control. Saffy had finally – tearfully – told her the story about the breakdown of her marriage. Poor girl. She had made a mistake and now she was paying for it for the rest of her life. Saffy seemed like a person with a tendency to self-sabotage. She was so hard on herself, so unforgiving. She reminded Mary of the boys when they were teenagers: all front but as vulnerable as fledglings underneath.

Mary can't bear people crying. It floors her. Whoever they are she just wants to make it all better. Jack the Ripper could be standing in front of her brandishing a knife, but if he shed tears she wouldn't be able to stop herself scooping him up and comforting him. She'd always been the same. When she was about six she'd crossed the floor of a restaurant where she was having a meal with her parents – her dad's birthday, she thinks – and climbed on to the lap of a woman who had burst into tears. Just clambered right up without saying a word and put her arms around the woman's neck. The woman had been so surprised she'd laughed, and the older lady sitting opposite had smiled too, and reached out a hand and placed it on top of the crying woman's own. Even at that age Mary had understood that she'd somehow helped break the moment. She'd always wondered what those tears had been about.

'Oh, you poor girl,' she'd said, when Saffy had told her her story. She'd walked over and grabbed her up in a hug. Saffy had stood rigid. People had become unused to hugging with everything that had happened. It had become both a luxury and, for a while, a taboo. A kiss of death. But she couldn't help herself. She'd become so fond of this girl and her brittle, spiky optimism.

The house felt cold and empty. Too quiet. It was too big for her. Too full of memories. But if she moved would all of those memories be lost forever? She didn't dare risk it. She'd lain awake till about two running What Ifs over and over again. What if Deirdre somehow worked out who she was? What if she had a violent streak and physically threw Mary out into the street? Or worse? But both Joni and Saffy had said she seemed like a nice woman. Friendly. And this was their last-ditch attempt to quiz her while she's still unsuspecting. Eventually they were almost certainly going to have to tell her everything and break her heart and that didn't sit easily with Mary at all.

Now she sits in Joni's car, parked five minutes away from Ant and Deirdre's house, breathing deeply to try and calm her nerves. Joni is talking to her softly, but she can't make out the words. Just the tone, which is soothing and reassuring but, to be honest, not helping. She's not sure her legs will even carry her the hundred or so metres she needs to walk to get to the main road. But Joni has taken a day off work for this. Mary can't let her down.

She realizes that Joni has gone quiet. That she's waiting for her to get out of the car.

'OK. Here goes,' she says in what she hopes is a confident tone. Isn't confidence 50 per cent telling yourself you feel confident? Fronting it out? She's sure she read that somewhere.

'I'll be here when you come out,' Joni says, laying a

hand on her arm. 'If I'm not in the car, text me, I'll only be walking round the block.'

Somehow she makes it to the shops, the little hairdresser's tucked between a takeaway chicken shop and a greasy spoon.

'Could I make an appointment with Deirdre Simons,' she'd said when she phoned. Saffy had told her that she'd seen a letter addressed to Deirdre when she'd viewed the house, and that she definitely used Ant's surname. It was the fourth hairdressers she'd tried, the first three having no knowledge of a Deirdre of any kind. Thankfully the estate agent had told Saffy that Deirdre worked locally, otherwise it would have been like looking for a very small needle in a very large haystack. Mary had found herself hoping the receptionist would tell her that Deirdre was fully booked till Christmas or that she'd just resigned. Instead, she'd said, 'Of course. What did you want done?' Mary had booked a full head of highlights, knowing that that would mean she'd be in the chair for hours. She was dreading it.

She steels herself, patting down her hair and brushing the front of her red top nervously. She had agonized over what to wear, as if it mattered. Deirdre would have no idea who she was, and she'd be spending most of the afternoon in a gown anyway. She'd settled on jeans with low boots and a soft red round-neck sweater under a short, thin cream coat. No jewellery. Very little make-up.

She pushes open the door. There are photos in the window of – presumably – happy customers, all women, showing off their bobs and wedges and balayage tones.

Mary hasn't even considered how competent Deirdre might be, if she might come out looking a fright. She knows it's the least of her problems, but still.

She announces herself to the young girl on the front desk. 'Sheila Marsden,' she says. It was the first name that came into her head when she booked the appointment. Her old friend from college. Afterwards she'd wondered what Sheila was doing now. Why, having not thought about her for nearly forty years, her name had been on the tip of her tongue. They had shared a room in halls in their first year, a flat in their second and third. Sheila had been at her wedding. And then life had slowly edged them in different directions and they'd lost touch.

'Have a seat,' the girl says. She has a complicated arrangement of plaits on top of her head. An inflated pout. Mary sits by the window, trying to calm her rapid heartbeat.

'Can I get you a coffee?' The receptionist is by her side now. Mary feels so hyper that she worries a coffee might send her over the edge. Full on Rambo.

'A tea would be lovely. Just a little milk. Thank you so much.'

She recognizes Deirdre from the brief glimpse she got of her as she spoke to Joni at the front door of the house. The cherry-red hair. She's over by the coat rack, saying goodbye to her previous client, who discreetly slips a five-pound note into her hand. She's wearing a wrap dress with low sandals. Pale legs. Chipped pink polish on her toes. She chats briefly to the woman as she pays.

Mary studies her. Of course this is the kind of woman Ant would go for. Young. Attractive. Vibrant. Not a sixty-three-year-old widow. She hadn't quite believed it herself when he'd been interested in her. She's constantly surprised by how old she is. She has a picture of herself in her head that is stuck at about 2010 and when she catches sight of herself in a mirror unexpectedly it's always a shock. Prepared, she's fine. She can arrange her face into something that resembles who she still thinks she is. It's those unguarded moments – a reflection in her phone screen or a shop window, a photo that she wasn't expecting, a rush to answer a FaceTime call with Oliver, the mobile held at the wrong angle – that take her by surprise. And she can't even look in her ten times magnifying mirror that George got her for Christmas without being armed with a pair of tweezers. Fully formed moustaches and beards seem to sprout up overnight. She has an appointment at her local beauty shop to get it all waxed off once a month but there are still battles to fight in between.

She knows she's being ridiculous. Objectively she understands that she looks good 'for her age' (always that caveat) but she's losing herself. If Andrew were still here she wouldn't give it a second thought. They'd laugh about how decrepit they were feeling. He'd tell her she looked beautiful. They had been looking forward to being grandparents. Laughing at the stereotypes they'd become when it happened. 'You'll have to get me a pipe,' Andrew had said when they'd been talking about it one night. 'I won't smoke it, obviously, I'll just walk round with it in my mouth so I look the part.' She couldn't bear that the boys' future children would never know him. If they had any. Neither of them seemed in any hurry.

'Sheila?'

Mary starts. Deirdre is standing in front of her, smiling broadly.

'Yes. That's me.' She stands up. Allows her coat to be taken and a shiny black gown wrapped around her.

'Come over,' Deirdre says. 'What is it you're after?' She runs her fingers through Mary's hair. It feels strangely intimate. This woman has no idea of the ways in which they're connected.

'Oh, just highlights and maybe a cut . . .'

'Do you want to stay the same sort of cool tone? It definitely suits you.'

'Yes. Whatever you think. I'll leave myself in your hands.'

'So, purple ombre?' Deirdre says, laughing.

'Maybe I should,' Mary says, going along with the joke. 'See if my sons even notice.'

'I think you should stay icy. It complements your skin. Very Scandi.'

She mixes up colour while Mary racks her brain for a conversation starter. What if Deirdre just isn't the chatty type? What if she likes to concentrate on her work and shuts down any question without even answering?

'How many sons do you have?'

'Oh,' Mary says, happy for the breakthrough. 'Two. Both grown up. How about you?'

'No kids. I'm just going to turn you round this way.' She swivels the chair so it faces her, starts sectioning Mary's hair. Close up she smells of a musky perfume. Something heavy and a bit sweet. There's the faintest hint of cigarettes on her breath, overlaid by mint.

Deirdre works in silence for a moment, pasting colour on, wrapping up the strands in foil. Mary struggles for something else to say. She settles on the weather. Better, she thinks, to keep a conversation flowing in any direction rather than let it dry up altogether. It might never get moving again. Deirdre seems happy to go along with it. Finally – maybe three minutes into what, to both of them she's sure, is a mind-numbingly dull exchange, Deirdre mentions her husband. Something along the lines of 'My husband always says they should have called it global raining and not global warming, then people might have sat up and listened.'

'What does your husband do?' Mary jumps in.

'He does maintenance at a day spa. Well, a chain of spas. Evoke? Have you heard of them?'

'I have!' Mary says, seemingly delighted. 'There's one in Kensington, isn't there?'

'There is. Three in London and one up in Manchester.'

'So which one does he look after?'

'All of them,' Deirdre says. 'But he's leaving soon. We're moving away, actually.'

'How exciting! Where to?'

'We're not sure where we're actually going to live yet . . . Oh, excuse me.'

Her mobile is ringing. She fishes it out of the big front pocket of the retro apron she's wearing. 'It's him – do you mind if I take it? It might be about our house sale.'

'No, go ahead,' Mary says, her heart starting to pound again. She picks up a magazine and pretends to be interested in a story about Selena Gomez.

'Hey,' Deirdre says into the phone. 'Anything? No . . . No . . . I'm with a client so I'd better . . .'

Mary looks into the mirror and accidentally catches her eye. Deirdre smiles and circles her hand as if she'd trying to speed whatever he is telling her up. 'OK. Yeah. OK. Is it Saffy or Lucy tonight?'

Mary freezes.

'Right. Are you going to finally seal the deal?' She laughs. 'You'll get over it. Just pretend it's me. See you tomorrow. Love you.'

She ends the call. Mary can hardly look at her but she feels as if she has to say something. 'Is he, um, away somewhere?'

'What? Oh, he has to go to the Manchester branch, so he'll stay over.'

'Right. Right.'

She keeps her head buried in the magazine, hopes that's a signal that she no longer wants to talk. She can't wait to get out of there.

Because – unless she's very much mistaken – she's just found out that Deirdre knows about Ant's other women. She's not the innocent wife they imagined, waiting at home with no idea what's going on.

She's not another one of his victims.

She's in on it.

37

The first thing Joni sees is Mary rounding the corner almost at a run. She throws herself into the car and slams the door way too hard.

'She knows about it. Us.'

'Wait – what?'

'We should go. Just in case . . . I don't know . . . but we should go.'

Joni starts the car obediently, pulls away. She'd been half asleep. She hadn't realized the appointment would take so long and she was dozing off. She shakes her head, trying to focus. 'Do you mean she's found out or she knew all along?'

'I don't know, but he called her while I was there, and she talked about you and Saffy. She said your names.'

'Jesus,' Joni says, swerving to avoid a cyclist. 'I need to pull over. I can't concentrate.'

'I didn't give anything away,' Mary says, pointing to a pub with a small car park. 'Park up there.'

Joni swings the Fiat 500 to the left and stops next to a skip. 'Tell me everything she said.'

'I felt so sorry for her. God, Joni, what have we got caught up in?'

Joni reaches over and holds her shaking hand. 'At least we don't have to feel guilty any more.'

Joni drives Mary back to hers and sends a text to Saffy, telling her to stop by on her way home. There's solidarity in numbers. She has no idea what they're going to do, but at least they can be clueless together. She orders Deliveroo and she and Mary sit in the kitchen both picking at their pizzas, waiting for Saffy's date to be over.

'Are either of your boys married?' Joni asks. They've been passing the time by filling in the details of their lives. There are only so many times they can try to unravel what Ant and Deirdre are playing at.

'George is. Three years.' Mary smiles at the memory.

'And did Andrew do a speech?'

'He—' She stops as Joni's mobile rings.

'Saffy,' Joni says, holding it up. She presses the button to answer. 'Hi . . .'

'I'm in the loo,' Saffy hisses. 'We're about to leave, but he keeps hinting he wants to come back with me. What do I do?'

'What do you want to do?'

'I mean, it's weirdly tempting because, you know, it's been a while . . . but no. I don't want him to know where I live, for a start.'

'So just tell him you're not up for it.'

'Shit. I've forgotten how to do this.'

Joni can hear water running in the background. 'Join the club,' she says; then she hears a woman's voice at

Saffy's end. 'Period pains,' it says. 'Works for me every time. They daren't question it because it grosses them out and they don't want the details.'

'Oh yes, that's a good one. Thanks,' Saffy says.

'Who's that?' Joni says, finding herself whispering.

'Have a nice night,' the woman says, and then there's a sound like the door shutting. 'Some random woman who was in the other cubicle.' Saffy says breathlessly. 'She must have worked out what I was on about. OK. I'll be at yours in about half an hour. How was Deirdre?'

'Awful,' Joni says. 'Worse than you can imagine.'

38

While Saffy is in the bathroom Ant checks his phone. Her incessant chatter is exhausting, but he feels as if he's making progress. She's horribly indiscreet about how wealthy she is. At one point – when she was describing a ring her ex-husband bought her – he'd found himself looking apologetically across at their table neighbours and giving a small smile that, he hoped, conveyed 'this woman is not my wife and I know she's being crass' but the couple had just looked away and carried on with their own conversation. She was attractive, though, and that was a bonus. When, that was, she stopped talking for long enough for you to actually see her face. Otherwise it was just a blur. He was looking forward to going home with her. His occupation definitely had perks.

To be fair, all three of them were good-looking women. He was looking for a fourth, just in case Saffy didn't come through, but she had to be the last. He and Deirdre had agreed no more. Originally, they had planned for the whole thing to be a bit more long-term. There was a seemingly endless line of lonely women out there looking for love, primed to fall for his flattery. But it was proving to be too much, too stressful, too combative. So they'd decided to cut and run. Neither of them had it in their hearts to be career criminals. Once they had the house in the countryside that they dreamed of he would stop. Not in the West Country as they'd told the estate agent and any prospective buyers who asked, but up in Yorkshire. They would be respectable. Untouchable. They would still need a mortgage for now and they'd both have to carry on working full-time, but they'd have a hefty – nicely laundered – nest egg that would change everything. And eventually the big fish would land. Eventually they would be rich. All they'd wanted at first was a step-up. A way to make their life better. And the women he was targeting would barely even notice the blip in their savings. Yes, they would probably feel foolish. In fact, he was relying on that. He knew he wasn't doing anything illegal – nothing provable at least – but he would still prefer the heat to be off and, for that, he was counting on them opting to shoulder the loss rather than have to explain to some patronizing young police officer that yes, they had handed the money over willingly. No, they had not asked for any kind of guarantee. No, they had not told their children/friends/parents at the time. He was relying on pride.

He wondered if Mary's house was a step too far. A con too big. Their ambitions had grown. But it was just too easy. He would kick himself if he didn't at least try. His last hurrah.

The sex was a bit of a bonus, he wasn't going to lie. He hadn't limited himself to good-looking targets – the money had been the only criterion. That and a certain vulnerability that you could only tap into after you had been talking to them for a while – but it certainly helped. And they were all so different. Like three separate species: soft, warm Mary; toned, lean Lucy; Saffy all bony angles. It was like some kind of weird anthropological study. Several times he'd been tempted to boast about what he was getting up to to his mates. Just the sex part, not the bonuses, obviously. But he would never do that to Deirdre. She didn't exactly find that side of the whole thing easy as it was, but she'd decided it would be worth it in the end. He wasn't sure she'd feel the same if she thought he was actually getting off on it.

He has no messages. Deirdre never gets in touch while he's out. They've agreed it should only be in an emergency. Life or death for one of them. And they never discuss the family business, beyond the basics of where he needs to be and when, anywhere except face to face. You can't be too careful.

He waves at the waiter for the bill just as Saffy emerges through the door to the stairs. She's wearing an expression like she's in pain, one hand on her stomach.

'Are you OK?' he says, all concern. He's already told her that he thinks they should take things further tonight – holding her hand across the table, massaging her fingers – and now he needs to follow through. To be fair, she didn't exactly bite his hand off saying yes. She'd claimed a sudden urge to go to the Ladies. He'd been surprised. Up till now their relationship had crackled with sexual tension. He'd warned Deirdre that tonight would probably be an all-nighter. Sighed when he said it so she would think it was all duty and no pleasure – he had definitely played down the attractiveness of all the women, and Deirdre had opted early on not to look at their profiles or pictures. She didn't want to be able to imagine him in the act, she'd said. She preferred to try for blissful ignorance. He had shared all their details with her though, so that she could help him select the ideal candidates. He needed her input. Except for Lucy, obviously: that had been a random stroke of luck and one that was about to pay off. Deirdre had felt uneasy about her from the start, out of control because she hadn't had a hand in finding her – as if that might make a difference to Ant's feelings.

'Tummy ache,' Saffy says now, grimacing. 'You know, girls' stuff . . .'

Ant cringes at the coy terminology. He's a grown man; he can handle the word 'period', for God's sake. 'Poor love,' he says. 'Maybe you should call an Uber. Or do you want me to go and find you a taxi?'

'I called one already, I hope you don't mind . . .' she says.

'Not at all. Let me just get the bill and I'll come out with you and make sure it's there.'

She gives him a weak smile. 'Thanks. Sorry. Next time, definitely.'

As he picks up her bag from the floor he would swear he feels it move.

He sends Deirdre a text before he hops on to the tube: *On my way. No go tonight.* He's not a bad person. He's just someone who didn't have the advantages or the education to ease seamlessly into a comfortable life. He works hard. Long hours. And so does Deirdre, dragging her brushes and hairdryer to friends' houses in a wheelie suitcase after a shattering day at work several nights a week to earn more money on the side. But the truth is they will never be able to earn enough, however hard they work. They will always be stuck in that shitty little house – he knows, by the way, that the fact they own a house at all, however tiny, however basic, however big their mortgage, puts them way ahead of millions of people in the privilege stakes – in that shitty street, gazing at the new wealth that has sprung up all around them and seemingly missed them by metres. It isn't that he wants flashy things – although, God, he had enjoyed driving that car for a couple of days before he'd put it up for sale – he just wants to stop worrying all the time. To ease off the pedal a bit. He just wants something to go his way for once.

He has to make that happen.

39

'So she knows he's been sleeping with you both?' Saffy screws her face up, trying to understand.

'I assume so,' Mary says. They've given in and opened a bottle of Sauvignon Blanc. It's officially the weekend and, besides, needs must. 'She knows your names – well, Joni's fake name – everything. I think she's as much a part of this as he is.'

'We're screwed,' Joni says, leaning her head back against the cushions. Jasper has taken her spot, so she's squashed up against Saffy in the middle seat. It feels oddly comfortable. Mary is curled up in the armchair opposite, shoes off, Tyson back on her lap. 'If we can't threaten him with telling his wife the truth then we've got nothing.'

'God, I'm knackered,' Saffy says with an enormous yawn.

'You can both stay here tonight if one of you doesn't mind sleeping in Imo's room,' Joni says, sitting back down. She surprises herself with how easily the invitation comes out.

'I'm OK with that,' Saffy says.

They all sit there in silence for a moment, staring at the half-full wine bottle on the table. Eventually Saffy speaks. 'Can we go to bed now? I don't think I can stay awake.'

'Me neither,' Mary says. She's looking pale, tired.

'Let me find you both something to sleep in,' Joni says, smiling at them. It reminds her of all the times Imo had a sleepover, hunting out spare toothbrushes and clean pyjamas for the friends who always seemed to have forgotten something crucial. They both follow her downstairs and she shows each of them to their rooms.

She delivers a clean T-shirt to Mary, who pulls her in for a hug. 'Thank you so much for this,' she says. 'You're both so kind.'

'Sleep well,' Joni says, allowing herself to relax into it. 'Help yourself to anything if I'm not up.'

By the time she takes Saffy's makeshift pyjama top – a T-shirt with Power Fit emblazoned across the front – in to her she finds her fast asleep on top of the covers, fully clothed. She folds the duvet over her so she's covered up, places Tyson next to her, and turns the light out as she leaves.

The Gibsons party is happening on a Tuesday evening, so Joni works through her lunch hour so she can leave before the collective hysteria that is co-workers getting ready to let loose together begins. She plans to sneak out without anyone noticing, although, to be fair, she's made her excuses already to anyone who asked.

At five to five she starts packing up her things. The corridor outside is already buzzing as if the idea of warm Prosecco and slightly stale canapés in a hotel basement has sent them all a bit giddy. Joni has heard the stories from previous years of drunken embarrassments and illicit hook-ups. Greatly exaggerated, she's sure, but Maureen in Catering apparently really did once fall asleep behind a trestle table and only woke up when one of the cleaners poked her with a hoover at five in the morning. There was photographic evidence.

She'd ended up spending most of the weekend with Saffy and Mary, lolling about on the sofas until Joni insisted they all go for a walk on the heath. They'd hardly talked about Ant. They were out of ideas. They were just three friends spending a couple of days together, she'd realized as she made toast on Saturday morning, and she'd found herself wishing Meg could see her, could witness the progress she'd made. And then she'd panicked. She was starting to care about both these women. She'd felt a wave of anxiety when Mary had talked about driving to the West Country to see her son and his wife – who sounded like a piece of work. Joni had always made an effort with Ian's mother, even though the woman had been vile to her. She couldn't imagine Mary being anything other than a doting mother-in-law – and started to lecture her about smart motorways and how unsafe they were before Saffy had jumped in and changed the subject.

She'd tried to persuade the two of them to go to the gym with her on Saturday. She had a collection of guest passes that she'd never used. But they'd both looked at her as if she'd offered them a threesome so in the end she went alone.

'You're late today,' Samira had said when she'd walked in, and Joni had felt almost proud of herself. She'd phoned Imo on her way back. She'd lied and told her that she'd finally ended things with Ant. She was worried she was setting a bad example, staying in a relationship that she had told her daughter wasn't working. Leaving things to fate instead of taking charge of her own life.

'What's weird is that you sound really happy.' Imo had said. 'Which is great, obviously . . .'

'Manic, probably,' Joni laughed. 'Drunk with relief.'

She had had messages from Ant, chatty, normal, confirming their next date for Sunday night. He wasn't giving up. In so far as he knew Joni was about to become his next fairy godmother and he wasn't going to let that one slip.

Saffy had heard from him too. 'You've got to hand it to him,' she'd said when she got a missed call and then a text from him in quick succession. 'He's dedicated. It's like a full-time job.'

'Let's make him an Employee of the Month certificate,' Mary had said and for some reason they'd all found that hilarious and laughed for way too long, like three over-inflated balloons who had just located their release valves.

On Sunday night she and Ant had gone to see *Strangers on a Train* at the Everyman. She'd bought the tickets in advance, and only told him when he'd called to ask her what she fancied for dinner. She knew she had to see him, but the thought of hours of conversation, of pretending everything was OK, was just too much. She wasn't sure she was that good an actress. He'd actually seemed pleased, presumably because he felt the same.

They'd eaten pizzas in a café beforehand and shared a carafe of white wine. Apart from the fact that he'd asked her how long there was to go until the fifty thousand pounds she had given the bank notice to withdraw from the fixed savings scheme became available, and the knot of tension that had taken hold of the back of her neck whenever Ant was around, it had almost seemed like a normal date.

Only when he'd left for work at half past seven in the morning did she relax, luxuriating in the thought that she didn't have to see him again until Thursday. She had a long, lovely day ahead of her, although she needed to do all the chores that she'd neglected, and to work out because she'd missed yesterday. But then Saffy had texted and said: *We're going to Harvey Nicks, why don't you come?* and she'd found herself thinking, Why not?

'What the fuck are you doing in my office?'

Joni jumps and drops the phone she's holding on to the floor. Her plans to leave early had been scuppered by a last-minute call from another party pooper at the Leeds branch who needed answers about the business rates bill. She clutches a hand to her chest. A man is standing in the doorway. Tall and skinny, all arms and legs. He's about her age, she thinks (which means he's probably anywhere from forty to fifty-five; her perception of her own age shifts daily, depending on how tired she is and if she's looked in the mirror or not that morning), with dark hair flecked with grey, cropped up the sides with a cluster of burgeoning curls on top, and a short beard that's more grey than brown. 'God, Jone, sorry,' he says flustered. 'I was joking. I didn't mean to give you a coronary.'

'Lucas?' She notices he has one leg of his blue suit trousers cinched in with a bicycle clip.

'It is. I am. I was just going to change into a shirt before the party. I forgot you might be in here.' He's wearing a T-shirt under his suit jacket and, she sees now, clutching a folded white shirt in his hand, along with a cycling helmet.

'Because it's really private in here,' she says, indicating the wall of glass on to the corridor.

He gives a little laugh. 'Yes, well, I hadn't really thought it through. I'll go and do it in the Gents. Does this mean you're coming? To the party? The fact that you're still here?'

'Definitely not. I'm on my way out.'

'Come,' he says. 'It's bound to be truly awful. It's worth experiencing once.'

'Ha! If you put it like that . . . but no, I'll pass. It's nice to finally meet you, though.'

'You look nothing like I imagined,' he says, leaning in the doorframe. He's thrown his suit jacket on a chair. 'I had you down in my head as a dead ringer for Queen Victoria.'

'Well, I'm sorry to disappoint.' Lucas full out laughs at that, she's gratified to see. 'Have you come in specially? I hope you're going to tell me you live round the corner because otherwise it's just tragic.'

'I don't,' he says. 'So, yes, tragic. This is the highlight of my social calendar. Honestly, you should come.'

'I didn't bring anything to wear. I can't just go like this.' She reaches for her coat.

'God, no. Imagine the people you work with seeing what you wear to work.'

Now it's Joni's turn to laugh. 'You know what I mean.' She shrugs her arm into a sleeve. 'You're not one of those men who cycles in Lycra, are you? The ones who think they're Jason Kenny but never go further than from home to the office and back.'

'I absolutely am. Clip-in shoes, heart-rate monitor, the lot.' She looks down at his feet. 'Not today, obviously,' he says. 'Please come to the party. Otherwise I'll end up having to talk to other people.'

'Isn't that why you're here?'

'I'm here for the free booze and blackmailing opportunities.'

'I really can't. I've been trying to leave for an hour.'

'Do you have somewhere else to be?' He flicks through a couple of piles of paper on the desk, messing them up. Joni fights the urge to straighten them again. 'Are you leaving this for me to do? Because I'm going to be in no fit state tomorrow.'

She ignores the second question. She notices that it's started raining outside and hunts for the tiny folded umbrella she usually keeps in her bag. 'I do have somewhere to be. And I'm late.'

'I hope you don't play poker: you're a terrible liar.'

Joni sighs. She feels exhausted. She's not up for bantering with a virtual stranger who she can't even ask to leave her office because he has as much right to be here

308

as she does. It's suddenly all too much. Ant, Mary, Saffy and now Lucas. Everything. 'She should have known that letting people into her life was a mistake. It felt as if once you opened the door a crack there was a stampede. You could never close it again.

'I just want to go home,' she says quietly and, to her absolute horror, a tear rolls down her cheek. She shakes her head in an effort to dislodge it before he sees, but it's too late.

'Shit, Jone, are you OK? I didn't mean to upset you, I was just messing . . .'

'I'm fine,' she says, so clearly not fine that she almost laughs. Outside in the corridor her colleagues have started heading for the lifts in a steady stream of rising hysteria. The hotel is only two minutes away, but they'll all be soaked by the time they get there. She can't leave until the rush is over, not if she wants to avoid more conversations about why she's such a killjoy. She wants to be on her own, though. 'You should go,' she says to Lucas. 'You'll miss all the excitement.'

'I'll live. Although I can get out of the way if you want to be left alone.'

She wants to say yes, but it sounds too abrupt, so she settles for a grunt. She doesn't really care what he does. She'll just wait until the crowd dies down and then leave. She sits down at the desk and slumps in her chair, willing him not to chat to her.

'I've got an idea,' he says. 'Wait here.'

He throws his shirt and cycling helmet on to the chair and goes out into the corridor, heading in the opposite direction to the crowd. Joni can hear people greeting him in amongst the raucous laughter. She thinks about sneaking out now while he's gone, but she can't summon up the energy. The giggling hordes are still outside. There's a bang on the glass wall and she looks up to see Caitlin from HR waving at her. 'You coming?' she shouts.

'Maybe later,' Joni says, not meaning it, but it seems easier than getting into another conversation about why she'd rather not. Caitlin moves on, satisfied. Joni angles the chair so it's facing away from the corridor, pretending to be absorbed in something on her phone.

'Here.' Lucas is back, now brandishing a bottle of red wine and two plastic cups from the water dispenser.

'Where did you get that?'

'Peter always has a couple in his office, I've noticed,' he says, naming their boss. 'I left a Post-it saying I'd replace it tomorrow.'

She raises a half-hearted smile. 'You're a braver man than me.' Office gossip has it that Peter laughed at something once, but no one has ever produced any proof. It's up there with sightings of the Loch Ness monster. 'I can't really drink red though.'

'Why not?'

'I get too drunk.'

'Isn't that the idea?' he says, and she realizes she doesn't really have an argument for that.

He pulls a chair over to the other side of the desk, sits down and pours two glasses of the red, then he scoots back and puts his feet up. Joni recoils slightly. 'We don't have to talk if you don't want to. We can just sit here and drink this till you feel up to the journey home. Although I am a good listener, just saying. Where do you live anyway?'

'Frognal. Off the Finchley Road,' she adds when she sees his blank expression. She takes a sip of her wine, looks at the label on the bottle. 'Is this expensive?'

Lucas gets out his phone. 'God knows. I hope not. I should take a photo of the label so I can get exactly the same thing. I did sign the note "John from IT" though, so if I can't, or it's too much, it's not really a problem.'

That actually makes her laugh. 'You didn't?'

'Of course I didn't. Although I might go and change it later.'

'Is there a John in IT?'

'No idea.'

They sit there in silence for a moment, and she's grateful that he's not trying to chat to her. The tide outside has reduced to a trickle. A few late stragglers. She should go. But suddenly she can't face the solitude. She just needs someone to tell her what to do.

'Do you really want to know why I'm upset?' she says, and she's sure she sees a brief look of fear on his face. It's one thing to offer to listen, it's a whole other to have someone take you up on it.

'If you want to tell me.'

'I want to tell someone. I don't know that it's necessarily you . . .'

'Wow, you know how to make a man feel special.'

'Sorry, that sounded way ruder than I intended it to. I

just mean . . . Well, I don't know what I mean.' She leans back in her own chair and mirrors his position, feet up. Rubs a hand over her eyes.

'Let's start again. You've got a lot on your mind and it might help to offload some of it. I'm not the ideal candidate but I am, at least, someone with no skin in the game who might be able to give you an impartial opinion. Plus I'm very discreet. About the important stuff, that is. I'm an awful gossip about trivia.'

She thinks about it. It would be a relief to just offload. To download the contents of her brain on to the table and leave them there. 'OK. You asked for it,' she says. 'How long have you got?'

Joni is grateful that Lucas doesn't interrupt once as she recites the whole story from the beginning right up to the latest bombshell about Deirdre. The offices are silent now, the last partygoers having finally left, everyone waving as they went on their way. It's only seven o'clock, but it feels as if they've been sitting there for hours.

'Jesus,' he says when she gets to the end.

'Is that it? That's the best you've got?'

'Probably.' He lifts his feet off the desk, grimaces as he bends his stiff knees, rubbing at the left one with his hand. 'Did her hair look nice, though?'

Joni screws up her face. 'Who?'

'Mary. Did she at least get a good haircut out of it?'

She laughs. It's impossible not to. 'Yes, actually. Deirdre clearly has skills.'

'What if you steal the car back?'

'He gets the insurance money and we're left with a stolen car.'

'Exactly. I was just trying to catch you out. More wine?'

She nods her assent. 'Thanks.'

'Get someone to buy it off him and then when he's signed it over stop the payment. Or, I don't know, steal the money back.'

'I don't even know if he's still got it. He probably cashed in straight away.'

'So, as far as we know, he has, what? Forty, forty-five grand sitting in his bank account, assuming Mary is his first target.'

'Depending on what he got for the car, yes. All legit apart from the fact that he owes it all to Mary – except that there's absolutely no evidence to prove that.'

They both sit and stare into the distance for a few moments. Suddenly Lucas slams his hand on the desk. 'I've got it!'

Joni's heart leaps into her mouth. 'What? Tell me!'

'Kill them both,' he says triumphantly. She looks at him for a second and then she begins to laugh, and so does he. She doesn't know why she finds it so funny, but it's such a relief that when she starts she can't stop. Lucas has a surprisingly booming laugh, like a skinny post-detox Santa, ho-ho-hoing away. They finally stop, and then they start again. And then, at exactly the same moment, they both stop once more, as if they've sobered up in a split second.

'We're actually fucked,' Joni says.

40

By the time she and Lucas leave at about half past seven – she to home, he to the party – she's feeling more than a little tipsy and no more optimistic than she was before. She does feel lighter, though. Unburdened.

'Oh, wait. We have to put the little fellas out,' Lucas says as she's about to turn the light out. He's clutching his shirt, his cycling helmet and trouser clip in a carrier bag that he found in one of the desk drawers. He decided he couldn't be bothered to change in the end. It has somehow evolved that Joni uses the drawers on the right and Lucas those on the left. Joni's are neat and ordered, Lucas's like an explosion in a rubbish tip. She tries not to think about them whenever she's sitting at the desk or the urge to tidy them would overwhelm her.

'Not really,' she says. 'Aren't you a bit . . . I don't know . . . old?'

He looks at her, confused. 'What?'

'For the toys. I mean, collectibles, whatever they are. Can't you live without seeing them for a day?' She hopes she doesn't sound too judgemental. She's not trying to be mean. She's just genuinely curious and a bit too drunk to be subtle.

'No. What? It's because of the memo . . .'

'What memo?'

'The memo about the desks . . . Didn't you get it?'

She screws up her face. 'I have literally no idea what you're talking about.'

'Wait. You thought . . .? You didn't get that memo from Judith about keeping our desks free from personal clutter?'

'No. It must have come on one of your days. Aren't we supposed to leave that kind of thing for the other one to read?'

Lucas looks up from setting out the figurines. 'This is too good. You thought I put these out because I like them? They're not even mine, they're my nephew's. He's a bit of a nerd, I'm not going to lie, but he's only seventeen so he might grow out of it. Or not. He's a good kid. There was a memo saying we had to leave our desktops clear. No personal items. Actually printed out and left on all our desktops. The irony. You really didn't see it?'

She shakes her head.

'This is my petty little protest. I like to imagine Judith's face every morning as she walks past and sees them. I'm still waiting for her to pull me up on it. I thought you were joining in with your animals.'

'I was trying to piss you off,' Joni says. 'I was annoyed at having to put your tat away every morning.'

'Ha! Brilliant. OK, let's put them all out.' He starts unloading them from the drawers. 'Hopefully I'll be here to see her expression when she staggers in with a hang-over in the morning and spots them.'

'What do you do the rest of the days? When you're

not here, I mean. If that's not too personal a question.' She's realizes she knows absolutely nothing about him and all they've talked about is her and her problems.

'Do you not know? I can't believe someone hasn't told you,' he says, sounding genuinely surprised.

'No. Should they have? Is it something exciting?' She's intrigued.

'Are you sure? God, I would have thought word would have got round . . .'

'OK, you have to tell me now,' Joni says, stuffing her umbrella back into her bag. The rain has all but stopped.

'Well . . .' he says, pausing for added suspense. 'On Tuesdays, Thursdays and Fridays I actually work in the accounts department of a firm of accountants. I know! You couldn't make it up!'

Joni looks at him to see if he's joking. 'You probably could make that up actually.'

'No, you really couldn't. It's too fucking boring. I'm not just an accountant, I'm some kind of double accountant. Accountant squared.'

She laughs. 'Strictly speaking you're Payroll and Infrastructure Services here.'

'Is that what our official title is? The glamour! I do payroll there too. I'm all about the payroll. Can't get enough of it. How about you? What delights do Mondays and Wednesdays bring?'

'Nothing.'

'What? Literally nothing?'

She shrugs. 'I go to the gym.'

'Is that a job?' Lucas says, dribbling the last of the

wine into his cup and knocking it back after Joni shakes her head no to any more.

'I wish. No, I . . . My life is very boring.'

'Join the club,' he says, standing back so she can go through the door before him. 'I'm actually quite envious of your conman drama.'

She makes an effort to have a normal Wednesday, not to get caught up in anything other than her own life. She goes to Waitrose in the morning, carries her shopping home in a taxi, and then the gym at precisely four o'clock. She struggles to lose herself in her session as she normally does. It feels like a chore. The day feels as dry and inflexible as a work day. So she ends up FaceTiming Saffy and Mary when she gets home to check in, and spending an hour alternately picking over the Ant situation again, and laughing at some outrageous exclamation of Saffy's. As she's preparing something to eat a text from Lucas arrives with a picture attached: *See what you missed out on!* The photo seems to be of Judith, the office manager, being sick into a shiny green parlour palm. It feels odd to get a message from him that's not about some half-finished piece of work he's intending to leave for her to do. How strange that he turned out to be the person she confided in, she thinks. She checks herself to see if she regrets it but, on balance – apart from feeling like an idiot that she cried in front of him – she's glad.

Damn! she replies. *If I'd realized it was such a classy do . . .*

A few seconds later there's a reply: *There's always next year.*

If I'm still working there by this time next year I'm the one who'll be throwing up into the foliage, she replies. *On a regular basis.* She really does need to leave her job, she knows that now. It's sucking the life out of her. But the idea of seven whole days without any kind of structure beyond the gym and food shopping terrifies her. She needs to work out what she wants to do with the rest of her life. She needs to take more risks, be spontaneous, embrace the changes that are happening in her life.

She breaks out in a cold sweat just thinking about it.

41

On Thursday morning there is a memo from Judith on her desk. *Good morning,* it says. *I'm sure you must have missed my note a while back asking that staff please refrain from cluttering up their desks with personal items, but please note that this is now an office regulation.*

She snaps a photo of it and sends it to Lucas with a smiley face.

Quick, let's buy some more! he sends back. *Maybe we can get them to sack you, put you out of your misery.*

Buy me a quick drink and you can tell me all about the party! she writes and then she deletes it immediately. What is she doing? Then she thinks, Sod it, why not? I'm supposed to be taking risks. So she types the same again and this time she presses send.

She waits. Answers an email about holiday pay. Her phone beeps.

Tonight?

She smiles to herself. *Can't. Date with Ant!*

Jesus! Lucas responds. *I'm getting blown out for a serial con artist. That's a dent in a man's pride.*

Tomorrow? I could meet you when I get off work, she sends before she gets cold feet.

Deal, he replies immediately. *I'll lurk around in the foyer at 6.*

*

Ant cooks her a curry with tofu and chickpeas and her kitchen fills up with warm, spicy aromas. She lights candles and stacks logs in the wood burner from a pile by the back door. It's chilly in the evenings now, but it's rare that she can be bothered with a real fire. It gives her something to do, though, a task that means she can avoid making small talk with him. Because their talk has always been small, she's realized that. They never really had anything in common besides working out and a few surface traits like their love of old films. Clearly their values couldn't be more different. Maybe subconsciously that was why she'd been drawn to him. There had been no danger of a deep connection.

She jumps as there's a knock on her door. It can only be Flick or the two from the top floor. She could try to ignore it, but Ant would want to know why.

'I'll get it,' she shouts, running to the door. Of course it's Flick. She's standing there with a casserole full of God-knows-what in her hands. When Joni had first moved in this had been a regular occurrence. Flick would materialize the second Joni arrived home from work with a spare loaf of bread she'd baked, or lumpy-looking oat cookies. Imo would feed them to the birds from the back window.

'Well, judging by the smell you've already got something lovely for dinner . . .' She pauses as Joni indicates for her to lower her voice. She's terrified Flick will say her name. She has a tendency to pepper her conversation with the moniker of whoever she is speaking to, just in case they forget who they are. '. . . but I made an extra pasta bake and I know you're always rushed off your feet, so I thought . . .' She obediently speaks in a half-whisper. Joni can think of little she desires less than Flick's leftovers, but she decides the best way to get rid of her quickly is just to accept. She reaches out a hand to take the pot. 'That's so kind of you. I can have it tomorrow. I'm just in the middle of . . .' She waves a vague hand in the direction of the kitchen. 'I have a friend here.'

'Ah,' Flick says as if the penny has dropped. 'Well, don't let me disturb you.'

'Thank you so much for this,' Joni says. 'I'll let you have the dish back.'

She's already closing the door as she says it.

'Who was that?' Ant asks as she plonks the casserole down on the counter.

'Upstairs neighbour. She's very sweet but completely barking. She brought me dinner.'

'You should have invited her in,' he says. 'I'd like to meet your friends.'

'God, no. I'd never get her out again. Thankfully she's allergic to Jasper or I'd be fighting her off every night.'

'I should go up and introduce myself,' he says, circling his arms around her.

'You'd regret it immediately,' Joni says, leaning into him. That had been too close for her liking.

It's odd watching him, knowing that his wife is on board with everything he's doing. It explains the confidence, the absolute security in the role he's playing. All he has to do is concentrate on being rich, successful, loving Ant. There's no guilt holding him back. No fear of exposure to anyone he actually cares about. What's the worst that could happen in his world? That one of them realizes he's not genuine? It would just be a mild inconvenience, a slight delay in the schedule while he sought out and groomed a new target. No big deal. You can achieve a lot if you have absolutely nothing to lose.

And it must be even easier if you know you have another fifty-thousand-pound car coming your way in a couple of weeks' time. There's not long left, she realizes. They need to move quickly.

By Friday evening she's exhausted and wishing she hadn't made plans to meet Lucas. She can't wait for it all to be over with Ant. To be officially single again with her evenings to herself. Not single in the way she was after Ian left – involuntarily single, feeling like a failure single – but by choice. Happily single. Able to concentrate on herself and getting her own life in order. Lucas is hovering near the revolving doors when she gets down to the foyer. Thankfully not wearing Lycra although he is holding his helmet, and when she looks down she sees the clip holding one leg of his jeans in tight. He's saying goodnight to everyone as they leave as if he's the new doorman. He's popular, she realizes. Much more so than she, who makes zero effort. She wonders if her colleagues ever compare them: *Oh thank God, it's Lucas in today. Get the party poppers out.* She wouldn't blame them.

'I knew you'd be bang on time,' he says when he sees

her. 'I bet you spend the last half-hour counting down the seconds every night.'

'Don't you?'

'I love my job,' he says with a wry smile. 'I live for accounting. Where do you want to go?'

She realizes she knows nothing about the local pubs. Has never once had a drink with a co-worker. 'Shall we wander towards Marylebone High Street? See what we find on the way?'

He nods. 'Let's do it.'

He's disappointed when she tells him she didn't display the figurines before she left. 'I don't want to get sacked,' she says, laughing as he tells her she's let the side down.

'Why not? I thought you were desperate to get out of there. We should have a competition. See who gets the chop first.'

'No one's going to fire Mr Life and Soul of the Party. They'll make an example of me. Put my head on a spike in the foyer as a warning to the rest of you.'

'I would knuckle down immediately,' he says, turning into a narrow side street. 'I'd become a model employee. How about in here?'

They're outside a tiny, ancient pub, all crooked wooden beams and with a door that lists alarmingly to one side. The lights glow a welcoming orange through diamond-paned windows.

'Lovely. Is there a table?'

They find a corner table that has just enough space for them to squeeze into. 'Shall I get a bottle?' Joni says when she realizes they both want white wine. 'Save us having to fight our way up there again.'

Lucas looks like a rabbit caught in the headlights. 'Let me buy it then. Otherwise you'll have bought me, like, three drinks and I'll have paid for nothing. I'll be as bad as Ant.'

She laughs. 'This one can be payback for the bottle in the office the other night. Did you ever replace it by the way?'

'Of course. But I found out the one we drank actually cost about two hundred pounds . . .'

'No!'

'Yes. Luckily I'd taken my note off first thing next morning, just in case. And then I bought something that looked similar but cost a tenth of the price. Hopefully he'll never even notice. And if he does he won't know it was me.'

'Did it taste like two hundred pounds' worth to you? I can't even remember.'

Lucas shrugs. 'It tasted like wine.'

'Exactly.'

'I've been thinking about your little problem,' he says. And?'

'No clue. Nothing.'

'Brilliant. Worst money I ever spent,' she says, moving off to the bar.

By eight o'clock they've finished the bottle and they each have an extra glass in front of them. Joni now knows that Lucas has never been married, that he lived with a woman called Ira for twelve years until a couple of years ago when he decided to call it quits – 'I felt bad, but I used to dread going home. Everything either of us did just drove the other one crazy. We get on really well now. I'm godfather to her twins' – and that he has a spin bike at home and does twenty kilometres every morning before he gets on his actual bike and cycles to work.

'Why cycling?' Joni asks. It's never been something she enjoys.

He shrugs. 'It makes me feel good. Why weights?'

'Good point. Same.'

Somehow they lose half an hour talking about their training programmes and nutrition regimes and recovery tips. Joni finds herself offering to show him round the machines in Power Fit and agreeing to try a Peloton class with him one day. She could chat about this stuff all night, she realizes. Never get bored.

'I shouldn't drink any more,' she says, once her glass is empty.

'Me neither.'

'You're not cycling home, are you?' she says anxiously. He's more than a little tipsy, and so is she.

'I'll come back and pick it up tomorrow.' He lives in Clapham, he tells her, south of the river. 'In the kind of glamorous home you might expect someone with two mid-level accounting jobs to have.'

They walk towards Wigmore Street. 'I'll think about your Ant situation over the weekend,' he promises as they say goodbye on the corner. 'I'll dedicate my every waking hour to trying to come up with a solution.'

'Anything,' she says, pulling the belt on her coat

tighter. 'However ludicrous. We need all the help we can get.' She sticks out a hand to flag down a taxi. 'Have a good weekend.'

'You too.' He waves as he turns and heads for the tube at Oxford Circus.

Joni calls Imo on the way home, checking first that it isn't too late because she knows her daughter has to get up extra early on Saturdays. Mary texts her with an invitation to lunch tomorrow – *I'm inviting Saffy too. It would be lovely if you could come* – and she accepts without even thinking about it. It would seem odd at this point not to see either of them for more than a couple of days, even without the common bond of Ant and his deception.

God, she thinks. I have a social life. It gives her a warm, fuzzy feeling.

She's already asleep when her phone buzzes. She reaches for it, plugged in on the bedside table, irritated. It's gone midnight: why would anyone be texting her at this time? She sees that it's Lucas.

Call me tomorrow, it says. *I think I know what you should do.*

42

Mary has barely seen Ant lately. For someone who claims he wants them to live together he hasn't been making much of an effort to spend time with her, and for that she's glad. It saves her from having to come up with excuses. She knows that he's concentrating his efforts on Joni and Saffy, waiting for those short-term investments to pay off. Meanwhile he's claiming commitments with his kids, and who is she to argue?

She has told him that she's registered her house with a private property company. That she doesn't want to put it on the open market until the new year if there has still been no interest by then. St John's Wood is such a desirable area, she reassured him. And so finite. She's sure it will sell in no time. Obviously, none of this is true. She's more determined than ever to remain in the home she and Andrew cherished.

They've been talking about where they might live. Mary has quite enjoyed the hypothetical conversations debating the pros of Hampstead versus Holland Park (more green space, fewer chauffeurs idling in the streets) or whether the relaxed pace of life in Richmond more than made up for the stress of the two hours stuck in traffic it might take you to get to the West End from there. A couple of times he had sent her links to properties he'd seen online – none costing less than 7 million, she'd noticed. She had told him the property consultant had suggested that would be a reasonable price to ask for her place and she had practically seen pound signs flicker in his eyes as if he were a walking one-armed bandit – and she had found reasons for them not to go and look at them (too small, too big, on a main road, miles from anywhere useful). She knew that he was trying to rush her before she could come to her senses – or speak to her children – and call the whole thing off.

Tonight, though, they are finally going to look at somewhere. A five-thousand-square-foot modernist box.

And she can't wait.

He has pored over the photos she showed him, attached to the email from the same private property finder who, she tells him, is hunting for a buyer for her place. It's standard practice that many high-end homes never even make it as far as an estate agent's website: their details get passed around a network of people hunting for homes for their wealthy clients who are willing to pay a premium for the service. 'Six point five?' he'd asked, his eyes like saucers. 'So we'd have money spare to change whatever we wanted. New kitchen? Sauna?' It was always 'we' when he talked about the new house, she'd noticed. She had linked her arm through his and rested her head on his shoulder.

They are meeting at hers and she'll drive them there. He didn't want to have to take his car to work, he'd said, so she's still none the wiser about whether he's sold it or not. The appointment is at seven. They could have waited until the weekend, but he's impatient. He needs to get this show on the road. Half of this six-point-five house securely registered in his name. She imagines he doesn't really care what it looks like or where it is. Just the price tag.

She's glad she's driving. It gives her something to focus on. She's nervous around him now. She has no idea what lengths he might go to, what else he could be planning. They're a little early so she takes a deliberate wrong turn and drives round in a circle. Phil the property finder is meeting them outside, she tells Ant. He has the keys so they'll have free rein with no owners breathing down their necks.

'I'm excited,' she says to him as they turn into the road at one minute to seven.

He reaches over and takes her hand. 'Me too.'

Phil is waiting outside, wearing an expensive-looking suit, leaning on a flash-looking silver car, checking his phone. He smiles as they pull in.

'Mary! How are you?' he says, extending a hand for her to shake. 'And you must be Anthony. Pleasure. So, this is it . . .'

Mary steals a glance at Ant. She can tell his eyes are popping out of his head even though he's trying to act blasé. After all, this is the world he lives in, or so he wants her to believe.

'You find it OK?' Phil says.

'Pretty much,' she says. 'It's lovely.' She looks at Ant.

'Stunning,' he says.

'Just quickly before we go in and then I'll leave you to explore, unless you have any questions – as I told you, Mary, the owners are moving to Dubai, so no chain and they want a quick sale. Hence why the price per square foot is so good. They might even come down a little if pushed. Right . . .'

He opens the front door and steps aside for them to go in. The airy hall smells of lilies. 'I'll be right here if you need me,' Phil says. 'The main living space is through there.' He waves his hand at a tall door. Mary opens it and they enter an L-shaped space that takes up most of the ground floor. She wishes they could have come in the day and seen the light through the wall of glass that looks on to the garden, but it's still breathtaking. Uplighters illuminate the walls outside with a warm orange glow. Two huge sofas sit either side of a large black coffee table in one end of the room with the kitchen at the opposite end of the L and a long dining table in the space between.

'Can you imagine us here with our families?' Mary says. The other day she had asked Ant about meeting his children, just to see what he would say, and he'd made a sad face and told her that Camille wouldn't allow it, not yet.

'I've tried to explain that you're not some casual fling,' he'd said. 'That we're moving in together. But she still says it's too soon.'

'She's just being a good mum,' Mary had said. 'I'm sure she'll be fine with a bit of time.'

He loops an arm round her shoulder. 'My two, your boys. Imagine Christmas.'

'Let's look upstairs,' she says, taking his hand. They pass Phil in the hall and he gives them a smile. 'All OK?'

'Fabulous,' Mary says, smiling back.

On the first floor there is a vast suite with two dressing rooms and two bathrooms. Only one of each seems to be occupied.

'Whoever she is she got the best end of the divorce,' Ant jokes. She can see him imagining himself living here, having this lifestyle. Nothing but the best. He's forgotten that the point would be to persuade her they should sell again as soon as was legally possible and disappear into the ether with a cool 3 million plus.

'I've always thought I'd like to do a bedroom in browns and coppers, maybe a bit of gold,' she says. They have never once discussed their personal taste in furnishings. He knows next to nothing about her beyond the bare facts. The idea of them setting up home together is ludicrous.

'That sounds a bit too much like the flagship Evoke,' he says, laughing. 'But you can decorate in any way you want. Whatever makes you happy.'

They wander up to the floor above: three more bedrooms, two more bathrooms. Each one a small work of art.

'Stunning, isn't it?' Mary says.

He pulls her into his arms. 'It's perfect. What if they can't wait till you sell yours?'

'If we give them a good enough offer Phil says they

will,' Mary says confidently. 'We could even exchange and then delay completion. I'm sure the bank would lend me the money. And then, by the time we complete you and Camille might have sold too.'

'Exactly,' he says, clearly knowing this will never happen.

'Let's go down and have another look at the main living space. Really get a feel for it. I think there's a study down there too, and a TV room. And there's the gym in the basement.'

'And then I'll buy you dinner,' he says.

'Lovely.'

Phil is still hanging round in the hall. 'It's perfect, mate,' Ant says. 'It's a very definite possible.'

'Good stuff,' Phil says. 'Take your time, while you're here. No rush.'

Mary wanders back into the living room, Ant ahead of her. He stops as he sees people gathered on the two sofas. Double-takes as he realizes those people are Joni and Saffy. Or Lucy and Saffy as Ant knows them.

'What the fuck?' he says, rooted to the spot.

'Hi, Ant,' Joni says with a smile. 'Isn't Saffy's house beautiful?'

43

It had been Lucas's idea. Lucas, who is now dressed in one of Saffy's ex's old suits that he left behind when he moved out so hurriedly. Lucas, who is doing a very fair impression of a property finder called Phil. It was Joni's brainwave to move Saffy's silver Aston Martin on to the drive for him to drape himself over.

'Very funny, ladies,' Ant says, trying to appear unconcerned. It's not working. Shock is written all over his face. 'What is this?'

'We thought it was time we chatted. All of us together,' Joni says. It feels natural that she's the one who takes charge. She started this whole thing, after all.

'We don't have anything to talk about,' Ant says, turning as if to leave. Mary and Lucas stand in the doorway. Not that either of them could block him if he was determined. ('You do know I'm a coward,' Lucas had said to Joni when she'd told him he might have to do this. 'And I have absolutely no muscles. You're probably stronger than me.' 'Definitely,' she had said. 'Anyway, it won't just be you. You'll have back-up.')

Ant looks as if he's thinking about making a break for it, but they all know there's no way he'll wrestle Mary to the ground. Even he must have some limits. They're counting on it.

'There's the small matter of the fifty thousand Mary lent you,' Joni says before he can change his mind. He turns round with a smirk on his face.

'Is that what she told you? She bought me that car; it was a gift.'

'It wasn't, Ant, you know that,' Mary says quietly. 'You promised to pay me back.'

'Is it my fault if you felt so insecure you had to buy my affection?'

'Whoa,' Saffy says, standing up. 'Fuck right off.'

Ant turns to her. 'I wondered when you'd pipe up. Don't tell me you didn't think it was laughable when you met her? That I'd be with some old granny because I'd actually fallen for her?'

'You really are a piece of shit,' Saffy says. 'She's worth ten of you.'

Joni pulls at Saffy's arm to get her to sit down again. It's not out of the question that she'll hurl herself at Ant, fists flying, and that definitely isn't part of the plan. She needs to get this back on track. 'If that's the case, why did you ask me to lend you money to buy a car too? Or did you lose the one she bought you?'

'I like cars,' he says facetiously.

'All you need to do is pay her back and that'll be that,' Joni says. The adrenaline is making her feel invincible. 'I assume you've sold the car, or you're going to. It's not as if you can't raise the money.'

'Mr CEO,' Saffy says. 'How's Camille? And Amelia and Jack?'

He ignores her. 'Prove it,' he says, addressing himself

to Joni. 'Prove it was a loan. It'd be my word against hers. Do you really think she wants her sons to have to hear the whole sorry tale?'

'You're right,' Joni says, calmer now. 'We can't prove it. I suppose I was hoping you might have a shred of decency in there somewhere.'

'Ha!' Saffy exclaims loudly.

'God, you're annoying,' Ant says, scowling at her.

'What about the fifty grand you were asking me for? Were you ever intending to pay that back? Or were you going to try to pretend that was a gift too?'

'Oh, Lucy—' he says, and Joni interrupts.

'My name's not Lucy, by the way.'

He screws up his face at her. 'What is it then?'

'Joni.' She waits to see if he puts the pieces together.

'Joni who stood me up?'

She nods. 'You're not the only one who can play games.' She has no idea what she means by this. She was never playing a game. She was looking for companionship. Love. But she thinks it might unsettle him. Leave him thinking he might not hold all the cards after all. She's gratified to see that he does, indeed, look rattled.

'So how did you three witches meet?' he says with forced confidence.

'Such a charmer,' Saffy says.

'Well, you obviously thought so.'

'Let's talk about the fact that you're trying to persuade Mary to buy a house and put it in both your names, then,' Joni interrupts.

'That's between me and Mary,' he says. 'Are you jealous that she's the one I wanted to live with?'

Saffy snorts. 'You never had any intention of living with her. You just admitted yourself that you weren't really interested in her. You just wanted half her house.'

'You thought you could steal the most from me.' Mary is holding herself steady with one hand on the door frame.

'Like taking candy from a baby,' Ant says with a smirk. 'Right, if this meeting is over, I'm leaving. But let's do this again sometime, it was fun!'

'How were you ever going to pay your share of the new house? From the sale of something that doesn't exist? Didn't you tell her that you were in the process of selling your own eight-million-pound home? You told me that. And Saff too, I think.'

'Didn't you tell me your name was Lucy?'

Joni just stares at him. Waits for him to continue.

'Mary and I are looking for a home together, yes. Well, *were*, I expect now. I think that ship might have sailed. If she wanted to put my name on the deeds what was I supposed to do?'

'No,' Mary says loudly. They all turn to look at her. 'I'm not having this. It was all your idea. And you said that when your own house sale went through you would pay me back. Just for the record I never believed it. I may be naïve but I'm not stupid. I was just stringing you along . . .'

Ant laughs. 'Like you were stringing me along with the car, I suppose? Not stupid, but you bought someone you'd known for five minutes a car and believed that they would pay you back one day.'

'So, you do admit that it was meant to be a loan?' Joni says.

'Who cares?' Ant says. 'She never asked me to sign anything so there's no proof either way. Go to the police, do your best, good luck. You have no fucking chance of proving anything. They'll laugh at you.'

'Poor Deirdre,' Saffy says. They've agreed not to let on what they know about his wife. See if he will trip himself up.

Ant's head whips around. 'Poor Deirdre? You think I was cheating on her? You think I was sneaking around behind her back? I would never do that.'

'I wonder if she would think sleeping with two other women and trying to shag a third means you're not cheating.'

'It would only be cheating if she didn't know,' he says.

Mary gasps theatrically. 'She knows? And she's OK with it?'

'She's more than OK with it. God, you really are stupid. She helped me pick you out.'

'So, basically, you trawled dating sites with your wife looking for wealthy victims, is that what you're saying?' Joni says, spelling it out. 'You set this whole thing up from the beginning as a way to con vulnerable women out of their money?'

'I think "con" is a bit of a strong word. If a woman is sad enough to believe I'm in love with her and wants to shower me with gifts, who am I to say no?'

'Except the car wasn't a gift, was it?'

'OK. So if she's sad enough to lend a virtual stranger fifty thousand pounds without anything in writing then. Is that what you want me to say?'

'It is, actually,' Joni says. They've done it. 'Thanks.'

44

They all stand in silence for a moment. Joni sneaks a glance at Saffy, who smiles and raises her eyebrows.

'I really am leaving now,' Ant says. 'And Mr Bean there isn't going to stop me.'

Joni gives Lucas a nod and he, in return, turns and gives a subtle thumbs up to someone behind him in the hallway. As Ant approaches, Mary edges out of the way and two boys of about nineteen or twenty, one of them built like Lennox Lewis in his prime, step into the gap.

Ant stops dead. 'Who are these clowns?' he says, but there's a nervous edge to his voice. It's only then that he notices one of them is holding a small camera, which is pointed his way, and the other a boom microphone. 'Is this a joke?' he says. 'Is it one of those stupid YouTube prank shows?' It's obvious that he daren't try to push past them though. The boys part to make the tiniest gap and a young girl slips through. Skinny limbs, long dark hair. Imogen. She's holding a smaller microphone and she thrusts it into Ant's face.

'I'm from Foot in the Door Productions,' she says, flashing him the ID badge that she has around her neck. 'And we're making a show about dating-site fraudsters. Do you have anything to say about the fact you've just admitted to stealing fifty thousand pounds from Mary here?'

Joni beams with pride. She had finally confided the whole story to her daughter, once Lucas had come up with his plan. Mostly, if she were being honest, because that plan was contingent on Imo's involvement – Joni loved that he'd remembered what she'd told him about Imogen's course: the fact that they buddied people up depending on their specialties. Camera or sound, presenting or directing. That they were expected to spend a couple of days a week working on their pilot series idea. That Imogen's interest was in factual shows. She wasn't sure Imo would actually use this footage as part of her submission – she rather hoped not, although she didn't feel she could say that – but she certainly had the skills and the friends to pull it off. Joni was pretty sure one of the boys – Rhys, the man mountain holding the boom – was more than just a friend. They both seemed like lovely boys and had jumped at the chance to travel down for the night and film something real. They were all staying at hers tonight. She couldn't wait to be feeding hungry teenagers again.

'I haven't admitted to anything,' he says. 'Give me that thing.' He reaches out for the camera. Rhys steps in front of him and he lowers his hand.

'I think you'll find we have the whole thing on tape,' Imo says. Joni finds herself hoping this isn't the field Imo decides to go into. Better she moves into directing nice period dramas. More hats; less chance of physical violence. 'There are cameras everywhere, in case you hadn't noticed.'

Ant looks round, and Joni sees the moment he spots the first Ring camera nestled on a shelf. There are three more, covering the whole room at different angles. Hardly professional, broadcast-standard footage, but perfectly acceptable in this case. Evidence. Ant nods. 'Clever. I know you can't use this footage though. Not unless I sign something.'

Joni has no idea if this is true or not, and she's not sure Ant does, but it's beside the point. 'But we can show it to the police,' she says. 'Mary can use it when she sues you to get her money back.'

'Do you still have the car you bought?' Imo says. Joni gives her a thumbs-up.

Ant looks at Joni, the penny dropping. 'Is this Dani?'

'Something like that,' Joni says.

'Unbelievable.'

'Do you?' Imo pushes.

He suddenly looks exhausted. All the bluff seems to go out of him; his shoulders drop and it's as if he actually deflates. 'No,' he says. 'I sold it.'

Imo flashes him a fake smile. 'So you have the money. You can pay her back.'

'Have you done this to anyone else before?' Mary says. She's sitting on one of the high kitchen chairs, by the central island.

He shakes his head. 'No.'

'So you say,' Saffy snaps.

Ant looks as if he's about to snap back but then checks himself. The footage is bad enough as it is.

'Like I said' – Imo takes a step towards him – 'you can pay her back.'

Ant ignores her, looks at Mary. 'I only got forty-four thousand for it. It was a quick sale.'

'Fine,' Mary says.

'Then you need to come up with another six,' Saffy says.

'No, Saffy, it's OK. If Ant pays me back forty-four now I'll accept it. I'll write off the other six to experience.'

'No. Fuck . . .'

'Yes,' Mary says firmly.

'You can't say fairer that that, Ant,' Imo says. 'How about we do it now?'

'Fine. Fuck it,' he says. 'And then it's over, right? Done?'

'Done,' Joni says. 'We'll keep the footage, obviously, just in case. I'd hate to find out some other poor woman had fallen for your shit.'

They all watch as Ant gets out his phone and asks Mary for her account details. Rhys stays firmly blocking the door until Mary has phoned her bank and confirmed that the money is there, awaiting clearance. They have to take it on trust that he won't call his own and stop the payment the minute he leaves the house – it's either that or keep him prisoner here for up to a day, waiting – but it seems unlikely. They have their proof. They know where to find him. He knows when he's defeated.

'This isn't who I am,' he says, looking between the three of them. He seems almost penitent.

342

'Oh, it totally fucking is,' Saffy says.

They all watch as he leaves, Rhys stepping out of the way to let him pass.

'Don't expect a Christmas card!' Saffy shouts as the front door slams.

'He's gone,' Hal, the trainee camera operator, calls from the hall. There's a collective sigh of relief and then Joni, Saffy and Mary throw themselves into a group hug.

'You were all brilliant,' Joni says, beckoning the others over. Lucas and Imo join the scrum, the two boys hovering on the periphery. 'You too,' she says, pulling them in. 'We couldn't have done it without any of you.'

45

Imogen, Rhys and Hal leave for the station before Joni is even dressed for work. She cooks them all a huge breakfast and hands them bags of sandwiches for the journey. She presses a twenty-pound note into each of their hands before they leave.

'Buy food,' she says. 'Or whatever.'

'I like it here,' Rhys says. 'I'm coming again.'

'You were brilliant,' she says to Imo as she squeezes her tightly. 'I can't thank you enough.'

'If he ever contacts you again, call the police,' Imo says.

'Or me,' Rhys chips in. 'I'll sort him out. Bastard. Treating old ladies like that.'

Joni manages to ignore the 'old ladies' remark long enough to make a wish that Imo and Rhys really do become a couple if they aren't already. She waves them off as they walk down the road towards the tube station.

She had thought she might have trouble sleeping last night, fretting about whether they'd done the right thing or if Ant might decide to take his revenge somehow, but she'd been out as soon as her head hit the pillow. They'd all spent the evening at Saffy's in the end – she, Saffy, Mary, Lucas, Imo, Rhys and Hal – eating takeaway pizzas and drinking wine. It had felt like a family party.

She wasn't sure what time they'd got back to hers. After midnight certainly. And then she and Imo had sat up talking while the boys slept in the spare room. This morning she feels as if she's got a hangover. Not from the alcohol – they were all reasonably restrained, even Saffy – but from the come down after the high. She doesn't want to sit in a stuffy room all day hunched over a calculator. She doesn't want to cram herself on to the tube in rush hour. She doesn't want to make small talk and watch the minutes tick by slowly, wishing her life away. She unplugs her mobile. Fuck it. She's going to ring in sick for the first time ever.

Saffy wakes up with a clear head and a clean house. She had told Mary they could leave the tidying up till the morning as she steered her towards the guest room upstairs, but she hates going to bed and leaving a mess. She knows if she does she'll end up getting up at four in the morning to deal with it before she can allow herself to go back to sleep. And besides, there's something therapeutic about putting the house back in order after a successful evening. She and Stefan used to have parties all the time. Big, small, friends, acquaintances. Any excuse. She had always booked caterers – no way was she going to spend her day trying to make fiddly little parcels of finger food that would probably be inedible anyway – but she'd always dealt with the aftermath herself. She had actually looked forward to it which, considering she hated most household chores with a passion, was, quite frankly, weird. She liked to use the time to think over the evening: half the fun of a party was reliving it the next day. Assuming it had been a success (and her and Stef's were always a success). It put a full stop on the night. Gave her a sense of achievement. She had missed that.

So she stayed up clearing away glasses and plates, stashing cold pizza slices in the fridge. She wiped down the tables and straightened the cushions. She was tempted to hoover but she was afraid Mary might hear even from two storeys up. And it wasn't as if it really needed it anyway; they had hardly been a marauding horde. The kids had been sweet. Imogen was adorable. Feisty and protective of her mum. And the boys were clearly both a bit in love with her. She suddenly felt winded as she always did when she thought about how old her and Stefan's son or daughter would have been now if, the one time she had actually managed to get pregnant, the pregnancy had gone to term and not ended in Selfridges of all places. A spot and then a rush of blood as she sat in the personal shopping area waiting for the attentive assistant to bring her an assortment of dresses suitable for a summer outdoor party. The staff had been fantastic. They'd sat with her until the ambulance came, but by then she'd already known it was too late.

Seven. She – in her head the baby was always 'she', she'd been convinced she was having a girl – would have been seven.

She hadn't wanted to try again. She couldn't face the disappointment. Worse, she couldn't face the fear if she actually did manage to conceive again. So, she'd reinvented herself as someone who had never wanted children. Who'd had a lucky escape. Only Stef had known the truth and, even though he'd been devastated too, he'd supported her. Because that was what he did. He just wanted her to be happy. She'd probably have been a terrible mother anyway. The kind of mother who goes home from a restaurant and forgets her baby.

She checks the time. One in the morning. Five in the evening in LA. She finds her mobile and dials his number even though she knows he won't pick up. He never does. She listens to his voice on the recorded voicemail message and then she hangs up without saying anything.

Mary lies in Saffy's spare bed staring up at the ceiling. She can't quite believe that they have pulled it off. That Ant is out of her life forever. At least, she hopes so. She has a vague low-lying unease that he knows so much about her, but Joni has convinced her that he's been rendered harmless. She doesn't think they'll hear from him again. Still, Mary thinks she's going to be cautious about answering her door for a while. Maybe change her locks. Not that she ever gave him a key, but you never know. She might get a dog, she thinks. A big, scary-looking hound who's soft underneath. She reaches a hand down and rubs Tyson's tummy. Saffy had plonked him into her arms when she'd said she was off to bed. She likes the feel of him there, this little life. She'll check out the charities. Find some sad old thing that no one else wants. A bit like herself, she thinks, and laughs.

She's made a decision that she really is going to sell

her house. Not because she's worried that Ant will bother her there, but because she needs a fresh start. She had always imagined a home full of grandchildren but she doesn't think that's going to happen any more. Even when George and Millie start a family she no longer believes they will bring them up to stay. Maybe a duty visit once a year. Millie will want to keep her at arm's length. She has no doubt she'll see them, that she'll be a part of their lives, but it's always going to be on her daughter-in-law's terms. She knows how she was with her own mother-in-law. She'd always got on with her, but she had never involved her in the boys' lives in the same way she had her own parents. That was just the way of the world. What was that saying? A son is a son till he takes a wife, but a daughter is a daughter all her life. Something like that. And as for Oliver, he's in no hurry to settle down, and why should he be? He needed to sort himself out first, work out what he wants to do with his future. She'll make sure her new place has room for all of them whenever they want to come and stay, but she'll find somewhere more manageable. It's not healthy to stay in a mausoleum. Her old life has gone, like it or not. She needs to make a new one. She's thinking she might move up here, to Highgate. She likes the villagey feel, the proximity to the heath. She'll talk it over with Saffy and Joni tomorrow.

Ant fumes. He's lost everything he's worked so hard for for months. All that time and investment. If anything he's worse off. He's paid out for dinners left, right and centre. Nothing but the best. And he's exhausted. Mentally and physically drained. He was so close. So fucking close. He should never have got greedy. He should have stuck with the car scam, fleeced the three of them and then disappeared off into the sunset six figures richer.

He didn't even know where he was when he left Saffy's house, furious with himself that he'd been intimidated by teenagers, conned by a bunch of housewives. He had no idea who the stick insect pretending to be some kind of estate agent was. He stormed down the road and then got lost in a maze of residential streets. He'd called Deirdre as he turned left and then right with no idea where he was going, telling her that everything had gone to shit. She'd talked him down. Told him to come straight home. Not to do anything he would regret. Deirdre always knew what to say. He'd be lost without her, that was the truth. He'd had to ask someone the way to the nearest tube station.

He'd lost it all. A year's work. Night after night of making mind-numbing conversation with woman after woman. All those loss-leader expensive dinners and theatre tickets. All that lost sleep. And for nothing. Everything had gone to shit. He was back where he started. Nowhere.

46

Joni stands on the street looking at the oh-so-familiar house. It's barely changed in the thirty-eight years since she first came here but, even so, it's hard to imagine this was once her second home. The cypress in the front garden is three times as big, and the paintwork is shabbier. She thinks the front door used to be red, but she's really not sure any more. She looks up at the first-floor window, on the left. Meg's room until she left home at eighteen. The room where they spent most of their teenage afternoons.

She tells herself not to cry. Picks up the roses that are lying on the passenger seat. She's a little early but she doesn't think Margaret will mind. She got the feeling when she spoke to her on the phone that she didn't have anything else to do today. Meg's dad – Gerald – will be at work. Still on the go at seventy-eight, serving in the hardware shop in town. 'It takes his mind off things,' Margaret had said.

Joni had been nervous when she called. She knew she'd been selfish not staying in touch, but she'd figured Margaret and Gerald had each other – and their two sons, Meg's brothers. And she just couldn't face piling their own grief on top of her own. It would be too much to bear. It was almost too much as it was. But she knew the second Margaret recognized her voice that she'd done the right thing. There had been no hint of disappointment or resentment. Just sheer delight to hear from her.

She walks up the path and rings the doorbell. Margaret answers immediately, as if she's been waiting in the hall just behind the door. She's aged in the last two years, Joni thinks with a pang. Of course she has. She opens her mouth to speak but nothing comes out. Margaret pulls her into a hug and they stand there in the doorway, tears pouring down both their faces. Margaret fishes in her pocket for a tissue when they eventually step apart. She smiles as she dabs at Joni's face. 'You need to invest in a good waterproof mascara,' she says, and Joni manages a laugh.

'You too,' she says.

'I'm sorry it's been so long,' Joni adds as she follows her down the hall to the kitchen. The house still smells the same. Furniture polish and baking. She hands Margaret the flowers. Margaret puts a hand on her arm.

'We all deal with things in different ways,' she says. 'There's no right or wrong way. So, nothing to be sorry about.'

Joni remembers how she always thought Meg's mum was the best at giving advice. 'She's like Yoda,' she remembers teasing Meg once. Meg had rolled her eyes. They had always been close, though, Meg and her mum. Right up till the end she'd visited every weekend for Sunday lunch, along with her brothers and their wives and kids. They had talked on the phone almost every day. Joni's mum used to ask if Meg was lonely living on her own, if she was maybe too fussy, but Margaret had never once questioned her daughter's choices. Meg had boyfriends – queues of them, it sometimes seemed to Joni – but she had never had any desire to hook her life up permanently to someone else's. It just wasn't for her. And her mother had accepted that unquestioningly.

'How are you?' Margaret says, a hand either side of Joni's face.

'Good. You?'

'Oh, you know. I have my moments. Tea?'

Joni nods. 'Please.'

She had said to Margaret on the phone that maybe they could go through old photos, and she can see a heaped pile on the kitchen table, and beside it Meg's mobile in its garish pink and orange case. She feels a lump in her throat. She knows it was found in the wreckage of the car, the screen not even smashed. She's not sure she can look at it.

'Let's talk while we go through them,' Margaret says, as if she's picked up on Joni's reluctance. 'Throw ourselves in at the deep end. I think that's better than building ourselves up to it.' She puts a hand on Joni's hand 'You'll be OK.'

Joni tells herself to get a grip. She's not here so Meg's mum can comfort her. If anything it should be the other way round.

'Here,' she says, taking charge. 'Let me show you these first.' She opens up photos on her phone. Scrolls back. 'This is the last one we took. Two days before . . .' She lets the words hang out there. Holds the screen up so Margaret can see the selfie. The two of them grinning up at the lens. They'd been at a day spa, both in the white fluffy robes and sliders that Meg hated wearing ('I feel like we're in *Cocoon*. All shuffling round like we've taken too many meds'). Meg had just had a facial and her skin was glowing. Hair pushed back from her face with a towelling band. Joni looks at Margaret and sees she has tears streaming down her face. 'I'll send it to you,' she says, wiping away her own.

By the time she leaves about two hours later she's exhausted. Wrung out. She's clutching Meg's mobile. 'Jerry found someone to open it up without the password, so now it doesn't have one,' Margaret had said. (Jerry, Meg's youngest brother, always knew a man who could do anything. They had often speculated about whether he might be involved in anything dodgy but had concluded he wasn't – he had a very respectable job in IT – but that quite a lot of his old schoolfriends were.) 'I've only looked at the photos, I can't face the rest. We . . . me and Gerald and the boys thought you should have it. Most of the pictures are of the two of you and I've copied any ones I want.'

Joni hugs her. She shouldn't have left it so long.

'Don't be such a stranger,' Margaret says. 'We miss you.'

'I won't. I promise.'

'Don't put things off. You never know . . .' She hadn't been able to finish the sentence. Joni had gulped so hard it made a noise.

*

She sits in Caitlin's office waiting for her to return from the kitchen with two coffees. She feels stupidly nervous, as if she might get told to stop being so silly and go back to work. Caitlin, she thinks, is expecting her to be making a complaint. Maybe about Lucas.

'So. I'm handing in my resignation,' she says when Caitlin returns, mugs in hand. Joni passes her the letter that she printed off at home this morning confirming her decision.

'That's a shame,' Caitlin says without really sounding as if she's the slightest bit surprised. 'Where are you going on to?'

'Nowhere at the moment,' Joni says, although the more she says it out loud the more it terrifies her. 'I just need some time to sort out what I want to do next.'

'Good for you. I wonder if Lucas would want to go full time,' Caitlin muses, already moving on to the problem of how she will fill the gap.

'Good idea,' Joni says, although she's pretty sure he'll say no. He's told her that the only reason he can bear either of his jobs is that he doesn't have to do them every day.

'Well, we'll miss you,' Caitlin says, effectively dismissing her. Joni carries her still full coffee mug back to her own office.

Meg would have been proud of her. She sends a text to both Saffy and Mary: *I've done it!*

About fucking time! Saffy texts back immediately. *We can be ladies who lunch!*

Well done, you x, Mary sends a couple of minutes later. Joni sends them both smiley faces.

47

Joni had thought that once Ant was out of their lives she, Saffy and Mary would slowly drift apart, but it seems, like it or not, she really has got herself a social life. Suddenly it's second nature to check in with them before the weekend, to call one or both of them with a funny story, a tiny bit of news or just to see how they are. They meet up for lunch during the week or drinks or dinner on a Saturday night. Joni has a spare key to Saffy's house in case she locks herself out (only once, so far, and thankfully in the daytime. She's waiting for a drunken 3 a.m. call although Saffy seems – at least for now – to be reining it in) and a handful of guest passes to the gym Mary has just joined. It's all fancy showers and fluffy white robes and Mary seems to be looking forward more to getting facials than working out, but she's asked Joni to accompany her for her first few sessions to show her what to do, and Joni said yes without even thinking about it. She's looking forward to it. They had asked Saffy if she wanted to join them – invitations to anything always naturally include the three of them, but there's no expectation that they have to be at one another's beck and call – and Saffy had laughed so hard she'd got a stitch.

Today they have their first session.

Joni stayed up late last night, working out a programme

that she thought Mary would both enjoy and benefit from. She'd googled a list of the gym's equipment, wanting to do a proper job. Mary keeps telling her she's only bothered about her arms – 'I want to be able to wear sleeveless tops,' she said, the first time they spoke about it – and Joni keeps trying to explain that she needs to tone her whole body to support those arms or she's in danger of looking like an overbalanced lobster.

Mary is waiting for her on the steps outside, wrapped up in a big brown coat and orange scarf and holding a large smart canvas bag. Shiny brand-new trainers on her feet. 'I'm treating you to a massage afterwards,' she says as she greets Joni with a kiss on the cheek.

They move from machine to machine slowly, Joni making sure Mary has her technique right, adjusting the weights to suit her. It's a learning curve, how far back to basics she has to go. Mary has never used a gym for anything other than classes and swimming. Ever. 'How is that even possible?' Joni had laughed when Mary had told her. 'It's like saying you've never been to the Post Office.'

'What's that?' Mary had said. Mary, it had turned out, had a fantastic deadpan.

They're there for over an hour, meticulously working every part of her body. Mary even seems to enjoy it, listening intently when Joni explains what they're going to do next and why. Joni hadn't realized she knew so much.

'I won't remember any of that,' Mary calls from the next-door shower cubicle.

'That's why I'm coming again next time,' Joni says. 'You'll get the hang of it.'

When they eventually meet up again in the hairdrying/make-up area Joni checks her phone. She has three missed calls from Saffy. Mary looks at her own and finds she has the same. 'I'll call her,' Joni says. She and Mary were planning to head to the Ivy on St John's Wood High Street for lunch, but something tells her they won't be going now.

'Stef is getting remarried,' Saffy howls as soon as she answers.

Joni pulls a face at Mary. 'Stefan,' she mouths. 'How do you know?' she says to Saffy.

'I bumped into a woman who works with him. I think she thought I already knew. He's moved back here and he's brought some . . . woman . . . with him.'

'OK. We're coming over,' Joni says, raising her eyes at Mary for confirmation. Mary nods, a worried expression on her face. Joni doesn't know how she's become this person who drops everything to rush across London to comfort a friend she's only known for such a short time, but she knows that that's what she has to do. They have been through so much together in such a short time. It's somehow wired into her brain now how much this news will have rocked Saffy.

Saffy is pacing behind the open front door when their taxi pulls up. She looks furious, but Joni knows it's an act. Not necessarily a conscious one, but a shield nonetheless. A self-preservation reflex.

'He didn't even have the fucking decency to let me know himself,' she says when she sees them.

Joni doesn't even bother to argue that that's Stefan's

prerogative. He was the injured party so he can call the shots. He and Saffy are divorced with no children so he can do as he wishes. She knows Saffy just needs to vent and she and Mary need to let her.

'Come and sit down,' Mary says, taking charge. She leads Saffy through to the kitchen. Joni stops off at the sink to fill the coffee machine.

'Is he back for good, do you know?'

Saffy sobs and says 'Yes' at the same time. And then something unintelligible that might be 'He's been made CEO' but could just as well be 'He's seen Dave's new toe'. Joni decides to assume it's the former.

Saffy flops down at the table. Joni puts a hand on her shoulder. 'Nothing's really changed. I know it probably doesn't feel like that but . . .'

The coffee machine stops whirring. Mary finds a capsule and puts a mug under the spout.

'I just thought he'd get stuff out of his system and then at least talk to me. I don't think I ever believed that would be it. Not really. Even after the divorce. I mean, you hear about people getting remarried all the time . . .'

'When was the last time you spoke to him?'

'The day he found out. He packed up his stuff and left, and that was it. Everything else was through solicitors.'

'And his family?' Joni slides the black coffee that Mary has put on the table over to Saffy. The Nespresso whirrs into action again.

'His mum hurled abuse at me down the phone a few times. I blocked her number in the end.'

'I think it's time to move on,' Joni says. 'I don't think you have a choice.'

'I tried to move on,' Saffy wails. 'Keepers was moving on.'

'On your own. Get things straight in your own head before you start thinking about anyone else.'

Saffy puts her face in her hands, elbows on the table. 'I don't want to be on my own. I've never been on my own.'

Joni accepts a coffee from Mary. 'What do you mean by never?'

'Never. Since I was fifteen. All my relationships have either overlapped or one's ended and another one's started within a couple of days. I joined Keepers the day after Stef left. Just so I wouldn't have to deal with it, really. And I got into this really intense thing with the first bloke I talked to, for a few months. I broke that off because he was getting a bit weird and started telling me how much he loved Jesus, and then I went straight into another exclusive thing with some other guy. Jax. He had a bit of 'roid rage, if you ask me, so I knocked that on the head after a couple of months too. I mean, they were online relationships, but you weren't allowed to meet up with anyone outside your bubble at that point anyway, so it was no different really. And then there were a couple more, and then there was Ant. I've never been officially single for more than a week in twenty-seven years . . . not till now.'

'Well then, it's about time you were,' Joni says, but then worries she sounds too stern. She softens her tone. 'I just mean, I don't think that's healthy, that's all.'

'Joni's right,' Mary says. 'Don't rush into anything. Not straight away.'

'I'm going to get old alone,' Saffy says petulantly. 'I mean . . . sorry, Mary, I didn't . . . God, I'm fucking ridiculous.'

'Ha!' Joni shouts. 'Well, we agree on something.'

Mary snorts. Saffy looks at her, hurt, and then starts to laugh herself.

'OK,' she says, once they all calm down. 'No more dating just for the sake of it. I'll live with my own horrible company.'

'And ours.' Mary puts a hand on her arm.

'Oh God,' Joni says, 'We're going to hug it out, aren't we?'

'Too fucking right we are,' Saffy says, reaching over and grabbing her. 'I'm starved of physical contact and who knows when I'll get laid again.'

'I'm glad to be of service,' Joni says, relaxing into it.

Later, when Mary is in the bathroom, Joni reaches out a hand and puts it on Saffy's arm. 'Yes,' she says. Saffy looks at her quizzically. 'You once asked me if I thought the reason I was such a control freak was because of Meg, and the answer is yes. I'm a bit scared of the unknown, of things happening that I'm not expecting. But I'm getting better. You and Mary . . .'

Saffy sniffs.

'Oh God, I've made you cry again.' Joni laughs through her own tears, just as Mary walks back in. She looks between them, confused. 'What have I missed?'

'Just that I absolutely love you,' Joni says. 'Both of you.'

48

With the holiday that she's owed Joni only has to work eight more days before she can be done with Gibsons forever. She had thought it would pass in a blur, but the days still drag as if they have no idea that anything's changed. Lucas ups his game with ever more elaborate tableaux involving both his figures and hers, holding signs declaring 'Please don't leave me alone in this shithole!' and 'Come back! All is forgiven!' She leaves them on display all day, a final act of rebellion.

Since his star turn as property consultant Phil, Lucas has been crackling with the desire to change his life, as if a moment lived in someone else's shoes has flipped a switch in his head. When Joni told him her news about handing in her resignation – over a post-work drink near Lucas's second job in Hanover Square – his first reaction had been to break into a huge grin and congratulate her. His second had been to stare morosely into his lager and say, 'I wish I had your courage. I'm destined to work in accounts forever.'

'It's not courage when you can afford not to work,' she'd said. 'I know how fortunate I am.'

'I'm going to drop dead one day checking the National Insurance contributions for the Sheffield branch. They'll engrave "He died doing the only thing he knew how to do. That's how sad his life was" on my headstone.'

Joni had laughed. 'I'll speak at your funeral: "Lucas loved payroll more than life itself . . ." Could you go part-time? Give up Gibsons and just keep the accountants?'

'Financially I actually could. It's not as if I have any dependants. What would I do, though? It's not as though I have a passion I'm desperate to follow.'

'Tell me about it,' Joni had said. 'I'm terrified I'm going to realize my life is completely empty. That I won't know who I am. Saffy keeps telling me we're going to go on regular shopping dates and I'm already trying to think of ways to get out of them. Not that . . . I adore her, don't get me wrong. It's the shopping I can't face.'

'I quite like shopping,' he'd said, draining the last of his pint. 'Maybe I should volunteer.'

'I don't mean going to Halfords and browsing the gadget section. I mean, "Let's try on every single thing in the shop and then buy it all whether we like it or not." She has wardrobes full of clothes with the labels still on. It's like an obsession.'

'OK. I'm out,' he'd said. 'I draw the line at clothes shopping of any kind. Do you want another?'

Joni had looked down at her nearly empty glass. 'Why not?'

He has taken it upon himself to organize her leaving do even though she's told anyone and everyone who'll listen that she doesn't want one. 'It's two hours out of your life,' he said when she first protested. 'What's the worst that can happen?'

'What's the best?' she'd said. She'd been hoping to sneak away, just saying a few quiet goodbyes. There was no one she felt compelled to stay in touch with apart from maybe Shona and Caitlin, and who knew how long that would last. Not that she wouldn't be happy for an impromptu catch-up if she bumped into them in the street, but she knew their fragile connections would soon start to fray from lack of contact. Their common interest gone. She would start to find it hard to feign interest in the goings-on at a firm where she knew fewer people as each month passed. Whoever she was speaking to would begin telling her a piece of gossip, and then realize that Joni had never met one or all of the parties involved. It was the way work friendships went. In the end few were built on anything more solid than proximity. She tells herself she'll make the effort. They're nice women. She needs all the nice people she can get in her life.

'You'll get presents,' he'd said. 'Well, maybe one present as you've not even been there two years and you're part-time, but anyway. You'll get something. Probably chosen by Caitlin, so start dropping hints about what you might like. And a card signed by thirty people you barely know. You can get drunk and tell anyone you don't like what you think of them or make a pass at someone you have a secret crush on.' Joni pulled a face. 'OK, so maybe not that,' Lucas said. Their relationship, thankfully, is completely uncomplicated by lust on both sides. There has never been a moment – a gaze held a fraction too long, a loaded silence – where the atmos- phere has felt charged, and for that she's thankful. She needs friends, a life, she's realized that. She doesn't need a relationship. Not yet.

She had found herself reluctantly agreeing, just to keep him happy. 'It'll put a full stop on it,' he said in his closing argument. 'Help you move on.'

'I know you just want to get drunk at the company's expense,' she'd said, laughing. 'Stop trying to pretend this is about me.'

Thankfully the party is in the offices, as those for all but the most long-serving are. Warm Prosecco, triangles of sandwiches on a plastic platter, their edges curling. A cake made by Judith who loves to show off her appalling baking skills, with 'Good Luck, Joan' scrawled on the top in piped pink cream.

'Is she taking the piss?' Joni whispers to Lucas.

'You know she's going to make you take whatever's left home with you? It's a tradition,' he whispers back.

She grimaces. 'I'll feed it to the pigeons.'

'Jesus,' he says. 'What did they ever do to you?'

There are about twenty people there, some of them, Joni is sure, just taken unawares and now afraid to look rude if they leave before the toast. Joni knows the drill. Caitlin will make a short speech, present her with a gift paid for by collection, and then ask everyone to raise their glasses. As soon as that's over with half the crowd will leave, with a diehard few staying to make sure the bottles are drained and the sandwiches eaten. There have been three such occasions since Joni started working here. Always the same, with a slight variation on the number of attendees and the size of gift depending on how long the escapee had worked for the company.

Caitlin taps a pen against a glass. The conversation stutters to a halt. 'So, we're here to say a big thank you and a sad goodbye to Joni . . .' The speech always follows the same lines: thank you, we'll miss you, one funny anecdote dredged up from the annals, here's a gift, let's drink. This one is no exception, except that Joni has no recollection of the humorous story about her borrowing a bottle of wine from boss Peter's office and then discovering how expensive it was and replacing it with a much cheaper one and an anonymous note. She glares at Lucas, who smirks.

'We had a whip-round for a little something,' Caitlin is saying. She hands Joni a wrapped parcel the size of a shoebox. 'And now we'd like to wish you good luck with whatever you decide to do next . . .' She holds her plastic wine glass aloft and everyone else follows suit. Joni utters her thanks and clinks a few glasses except that they don't clink, they make a dull thud. She hugs Caitlin and Shona.

'Open your present,' Lucas says. She notices he's still looking pleased with himself. She tears off the paper and reveals the box which turns out to be the giveaway yellow of Selfridges.

'We had no idea what to get you,' Caitlin says. 'But we know how much you love your . . .'

Joni opens the box. Unravels tissue paper, feeling a hard object inside.

'. . . figurines.'

It's a china statue of a cat with three kittens wrapped playfully around its legs. Some kind of Persian by the look of it, with ripples in the surface representing its long hair. Huge blue eyes. It's hideous. Lucas snorts and tries to turn it into a cough. 'Did you choose this?' Joni says to him, smiling sweetly.

'It was Lucas's idea,' Caitlin says, clearly pleased that their choice has gone down so well.

'It's . . . well, it's fabulous. Thank you. I'll treasure it.'

Thankfully she's saved from having to say any more by Judith announcing she's cutting the cake, at which point several people start to put their coats on.

'What the fuck am I going to do with it?' Joni laughs helplessly as she and Lucas share the lift down twenty minutes later.

'Build a shrine,' he says. 'The Gibsons memorial.'

'You're taking it home. I can't live with it in my flat.'

'How gracious. Shall we get another drink first or don't you want to be seen in the pub with it?'

'I'm desperate for another drink,' she says, pulling her coat tighter. 'Shit, we forgot the cake.'

'Do you care?' he says, pushing open the front door and grimacing as a blast of cold wind hits him in the face.

'Not enough to go back up.'

She wakes up early, disturbed by the honking of cars and a siren screaming past outside the window. Something feels off. There's a different smell. Not unpleasant, just different. Not the Le Labo Verveine candles she favours, something more earthy. Like Christmas trees. She opens her eyes. It takes her a second to realize she has absolutely no idea where she is. She throws back the covers – slate grey with a deep aubergine throw across the bottom – and looks at the bed she's woken up in. A dark wooden double. King-size, she would guess. The other pillows are thankfully unruffled. There are thick curtains across the window. Close to but not too matchy with the grey of the sheets. The walls are white. The only light is coming from the en-suite bathroom, the door to which is open and the window blind up. She looks down at herself. She's still wearing everything she had on last night bar her coat and shoes. Last night. Her leaving do. She remembers heading for the pub with Lucas, ordering a bottle of wine. Oh God. She can't have . . .

She locks herself in the bathroom and has a pee, then creeps out into the hall. Flashes of the evening come back to her: laughing, a taxi, tripping up some steps. She needs water and a paracetamol and to face up to whatever it is that has happened.

The first door she comes to is a large square living room. Huge mullioned windows look out over a busy road that she doesn't recognize. She remembers that Lucas lives in Clapham – or is it Balham? Somewhere she's not familiar with. As she walks towards the light for a better view she jumps as she sees a figure lying on the sofa. He's snuggled under a throw, but she can see he has his socks on and also the hem of his trousers. His shoes are lined up under the coffee table. Two empty wine bottles sit on the table alongside two glasses and the detritus of a takeaway pizza. Joni remembers the shop. The harsh light and the menu displayed behind the counter.

Her head hurts.

She starts to retreat towards the hall as a croaky voice says, 'What did you do to me?'

Damn, she'd been hoping to sneak out. She can feel her spiritual hangover descending. Did she make a fool of herself? Fall over? Slur her words? Cry? She sometimes cries when she gets really drunk, she doesn't even know about what. Was she so out of it that he felt he had to put her to bed rather than risk sending her home? Hopefully he was in as bad a state and this time tomorrow they can relive the whole thing and find it hilarious. For now she just wants to be on her own and sleep.

'I'm getting water,' is all she manages to say. He says something that sounds like 'Me' so she finds the kitchen – Shaker units in a pale blue, black worktops and a huge wooden table in the middle of the room – locates two glasses, fills them both and drinks a whole one down before refilling it and carrying them both to the living room. Lucas is sitting up, hair standing up at an angle. He holds his hand out for a glass, grunting a thanks.

'Did we drink all that?' Joni says, grimacing.

'One of them was open already, but more or less.' He rubs his hands over his eyes. 'You OK?'

'I've been better.' Something is worrying away at the

edges of her memory. Being hungover always does this to her though. She and Meg used to call it the Shame Train.

'I'll make coffee,' he says, standing up. 'And then my suggestion is we sleep for a couple more hours.'

She flops into an armchair, too exhausted to make a move. 'Go on then.' She looks round when he leaves the room. His flat is more tasteful than she imagined it would be. Not that she's ever really given it any thought. The floors are a deep red-brown wood, there is a turntable and a shelf of LPs, framed tour posters and cover artwork from the seventies and eighties, a whole wall of books. She leans her head back and closes her eyes.

'It was a laugh though, wasn't it?' Lucas bangs a mug down on the small round table beside her. She jumps.

'God knows. I don't even remember coming back here.'

He raises his eyebrows. 'It was your idea.'

'Was it?' she groans. 'Never listen to me when I'm drunk.'

'It was your leaving do. You were allowed to get wasted. I'm not sure what my excuse was. Did you find the paracetamol?'

She shakes her head and he goes off into the hall, returning a minute later with a packet of pills. He pops two for himself and offers her the packet.

'Thanks.' She starts to feel a bit better just at the thought of taking them. 'I really don't do this very often. I think I've only been that drunk twice in the last twenty years and the other time was Saffy's fault.'

'Oh yes. Always blame someone else.' He laughs. 'You were fine. I was just as bad.'

'Good.' She sips her coffee.

'So, you fancy me when you're pissed then?' Lucas says with a wry smirk.

'What? No. What?' Oh God.

'Ha! I knew you wouldn't remember.'

'We didn't . . .?'

'No! God. I knew it was the drink talking.'

She buries her head in her hands. 'I don't . . . not you . . . I mean, that sounds rude, sorry, but . . .'

He puts the back of his hand to his forehead. 'I'm cut to the quick. I was tempted though, I admit it.'

'Ah, so you fancy me then?' she says, trying to make a joke of it. Laughing it off seems to be the only way to deal with it, otherwise she'll die of embarrassment. She can't even imagine what she was thinking.

'When I'm paralytic, apparently I do.'

'Worst compliment ever.'

'Makes you wonder though, doesn't it?' he says, waggling his eyebrows.

'No,' she says, laughing. 'It doesn't.'

The truth is, though, that however much she tries not to think about it, it's there now. Whether she likes it or not.

49

She throws herself into her new life, relishing those mornings she doesn't have to get up and force herself into the office. She makes plans to fill every day: upping her gym workouts to six, lunching with Saffy and Mary, ticking off museums and galleries on her and Meg's list at the rate of two or three a week. She travels up to Manchester to stay with Imo for a couple of nights, taking her, Rhys (now officially Imo's boyfriend) and Hal out to dinner, then top and tails it with Imo in her tiny bed. She worries that she's derailed her burgeoning friendship with Lucas with her stupid drunken pass – they haven't met up for a drink since although they've exchanged texts, but their easy teasing has fizzled into a slight awkwardness that threatens to dull their relationship completely. She's hanging in there, hopeful that they can claw it back before it's too late.

Occasionally she has slightly inappropriate dreams about him that have her waking up discombobulated. She pushes them to the back of her mind, knowing they're just her subconscious trying to embarrass her.

She talks it over with Mary and Saffy – her 'girls'. She talks everything over with them now. After two years of bottling up anything personal, anything she used to share with Meg so lightly, she finds she can't stop. They know everything about each other; nothing is off-limits. Their advice might not always be helpful (Saffy's in particular is always of the 'have sex/get drunk' variety), but nothing can beat the cathartic relief of not only getting her worries off her chest but laughing at them. She can't remember when she ever laughed so much.

Still, there's something missing.

She's waiting in the reception of Power Fit one afternoon to talk to Samira about permanent locker hire – she knows that some of the regulars have negotiated a deal for a long-term lease on their own slice of changing-room real estate. She likes the idea of being one of those people, regardless of whether she needs it or not. She has no idea what she'd keep in it, but having your own locker key is like a membership badge or a Masonic handshake. Like showing up at a club and saying, 'I'm on the list.'

Samira is chatting to a woman about personal-training sessions. The gym has a small staff of part-time trainers. Unlike the big chains where the PTs are mostly doing inductions for new members or occasional courses of sessions in the run-up to a wedding or a holiday, Power Fit PTs tend to focus on regular clients, helping prepare them for competitions or photo shoots. Serious stuff. Joni loves watching them, loves seeing the progression over the weeks as their charges gradually emerge from their off season and evolve into a bronzed god or goddess. She always listens in to the tips, the nutritional advice, soaking it all up.

'I used to compete,' the woman is saying. Joni looks at

her with interest. She's in her fifties, still in shape but soft around the edges. 'Years ago. But when I had kids . . . you know . . .'

'It's hard!' Samira says. 'It's like having a full-time job!' Samira is young and lean and lovely, but she has a seemingly boundless capacity for empathy with those who aren't so blessed. She speaks in infectious exclamation marks. She's a judgement-free zone.

'Anyway, I'm on a mission to get back in shape. I need some serious training. Do you have any female trainers?'

'We do!' Samira says. 'When were you thinking of starting?'

The woman looks over her shoulder, slightly embarrassed. She relaxes when she sees that the only person in earshot is a woman of a similar age to herself. Joni smiles at her encouragingly. 'Are any of them a bit older?'

'Well,' Samira says, thinking for a second. 'Kai is thirty-four. She's the oldest, I think.'

The woman sighs audibly. A lightbulb flickers into life in Joni's head. Like a fluorescent strip it flares and then dies a couple of times before catching hold.

'OK. Let me think about it,' the woman says. She thanks Samira and leaves, Joni watching her go.

'Do you often get that?' Joni asks, forgetting all about the locker key. 'People wanting older trainers?'

'We do!' Samira says cheerfully. 'Mostly women. Wait . . . you should totally do it!'

'I was just thinking . . . should I? I don't even know how . . .'

'Oh my God, you'd be amazing! You need Level Two

Gym Instruction and a Level Three Diploma in Personal Training . . .'

'I don't know, Samira . . . I don't even have Level One anything.'

'I don't think there is a level one, to be honest. This place is great,' Samira says, fishing in a deep drawer and coming out with a leaflet. 'They're based in Finsbury Park, but it's all online these days. It takes a few months, but you don't have to do full-time. It might just take a bit longer . . .'

Joni feels light-headed. Is this it? Is this her 'thing'? 'Would people use me, do you think?'

Samira shrugs. 'Why not? I mean, there are no guarantees, but I'm pretty sure Mo would put you on the roster if he knew you were qualified. Especially if we're missing out on custom because we don't have anyone suitable for some clients.'

Mo is the manager. Joni has known him for years to wave to and say hello. He knows how dedicated she is. Even if it was only a few ad hoc hours a week she would be doing something she loved. She would have a purpose. She would have an answer to the question 'What do you do?' that she was proud of. She can't wait to get home and google the course. She and Saffy are spending the evening at Mary's: she doesn't feel as if she can make such a big decision without consulting them. And Imo. She needs to call Imo. And Lucas, she thinks with a pang of regret. She wants to know what he thinks. When did her life become so crowded with people she feels she can't do without? she thinks. Six months ago – less – it would have driven her to distraction. Now all she feels is a warm glow.

50

She's decided against a big birthday bash. She wants a small gathering. Dancing. She wants it in her flat, not just because she doesn't want the fuss of a venue, but because she has never had a celebration here and it feels like time. She wants to decorate it herself in a brazenly amateur fashion (Saffy keeps handing her the numbers of party planners) and leave all the cooking and clearing up to someone else.

Her course starts on Tuesday. Part online, part in person at practical workshops and assessments. In three months she'll be qualified. She's already thinking she might tack on a top-up course at the end, specializing in the specific needs of perimenopausal and menopausal women. She wants to attract all those who feel too embarrassed to show up at a gym – let alone a hardcore operation like Power Fit – and she wants to knock them into shape but, more importantly, to help them get their confidence back. She wants to make them strong and lean and fabulous and ready to take on the world that has somehow become intimidating just by virtue of a few hormones, or the lack of them. She can't remember when she felt so energized about anything. She's going to practise her new skills on Mary as she acquires them.

For now they are overnighting at a spa hotel – Saffy

and Mary's birthday treat – and she and Saffy are lying beside the steaming indoor pool waiting to be called in for massages. The two of them have already presented her with a set of beautiful embossed notebooks and a monogrammed Mont Blanc pen. 'For your studies,' Mary had said as Joni tore the wrapping paper off. Joni had almost cried.

'I have news,' Mary announces as she shuffles up to them in the towelling sliders that the hotel provides. Joni is refusing to wear them as an homage to Meg. 'I just spoke to George. He and Millie are separating.'

'Oh . . .' Joni isn't sure how to react. 'Is he OK?'

Mary gives her a big smile. 'He's fine. All his decision. He said they've been growing apart and he just couldn't see himself having children with her.' She sits on the edge of a lounger. 'And he said he really wants to have children. Lots of them.'

'Result,' Saffy says, sitting up.

'He's coming to stay with me next week. He said he feels as if we haven't seen each other properly for ages.'

Joni reaches out a hand and puts it on Mary's arm. 'I'm really pleased for you. I mean, so long as George is OK and, obviously, I feel sad for Millie . . .'

'Stop being so fucking nice,' Saffy says, but it comes out jokey not accusatory. 'We all know Millie's a massive bitch.'

'She is,' Mary says, agreeing.

Joni holds up the green juice she's been presented with by a white-coated therapist. 'Let's drink to the break-up of your son's marriage. Why not?'

'He's going to meet someone lovely. And they'll have hundreds of babies and you'll be the best granny,' Saffy says. 'And I can be their mad old auntie. I've always wanted mad-old-auntie status.'

The party is on Saturday night. Imo and Rhys arrive in the early afternoon straight from the studio and set to work hanging fairy lights despite Joni's protestations that it's supposed to be their afternoon off. Joni has been cleaning since first thing. The flat has never looked so tidy. She's been burning candles all day infusing the soft furnishings with the heavenly scent. At five thirty, two women from Perfect Party Catering arrive and unload platters of delicious-looking bite-sized treats on to the kitchen table. They sprinkle micro herbs on top of the savoury selection and dust edible glitter on to the sweet plates. Then they weave bits of evergreen foliage between the trays. Joni tries to pretend she hasn't noticed as one of them hands Imo a cake box that she stashes in the cupboard where the glasses are kept. All the wine glasses Joni possesses are currently lined up beside a couple of wine coolers that are waiting for the crushed ice that Joni bought in Morrisons yesterday. Tomorrow the Perfect Party ladies will return to collect the platters and the small gold plates that they have provided. They leave Joni with strict instructions not to wash any of it, but she knows she will. There's no way she's handing dirty crockery over to someone to take home.

Once they've left she has a shower and takes her time getting ready. She can hear music coming from the living room upstairs. Travis singing about flowers in the window. Happy. Hopeful. It's perfect. She dresses in the silky dress that Saffy helped her pick out. Short with cap sleeves and a flared skirt. Tiny buttons down the front and a belted waist. It shows off her gym-honed limbs. It's utterly inappropriate for the weather, which is cold and crisp but, as she's not intending to go outside, who cares? She doesn't bother with shoes. It's her party, she can do what she likes. Her toenails sparkle with gold shellac. She brushes her hair out and leaves it loose.

Saffy and Mary arrive first as they promised they would, in a cloud of expensive perfume. Rhys has offered to be on drinks duty all evening, and when Joni tried to refuse the offer – 'You're a guest, not the hired help!' – Imo had laughed and said, 'Let him, Mum. It means he doesn't have to make conversation. He's terrified.' All six foot two of Rhys had blushed.

'OK,' Joni said. 'Well, if at any point you can't be bothered any more, just stop. I don't want you to feel you're here to work.'

Lucy and her husband Giles, and their three kids – fifteen-year-old Netta, Jemima thirteen and just-turned-twelve Carey – are next and with them Joni and Lucy's mum, Maura, resplendent on her walking frame, Happy Birthday helium balloons tied to the handles. Joni has sworn Saffy and Mary to secrecy about her using Lucy's photos. She can't prevent her mother from hearing whispers of the Ant saga, but Joni stealing her sister's identity would be a piece of information too far. Lucy

presents her with a beautifully wrapped gift (too beautiful for her to have done it herself, undoubtedly). Joni
tears the paper off as Imo takes their coats. Inside in a
soft case is a shiny leather handbag on a gold link chain.
She knows it's unthinkably expensive; the prominent
logo tells her that. It reminds her just how little her sister
knows her.

'It's beautiful, thank you,' she says, hugging her. She'll
give it to Saffy, she decides, unless Imo wants it, although
she finds that hard to imagine. Imo wears a small red
vegan backpack when she goes for a night out.

Her mum presents her with a photo in a beautiful silver frame: Joni and Meg when they were thirteen. Joni
can remember the night. Their first school disco. She
bursts into tears. 'That's so lovely, Mum,' she says.

'Oh no, lovey. I didn't mean to upset you,' Maura says,
looking stricken.

'It's the best present ever,' Joni tells her. 'I love it.'

Lucas is next, with Caitlin and Shona. Joni knows they
were meeting in the pub up the road first. He presents
her with a wrapped box and, when Joni opens it in front
of the other guests, it turns out to contain a companion
figurine to the one she was given at her leaving do. It's
even more horrific. A giant marmalade tabby with a ball
of yarn dangling from a paw. Lucas smiles at her with a
glint in his eye. 'It's from all three of us,' he says.

'It's fabulous,' Joni says, for Caitlin and Shona's sake.
'Thank you.'

'We know how much you love your ornaments. Where
are the others?' Shona says, looking around.

'Oh. Well, I put everything away before tonight, just in case.'

She sees Lucas stifle a grin and the relief she feels almost knocks her off her feet. They're back. She looks over at Saffy and Mary and sees them both, eyebrows raised, staring at the china monstrosity. She winks at them, hoping they get the message and introduces everyone.

There's a tap on the door and Flick lets herself in. Joni felt she couldn't get away with not inviting her – she could hardly pretend the party wasn't happening, after all – but she told her it was starting an hour later than it was, knowing Flick would show up early to offer help. She's going to be kinder to her neighbour, she's decided. She can spare the odd hour or two out of her life to listen to Flick over a cup of tea. She'll just need to find a way to mark the boundaries so it doesn't become a full-time occupation.

'You're in full swing,' Flick says as she walks in brandishing a large plate with what looks like shortbread fingers on it, and another with tiny individual mince pies. Joni could smell baking all afternoon, so she'd guessed what was coming.

'Is that the marmot?' Saffy whispers in Joni's ear.

'It is. Be nice to her.'

'Of course I will.'

'Flick, hi!' Joni says, taking the plates from her hands. 'Look at those treats, thank you. Come in and meet everyone.'

More people trickle in. Samira from the gym, Margaret and Gerald, looking round nervously until they spot

Maura and wave enthusiastically. Joni had been trying to work out when they last would have seen each other. Maura had been too unwell to attend Meg's funeral, so it was probably more than ten years ago, before her mum moved to be nearer to Lucy. There are seventeen of them altogether. A cross-section of Joni's life. Worlds that only overlap at all because of their relationship to her.

There's music and toasting and, later on, dancing. It's everything she hoped it would be. Her face aches from smiling.

'Do you want to talk about the elephant in the room?' Lucas says quietly as she recovers after giving it her all to 'Dancing Queen'.

'There's an elephant here?' she says. She's feeling exquisitely tipsy.

'Funny.' He smiles. 'I need to be a bit drunk to have this conversation, but not too drunk, so we have to get it over with now. I'm at the tipping point.'

'You're taking that cat home with you,' she says. She's not sure she wants things spelled out. She doesn't want to be reminded that she messed things up.

'Deal,' he says. 'Two minutes, I promise.'

'Come on then,' she says. She leads him towards the hall. Taking him downstairs where the bedrooms are feels as if it's giving off the wrong message. She wishes she'd filled her glass on the way.

'Oh, I have a proper present for you, by the way. Just don't tell Caitlin and Shona.' He fishes in the inside pocket of his jacket and pulls out an envelope. 'It's tickets to a fitness expo at the O2. I got three so you didn't have to go on your own like a saddo. I talked to Imogen and she said Rhys is a big fitness buff so they'd like to go, so I got Sunday tickets . . .'

'That's fantastic. Thank you.' She's slightly blown away by how thoughtful a gift it is. She puts the envelope on the hall table. Waits.

'OK. I shouldn't have told you about what happened the other week,' he says, leaning back against the wall. 'I don't want it to ruin everything.'

She sighs. 'I probably would have remembered eventually. And that would have been even worse, wondering whether you did too. So, it's OK. I shouldn't have drunk so much. I'm not used to it.'

'You and me both,' he says. 'The thing is . . .'

Flick suddenly appears at the door to the living room. 'Sorry. Just need the loo.'

Joni gives her a smile, almost grateful for the interruption. 'Are you having a good time?'

'Marvellous,' Flick says. 'Your friend Saffy is a hoot.' She sneezes. 'Is the cat nearby? I thought you would have shut him in somewhere.'

'He's down in my bedroom.'

'Poor love,' Flick says, as if she isn't the main reason Jasper has been incarcerated. She sticks a hand through the bathroom door and waves it around searching for the light switch. 'Don't mind me.' Finally the over-mirror bulbs flash on and Flick closes the door. Lucas opens his mouth to continue, but Joni shakes her head and uses her

382

hand to imitate flapping ears. She has no doubt Flick will be listening in.

'Anyway,' she says loudly. 'It's three months, mostly online, but you go in every now and then for an in-person assessment . . .'

'I'm jealous,' he says, playing along. 'You've found your calling. I wonder how I could make cycling my job.'

'Become a Peloton instructor,' she says and he laughs and says:

'Yeah, just like that.'

'Get a job in a bike shop then.'

'I've actually thought about it but I don't think I can face going to the bottom of the food chain again, even if I could afford to. I thought about opening one too. There isn't—' He stops as the toilet flushes. The tap runs for a second.

'That would be a great idea. I mean, risky . . .'

The bathroom door opens and Flick appears. 'Last thing we need is more cyclists on the road. One nearly ran me down on the way back from Tesco the other day,' she says. Thankfully she carries on walking back into the living room. Joni laughs.

'I knew she'd listen in. That is a good idea, though. Bike shop. Did you mean it?'

He nods. 'There isn't one anywhere near me. Gap in the market. Anyway, let's get back to the horrendously awkward conversation we're supposed to be having. I think part of the reason I told you about what happened – apart from that I thought it would be funny to embarrass you, obviously – is that I wanted to see how you'd react. In the cold light of day.'

'Right . . .' She's not quite following.

He puffs out his cheeks. 'I think because I thought . . . I wondered . . . for a moment there, I was . . . well . . .'

'Don't start a new career where you have to speak for a living, will you?'

He ignores her attempt at a joke. 'I'm going to say this once and then I'll never say it again, but it needs to be said. If you'd been sober I definitely wouldn't have said no. I don't think. And what if . . . you know . . . what if it turned out to be what we both want. There. That's it. I've got it off my chest.'

He can't look at her. He stares at the floor, waiting for a response. Joni tries to work out how she feels about what he's just said. Her immediate response – her default position – is to be mortified. To back away. But her heart has speeded up without her head's consent. She closes her eyes. 'OK. Um . . . it's too soon, you know that, don't you? I need some time on my own . . .'

'Of course,' he mutters. He looks so crestfallen she wants to hug him. She has to keep her hands glued to her sides.

'But that's not to say never. I mean, I've thought about it since, don't get me wrong . . .'

He looks at her at last. 'Have you?'

'A few times, if you get my meaning . . .'

'Eew. TMI,' he says, and Joni laughs so hard she starts coughing. It's helping. The laughing is definitely helping.

'Shit. Anyway, one day, if it happened again . . . I

mean, if you initiated it this time, I probably would . . .
One day . . .'

He smiles at her. 'OK.'

'But not yet.'

'I know. Can you give me an idea of timescale, though?
So, you know, I can keep my diary clear.'

She laughs. 'There's nothing in your diary anyway,
don't kid yourself.'

'Harsh,' he says.

'Let's forget about it till after my course, see how we
feel then. But I mean, really forget about it. Be our normal selves.'

'So, what . . . end of February? Say beginning of
March as February is a short month?' He fishes his
phone out of his pocket and goes into calendar. Types
something. He holds it out for Joni to see.

Find out if Jone fancies me when sober, she reads on 7
March. 'OK, it's a deal.'

'And vice versa, you know,' he says. 'Because I could
have transferred my affections on to Flick by then or
something. Or Judith.'

She smiles. 'March seventh. Absolutely no mention
of it till then.'

'Definitely not. Thank God.'

'And we can go out for a drink and there won't be any
awkwardness? Or subtext?'

He nods enthusiastically. 'Only if you jump me again,
obviously. And there's not a lot I can do about it if I'm
that irresistible.'

'I'll try to contain myself.' She hears the strains of

'Stayin' Alive'. 'I'm dancing to this. I haven't made enough of a fool of myself yet.'

'Oh good. Can I film it and put it on YouTube?' He follows her back in. Saffy is dancing with Mary and Flick, throwing fabulous shapes in her three-inch heels. She reaches over and pulls a reluctant Lucy into the throng. The kids watch, horrified. Maura claps along on the sidelines. Margaret and Gerald wave their glasses. Imo chats with Samira and Shona while Rhys dodges between the dancers with a bottle of champagne in each hand, filling glasses. Joni smiles. This is a good night. She inserts herself between Saffy and Mary, arms over her head, singing along.

51

There have been no offers on their house yet. Not a single one. The problem is, Ant knows, that there is nothing about it to make it stand out. It's a rundown house in a rundown area, exactly the same as all the other houses in the street. If you were looking at similar properties for a similar price you'd search for the surprise positives: it's near a school, it has a new oven, the tiny garden faces south. None of these apply to his and Deirdre's home. No one is going to buy it until the price is reduced to an irresistible low. Less than it's worth. Less than they need to make their new life any better than this, their old one. Without their windfall, moving away seems less attractive. What's the point? Their new life will be just the same as their old life, only with nicer countryside.

He's still smarting from the humiliation of being set up. His plan had been almost perfect. But he'd overestimated how desperate Mary was, how naïve. And he'd most definitely underestimated Lucy. Or Joni. Or whatever her real name is. She seems to be the one who masterminded the whole thing. He cringes at the thought of how scared he'd been when confronted by what was, to all intents and purposes, a kid. A huge muscle-bound kid. He'd almost pissed himself. Physical confrontation has never been Ant's thing.

The overzealous agent is asking him if he wants to reduce the price once more. 'I know you have timing issues,' she says. She's right. He has already left Evoke. His new job starts in a week and a half. Someone at the leisure centre where he'll be working has sent them a list of flats and houses they could rent, but so far he's done nothing about it. He's skim-read the list, to be fair, but it was hard to get excited about the kind of places they could afford. The plan wasn't to move to a strange place to live in another shithole. The plan had been to make a life where they came back to a lovely home at the end of a hard day at work, with a decent garden and space for them to relax. It was hardly a pipe dream, although, for them, it seemed as if it was.

He doesn't care about revenge. He wants to get as far away from Mary, Saffy and Joni as he can. Put it all behind him. Start again.

He'll know better next time.

He's nervous that they might keep looking for him. Obviously, there are hundreds of dating sites – probably thousands at this point – but he wouldn't put it past the three witches to sign up to them all and scour each and every profile for his face or his name. For the rest of their days. It would probably give them a purpose in life. A reason to get out of bed in the mornings. But he knows what they won't be expecting.

He fills in the interminable questionnaire the way he suspects everyone does – using ideals rather than truth. Who the hell ever answers the questions like 'Have you ever had a problem with drugs or alcohol?' or 'Do you have a criminal record?' with yes rather than no? He flicks through the photos and selects the three he and Deirdre have agreed on: wholesome (windblown on a hill), kind (cuddling their neighbour's dog, Vinnie), a hint of sex (long bare legs in a body-skimming dress, high heels. Nothing too much). He adds them to the profile.

He hands the phone over to Deirdre. 'That look OK?' He's already sent her all his photos of his brother Trevor's kids.

She reads it through carefully.

'Perfect,' she says. Her mask is a soon-to-be-wealthy widow, awaiting probate. Rich but with limited access to her money for a short time. 'If it ain't broke . . .' Ant had said.

'OK, I'm pressing send. Are you sure you want to do this?'

'I'm sure,' she says, leaning her head on his shoulder. 'It's my turn.'

Early next morning Deirdre opens the app. She has no idea what to expect, but she has received three hearts. She looks at who the first one is from – a teacher – and dismisses him immediately. Number two works in the City. He has a Rolex on his arm in his profile picture.

She returns with a heart of her own. Clicks on the box to open a chat with him.

52

Joni flops onto the sofa, too tired to move. She's had the best night. The absolute best night. Now, everyone has left. Lucas was the last, helping to see them all into their taxis and make sure Flick negotiated the stairs without incident. They're having a drink on Tuesday evening – Lucas and Joni, not Lucas and Flick, at least she hopes not – so she can tell him all about her first day as a student. Lucy and Giles are staying at a hotel in Mayfair, along with Maura, and will deliver her home tomorrow. Margaret and Gerald are in a B & B near Marylebone. Imo and Rhys have staggered off to bed downstairs, insisting they will do all the cleaning tomorrow. It's just Joni and her girls, Saffy and Mary, sharing a pot of coffee and a small brandy on the side. 'The oldest girls in town,' Mary had said, laughing when Joni had declared her love for them in the – very short – speech Imo had forced her to make. 'OK, my women,' Joni had said. 'My dearest friends.' They'd all raised a glass to Meg, the only other person in the world she wished had been there. Imo, Margaret, Gerald and Joni's mum had all shed a tear at that point and Joni had choked up. It had felt cathartic, publicly acknowledging her loss like that.

'I could sleep right here,' Joni says. 'Saffy, you take my bed.'

'I might stay here too,' Saffy says, reaching down and pulling off her shoes.

Mary stretches out on the other, smaller, couch and pulls a throw over herself. 'Me too.'

Joni is too tired to argue, even though she's made up the spare room in anticipation of one of them needing it. 'We should have toasted Ant for bringing us together,' she says sleepily.

'Fucker,' Saffy says.

'Absolute fucker,' Mary says. The word sounds so wrong coming out of Mary's mouth that Joni starts to laugh.

'You're turning into Saff.'

'I've got my mojo back. If I ever had a mojo, that is. I'm not even sure what one is.'

'I like Lucas,' Saffy says. 'Not, you know, in that way. He's funny. And he clearly has the hots for you, Jone.'

'Nice man,' Mary says. 'I'm buying a hat.'

'Please don't talk about it. If it happens, it happens. But mostly he's my friend. For now at least. I don't want to make things weird.'

Saffy shuffles further down on to her back. 'My lips are sealed.'

'Promise?'

'Promise. I wonder what Ant's doing right now.'

'Crying into his beer, I hope,' Joni says. 'Wishing he'd never started it.'

On Tuesday morning Joni sits at the kitchen table, her laptop in front of her. This morning she got up early, showered and was dressed and ready two hours early. She had to go for a walk in the end to calm herself down. She has one of her new notebooks and a pen on the table, a carafe of water and a coffee. She checks behind her to make sure nothing embarrassing will show her up in the Zoom background. She tried banishing Jasper to the other room, but he yowled so loudly she's had to let him in and risk him appearing on her lap at some point. Her first class starts at nine. Yesterday Imo sent her a huge bunch of flowers. A few minutes ago she received a flurry of good-luck messages from Saffy, Mary and Lucas. Her gang. She puts her phone on silent. She feels exhilarated. Happy. Nervous. Alive. Ready for the rest of her life to begin.

She checks the time. Clicks on the link.

Here goes.

Acknowledgements

Thanks as ever to my stellar team at Michael Joseph, above all Louise Moore and Maxine Hitchcock. Special thanks this time to Gaby Young for her stellar work in publicizing me and my books, and to Bea McIntyre who has made the whole copy-editing process so much less painful. Everyone at Curtis Brown – Jonny Geller, Viola Hayden, Ciara Finan, Nadia Farah Mokdad – I'd be lost without you. And to Charlotte Edwardes, thanks as always for spotting the inconsistencies.

'What was that?' I said. I'm not sure, looking back, what I expected from Maia, but I think, for one absurd moment, that I hoped to engage her in some shared moment of bewilderment or wonder, as if, by doing that, I could have made a friend of her, somehow, in spite of what we both knew.

'What?' She looked off to the side, as if searching for a clue to what I meant – but it wasn't real. She was mocking me.

'The feathers –' I said, then I forced myself to stop. I was annoyed with the way I was falling into her trap. Annoyed at being so easy to fool. I could see the way she was looking at me, and I was angry that I had somehow ceded the advantage to her. I had wanted to confront her, to ask what she was doing hanging around our house, or maybe remind her, coldly, and without the least trace of annoyance or irony, that Mother didn't have any further use for her. Now she had the upper hand.

She looked down. A few greyish wisps had settled on the path, just by her feet. 'Yes,' she said. 'I see.' She looked at me and smiled. 'You're right,' she said, in what I took to be mock surprise. 'Feathers.'

I shook my head. 'No,' I said – and for one ridiculous moment, I was about to explain, before I caught myself.

All the while, she had been regarding me with that same good-humoured contempt that the teachers had shown Mats Sigfridsson when he was lost for words in the classroom. For a moment, she was silent, lingering on that feeling, letting it sink in. Then she spoke, her voice suddenly bright. 'Going out?' she said. 'Are you sure you're well enough?'

I didn't respond to that; though now that she asked the question, I realised I'd had no idea where I was going, and all of a sudden, I didn't want to leave the house. It may have been fear, in part, that I would be exposed, out in the open – a fear I had never once felt, day or night, in my life – but it was also a reluctance to leave this girl alone, so close to where Mother was working. Because, at that moment, I was afraid for Mother. It sounds ridiculous now, but I suddenly had the notion that Mother really had fallen under the *huldra*'s spell, just as the Sigfridsson boys and Martin Crosbie had done. Why else would she allow this creature into our house? Why had she suddenly returned to portrait painting? Why did she seem so indifferent to my feelings about the intrusion? I could think of no other explanation than enchantment and, while I realise now that, when someone claims they can think of no other explanation, it's only because they haven't really considered the alternatives, I felt sick at heart and hopelessly undecided – which I was desperate for her not to see. But she did see, and she would have prolonged the moment – pretending, say, that she had another appointment with Mother – if Kyrre Opdahl hadn't appeared at that very moment, walking slowly up the path towards us, his face fixed in what he must have imagined was the semblance of a friendly expression.

'Good morning, young ladies,' he said, his voice not like his usual voice at all, the tone strained, the language artificial. I couldn't have imagined him using the words 'young ladies' until that moment and, of course, I knew he didn't think Maia was any kind of lady. 'What a beautiful day it is!'

Maia turned to him – and because I thought, at first, that she didn't know him, it seemed to me, preposterous as it sounds, that she was underestimating him. Because Kyrre Opdahl knew exactly who *she* was. 'A beautiful day,' she said, echoing him, with only the slightest hint of mockery in her voice. '*Akkurat*.'

The word sounded odd, coming from her – and he almost

300

smiled. Then his expression altered. 'Well,' he said. 'Better make the most of it. Because it won't last much longer.'

Maia detected the change of tone – and at that moment she understood, if she hadn't guessed before, that this old fool wasn't what he pretended to be. She didn't appear to be disturbed by that knowledge, however. On the contrary, she was, or gave the appearance of being, amused by him. 'You're absolutely right,' she said. 'Winter is coming. And what will a poor girl do then?' She was smiling, but there was no mistaking the provocation in her voice – and, of course, I saw then that she knew who he was. She had to know. She'd probably seen him about the place, and she would no doubt have heard about him from Martin. Maybe she'd even seen him come to the *hytte* that day, just after the last drowning, to clear everything out and secure it against intruders. Against *her*, in other words. I wondered again where she was sleeping, and what she was doing for food.

Kyrre shook his head. 'Well,' he said, 'there's shelter down below, for anyone with nowhere else to lay her head.' He wasn't smiling. He said what he had to say, then he stood with his eyes fixed on hers, his mouth set, waiting for her reply – but he wasn't speaking to a young girl, he was addressing the *huldra*. 'It's not much,' he said. 'But there's room enough for a winter guest.'

It was absurd, of course, but that was how he framed his invitation. He just came out with it, and he didn't seem to mind that it sounded completely inappropriate, a transparent case of a dirty old man propositioning a young girl, trying to take advantage of her, when she was at her most vulnerable. And even though I knew what he thought of her, even though I knew that, in his own mind, he was addressing the *huldra*, I couldn't help but notice a trace of excitement – an

301

infinitesimal trace of dark pleasure – that was almost, but not quite, concealed behind that casual invitation. Of course, I knew what he wanted to do right away. He was protecting me, protecting Mother, by playing decoy, putting himself in harm's way to divert the *huldra* from her intended prey – and in that moment I had a sudden glimpse of Maia through his eyes. A glimpse, no more, of someone, or something, as alluring as she was repugnant to him and his assent to this allure seemed, at that moment, as real as his determination to draw her away from Mother and me.

I was appalled. What did he think he was doing? Did he really hope to deceive her? Was he imagining that he could *charm* her? How could he have believed that such a thing was possible? Maia was still smiling, but I could see in her eyes that she was suspicious, too – suspicious, but not afraid, because she had to know that she had nothing to fear from a silly old man who believed in trolls and sprites. Besides, she really did need a place to stay, now that Martin was gone. Maybe she had been trying to win Mother over, by sitting for her, but I can't imagine she received anything in exchange. If she had, it had come to nothing and winter was approaching fast.

There was a moment's pause – and I don't know, now, why I didn't intervene. I wanted to take Kyrre by the arm and lead him away, I wanted to give him a good shake and make him see how ridiculous all this was, but I simply couldn't. I just stood and watched, as he made what he must have believed was a pact with the devil. Then, having taken that moment to work out what was going on – I look back now and I don't think of her as a girl any more, I see what Kyrre saw: I see the *huldra* – Maia laughed. She turned to me briefly, then she looked back at Kyrre, and her manner changed again. A moment before, she had been suspicious, as any eighteen-year-old might be when presented with such an offer; now, she was flirtatious, and quite brazen. 'Well, I don't know,' she said. 'How much room is there?'

Kyrre's head shook almost imperceptibly. 'Enough,' he said.

Maia studied his face. I didn't think she was going to accept Kyrre's offer, but she wanted to know why he had made it. She wanted to know what *he* knew, or thought he knew, about her. 'I wouldn't want to inconvenience you,' she said.

'No inconvenience.'

'Well,' Maia said, 'I'm not sure . . . I mean, I don't even know you –'

'Nor I you,' Kyrre said, 'But that's not a problem, is it? And I'm sure we could come to some arrangement –'

Maia jumped at that. 'What arrangement?' she said.

'Well,' Kyrre said, 'come and have a look. It's not far. We can talk about that while we walk.'

I couldn't believe it. What was happening was grotesque, and I *wanted* to say something. I wanted to stop him pursuing this mad course, but I didn't know how. Besides, I was sure, still, that Maia would refuse his offer. She would string him along, till he did something stupid, then she would show him up and let everybody know what a dirty old man he was – because surely that was what she was thinking, surely she had assumed that he wanted something from her, the one thing that was hers to give, now that she was alone in the world. The one thing that, presumably, she had been able to offer Martin Crosbie. There was no way for her to know how badly she was misjudging him. Or was there? Maybe she knew exactly what he intended and, maybe, she enjoyed the challenge. Maybe, as the *huldra*, she wanted to show him how invulnerable she really was. Maybe she had it in mind to seduce this

303

foolish old man, just as she had seduced the others – and I wasn't altogether sure that Kyrre Opdahl was beyond seduction. I was ashamed of that thought but, considering what happened afterwards, I cannot rule out the possibility that my suspicions were justified. At the time, though, it was nothing more than an idle thought, a flicker of mischief and superstition that would, I knew, be immediately dispelled, when Maia laughed off this bizarre invitation.

Only, she didn't laugh it off. Not at all. She regarded him for a long moment with a mix of suspicion and amusement; then her face softened, and she moved over to where he was standing and took him lightly by the arm. 'All right,' she said. 'I'll take a look at this *shelter*.' She glanced at me, as if we were together in some girls' conspiracy, then she laughed. 'Though I warn you,' she said. 'You don't know what you're letting yourself in for.'

I turned to Kyrre. I could see that he hadn't fallen under her spell. He was clinging to some plan that he had hatched over the last few days, ever since he'd first seen Maia at our house and decided Mother was in danger. I could see that he was up to something and I could also see that his cunning plan was just as obvious to Maia. She had put on a face – an expression that she must have thought made her seem the gullible and needy girl that Kyrre so clearly believed she was not – but there was, in the dark glitter of her eyes, a knowingness that made me afraid, for Kyrre, of course, but also for her. He was pretending that he wanted to help, but he wasn't making a very good job of it, not because he wasn't good at pretending, but because he couldn't care less whether she trusted him or not. All he wanted was for her to go with him, away from this house, away from the only people he loved in the whole world. I didn't know what he intended – did he think he could save Mother from her grim fascination with the shadow that she saw in this disturbed girl, the shadow that he knew, against all reason, was the *huldra*? If he did, how was he going to do it? I don't recall, now, how much I suspected at the time, and how much came later, but I think, even then, when something could still have been done to divert him, I already knew he wanted to destroy her. What was worse was that Maia knew it too. She wasn't deceived for a second – which meant that, for her, whatever Kyrre had in mind was a challenge she was prepared to accept, quite gladly. A challenge that she welcomed. She thought that she was stronger than him. She knew it, in fact, because she was the *huldra*, and he was just an old man.

I don't recall how much of this I believed at the time, but I do know that, just as he had deceived himself, Kyrre had deceived me, because I was thinking of this girl – who, in the plain light of day, seemed nothing more than a lost, possibly abused child with nowhere to go – I was looking at this lost girl and I was seeing the *huldra*, seeing her with Kyrre's eyes, making her a character from one of the old stories, a creature possessed, whether temporarily or intrinsically, by some random wave of malice. Maia had always been strange, and there were questions about her that I couldn't answer; she had invaded my home and she had taunted me with what she must have imagined was a power that I envied; she was inextricably connected to three unexplained deaths, at least one of which she had watched, without lifting a finger to help or to raise the alarm; but surely common sense should have told me that she was still nothing more than a young girl – troubled no doubt, malicious even, but only in the way that damaged children often are. Common sense should have told me that she wasn't the *huldra*, because – why did I forget it,

305

even for a moment? – the *huldra* did not exist. The *huldra* was just a notion, a metaphor no doubt, for something harder to pin down and more painful to consider, an ugly spirit from an old story, told to keep young men in line, or to explain away the darkness. A story, a warning, a zone on the map that allows us to navigate an impossible world.

I looked at Kyrre, and I could see, in the set of his mouth, in the fixity of his eyes, the expression of a man who has made up his mind to do something terrible – and, beguiled by a fairy tale, I did nothing to stop him. Instead, I turned to Maia and, through a fog of doubt and absurd fantasy, I made a desperate appeal to the plain light of day in her that I had already given up on. 'You can't go now,' I said. 'I don't think Mother's finished the painting yet.'

Maia laughed. 'I think she has,' she said, without a hint of regret. 'I think it was finished on the first day. In fact –' she looked at Kyrre and then back to me with a defiant smile – 'I think she knew what she was going to paint even before I sat down in that lovely studio of hers.' She slipped her hand into her jacket pocket – and I knew that she had something in there, something that Mother had given her, or possibly some small treasure that she had stolen. She looked at me, and her face was pleasant, and utterly calm – yet I knew that she had sensed my suspicion and she was hurt by it. 'I think,' she said, and there was no shift in her manner, no shadow of malice or judgement in her voice, 'if I'm not mistaken, your mother began that painting a long time ago, and has only just got round to finishing it.'

That stung me – and, for the first time, I realised that, to sit for Mother, Maia would have had to climb the stairs, to pass the door to my room and cross the landing and, as she did, she would have seen the portrait of me that Mother had begun so long ago, begun and abandoned, without ever offering a word of explanation. She had seen it, and she had seen through it – or so she thought. But what she had seen wasn't the truth. How could it be? I wasn't like her, and Mother knew that. She *knew* – and what she wanted to capture in this portrait was the same thing, more or less, that Kyrre had seen when he decided that Maia was the *huldra*. She would have laughed at the old man's superstitions, no doubt, but what she saw in Maia was a girl touched by a darkness that could have been ordinary bad luck – a talent, almost, for tragedy – but might just as easily have been a form of possession, a weakness of spirit or resolve that allowed the darkness to work through her. A weakness that had allowed her to welcome the darkness in, perhaps unwittingly – and that was what Mother had wanted to capture. *Susceptibility*, in the abstract – not this lost girl.

I shook my head, but I refused to respond to the provocation. Perhaps I saw in it a wish to draw me into whatever was about to unfold with Kyrre, a wish to drag me down with the old man and make me an accomplice in whatever she imagined he was planning. 'I'm sure, when she's finished, she'll let you see the picture,' I said. 'Don't you want to see –'

She burst out laughing then. 'It's all right,' she said. 'I don't have to see it. But you take a look, and let me know what you think.' She turned to Kyrre, with a sweet, absurd smile. 'Thanks to your kind neighbour,' she said, 'I'll just be down the road . . . For a while, at least.'

Kyrre nodded. '*Akkurat*,' he said.

Maia nodded back and made to leave. Then, as if as an afterthought, she took what she was clutching from her pocket and held it out to me. It was money, of course. She hadn't stolen it – and she wanted me to see that my suspicions had been unfounded. It was payment for the sitting. 'Give this back to your mother,' she said, with that same mocking glitter in her eyes. 'I didn't earn it.'

I shook my head again, but I didn't say anything. I didn't want to touch the money. I didn't want to touch anything she had touched – and, at that moment, I had a sense of the house behind me as contaminated, everywhere, by contact with her. With her fingers, her breath, the scent of her and, most of all, those dark, glittering eyes. 'Keep it,' I said, at last. 'You might need it.'

Her hand wavered a moment, then she slipped the money back into her jacket. All this time Kyrre had been standing by, watching, waiting, patient with the dull resolve of the desperate. For a split second, I thought I had one last chance to intervene, one last chance to dissuade – and then even that moment was gone. Maybe it hadn't existed anyhow. Maybe everything was already decided, the way it is in fairy tales. For too long, I had flickered back and forth between that world where nothing can be done and the plain light of day, where reason is supposed to prevail and now it was too late. Ryvold had said, once, that trolls exist, whether we like it or not, but we had a choice about the forms they took, and the powers they could assume. It all depended on whether we allowed ourselves to be deceived, on whether we succumbed to super-stition – but at that moment, and just for that moment, I didn't believe him. And by the time I did, there was nothing I could do.

I watched them walk away. In some far part of my mind, I was praying, or hoping at least, that Kyrre would abandon whatever plan he had made to divert the *huldra* away from us, but I knew it was too late. He was determined to see this through, they both were – and all of a sudden I pictured them together, in that house of his, a few hundred metres along the shore, sitting at the kitchen table over coffee, as Kyrre and I had always done, surrounded by cogs and spark plugs, in a fug of engine oil and white spirit, each waiting for the other to make a decisive move. It was a terrible image – and I wondered what Kyrre thought he was doing, inviting the *huldra* into his house, when he, of all people, knew that she could not be contained or defeated. They walked slowly, side by side, neither talking nor even looking at the other – and yet, for a moment, just before they disappeared, they looked, not like strangers who have only just met, but like kith and kin, family members who, whether they were fond of one another or not, would always be irreversibly united by blood and history. That impression lasted for a few seconds, no more, before they disappeared at the first curve of the track, but it was undeniable. Then, for a long moment, I was gazing at nothing but leaves and air, the birches paler now, and touched here and there with streaks and blemishes of gold, the light thin and unconvincing at the far end of the track, as if something that had been there for years, some high tree or carved stone, had been uprooted overnight, leaving only a gap where substance should have been. I waited there for a long time – several minutes, I think, though it is hard to tell, looking back – and all that time I was in doubt, ready to believe that what I had just witnessed hadn't happened at all, or was, at least, capable of being reversed. Then, with a sense, not so much of having been defeated as of having given up too easily, I turned to go in. I was still there, at the gate, just a few yards from the front door, but I suddenly felt exposed and, as ridiculous as it sounds, in danger – and it took a considerable effort not to give in to that sudden fear, a sense of apprehension that, in the space between one breath and the next, was transformed into blind, unreasoning panic.

I was almost inside, almost out of harm's way, when I heard the scream. It was a sound unlike anything I had ever heard before, a scream, a shriek, a wild cry laced with horror that seemed just inches away for one awful moment, before I placed it, and realised that it must have come from further along the track, in the direction that Kyrre and Maia had taken a few minutes earlier. It was a sudden, high-pitched shriek, the last cry of something that had been caught and pulled down, and it was startling in its finality, but I couldn't have said whether it was the scream of a girl, or an old man, or an animal that some predator had taken, down in the meadows or somewhere in the woods. It could have been any one of those, and it could have been none of them – and in the old stories, certainly, it would have been the cry of no living thing, but the other-worldly shriek of a harpy or a fetch, echoing on the still air of an afternoon that, by some logic that no mortal could follow, had turned out to be cursed.

I try to think that, on any other day, I could have been rational about what I heard. As that shriek died away – though that's not an accurate description for the sense I had of something moving off into the distance, not fading so much as being absorbed into the land for miles around, absorbed by the birches and the meadows and the white air out over the Sound, absorbed so thoroughly that it would never disappear – as that terrible scream soaked into the fabric of the world around me, I should have tried to explain it as a natural event of some kind. A kill, in the far grass, say, where some predator had pulled down a bird or a hare, or the sound a foreign ship might make, as it navigated its way out of the channel into open water. I could have said it was a tyre blowing out, down on the Brensholmen road, or a seabird calling from further up shore. I had heard sounds here that I couldn't explain often enough, odd wailings in the wind in the small hours of *midnattsol*, a high-pitched keening over the snow in the dark time, bird calls where no bird could have been, animal cries in the woods when I was out in the noonday darkness and imagining the wolverine, come down from the far north to track me by my torchlight. No sound is improbable, here – but *that* sound was impossible and, as it faded away, sinking into my skin and my bones as surely as it was soaking into the land around me, I knew it had come from some point along the track between our house and Kyrre Opdahl's. It startled me, that cry, and it held me for a moment, as it faded – but it was only a moment and, as soon as that moment passed, I was running blindly towards it, running out through the gate and along the path towards the scene of whatever crime had been committed within calling distance of the house where Mother was, no doubt, standing in front of a canvas, putting the finishing touches to a picture she should never have begun, and, absurd as it sounds now, I had a vision of her in what Maia had called her lovely studio, smiling at the finished portrait, happy to have captured whatever it was she had set out to capture, in features that were both girlish and inhuman. It lasted no more than a second, that fleeting vision, but it was as vivid as the cry had been – a cry she probably hadn't even heard, at work on the far side of the house, oblivious to everything, as she always was when her work absorbed her.

The ground is steep and uneven on the track to Kyrre's house, but it couldn't have taken me long to reach the place where the cry had originated – and though I found nobody there, and no immediate evidence of violence or harm, I knew

311

it was the scene of whatever had happened. The place, not where Kyrre and Maia were, but where they should have been. Where they *had* been, moments before, when that shriek pierced the air. There was nothing to detain me at that place, or nothing that I could see at first glance, as I hurried along the track, but I felt sure they had gone no further. This was the place where they had stopped, for whatever reason, and it was here that they had disappeared.

There was nothing there, though. Or nothing I could see. Yet if they had stopped there, if they had gone no further, then it stood to reason that they *had* to be there still, and if they weren't, then they *had* to have vanished. They couldn't have just vanished into thin air – and that was what confused me, because *that* was impossible. That was what confused me – that, and the smell. I didn't catch it at first, but then it was everywhere around me, strong and dark and almost over-whelming, just for a moment, so close that I felt dizzy, and I had to bend, my hands on my knees, my head down, not gasping for breath, quite, but suddenly clogged with that dark, water-and-smoke scent, like the smell you get after a doused fire, when the wood is still smouldering here and there amid the wet timber, a chill, dark scent that made me feel – I don't know what to call it, not sad exactly, but disappointed. Disappointed at some extreme, physical level. Or dismayed – yes, that would probably be the right word. Dismayed. Dismay in the pit of my stomach and in the marrow of my bones, dismay in my throat and in that smoke taste in my mouth and nose, dismay that seemed like it would last forever, that had always been there, waiting on that path I had walked hundreds of times, going down to Kyrre's house to sit in his kitchen and drink strong coffee while he sat opposite, working on an outboard motor and telling me stories from the old days – and though there was no evidence that something bad had happened, other than that black, smoky scent hanging on the air among the birch trees, I think that was when I first knew he was gone. I look back and I see that I knew from the first. I knew, even before I smelled that smell, or saw the spots.

I didn't notice them at first. They only became visible when I bent down, eyes closed, trying to catch my breath and then, when I had gathered my strength and opened my eyes again, I caught sight of the first thick, black spots on the grass at my feet. Then, as I raised my head and started breathing again, I saw that they were all around me: on the grass, in the dirt, on the leaves of the trees, inky black spots that, at first sight, looked like soot or dust but, when I stretched out my hand and brushed the tip of my finger over the surface of a yellowing birch leaf, felt oily to the touch. Oily, like something live. Like the traces you find out in the woods after something has been there in the night, feeding or suckling on its prey. I pulled my hand back and looked around. The spots were everywhere, thick and black and sticky, touched with the dark, smoky scent that had forced me to stop at that turn in the path, almost halfway between our house and Kyrre's. I stood a moment, staring, my head filling again with the smell – and then I was hurrying on, knowing it was pointless, but also knowing that I had to check, because nothing here offered an explanation for what had happened. Nothing here made any sense. I knew that Kyrre and Maia had stopped at that very spot, and that the smell and the black spots had something to do with what had happened next, but I also knew that this was ridiculous, and I ran on for several metres, like a lost dog, ran then walked then ran again, my head craning forward to see whatever I might see before it slipped away and, all at once, it was like being in the middle of a huge and elaborate conjuring trick, as if the whole world had been set up to deceive me, but I could see through it, if I could only find the right clue.

So I ran and walked and ran all the way to Kyrre's house – and as soon as I got there, I felt anxious. Now that I was away from the scene, I thought I must have missed something at that turn in the path, and I had to go back right away, before it was too late. There was something I hadn't understood, something I hadn't seen, or maybe something that I *had* seen that hadn't really been there at all, and I had to retrace my steps and catch whoever or whatever was playing this trick on me, catch it out, see through it, find the real explanation. Even before I got to Kyrre's house and looked in at the kitchen window, I could see that nobody was there, and I realised that, in my hurry, I must have tricked myself, at the turn in the path – and I started back, running now, in a panic, I suppose, and close to tears, not because I knew Kyrre had gone, but because I had been tricked, and I was upset at not knowing how. It was like being in school, doing some complicated equation and not being able to get an answer: you go over it again and again and when nothing comes this astonishing anger rises up in your blood. That was what I felt then: that same anger. I came back to the place where I had seen the spots of black ash on the grass – and at that very moment, quite unexpectedly, it started to rain. That far northern rain, the kind that comes out of nowhere and goes on for days, without stopping. Huge, cold drops, inky and black and sudden, loud on the rooftops, cold on your face and hands, chaotic out among the trees, pouring through the branches, bouncing off leaves, washing everything clean, every trace of warmth, every stain, every mark of what has been and gone over an entire summer, till nothing at all remains. I stood still, unable to move, watching as the black stains on the leaves were washed away. And I couldn't move. I still felt angry, but I was frightened now too, because I knew that, whatever had happened to Kyrre and the *huldra*, it wasn't a trick. I stood a long time, perhaps several minutes and then, when I had started to gather the resolve to make my way back to the house, I heard a sound off to the right, in the birch wood. A soft, rustling sound, like someone coming through the trees towards me. I turned. I thought it was a person – and I suppose I must have thought that it was Kyrre Opdahl, because I took several steps in the direction of the sound, scanning the gaps between the trees, expecting to see a human shape coming through the birches. I didn't see anyone, though. I could still hear the noise – a soft, creeping sound – but there was nothing there that I could see. Or not at first. I had taken five or six steps into the birches, certainly no more, before I came to a stop and stood there, watching, listening, but I was looking for something at eye level, I was looking for a person, and it was only when I heard the sound – a soft, plaintive snuffling, like a dog trying to find its way into a hole where something is hidden – that I looked down. There, ten or maybe twelve metres away, I saw what I took for an animal. I say *took for* an animal, because it was crouching down, its snout reddened with blood and it had something in its mouth – hair, bone, the remains of some creature it had hunted down and killed – but I couldn't have said what kind of animal it was. Certainly, it resembled nothing I had seen in the meadows before. Yet it was an animal, nevertheless: of that there could be no doubt. It wasn't a person, it was an animal, and when it saw me, or maybe when it caught my scent, it looked up, its eyes dark and bright, the piece of carcass still clenched between its teeth. It looked at me – and, for a moment, it was as if it *knew* me. The thing looked up and made a soft, hoarse sound, and though I didn't know what kind of animal it was, I could see its face – or, no, it wasn't a face I saw, it was an *expression*. An expression of – what? Triumph? I think it was that. Triumph. It looked at me, and it made that soft, hoarse sound – and then it turned and hurried away through the long grass, moving so quickly that I could make nothing out, other than a few fleeting and possibly inaccurate details. I thought it was black, or dark brown; I think it was about the size of a large dog – though it wasn't a dog, of that I am sure, and I am almost certain that it wasn't native to the island, but had strayed in from elsewhere. Maybe it was an illegal pet that had escaped from one of the houses further along the coast, maybe it was something that had strayed here from the high tundra – whatever it was, all I could have said for sure was that it wasn't a person. I walked over to where it had been when I saw it first, and it's strange, I wasn't really afraid, I felt numb – maybe I was in shock – and when I reached the spot I found nothing. No bones, no matted hair, no dead creature with its throat torn open or its eyes picked out. There was nothing – not even a spot of blood. Whatever it had killed, it had carried the thing away with it – and though, at that moment, it seemed that this vision was nothing more than a coincidence, even though it didn't even occur to me that there was any connection between this animal and what I had witnessed earlier, I felt sick with fear, all of a sudden, because I knew that something terrible had happened. I didn't know what it was, or who it had happened to, but I suddenly became aware of myself, alone in the woods, and I felt something was watching me still: the animal, or something else, I couldn't have said what. Something was watching me, with my scent in its nose and mouth, and at any moment, it would attack.

316

I wasn't conscious, then, of how I came to be running. I don't recall making the decision – if I had thought about it, I would have known it was the wrong thing to do because, as I crashed away through the trees like a startled deer, I felt something ebb from my mind, and then everything was dark, not black, but dim, as if seen through smoked glass, and then I was running blind, in utter panic, unable to think, and unable to stop myself. I ran through the trees and back along the path towards the house and, all the way, I was terrified something would appear at the gate, or halfway up the garden path, and swallow me up, in one bright, triumphant movement. In fact, I was convinced that it would come, and I knew I was running straight into its arms, and still I couldn't stop running. I didn't see anything until I reached the gate, and then I saw the door – it was open, and that shocked me, because I had no memory of that, and I thought that whatever was pursuing me was waiting there, inside the house now, the stink of it in the hallway, or on the stairs, but even then I didn't stop running. I didn't stop, in fact, until I was inside and, clawing desperately at the latch, managed to push the door shut behind me – and then I collapsed on the floor, everything going white, and then dark, and then, as I understood finally that I was safe, as I realised that I had escaped, there was nothing.

It's nine o'clock. I have been working since early this morning, drawing a new map of the path that runs from our house to Kyrre's, a map that is almost infinitely detailed: every tree, every rock, every patch of wildflowers marked out, the way the objects are marked out at a crime scene, everything doused in possibility, every shadow, every scuff in the grass, every fallen twig laden with a significance that has yet to be seen. It's ten years, now, since that day, and I am still trying to find some factual basis for what I saw, because, when I look back, I don't believe that what I am telling is completely true. How could it be? What happened that day was impossible. It doesn't matter that I remember it all just as clearly – just as *factually* – as I remember everything else: what happened out there, on the empty path, remains an impossibility and there is nothing I can tell myself that will change that.

I was ill for a long time after my vision of that day. Mother found me in the hallway, right at the foot of the stairs, and she saw that something was terribly wrong. I wasn't unconscious, but I didn't respond when she asked me what had happened, so she didn't know that Kyrre and the girl were gone. All she knew was that I was very ill, so she got me out of my wet clothes and half carried me upstairs to bed. I don't remember any of this – I don't remember anything that happened for a long time after that morning – but this is what she told me when I was well, and I have no reason to doubt her. She told me that I ran a high fever that night, and she couldn't get me to eat. I was shivering, and I couldn't talk for a long time, but I did drink, when she brought me water, which she took as a good sign. I also slept off and on, and that was better still. Mother has always believed in the healing power of sleep. There have been times when she's slept for twenty-four hours, thirty-six hours, or even longer. Dreams mend us, she says. Without dreams, we would all be insane. At the high point, when things were at their worst, she said, she sat with me while I slept and she noticed that my eyes were moving, which meant that I was dreaming, and though I struggled in my sleep and sometimes cried out, she let me sleep on. Dreams are the stories we tell ourselves to make sense of the world, she says. The only difference between the mad and the sane is that the mad do not dream well enough.

No doubt she is right and, whatever else is true, she brought me through the madness of the next several days alone and unassisted – but, to this day, there *is* no story I can tell myself that will make sense of what I saw. I can tell myself other things about what happened that summer; I can make certain statements about what I know to be true, in the ordinary way of things, but these are mere facts, and though any story conveys, or claims to convey, a factual history, what I can tell myself, what I can say is factually true, is really neither here nor there. I can say that Martin Crosbie's body was never found; I can say that, when his car disappeared, everyone assumed he had left the island – everyone, that is, who had any interest in the matter. I can say that Ryvold never returned to Kvaløya, though he did write and, later, sometime during the following spring, as I recall, he sent Mother the manuscript of a book he had written, a book that was later published, not only in Norway, but in several other territories. It was a book about the old stories, of course, though it was also a series of personal memories and reflections, and I read it carefully for what it might reveal about his mind but, though he touched upon art and the Narcissus story, and though he included a long section about his time in the north, he didn't mention Mother once. I was surprised, at the time, but I was glad he left her out of his story. There were too many stories about Mother and not one of them – not even Frank Verne's – was true.

After Ryvold left, the suitors gradually fell away – and Mother finally became the recluse that those stories had always described her as being. She is still painting, and the man from Fløgstad's travels up and down the country with her pictures, stopping off on the way at his sister's house in Mo I Rana, and even though the work has grown darker – as some critics see it, though what I see is quite the opposite of darkness – it continues to sell. Meanwhile, I decided what to *do* with myself. It took some time, but I knew, after that summer of drowning, that I belonged to this place, and I have no intention of leaving, or of ever becoming distracted from the work I have chosen. I can happily say that I never received any more gifts from Kate Thompson, though I also have to confess that I find myself thinking about her from time to time. It struck me as odd, to begin with, that it was Kate I thought about, not Arild Frederiksen, but then, I never met Arild Frederiksen and, other than a character in a book, he has never existed for me.

It was some time before Mother accepted that Kyrre Opdahl had just disappeared off the face of the earth. To begin with, when I was still ill, she had wondered why he didn't answer the phone, and I think she even walked down to his cottage on the shore to see if he was there. Then, when it was obvious that he was missing, she seems to have told herself that he'd gone off to visit a friend. Maybe he'd gone to Narvik again, or up north somewhere. It wasn't a very likely explanation, but she was preoccupied with me and I think she didn't want anything else on her plate. As far as I know, she didn't even register that Maia had also disappeared. She probably just assumed that the strange girl had gone away – she had been something of a vagrant, after all – and she was probably glad of it for, though she never did understand why, she quickly came to understand that Maia's presence in our house had been one of the main causes of what she later referred to as my *crisis*. She didn't say breakdown, though that would have been the conclusion anyone else would have come to, had they been present to observe my condition over the next several weeks. But there *was* nobody else. At no point during my illness, even on that first day, when she found me, mute and helpless with panic at the foot of our stairs – at no point whatsoever did Mother think of calling a doctor. Instead, she nursed me herself, day by day, till I was well enough to speak. And even then, when the slow process of recovery began, she didn't ask me about what had happened. She didn't want to know what I had seen – or, if she did, she didn't allow herself to ask the questions that must have been in her mind. Later, when I was able to get up and go about my normal business, I remember being shocked by that. How could she stop herself from asking those questions? Was it because she was afraid to reawaken the terror she had seen in my face? Or was it just her usual discretion? I couldn't say. All I know is that I wouldn't have been able to tell her anything, if she had given in to her curiosity. There was no story, no explanation that I could offer, whether to her or to myself – or none, at least, that made any sense in the plain light of day. Still, I was always aware of a gap – a dark, clean tear – in the fabric of the world, which I expected first Mother and then everyone else to notice at any moment. And maybe that was why I said nothing, because that gap seemed so obvious. I didn't say anything about what I had seen – or rather, what I hadn't seen at all, but surmised from events and clues that were lost in the rain or too preposterous to repeat. Besides, even before the rain, what evidence of actual mischief had there been? A few spots of dust or grease, a cry that could have been an animal or a bird, and a solitary teenager's sense that something was wrong. I don't remember making a conscious decision to keep back what I knew – though, in retrospect, it isn't so surprising. In fact, I don't think I decided anything at all. I was waiting, I suppose, for that tear in the universe to become visible enough to betray itself and maybe part of me was waiting for someone to find real proof – a body, say, or some sign of violence out in the woods – but at the back of my mind, even then, I knew there would never be conclusive proof of anything. What had happened belonged to Kyrre's world, the world of stories and fatal magic, and any attempt to tell what had happened in that world would only convince people that the old man had turned my head with his nonsense. I would be an object of scorn or pity, a hysterical girl who'd come upon a kill-site in the birch woods and panicked. Sometimes, I even told myself that I was exactly that – because what had happened, what I had almost but not quite witnessed, was impossible, and there had to be some other explanation that I was unaware of, something that would reconcile the world I knew with the world that Kyrre had always believed was out there, and that I had always believed was nothing more than a story.

It's nine o'clock, and I have been at work for several hours – which is how the days usually unfold, now. I get up early and I have a cup of coffee, then I go upstairs to what used to be the spare room and is now my workroom. I don't call it a studio, because that isn't what I do. I'm not an artist, like Mother: I'm a map-maker. I don't deny that my maps are shown in galleries, or that people buy them, but I never think of them as art. I consider them to be functional, though not in the usual way: they are maps, but you can't use them to drive from one end of the island to another – not unless you go *very* slowly – and their scale is such that you are more likely to get lost in the detail than to use them to find your way home. They also differ from other maps in the way they accommodate time. Every map has a limited lifespan, of course: roads are replaced and buildings are demolished, what was once woodland or meadow is now a supermarket or a car park. Maps provide snapshots of places, pictures that can last for weeks, or centuries, depending on how detailed they are, but nothing about them is truly permanent and there are times when what they leave out is crucial. My maps leave nothing out, though: they are so detailed that they are immediately obsolete, at least as navigational tools and, in that respect, I like to think of them as a commentary on how carelessly we look at the world. I've been making them for eight years now, in various forms: I began with this island, working outwards, one metre at a time, from Kyrre's *hytte*, in an infinitesimal charting of every object I found, every rock and pebble and bird's nest, searching – square by square, coordinate by coordinate – for the unseen, adjacent space that the stories unfold in. It sounds odd, no doubt, to suggest that the unseen could be mapped, but that is what I am attempting to do, not as fantasy, but as invention – invention, in the old sense, which is to say: revealing what there is, seen and unseen, positive and negative, shape and shadow, the veiling and the veiled. Some things can only be seen in negative, some bodies only become perceptible in the interference they create. About some – Kyrre Opdahl, say, or the *huldra* – the only location I can propose is what is not present in the map of where they do not occur. No one else knows this, but that doesn't matter. People buy the maps to hang on a wall, as if they were pictures, but they also suspect, even when they don't know why, that they are buying something that could be used. And that is what my maps intend – they try to give a sense of the world beyond our illusory homelands. Not for navigation, but for seeing. Because there are two ways of looking at the world and two kinds of seeing. The first is the way we learn from infancy onwards, the way of seeing what we are supposed to see, building the consensus of a world by looking out for, and finding, what we have always been told is there. But there's another way – and that is what I am after. It's the way we see when we go out alone in the world, like a boy going out into the fields, or along the shore, in some old story. When he's at home, he sees what he is supposed to see, but as soon as he leaves the safety of the farmhouse, or the village school-room, everything is different. He tries to go on seeing what he expects to see, but something creeps in at the edge of his vision – and he begins to realise that, out here, *anything* can be the *huldra*. Every thing he knows, every illusory detail of home, melts away, leaving him alone with a world too strange to witness. The *huldra*'s world – the real world – that the farmhouse and the village schoolroom try so hard to conceal.

I have never discussed this with Mother – or rather, I have never told her what it is I am attempting to do – but even if she doesn't know what I am trying to create, she seems happy for me. I am her equal now, not so much in her eyes, but in what she thinks is my own estimation, and that has made a big difference in how we live together. I am her equal, not because I have found something to do with my life, but because I have been permitted a terrible privilege. I have been allowed to witness something that could never have happened, and this event is always with me, like an invisible companion or a scar. I am her equal, in a way that doesn't matter in the least, because I have seen through the fabric of the world that everyone else agrees upon, and I have been obliged to start again, with measurements and pencil marks and blocks of colour on the finest paper that money can buy – and that simple, absorbing work has given Mother permission to stop worrying about me, once and for all. It wasn't something I would have thought of before, but now I can see that she *was* very worried about me, when she didn't know what I was going to do with my life – not because it mattered to her, but because she knew it mattered to me. Now she feels she can relax – maybe we both do – because she knew, all along, that I *needed* something, so I wouldn't just be her daughter.

I'm not making some grand claim to happiness or fulfilment here, though. I'm not saying I have a happy life, in the way someone else might understand it. I don't have *any* other life, in fact, outside my work. I don't need what other people seem to need, and I never miss what I have never wanted, but once a week, I take the track through the birch woods where Kyrre and Maia vanished, then I follow the Brensholmen road to the point where Kyrre's track veers off, on the shore side. The house was never locked when Kyrre was here – he didn't have anything anyone would want to steal, he'd say, though that wasn't strictly true – and I keep it just the way he left it. If he ever comes back, it will be as it always was: the cluttered kitchen, the old pots and pans, the spare room full of engine parts and old clocks, the wide alcove off the hall that was nothing but shelves, like some troll-child's secret library. I go once a week, and I keep the place clean, but I don't tidy up, and I only move what I have to move, when I'm dusting or using the vacuum and, afterwards, I put it all back exactly as it was.

Usually, I go on a Wednesday, first thing after breakfast. I let myself in and I make coffee – strong, the way he used to make it – then I give the place a bit of a clean, and make sure it's all sound. I work for a couple of hours – it doesn't take much – and I keep it brisk. Sometimes, there are small repairs to attend to, and occasionally, when I'm in a sentimental mood, I bring out Kyrre's old books and albums and flick through the pages, trying to make out who is who, or who *might* be who, in the photographs and clippings. Mostly, they show local events and family gatherings, but sometimes there are old stories out of the newspapers – local mysteries that kept people guessing for a while, thirty or fifty years ago, then got forgotten at summer's end. I sit for a while and look at the photographs, trying to make out which of the young men might be Kyrre, and who, among the people standing round, could be relatives of his, or maybe a sweetheart. I'm sorry, now, that I didn't ask him more about those pictures. Who was who, when and where they were taken, what the occasion was. I suppose I just took him for granted – though when I look back, I see that I was longing for answers to all those questions; it was just that I didn't know how to ask.

I miss him, of course, even though I don't wholly think of him as gone. Every now and then I turn round, or I look up from one of those picture books, and I half expect to see him coming through the door, or sitting in his big, creaky chair, surrounded by cogs and flywheels. There will be times when a thought passes through my head and I almost hear him listening in. '*Akkurat*,' he will say, in that way he has. Or that way he had when he was living. I don't think of him as gone, but I don't think of him as living any more, and I know, if I ever do see him, it will be something other than a man that I will see – which is odd, because I don't really believe in ghosts. I know he is dead, I am quite certain of it, and I don't believe that the dead come back to haunt us, yet I still expect to see him, one day, back home and safe in his own house. It's a kind notion, for me at least. I like to think there is something that he was working on, something he needs to come back and finish, and I like to think that I'll be there when he returns, drawn home by the smell of coffee and a last promise to keep. I always think I'll see him here, in the house – and I suppose, if the dead ever did return, then this would be the place they'd choose: low and set back from the road among

326

its own stand of trees, Kyrre's house is almost invisible, and though I have spent my entire life going back and forth between this house and my own, I never noticed, before, how isolated Kyrre was. Isolated – and safe.

I go to the *hytte* too, and I do my best to maintain it. I don't like being down there for too long, though. I don't really understand why, but I feel uneasy. It's ridiculous, I know, but I can't help thinking that I am being watched. Like you do in the woods sometimes, or when you're walking out on the beach in the middle of the day, and you can't see anybody, but you can't quite shake off the notion that someone is watching, either. Of course, that's natural – it's far more exposed there and, sitting out front, on the lawn by the shore, I know I am visible to every single passenger on the big boats that chug up and down the Sound, just as I know all too well that I can be seen from the landing outside my room. Though I also know that there is no one there to spy any more. As always, Mother is hidden away in her studio and, without me, the house might as well be empty. Sometimes, sitting there on the old elmwood chair looking out across the water, or away along the shore, it feels as if the whole world is empty. All except for me, and whatever ghosts I choose to entertain – and I don't entertain ghosts very often. Yes, there are times when I half expect Kyrre to come driving down the track in his old van; if I'm not careful, I can even imagine that Maia is about to return, walking across the meadows, looking for another boy to drown – but, mostly, I stay away from those thoughts because, to be perfectly honest, I am not sure which of them I think I will see. Or which of them I *hope* to see. In the summertime, when the nights are white and long, I might go down and read for a while, the way the visitors always loved to do, sitting in a deckchair at three in the morning

with a book and a cup of coffee under the midnight sun.
When I do, I read old myths and legends, fairy stories and
cautionary tales, to keep the ghosts at bay. They need somewhere to be, though, and if you don't find a home for them
out in the wind somewhere, if you don't bed them down safely
at the edge of the sea or the once upon a time, they spill back
into this world and turn into ghosts and monsters, resentful
and neglected and intent on doing harm. I am no more of a
believer now than I ever was, or not, at least, in the way people
usually imagine. I just need to know where everything is, and
then, when I am sure, to make a little space for the mystery.
I have no better word for it than that, but it's not a bad word,
when all is said and done. I'm not crazy – I know enough,
after all, not to talk about these things to the living – and I'm
not an old-time believer, like Kyrre, but I am getting used to
the fact that, in my house, there are shadows in the folds of
every blanket and imperceptible tremors in every glass of water
or bowl of cream set out on a table – and, some days, there
are tiny, almost infinitesimal loopholes of havoc in the fabric
of the given world that could spill loose and catch me out
wherever I am. I know this – and I spend the best part of my
time making such maps as I can, maps of the world as it is
between one moment and the next, charging myself with the
impossible task of finding, among the pencil marks and
shading, some cold angle of meadow or fjord where old
Bieggaålmaj, or some other restless and hungry god, gathers
them all in, one after another, Mats and Harald, Martin Crosbie
and Kyrre Opdahl, the girl Maia and the *huldra* she became,
hidden away in the folds of the wind, where only the most
careful of storytellers could find them.

NOTES AND ACKNOWLEDGEMENTS

I would like to thank the Scottish Arts Council and the Creative Scotland Awards for their invaluable support at the research stage of this novel.

Acknowledgements are due to Dag Andersson and Harald Gaski, in particular, for their advice, stories and suggestions, much of which informed the writing of this book, and to all my friends in the north, for their profound generosity of spirit, immense hospitality and quiet encouragement.

Tusen takk!